Tanya Huff

THE BETTER PART OF VALOR

DAW BOOKS, INC.
DONALD A. WOLLHEIM, FOUNDER
375 Hudson Street, New York, NY 10014
ELIZABETH R. WOLLHEIM
SHEILA E. GILBERT
PUBLISHERS
www.dawbooks.com

Cover art by Paul Youll.

DAW Book Collectors No. 1217.

DAW Books are distributed by Penguin Putnam Inc.

First Printing, March 2002
3 4 5 6 7 8 9

DAW TRADEMARK REGISTERED
U.S. PAT. OFF. AND FOREIGN COUNTRIES
—MARCA REGISTRADA.
HECHO EN U.S.A.

PRINTED IN THE U.S.A.

The worst of times bring out the best of people.

This is for the rescue workers who died
going *up* the stairs.

ONE

"AND the moral of the story: never call a two star general a bastard to his face."

Stretching out his regenerated leg, Captain Rose leaned away from his desk and drummed his fingers against the inert plastic trim. "I'm a little surprised you didn't already know that."

"You and me both, sir." Staff Sergeant Torin Kerr stared down at the general's orders on her slate. "You and me both."

"Still, I suppose you could consider it a compliment that General Morris wants you on this reconnaissance mission."

"Yes, sir, but somehow when I think of 'an unidentified alien vessel drifting dead in space,' the word that tends to stick is *dead*. And I've barely recovered from the last time the general took a personal interest." Before looking up, she cleared her screen with more emphasis than was strictly necessary. "Considering how the *diplomatic* part of the last mission got redefined as getting our asses kicked, I just hope I can survive what he considers recon."

The captain smiled, pale skin creasing at the corners of both eyes. "You kicked some ass yourself, Staff."

"Yes, sir, I did. Although I admit I had help from a

platoon of Marines and Lieutenant Jarret. Both of which," she added, "I wouldn't mind having with me this time."

"Should I authorize an armored unit as well?"

"I wish you could, sir." Hooking her slate onto her belt, Torin drew in a deep breath and accepted the inevitable. She'd made herself memorable to the top brass and would have to live with the consequences—although the little information she had made *survive* the consequences seem more accurate. "He wants me on the next coreward shuttle. There'll be transportation arranged once I reach MidSector but he doesn't actually say where I'm going."

"He's a general, Staff. He doesn't have to say. Ours is not to question why."

"Yes, sir. The next shuttle leaves in just under two hours. Unless the general's arranged for me to skip decontamination, I'll have to hurry."

The captain nodded, agreement and dismissal combined. "See that you hurry back, Staff Sergeant. I've got a new First, and he's got a shitload of new recruits he could use your help with. This is a lousy time for you to go gallivanting around the galaxy."

"I'll be sure to mention that to the general, sir."

"I'm hoping you're smarter than that, Staff."

"Yes, sir."

"Staff?"

She paused, just outside the door's proximity sensor.

"General Morris' parentage aside, it's entirely possible he recommended you for this mission because you're the best person for the job."

"General Morris' parentage aside, sir, I never doubted that."

* * *

And it started out as such a good day, Torin growled silently as she walked to the nearest vertical. Admin had finally cleared the files sending Binti Mashona to sniper school, Corporal Hollice was getting a well-deserved promotion to sergeant, a number of the new recruits actually seemed to have arrived with half their brains functioning, and, thanks to the situation on Silsviss, Sh'quo Company was so far down on the rotation that the Others would have to overrun the entire sector before they were sent back out. *I should have known something would happen to fuk it up.*

Report to shuttle bay twelve for decontamination in forty-six minutes.

Years of practice kept her from visibly reacting to her implant's sudden announcement. It hadn't taken Captain Rose long to post her orders to the station system.

A quick glance up and down the vertical showed a cluster of people descending but a clear fall below them all the way to C deck. With every intention of using General Morris' name not only in vain but in any way possible should the necessity arise, Torin dove headfirst down the shaft. The turn in mid-fall slowed her slightly, but she was still moving fast enough to set off the safety protocols when she grabbed the strap and swung out onto the deck.

Please exercise more caution in the verticals. This is a level one warning.

Torin tongued in an acknowledgment without breaking stride. She could live with a level one. It took three in a Tenday before the station reported them and she'd be gone long enough that this particular warning would have been wiped by the time she returned.

Unhooking her slate, she began locking down her desk as she walked—sealing her personal folders and encrypting the rest to Sergeant Chou's access codes. Anne Chou would be senior noncom for the platoon while she was gone and would at least give Lieutenant Jarret someone he'd already . . .

"Is it true, Staff?"

She looked down at the Krai private who'd suddenly appeared beside her. Given their difference in height, all she could see was the mottled top of his hairless head which gave no clue at all to the meaning of his question. "Is what true, Ressk?"

"That instead of a promotion and comfy tour at Ventris Station teaching *diritics* how to survive, General Morris has detoured you to a Recon mission."

"I'm impressed; those orders have been on system for less than ten minutes."

Ressk lengthened his stride to keep up, bare feet slapping against the floor. "I guess once you pull somebody's brass out of the fire they expect you to keep doing it."

"That is the way the universe tends to function." At the lock leading to SRQ, she paused. "You got a reason to be on this level, Ressk?"

"Sergeant Aman wants to see me, Staff. And when I saw you, I thought I'd say . . ."

The pause lengthened.

"Private?"

His nose ridges flushed. "Could you talk to the general, Staff? Exploring an unidentified alien vessel floating dead in space—that's always been my dream!"

Torin blinked. "You're kidding?"

"No, Staff, I'm not. You know there isn't a sys-op I

can't get into. I could be useful on this kind of a mission."

"I don't doubt that, but I'm sure there'll be specialists . . ."

"I'm faster. If it's a matter of life and death, you're not going to want some specialist . . ." The word emerged somewhere between an insult and profanity. ". . . taking their time, doing everything by the book."

"Ressk . . ."

"I haven't even read the book!"

Report to shuttle bay twelve for decontamination in thirty minutes.

"If I can, I'll talk to Captain Rose before I go."

"Thanks, Staff. You're a real *chirtric.*"

It wasn't every day she was called a delicacy, Torin reflected as she continued toward her quarters, but even if she managed to talk to Captain Rose he'd have no time to speak to the general before the shuttle left the station.

The captain's Admin clerk agreed to pass the message along. "You do know that captains aren't in the habit of paging two star generals and suggesting they should make use of personnel with what amounts to illegal computing skills, don't you, Staff?"

"Not my problem." Torin thumbed her kit bag closed. "I told him I'd try to talk to Captain Rose. The captain was unavailable, I spoke to you. My conscience is clear." Her slate made a noise somewhere between a snort and a snicker. "You have something to add, Corporal?"

"Just my best wishes for a successful mission and a safe return, Staff Sergeant."

"Thank you. Kerr out."

"The double tone closing the connection sounded as she glanced one last time around the room, noted both living and sleeping area would pass at least a cursory inspection, and crossed to the door. The empty sockets of the Silsviss skull on the shelf over her entertainment unit seemed to follow her every move. A couple of the more politically correct Battalion NCOs had objected to having the skull of a sentient species mounted in the Senior Ranks' Mess, so rather than stuff it into a recycler, she'd brought it home.

"Don't look so concerned," she told it. "I'll be back."

Report to shuttle bay twelve for decontamination in twenty minutes.

In spite of a crowd on the lower beltway, she made it with seven minutes to spare and could walk across the lounge to the shuttle bay without challenging the belief, widely held by the lower ranks, that sergeants and above controlled time and therefore never had to hurry.

"Staff Sergeant Kerr!"

Torin checked her watch, then turned. His lilac eyes a couple of shades darker than his hair, Second Lieutenant di'Ka Jarret, her platoon commander, rushed around the end of an ugly gray plastic bench and hurried toward her. As incapable of looking awkward as any of his species, he didn't look happy. "Sir?"

"You were just going to leave?" He didn't sound happy either.

"The general's orders were specific, sir. I had forty-six minutes to get to decon and you were at Battalion. Captain Rose sent you a copy of the orders."

"I received the captain's transfer, Staff Sergeant," the di'Taykan informed her, drawing himself up to his full height. Torin stared at the pheromone masker prominently displayed at his throat and just barely resisted the urge to crank it up a notch. A small indiscretion some months previously had left her more susceptible to the lieutenant's chemical invitation than she should have been. One night he's a pretty young di'Taykan—one of the most enthusiastically undiscriminating species in the galaxy—and next morning he's her new second lieutenant. There were times Torin thought the universe had a piss poor sense of humor.

Had her time been her own, she could—and would—have waited indefinitely for him to continue. His last declaration had exhibited an indignation junior officers needed to be trained out of—the greater portion of the universe, not to mention the Marine Corps, ticked along just fine without them ever being consulted.

However, as she was currently on General Morris' clock . . .

"I sent a message as well, sir. Wrote it on the beltway. Station should have downloaded it to your slate by now."

She half expected him to check his inbox. When he didn't, she allowed herself a small smile. "I appreciate the chance to say good-bye, sir. You must have really hauled ass to make it all the way down from Battalion in time."

"Well, I . . ."

"Staff Sergeant Torin Kerr, report to decontamination at shuttle bay twelve."

"Tell the whole station," Torin muttered, as her name, rank, and destination bounced off the dull green metal walls of the lounge.

"I think they did." The lieutenant's hair and ears

both had clamped tight to his skull. "You'll, uh . . ." When Torin lifted an eyebrow in his general direction, a skill that had been well worth the price of the program, he finished in a rush. ". . . you'll be coming back?"

"I always plan on coming back, sir." She took a step closer to the decontamination lock. "Every time I go out."

"I know. I mean . . ."

"I know what you mean, sir." One of the most important functions staff sergeants performed was the supporting of brand new second lieutenants while they learned how to handle themselves in front of actual—as opposed to theoretical—Marines. The realization that this relationship wasn't necessarily permanent, that said support could be pulled out from under them at the whim of those higher up the chain of command, always came as a bit of a shock to the young officers. "During the time I'm temporarily detached from the company, you can have complete faith in Sergeant Chou's ability to handle the platoon."

"I do." He opened his mouth to continue, then closed it again. After a moment's thought, he squared his shoulders, held out his hand, and said only, "Good luck, Staff."

"Thank you, sir." When, like any di'Taykan, he tried to extend the physical contact, she pulled her hand free and moved into the decontamination lock's proximate zone.

"Staff?"

A half-turn as she stepped over the lip and into the outer chamber. The lieutenant was smiling, his eyes as light as she'd ever seen them.

"Is it true you called General Morris a bastard?"

* * *

Torin stowed her bag in the enclosure over her seat and took a look around the military compartment. Forward, a pair of officers sat on opposite sides of the aisle. The Human artillery captain had already slid his slate into the shuttle's system and, from the corner of screen Torin could see, had accessed the hospitality file—although it wouldn't dispense his drink until they were in Susumi space. Her seat on full recline, it appeared that the di'Taykan major had gone to sleep. Torin wondered if she'd already made the captain an offer and was resting up. And if that's why the captain was drinking.

In the aft end of the compartment, half a dozen privates and a corporal were settling in. According to their travel docs—available to sergeants and above from the shuttle's manifest—the corporal from Crayzk Company's engineering platoon was heading Coreward on course and the six privates were on their way back to Ventris Station to be mustered out.

She had the NCO compartment to herself.

As the shuttle pulled away from the station, the walls separating the sections opaqued. Although the center aisle remained open along the length of the compartment, it was easy enough to maintain the illusion of privacy between the ranks—an illusion Torin was all in favor of. She as little wanted to be responsible *to* the officers as she wanted to be responsible *for* the junior ranks.

Half an hour later, the shuttle folded into Susumi space. Since little changed from trip to trip, they'd be spending only eight to fourteen hours inside, emerging four light-years away at MidSector at the same time they left. Torin pulled a pouch of beer from her alcohol allotment and settled back to watch the last three episodes of *StarCops*, one of the few Human produced vids she hated to miss.

But neither Detective Berton's attempt to find the smugglers bringing the highly addictive di'Taykan *vritran* into Human space nor Detective Canter's search to find the murderer of a Krai diplomat could hold her attention. She might as well have been watching H'san opera. When the third episode featured a government official throwing his weight around, she thumbed it off and glared at her reflection on the screen.

If General Morris wanted a recon team to investigate an unknown alien spacecraft, the Corps had plenty of teams he could choose from. Torin didn't know whether he wanted her to replace the staff sergeant from an established unit or to be a part of a team he'd built from scratch, but either way she didn't much care for the idea. It was inefficient. And bordered on stupid.

She could do the job. She understood that as a member of the Corps, she was expected to pick up and move on as the Corps saw fit. And she took full responsibility for the actions that had lodged her in the memory of a two star general.

But stupidity at high levels really pissed her off.

Because stupidity at high levels was the sort of thing that got people killed.

A Krai territorial cry sounded from the rear compartment, closely followed by a stream of happy Human profanity. Jerked out of her mood, Torin was startled to see she'd been brooding for almost an hour.

The profanity got a little less happy.

Not her problem.

She heard the corporal's voice rise and fall and

then the unmistakable sequence of flesh to flesh to floor.

Now it was her problem.

Standing, she shrugged into her tunic and started down the aisle. *No point in letting a bad mood go to waste . . .*

The corporal was flat on his back. One of the Krai privates—probably the female given relative sizes—sat on his chest, holding his arms down with her feet. He wasn't struggling, so Torin assumed he'd taken some damage hitting the floor. The smaller Krai had a pouch of beer in the foot Torin could see and was banging both fists against the seat in front of him, nose ridges so dark they were almost purple. The di'-Taykan were nowhere to be seen—all three of them had probably crammed themselves into the tiny communal chamber the moment the shuttle had entered Susumi space—which left, of the original six privates, only a Human who seemed to find the whole thing very funny.

He spotted Torin first. By the time she'd covered half the distance, his eyes had widened as the chevrons on her sleeves penetrated past the beer. By the time she'd covered the other half of the distance, he'd stopped laughing and had managed to gasp out something that could have been a warning.

Too late.

Transferring forward momentum, Torin wrapped her fist in the female Krai's uniform, lifted her off the corporal, and threw her back into a seat.

The sudden silence was deafening.

She reached down and helped the corporal to his feet.

Someone cleared his or her throat. "Staff, we . . ."

Her lip curled. "Shut up."

The silence continued.

"If I hear one word from any of you while Corporal Barteau . . ."

No one seemed at all surprised she knew the corporal's name.

". . . is telling me what the hell is going on back here, I will override your seat controls and you will spend the rest of the trip strapped in." Eyes narrowed, she swept the silent trio with a flat, unfriendly stare. "Do I make myself clear?"

"Yes, Staff Sergeant."

"Good. Corporal."

They walked back to the wall dividing the lower ranks from the NCOs.

Torin pitched her voice for the corporal's ears alone. "You all right?"

"Just a little winded, Staff. I didn't expect her to jump me. They'd been drinking, and I think she was showing off for Private Karsk. I was studying." He nodded toward the schematics spread out over the last two seats. "I asked them to keep it down. Next thing I knew . . ."

An unidentifiable sound from the back of the compartment pulled Torin's head around. All three privates, sitting exactly where she'd left them, froze, wide-eyed like they'd been caught in a searchlight. She held them there for a moment—half hoping they were drunk enough to cause more trouble—then turned slowly back to Corporal Barteau.

He shrugged. "They're on their way home, Staff."

"I know."

"Privates Karsk and Visilli were at Beconreaks and Private Chrac, she was aircrew, Black Star Evac. They flew at . . ."

"I know, Corporal, I was there. Your point?"

"I don't think they deserve to be put on report. Not for celebrating the fact that they're going home."

"I agree."

He looked surprised. "You do?"

Torin exhaled slowly and forced the muscles in her jaw to relax. From the corporal's reaction, she suspected she'd looked like she was chewing glass. "Yes. I do. I'll have a word with them and, *if* we get to MidSector without any more trouble, that'll be the end of it."

"You've already scared the piss out of them," the corporal acknowledged.

"Yeah, well, I'd say that was my intent except the shuttle service would make me pay for having the seats cleaned."

Feeling considerably more clearheaded, Torin accessed the hospitality screen and a moment later pulled the tab on a pouch of beer.

Ours is not to question why.

I'll do, she said silently, with a sarcastic toast to absent brass, *but I'll be damned if I'll die.*

The detoxicant Torin had taken when they folded out of Susumi space had done its job by the time the shuttle docked at MidSector. Although the military and civilian passengers had been kept separate during the trip, exit ramps emerged into the same crowded Arrivals' Lounge.

There were a lot fewer uniforms in the crowd than Torin was used to.

"Excuse me."

Torin had a choice. She could stop, or she could

walk right over the di'Taykan standing in front of her. She stopped. But it was a close decision.

The di'Taykan had lime green hair and eyes, the former spread out from her head in a six-inch aureole, the latter so pale Torin wondered how she could see since none of the light receptors seemed to be open. Her matching clothing was unusually subdued—in spite of the color—and the combined effect was one of studied innocence.

Torin didn't believe it for a moment. Anyone studying that hard had to be working against type.

"One of my *thytrins* was supposed to be on that shuttle, Sergeant di'Perit Dymone. I didn't see him get off so I was wondering if he, well, missed his flight again." Her hair flattened a little in embarrassment. "He missed the last flight he was supposed to be on."

Looking politely disinterested, Torin waited.

"I thought maybe, if he didn't miss this flight, he might still be on board."

"No."

"Are you sure . . ." She dipped her head and her eyes went a shade darker as she studied Torin's collar tabs. ". . . Staff Sergeant?"

"I'm sure."

"But . . ."

"I was the only NCO of senior rank on board. Your *thytrin* missed another flight."

"Oh." Her hair flattened farther as she stepped out of the way, one long fingered hand fiddling with her masker. "I'm sorry to bother you then."

Torin swung her bag back onto her shoulder. "No problem."

"Um, Staff Sergeant, would you like to . . ."

"No. Thank you." When a di'Taykan began a question with *would you like to,* there was only ever one ending. And that was probably why the girl's *thytrin* kept missing his flight.

By the time Torin reached the exit, she'd been delayed long enough for the lines to have gone down at the security scanners. Wondering why the Niln next to her was bothering to argue with the station sysop—top of the pointless activity list—she slid her slate into the wall and faced the screen. In the instant before the scan snapped her pupils to full dilation, she saw a flash of reflected lime green. The di'Taykan? Scan completed, she turned.

On the other side of the lounge, now nearly empty of both the shuttle's passengers and those who'd come to meet them, the di'Taykan had crouched down to speak to a Katrien. Although conscious of being watched, they glanced up and smiled. For an omnivore, the Katrien had rather a lot of sharp-looking teeth in its narrow muzzle and although Torin couldn't see much of its face around an expensive looking pair of dark glasses, something about its expression made her fairly certain she'd seen that particular Katrien before. She just couldn't put her finger on where.

You have been cleared to enter the station. Proceed immediately to docking bay SD-31. Your pilot has been informed of your arrival.

Torin tongued in an acknowledgment and stepped through the hatch, the Katrien's identity no longer relevant.

Facing the lounge exit was a large screen with a three-dimensional map of the station. As Torin stepped closer, a red light flashed over her corresponding place on the map and a long red arrow led to the legend; *"You are here."* Torin would have bet her pension that the graffiti scrawled next to it in a script she didn't recognize said, *"And your luggage is in Antares,"* or a variation thereof.

Shuttle departures were down one level. Unfortunately, SD-31 was not a shuttle bay. All MidSector and OutSector stations had a squadron of two-person fighters for station defense plus a few extra bays in case of fighters arriving without their ships. As no MidSector station had ever been attacked, their squadrons were on short rotation. There were few things more disruptive to a sentient society than a squadron of bored vacuum jockeys.

"Docking bay SD-31."

The map rearranged itself. A second red light appeared. A green line joined them.

Okay. That was going to take some time.

"Shortest route. Species neutral."

Not significantly shorter.

The MidSector stations had been in place longer than Humans had been part of the Confederation and over time they'd grown almost organically.

"Like a tumor," Torin muttered, heading for the nearest transit node. OutSector stations had been designed for the military after the start of the war and were a lot more efficient. She hoped that when informed of her arrival her pilot had kept right on with whatever it was a vj did when he wasn't flying or fighting with Marine pilots because they wouldn't be leaving any time soon.

At the node, she wasn't really surprised to find a link had just left. Given the way her day had been going, she wouldn't have been surprised to have found the links shut down for unscheduled maintenance and that she was supposed to cover roughly eight kilometers of station on foot.

Ours is not to question why.

A trite saying rapidly on its way to becoming a mantra.

By the time the next link arrived, the platform had become crowded. A trio of di'Taykan officers at the far end—pink, teal, and lavender hair—provided a visual aid for anyone who wondered why the Corps had switched to black uniforms and about forty civilians filled the space in between, including four representatives of a species Torin couldn't identify.

There were also a number of Katrien. Hard to count because they were shorter than many of the other species but easy to spot since every single one of them appeared to be talking—sometimes to other Katrien, who were also talking. MidSector was close to their home system, which explained the numbers. Torin watched only the occasional broadcast coming out of the Core but she seemed to remember a Katrien news program announcing that their Trading Cartel had taken over a significant number of both X- and Y-axis routes.

When the link finally arrived, Torin took a center seat, plugged her slate into a data console, and ran "alien ship dead in space," then "ship of unknown origins," paying a little extra for a secure search. Nothing. *Great, the one time I could use a little help from the media, General Morris managed to keep the lid on.*

Impressive if only because the Marines had arrived in more than one contested system to find the media there first.

At her final node, Torin had her link to herself and at the end of the line stepped out onto an empty platform. Four Katrien bounced out of the link behind her and one out of the link behind that. Although she hadn't paid much attention to fur patterns, the dark glasses on the single Katrien, now hurrying to join the others, seemed familiar.

I'm in friendly territory, Torin reminded herself. *No reason to assume I'm being followed. Two different people could easily be wearing the same expensive eyewear.*

But she crossed the platform toward them anyway—paranoia and survival instinct were two sides of the same coin when the job description involved being targeted by projectile weapons. The single Katrien cut off a high-pitched and incomprehensible flow of sound as she reached the group, and all five turned toward her.

She scowled down at the source of her disquiet. "Do I know you?"

A heavyset individual—Torin didn't know enough about the Katrien to assume gender—spread hands that looked like black latex gloves extending from the sleeves of a fur coat, and replied in a friendly sounding torrent of its own language.

Translation not available.

"Do any of you speak Federate?"

A second torrent, even friendlier sounding than the first.

Translation not available.

All five were now smiling toothily, the Katrien who might or might not have been following her, a little toothier than the rest. Torin knew better than to make cross-species generalizations, but it looked smug. If they were living on station, they spoke Federate; no question they were being deliberate pains in the ass. Maybe they disliked the military on principle. Many of the Elder Races were pacifists—to the point of extinction when the Others showed up which was, after all, why the Humans, Taykan, and Krai had been invited in.

Maybe the Katrien *was* the same Katrien she'd seen in the lounge. Maybe it told the others to play dumb for the soldier. Fuk it. It was a free station. She was not going to get involved in the game.

But this time, she noted the fur pattern. If she saw this particular smugly smiling Katrien again, she'd know it.

Her answering smile was less toothy but more sarcastic, "Thank you for your time."

They shouted something after her as she left the platform. Torin tongued off her implant before it could tell her once again that a translation was unavailable. Some things didn't need to be translated.

There was a vacuum jockey leaning against the orange metal bulkhead outside SD-31. Torin wondered how the Navy flier could look so boneless and still remain upright. He straightened as she approached.

"Staff Sergeant Kerr?"

"Yes, sir."

"Lieutenant Commander Sibley. I'm your ride." He palmed the lock and stood aside as the hatch opened.

Torin peered into the tiny suiting chamber and looked back at the pilot in time to see him slide a H'san stim into his chest pocket. Humans chewed the sticks as a mild stimulant. They were nonaddicting and completely harmless although they had a tendency to stain the user's teeth and, in extensive use, turn subcutaneous fat bright orange. Although the sticks were frowned on, they weren't actually illegal, and Navy pilots, operating in three dimensions at high speeds, often chewed to give themselves an edge. Navy flight commanders, who preferred their pilots alive, usually looked the other way.

Lieutenant Commander Sibley followed her gaze and grinned. "I know, Staff, it's a filthy habit. And I'm not trying to quit."

"Not my business, sir."

"True enough." He stepped into the chamber. Torin followed. "We've got a one-size-fits-most flight suit for you. I take it your suit certifications are up to date?"

"Yes, sir. If either branch of the military uses it, I'm certified to wear it."

The suits were designed to fit loosely everywhere but the collar ring and the faceplate so one size fit well enough. Exposure to vacuum caused a chemical reaction which stiffened the suit and filled the spaces between it and flesh with an insulating foam capable of maintaining a constant temperature of 15°C for thirty minutes. Since the suits came with only twenty minutes of independent air, pilots who found themselves free of their fighter's life-support pod didn't have to worry about freezing to death.

Among themselves, Torin knew the vacuum jockeys referred to the suits as buoys—markers to make it easier for the Navy to find the bodies.

Theoretically, pilots weren't supposed to come out of their pods even with their fighters shot to hell all around them. In Torin's experience, theory didn't stand a chance up against reality. Theoretically, species achieved interstellar space travel after they'd put war behind them, but apparently no one had told the Others.

They checked each other's seals and packs, then Lieutenant Commander Sibley opened the outer door. SD-31 held, as expected, a two-person Jade although for the moment all Torin could see of it was the access to the pod.

"Ever ridden in one these jewels, Staff Sergeant?"

Torin's stomach flipped as she stepped out into the docking bay and the gravity suddenly lessened. "No, sir."

His hazel eyes held a gleam of anticipation as he showed her where and how to stow her bag, then he waved at the tiny rear section. "We're point five gees in here, Staff, so just step in, feet about this far apart . . ." He held out white-gloved hands. ". . . and settle into place. Your pack fits into the back of the seat and, if you do it right, all hookups are made automatically."

And if I do it wrong? Torin wondered as her feet hit the deck and she sat down on a disconcertingly yielding surface. Apparently, she'd have to find out another time as straps slid down around her shoulders and disappeared into the seat between her legs. *Great. We can fold space, but we can't improve on the seat belt my father uses on his tractor.* The screens to either side of her remained dark, but on the curved screen in front, half a dozen green telltales lit up.

"You're in." The pilot leaned up out of her section and dropped into his own, considerably faster than she'd done it. "Probably best if you keep your hands in your lap, Staff Sergeant. None of your controls are live, but you're in my gunner's seat and I'd just as soon we didn't shoot off bits of the station. Navy frowns at that."

Every time it happens, Torin snorted, but all she said aloud was, "Hands are in my lap, sir."

Almost before he was strapped in, the pod sealed. An instant after that, they dropped out into space.

Zero gravity flipped her stomach again. Torin swallowed hard as acceleration pressed her first against the straps and then down into the seat. Lieutenant Commander Sibley had cleared launch on his implant, probably so he could hit space without giving her warning. Two diagonal moves later, they were upside down relative to the station.

"Be about an hour and a half before we reach the *Berganitan*. I hope you're not claustrophobic."

Well, sir, if I was, I'd have probably found out years ago crammed into the troop compartment of a sled with a couple of dozen muddy Marines while the enemy tried to blow us the hell up. At least you've got windows.

But all she said aloud was, "Not that I know of, sir."

She spared a moment wondering if there was any significance in General Morris' apparent fondness for the *Berganitan*. Maybe it was the only ship the Admiralty would let him play with.

The Jade suddenly dropped away from the station. About thirty meters out, it flipped over.

Shouldn't have told him I'd never been in a Jade before. She'd probably thought a lieutenant commander was a little old to play "let's see if we can get the Marine to puke." More fool her. All vjs were crazy, from raw ensigns right up to Wing Admiral di'Si Trin herself—something she should have remembered. *Well, counting the ten hours and forty-seven minutes in Susumi space, it has been a long day.*

Lieutenant Commander Sibley added a few final flourishes as he brought the Jade up to cruising speed.

"If you have to hurl, Staff Sergeant, bite the black tab at the base of your faceplate. It'll open a pouch."

No answer. Not even the sound of a lost lunch.

"Staff?"

Her telltales were green. She was conscious. Heart pumping at sixty/sixty. Respiration slow and steady.

Then it dawned on him. While he'd been flying a pattern designed to test the limits of Human physiology, his passenger had gone to sleep.

Two

"STAFF Sergeant Kerr?"

"Yes, sir." The lieutenant waiting outside the fighter bay had hair and eyes the palest blue Torin'd ever seen on a di'Taykan. His Class Cs had been perfectly creased, his boots and brass magnificently shined, even his masker gleamed.

He seemed momentarily disappointed that her spit and polish matched his.

"I'm Lieutenant Stedrin, General Morris' aide. The general wants to see you right away."

She'd been traveling for the last fifteen hours. What *she* wanted was a shower—although perhaps wanted wasn't the most accurate word.

Stedrin's eyes darkened, as though he were trying to see her expression in more detail. Then he stepped back and gestured to the right. "The Corps' attachment is this way."

They walked in silence, watched covertly by the *Berganitan*'s crew. Torin and a warrant exchanged nods as she passed his work party, but the lieutenant might as well have been moving through an empty ship. She wondered if he'd have shortened his stride had she not been tall enough to keep up and decided, after casting a quick glance at the rigid muscles of his jaw, he probably wouldn't. *Must make him real popular with the Krai. Why the hell didn't he just message my implant?*

"The general thinks highly of you." Stedrin made the sudden announcement in a tone that suggested the general was alone in that regard. "He says that without you, it's doubtful we'd have gained the Silsviss as allies." The pause was too short for a reply. Too long to have been anything but deliberate emphasis. "I think you've taken as much advantage of that as there is to be taken. Do you understand me, Staff Sergeant Kerr?"

"Yes, sir." And that answered the message versus personal touch question. He'd come all the way down to the fighter bay to warn her to play nice or she'd have him to deal with. The overachieving, armament up the butt attitude was unusual for a di'Taykan. Willing to lay odds that he had a minimum of eight letters in the unmentioned half of his name—which would put his family low in the Taykan caste system—she kept her face expressionless under the weight of his regard.

"I get the impression you're not taking this seriously, Staff Sergeant."

Stepping forward, she checked that the lock lights were green and opened the hatch separating the Marine attachment from the *Berganitan* proper. "Sorry, sir."

"For what?" he demanded, walking over the seals with the self-conscious care of one who'd spent very little time in space.

"For your mistaken impression, Lieutenant." She dogged the hatch closed and turned to meet his eyes. "I take everything I do seriously. It's how I keep my people alive." After a moment, she let him look away.

Hair clamped tight to his skull, the lieutenant took

a step back, opened his mouth, then snapped it closed again. Torin gave him credit for recognizing he was in a battle he couldn't win and waited patiently while he brought his emotions under control. The general's compartment was barely three meters down the passage, and the last thing he'd want was to have General Morris inquiring about his temper.

Or wondering where the hell he'd been.

Seconds before Torin was about to point that out, the di'Taykan turned on one heel, and marched down the passageway, graceful in spite of a rigidity of spine that promised they weren't through.

"You're looking better than the last time I saw you, Staff Sergeant."

"Thank you, sir." So was he. Last time she'd seen the general, he'd had two black eyes, a broken nose, and a poleaxed expression—all of which she'd been essentially responsible for.

Given his current expression, he was thinking pretty much the same thing. "Yes, well, we've a new situation here, so let's put the past behind us, shall we?"

"Yes, sir."

It was more neutral noise than agreement, but General Morris took the words at face value, smiling and nodding—both of which put Torin on edge. Damn, she hated smiling generals.

"You're probably wondering why I had Lieutenant Stedrin bring you to me."

She was, but she wasn't expecting an explanation. The pause went on long enough so Torin began to think the general himself was also wondering. She was about ready to throw in another *Yes, sir,* to prod him forward, when he squared beefy shoulders and said, "You'll be Senior NCO for this mission and, as you were my personal choice, I felt I should be the one to introduce you to the officer commanding." He touched the edge of his comm unit. "Lieutenant."

"Sir." Stedrin's voice snapped out of the desk so crisply Torin knew he'd been hovering over it, waiting for the call.

"Have the captain report to my office immediately."

"Yes, sir."

Generals did not make introductions for staff sergeants.

Staff sergeants did not ask generals what the hell they were up to.

Unfortunately.

General Morris sat back in his chair and steepled his fingers, looking over their blunt ends at Torin. "How much do you follow politics, Staff Sergeant?"

"I don't, sir."

"You just do your job?"

Best to ignore two star sarcasm.

"Yes, sir."

He nodded and continued. "As you're well aware, politics are a part of my job. The balance of power in Parliament is very tenuous right now. Many of the old races feel the Confederation isn't making enough effort to deal with the Others diplomatically—in spite of the fact that diplomacy so far has resulted in nothing but dead diplomats. There's a very real possibility that the arguments between the various factions could result in the same crippling of the government as happened back in '89 when, with defense spending stalled, the Others took over most of SD38 including the Ba'tan home world. It would be nice," he continued dryly, and Torin got the impression he was talking as much to himself as to her, "if this time, things could stabilize without such a drastic kick in the collective ass. Surprisingly enough, it's been the Krai who've been causing the most trouble of late, throwing one faction against the other so that the military will take notice of their complaints that there aren't enough of their people in top positions. They've been insisting Krai officers, Navy and Marine, receive more chances to serve in those places where promotions are most likely."

"The front lines, sir?"

The general looked startled by her question. "No, not the front lines. They're looking for a higher survival rate."

Aren't we all.

"Sir!"

Torin wondered if Stedrin stood at attention when he addressed the general over the comm. It certainly sounded like he did.

"Yes, Lieutenant?"

"The captain is here, sir."

"Send him in." General Morris stood, tugged his tunic into place, and came around the desk, shooting Torin a look that seemed almost apologetic.

Bugger it. That's not good. She'd been standing easy, so when the door opened behind her, she came around ninety degrees, presenting her back to neither the general nor the entering officer.

He looked vaguely familiar. Which wasn't necessarily relevant since the Krai as a whole had very little color or size variance and, to any species without a highly developed sense of smell, all looked pretty much the same.

"Staff Sergeant Kerr, I'd like you to meet your commanding officer for this mission, Captain Travik."

Oh, crap.

Captain Travik's rescue of the besieged research station on Horohn 8, his reckless charge through the Others' perimeter recorded by the station's sensors, had captured the attention of the public and made him a celebrity. He'd been feted all through the sector, his image turning up every time the Corps got mentioned on any kind of a popular broadcast, his reputation growing as every new program fed on the one before it, his ego growing with his reputation.

Most of the Marines who landed under the captain's command hadn't survived.

To the public, that made him even more the hero.

To the Corps, particularly those who'd studied the recording, that made him a reckless hotshot who knew how to manipulate the media.

And here he was.

Because the Krai government wanted more Krai in top military positions.

Torin glanced over at the general and thought of a few more things to call him.

They folded into Susumi space early evening ship's time when the last two members of the recon team finally arrived. According to the data on the desk in Torin's small office, the twelve Marines had been detached from as many different units for security reasons. A decision had been made at the highest levels to keep the media away from the alien vessel and individual Marines moving about the Sector were deemed a lot less noticeable than a squad taken from one location.

From a combat perspective, it *was* inefficient, but Torin couldn't fault the security reasoning. She only hoped they'd be spending enough time in Susumi space to make the word *team* relevant. Even with specialized training in common, it was going to take a while to shake three different species and twelve different personalities into a smoothly functioning unit.

Although there'd be common ground the moment they knew who was commanding.

Might as well get it over with.

"That was Staff Sergeant Kerr giving us a ten minute warning," Corporal di'Marken Nivry announced, upper body leaning through the hatch. "She wants us all. You two better get some clothes on and get in here."

The two dripping Marines on the shower platform exchanged glances as identical as Human and Krai physiognomy allowed.

"Briefing's tomorrow morning," Werst growled, turning the air jets on. "She can't wait?"

"She doesn't have to," Nivry reminded him and disappeared.

Lifting both heavily muscled arms over his head, Werst turned and scowled at the man standing next to him. "What?"

August Guimond scrubbed his fingers through the maximum amount of thick blond hair the Corps allowed, smiling broadly. "She was checking out my package."

"Dirsrick anbol sa serrik tanayn."

"That's Krai, isn't it?" Guimond turned off the air and stepped down. "What does it mean?"

"Roughly: who the fuk cares."

Torin glanced around the compartment. Five di'Taykan, five Humans, two Krai—pretty much the usual split for the Corps. The engineers, Lance

Corporal Danny Johnston and Corporal Heer, were sitting together, slates out. The two highest caste of the five di'Taykan—Privates First Class di'Por Huilin and di'Wen Jynett—appeared to be playing "my family compound is bigger than yours," and looked as though they'd been interrupted in the midst of getting to know each other better. Which was pretty much standard operating procedure for di'Taykans and a heartbeat after she left all five would be in the communal compartment. For a moment it looked as though Pfc di'Sarm Frii was having a small spasm and then she saw the earphones almost covered by swinging ocher hair—although his hair seemed to be keeping a different beat than either hands or feet.

And Private First Class August Guimond, who was one of the biggest Humans Torin had ever seen, must have found something or somebody pretty funny given the size of his smile.

The rest were waiting more or less attentively for her to speak. The other Krai, who therefore had to be Pfc Werst, cradled a mug of *sah* in both hands. It took a security scan to release the stimulant to the Krai and, given the effect on Humans, Torin was glad to see Werst also wore an expression that promised critical damage should anyone try to take it from him.

She drew in a deep breath, noted that the silence became more attentive, waited for a blocky blonde—Lance Corporal Lesli Dursinski—to drive an annoyed elbow into Frii's ribs, and began. "My name is Staff Sergeant Kerr and I am your Senior NCO for this mission. Like you, I got dragged away from my team and my friends and the job I was doing and, like you, I know that doesn't matter one goddamned bit. The Corps calls—we answer. This is your new team . . ." A sweeping gesture with her right hand. ". . . these are your new friends . . ." Followed by a sweeping gesture with her left. "I don't care if you like each other, but you will respect each other's abilities and you will work together as Marines. Whenever that seems too difficult for you, remember there's sixteen of us and over two thousand sailors out here." Her left eyebrow lifted and her tone dried out. "I'm not saying that it's us against them, I'm just saying that sixteen Marines, working together, should have no trouble with two thousand sailors."

"Bring 'em on, Staff!" Pfc di'Benti Orla was on her feet. "I could do two thousand sailors myself before breakfast!"

One of the Humans, Corporal Harrop, snickered. "Yeah, I've heard that about you."

Orla flipped him the finger, a Human gesture the di'Taykan had adopted wholeheartedly. "Fuk you!"

"After breakfast."

"Deal."

When Harrop looked startled, Torin grinned and shook her head. "You *have* served with di'Taykan before, Corporal?"

"Sure, Staff. Hundreds."

"Then stop looking so damned surprised. At the moment," she continued, now that the room's attention had returned to her, "I know little more about this mission than you do; we'll be first on an alien, deep-space craft found drifting by a civilian salvage operator. Briefing's tomorrow morning, 0900 hours, across in the *Berganitan*. General Morris would like us all to attend." Torin paused long enough for the expected rumble of complaint but not so long that the rumble turned into something more. "Whether he expects our presence to reassure or intimidate the civilian scientists who will also be in attendance remains unclear at this time."

Lance Corporal Ken Tsui snickered—there was one in every team who always got the joke—and several Marines smiled.

"At the briefing," Torin continued, "we'll meet our commanding officer, Captain Travik."

Johnston's slate squawked as he closed his fist around it. A heartbeat later, eleven of the twelve started talking at once.

". . . *serley* asshole couldn't command his way out of a wet . . ."

". . . had a *thytrin* with him at Horohn . . ."

". . . part of a fukking PR show . . ."

". . . bastard tries that 'hero' shit on me . . ."

". . . General Morris trying to get us fukking killed . . ."

Torin folded her arms and met Werst's eyes across the room. He took a long drink of his *sah*, expression no different than it had been before she'd started speaking. One by one the other Marines noted her position and their protests trailed off.

"All right, now that you've got that out of your system," she told the renewed silence, "let's get a few things clear. One, General Morris is not trying to get us killed. The Krai in Parliament want more senior officers, and Captain Travik was the politicians' choice. Unless the general wanted a repeat of '89, his hands were tied."

"Fuk the politicians," someone muttered.

Torin snorted. "Thank you, but no. Two, this is not a public relations show. Until we've determined exactly what we're dealing with, we're under level four security and a full media lockout—which is why they didn't move in an existing team. The media watches troop movements, they don't watch individual Marines."

"Staff?"

"What is it, Dursinski?"

"Why a full media lockout?" The lance corporal's frown fell into two well-defined vertical lines in the center of her forehead. "Is there something about this ship they're not telling us?"

"Probably. But I'm sure if you all put your little minds to it, you could come up with an infinite number of reasons for command to keep the discovery of this ship away from civilians until we've determined what it is."

"Well, if it's one of the Others' ships, they could get hurt."

"While I appreciate enthusiasm, Private Guimond, I wasn't actually asking for reasons."

Head cocked to one side, his lips moved as he silently repeated her previous statement. "Oh." His smile grew a little sheepish. "Sorry, Staff."

"It's okay. Three . . ." She swept the room with a flat, emotionless gaze. ". . . Captain Travik is a Marine Corps officer and his orders, passed to you through me, will be obeyed. What you think of him personally is irrelevant. Do I make myself clear?"

A ragged chorus of, "Yes, Staff." Scattered nods. Werst took another drink.

"Good. Form up in the passageway at 0830. I'll see you then." She paused, one hand on the hatch, and turned back to the room. "Private Orla."

"Staff?" The young di'Taykan looked startled to be singled out.

"I'm sorry to hear about your *thytrin*. For what it's worth, I expect your contact with the captain will be minimal." When Orla nodded, Torin stepped out of the compartment and closed the hatch behind her.

"You told them?"

Torin pivoted on a heel, just barely resisting an urge to ask Lieutenant Stedrin why he was lurking about the enlisted compartments. "Yes, sir. I did."

"Why?" The question held equal parts curiosity and challenge.

"If they found out about Captain Travik tomorrow at the briefing, that's all they would have found out. Now, it'll be old news, already dealt with, and they'll be able to concentrate on information that might keep them alive."

"I doubt the briefing will be that dangerous, Staff Sergeant. Good night."

"Good night, sir." Torin watched until the lieutenant turned the corner, trying to decide if he had the sector's driest delivery or the Corps' worst grasp of tactics.

"You've been pretty quiet, Werst," Guimond observed as the horror stories and complaints began to die down. "What do you think about serving under Captain Travik?"

"Why do you want to know?"

"I just . . ."

"You think because I'm Krai, I'm going to defend him?"

"No, I . . ."

"I think he's a grandstanding asshole at best and a murdering asshole at worst, but we won't be dealing with him." Werst scowled into the depths of his *sah*. "We'll be dealing with Staff Sergeant Kerr. He's her problem."

"Okay." Guimond grinned. "What do you think of her?"

Werst shrugged. "*Chrick.*"

"What don't you find edible?" Ken Tsui demanded getting himself another beer. "She's not recon."

"She was. She started out Fifth Re'carta, First Battalion, Recon. Went in half a dozen times, got wounded, made corporal, got transferred. What?" Nivry demanded of the room as whole. "I looked her up." The corporal held up her slate. "It's all in the attachment's database. You can bet she's downloaded everything in there on us."

No one took the bet.

"I heard the general picked her personally," Johnston offered, scratching at the faint shadow of whiskers across his chin.

"And we were randomly generated?" Nivry snorted. "With the whole sector to choose this team from, they'd have picked the best."

"And you think you're proof of that?"

"Damned right. Anyone in here think they're not?" She paused for effect and got an answer.

"He's not." Jynett jabbed her elbow into the ribs of the di'Taykan beside her.

"Suck up," Huilin grunted, rubbing at the damp patch of spilled beer on his shirt.

"Slacker."

"All right, let's be . . ."

"Relax, Corporal, we took our HE1 course together. This one . . ." Huilin raised the remains of his beer in an exaggerated toast. ". . . placed top in the class."

Jynnet's glass rose to touch his. "Which means poor Huilin had to settle for second."

"I was robbed."

Nivry's eyes lightened. "Which proves my point.

We were picked because we're the best. Staff Sergeant Kerr was probably picked because she could get the job done even under the handicap of Captain Travik."

Across the room, Corporal Harrop said something that sounded distinctly rude in one of the remaining Human languages. With all eyes on him, he shrugged and translated. "No one's that good."

Werst drained his *sah*, stood, and tossed the cup into the recyler. "She'd better be."

Craig Ryder held a full house, kings over threes, when his ship, parked in one of the *Berganitan*'s shuttle bays, informed him it was 0600 hours. He tongued in an acknowledgment, then looked up and swept the table with his second best smile, the one designed to distract from the situation—which was, at the moment, the happy fact that he'd taken a month's pay or better off everyone at the table. "Afraid this'll have to be the last hand, mates. Duty calls."

"Duty?" One of the two watching di'Taykan, long since tapped out, stared up at him from under a moving fringe of lavender hair. "Calling *you?*"

"As it happens, I've got a briefing to attend in under two hours and—you know how it is—I'd like to make a good impression."

"On who?"

"On whoever it would do me the most good to impress, of course."

"Well, as it happens," Lieutenant Commander Sibley echoed, tapping his own cards on the edge of the table, "it's up to you."

Ryder allowed his smile to pick up a slight predatory edge as he aimed it directly at the vacuum jockey. "So it is. I see your hundred and I raise you . . ." Eyes locked on the opposition, he picked up a stack of markers and threw them into the pot. ". . . three hundred more."

The Krai between them glanced at the cards in her right foot, took a long draw on a pouch of beer, and shook her head. "I fold."

"Down to you and me, Sibley."

"You wish," he muttered, frowning at his hand.

The second di'Taykan made a suggestion.

Both Humans ignored him.

"Well?"

"Why not." Sibley looked up and grinned, pushing his last markers into the center of the table. "I call. What've you got?"

Ryder laid out his cards.

The grin slipped sideways but held. "Buh-bye," he sighed throwing in two jacks, two tens, and a seven.

The Krai, who'd played cautiously all night, still had a few markers left, the rest Ryder scooped up and dumped into his belt pouch. "Always a pleasure doing business with the Navy." He lifted his beer in a flourishing salute, drained it, and tossed the empty pouch down on the table. "Hope you lads don't mind cleaning up . . ."

It was almost a question.

He was gone before anyone answered.

The markers were a comfortable weight against his hip as he made his way back to shuttle bay four—nothing like turning a profit to improve the time wasted in Susumi space. Later, he'd head down to QSM and cash in, but right now he needed to reach his ship before someone in Navy gray checked his pass and discovered his clearance didn't include this part of the *Berganitan*.

They—they being the anal retentives in uniform running the show—hadn't wanted him along. Too bad. He alone knew where they were going, and he had no intention of handing that information over gratis. Restricting his unescorted movements beyond the confines of the shuttle bay had been their way of taking a petty revenge. The sergeant at arms had made it quite clear they'd slap a security chip in him if they found him where he didn't belong.

That said, he still preferred to play on the other guys' turf—it made the opposition overconfident and kept the repair bills from coming out of his account if the game got out of hand. As friendly little games so often did.

A couple of techs on morning watch looked up from an open panel as he passed, but he made it back to the *Promise* without attracting any unwelcome attention. He'd refused the generous offer of access to the *Berganitan*'s system—and the reflective access that would give the *Berganitan* to him—and, because he'd always been a *cautious* man, he'd locked his implant and his ship down tight. A quick check after boarding proved the security protocols on both were intact; as far as anyone who might care would ever know, he'd spent the night sound asleep.

"And wouldn't that have been a waste of time?" Tossing the belt pouch onto his bunk, he stripped off for the shower.

He'd sincerely meant it when he'd said it was a pleasure doing business with the Navy—a vacuum jockey's idea of saving for retirement was drawing to an inside straight. Probably a result of too much time spent in zero gee.

He had a feeling the Marines weren't going to be half so much fun.

* * *

Torin had her team in place well before the briefing was due to start. The twelve Marines filled the last two rows, the double line of service uniforms creating a matte-black shadow at the back of the room. With the exception of Guimond, the rest—even the two engineers—wore the sort of blank expressions usually seen after the words, "We need a volunteer for . . ." Guimond looked fascinated by everything he saw.

She had no doubt that each and every one of them had not only marked the exits but carried a complete mental map of the route back to the attachment and the armory—Marines being Marines and Recon even more so.

When General Morris, Captain Travik, and Lieutenant Stedrin entered, she brought them to attention. There was nothing of the parade ground about the movement, but they all ended up on their feet more or less at the same time. The general made a sotto voce suggestion to the captain who then sauntered—there really could be no other word for it even given the natural gait of a species with opposable toes—back to Torin's side.

"So this is my reconnaissance team, is it, Staff Sergeant?"

He hadn't actually looked at them. Hadn't actually looked anywhere but at her. "Yes, sir."

"Excellent." His smile showed almost enough tooth to be considered a challenge—which would have been a lot more relevant had she been another Krai. "I assume you've gone through their records, checked them all out, made sure they're the best?"

"They were chosen for this mission because they *are* the best, sir."

"I know I was."

Jolly tones suggested he was making a joke. Torin decided not to get it. "Yes, sir."

"Well, I'm not sure why the general wants them here—that is, right here, right now. I'm quite sure you'd be capable of briefing them after it's all over, but ours is not to question why."

Torin managed not to wince. *Wonderful. Now, it's a theme.*

"Have them sit down. They can take notes if they feel it's necessary. I'll speak to you later."

"Yes, sir." After he'd turned and walked away, she turned herself, saying quietly, "As you were." Expressions as the team sat ranged from blank to bored. The one murmured observation had been too low for her to hear content, so she ignored it. All things considered, it hadn't gone badly.

Based on their two short meetings, Captain Travik seemed more an idiot than a murderous glory-hog. *Not,* she acknowledged, *that those personality traits are mutually exclusive.* She'd be able to form a more relevant opinion after she saw him in action.

A number of civilians filed in as she sat and the front rows filled quickly.

"We're not taking them *all* in with us, are we, Staff?" Guimond wondered, his voice a bass rumble by her left ear.

Torin sure as hell hoped not but all she said was, "We'll do what we're ordered to do, Guimond."

"Yeah, but . . ."

"We'll find out soon enough." She heard his seat creak as he sat back. He had reason to be concerned. There were eight or nine Katrien, all talking at once, a half a dozen Humans, three di'Taykan, three Krai, four Niln, and a Ciptran—sitting alone, antennae flat against his/her head, one mid-leg fiddling with the controls on the inhaler implanted over the gills on both sides of his/her carapace. The Katrien and the Niln were local to this sector, the Humans, di'Taykan, and Krai had probably been chosen because of the military presence in an effort to keep species numbers down. Torin had never seen a Ciptran before but had been told they were the exception to the rule that said only social species developed intelligence.

When Captain Carveg and two of her officers arrived to represent the *Berganitan* and things still didn't get started, Torin wondered who else they were waiting for.

He made his entrance at 0759, stepping through the hatch as though both the scientists and the Marines had been gathered in this room, at this time, for his benefit. A civilian, a Human male; just under two meters tall, with broad shoulders and heavy arms, almost broad and heavy enough to be out of proportion to the rest of a muscular body. Torin watched him cross to the general through narrowed eyes. She didn't know much about civilian styles, but she knew attitude when she saw it. And she was seeing it. In spades.

When he reached the officers, he smiled broadly, spread his hands, and said something too low for Torin to catch.

"The exact same thing happened to me." Captain Travik's voice carried clearly over the room's ambient noise. "That's the Navy for you, can't draw a straight line between two points. You ought to come stay with the Marines."

Torin glanced at Captain Carveg who gave no indication she'd overheard the comment. If Parliament wanted to promote a Krai, why didn't they start with Carveg? A Navy captain held rank equivalent to a

Marine colonel; Travik had a way to go to even catch up. *On the other hand,* Torin mused, her gaze flicking between the officers, *if they leave Carveg where she is, she can keep doing a job she's good at, and if we're very lucky, they'll stuff Travik where no one on the lines'll miss him.*

General Morris moved out beside the large vid screen at the front of the room and various conversations trailed off into an anticipatory silence. "We all know why we're here," the general began without preamble. "A vessel belonging to no known species has been discovered drifting in space. It is, or rather will be, our job to find out everything we can about this vessel. At this time, I will turn the briefing over to Mr. Craig Ryder, the CSO who made the discovery."

CSOs, civilian salvage operators, haunted the edge of battle zones where they dragged in the inevitable debris. Some they sold back to the military, the rest to the recycling centers. The overhead of operating in deep space being what it was, even the good ones never made much more than expenses.

Like all scavengers, they performed a valuable service and, like all scavengers, they profited by the misfortune of others. Since most of that misfortune happened in combat to people who were never strangers, Torin decided she didn't much care for the man now crossing to General Morris' side.

"Thank you, General." As the general moved back to the small knot of officers, Ryder turned to face his audience. His eyes were deep-set to either side of a nose that had clearly been broken at least once away from medical attention, brown hair curled at his collar, and he wore a short beard—unusual in those who spent a lot of time in space and therefore expected to be suiting up regularly. He had a deep voice and an accent Torin couldn't quite place. "G'day. I hope you all understand why I'm unwilling to give out specific coordinates at this time but I can assure you, this ship is a good distance off the beaten paths. I found it by accident . . ." His smile suggested further secrets he wasn't ready to share. ". . . thanks to a small Susumi miscalculation . . ."

Torin heard several near gasps and even the Ciptran's antennae came up.

Susumi miscalculations usually ended in memorial services. *This guy's got the luck of H'san.*

". . . that popped me back into real space some considerable distance from the system I'd been heading for. After I got my bearings—and changed my pants . . ."

And the sense of humor of a twelve-year-old.

Behind her, Marines snickered.

He acknowledged the response like a seasoned performer and continued almost seamlessly. ". . . I thought I might as well have a look around. Imagine my surprise when I read a very large manufactured object a relatively short distance away. Which was, of course, nothing to my surprise when I went to have a look . . ." Half turning toward the screen, he ran his thumb down the vid control. ". . . and found this.

"That little shape down in the lower right is the *Berganitan.* I pasted it in to give you lot some idea of scale."

It was bright yellow. And it was big, close to the size of the OutSector Stations, longer than it was wide—20.76 kilometers by 7.32 kilometers—with a high probability of the dimpled end representing some kind of a propulsion system. The Confederation database had declared it alien, but—in spite of the color—Torin thought it looked a lot less alien than a number of ships she'd seen.

There were a number of identifiable air locks, one on each side up near the bow, one topside, one on the portside about two thirds of the way back, and one in the belly in the aft third. There were no identifiable exterior weapons. Unfortunately, air locks had limited design options, weapons did not. They could be looking at enough firepower to rebang the big one and never know it.

Scans showed no energy signals—in fact they showed nothing at all inside the yellow hull although Ryder admitted his equipment was perhaps too small to penetrate.

Which brought the expected response from the di'-Taykan present.

When the *Berganitan* arrived after four days in Susumi space, there'd be more scans, and then the Marines would be sent in to discover what the scans missed.

Simple. Straightforward.

Or it would have been had the scientists not argued every point—with each other, with Ryder, and occasionally with themselves. A half an hour later, when General Morris walked back out in front of the screen, now showing a dozen different views of the ship, his presence front and center had no noticeable effect on the noise level.

"Think he's going to order us to strangle them, Staff?"

Torin grinned at Guimond's cheerful question. "It would explain why we're here, but, somehow, I doubt it." She kept her attention locked on the general's face. When, eyes narrowed in irritation, he met her gaze and nodded, she stood.

"MARINES, ATTEN—SHUN!"

Her voice filled the room, wall to wall, deck to deck. It filled in every single space that wasn't already occupied by a physical form.

Twelve pairs of boots slammed down on the deck as twelve Marines snapped up onto their feet. This time, because it counted, it was a textbook maneuver.

The silence that followed was an unsure and tentative thing. Faces furred and bare stared from the general to the solid wall of black so suddenly behind them and back to the general again. Craig Ryder and the Navy officers had moved from Torin's line of sight, but Captain Travik was obviously amused by the scientists' discomfort. If Lieutenant Stedrin found the situation amusing, he didn't show it. The latter went up, the former down in Torin's regard.

General Morris swept a stern gaze across the first three rows of seats. "I would like to remind you all that until we are one hundred percent certain this vessel does not belong to the Others or one of their subject races, this will remain a military operation. Mr. Ryder's scans as well as information extrapolated from them have been downloaded into your laboratories or workstations where you may go over them in as much detail as you wish. When you have chosen the four scientists who will be first to board the vessel after it has been secured, have them report to Staff Sergeant Kerr so that she can ensure they will be neither a danger to themselves or to her team. That is all."

The Ciptran unfolded its lower legs and stalked out of the room.

The remaining scientists shuffled in place for a moment, then the Katriens—all trilling loudly—led the exodus.

A moment later Captain Travik waded through the stragglers and headed for the back of the room.

"Staff Sergeant Kerr."

"Sir."

"General Morris would like a word with you after you dismiss the team."

"Yes, sir."

"Nice to see the fear of the Corps in the eyes of those *serley chrika*. I told the general he should use the Marines to keep the civilians under control." He sounded like he believed it, too.

"Yes, sir."

She sent the team back to the Marine attachment under Corporal Nivry and followed the captain to the front of the room where General Morris was speaking with Lieutenant Stedrin.

"Staff Sergeant Kerr?"

Most of her attention still on the general, she half turned to find Craig Ryder smiling at her. Up close, she could see that his eyes were very blue and the secrets in his smile had taken on a strangely intimate extension.

Intimate? Where the hell was that coming from? She'd never met the man.

"So, Captain Travik tells me you'll be helping him out on this little excursion."

Torin shot a look at the captain who showed teeth. It was quite possibly exactly what the captain had told him. Verbatim.

"I'm Captain Travik's senior NCO, Mr. Ryder, if that's what you mean."

"Is it?" Both brows flicked up. "All right, then. Well, as Captain Travik's senior NCO, I thought you should know that I'll be heading inside with you on that first trip."

"No, Mr. Ryder, you will not."

"Yes, Staff Sergeant, he will."

She slowly pivoted to face the general. "Sir?"

"It was one of the conditions Mr. Ryder imposed when he agreed to take us to the ship. And what I intended to speak with you about. As Mr. Ryder has beaten me to the punch, you two might as well carry on with your discussion." The general's expression made it clear, at least to Torin, that he appreciated the CSO's interference. "Lieutenant . . ."

"Sir." The di'Taykan fell into step beside the general as he left the room. After a moment's hesitation, Captain Travik hurried to catch up.

"Alone at last."

Torin pivoted once more, a little more quickly this time. "Are you out of your mind? You have no idea what's in that ship."

His eyes sparkled. "Neither do you."

"But *we* are trained to deal with the unexpected, the dangerous unknown." Torin held onto her temper with both hands. "You, Mr. Ryder, are not."

"I intend to protect my investment, Staff Sergeant."

"From what? We don't want your *salvage*."

"Nice try, but I've worked with the Marines before. You don't know you don't want my salvage until you've had a good look at it. Just to keep things on the up and up, I'll be looking at everything you do. Might as well accept it graciously."

"Graciously?"

"Kindly. Courteously."

"Mr. Ryder, if your presence endangers any of my people," Torin told him in as gracious a tone as she could manage, "I'll shoot you myself."

"Woo." He rocked back on his heels, both hands raised in exaggerated surrender. "I don't like to criticize, Staff Sergeant, but have you ever considered cutting back on your red meat?"

A moment later, watching the rigid lines of the staff sergeant's back disappear out the hatch, Ryder grinned. "Well, when I'm wrong, I'm right wrong—looks like I'll be having fun with the Marines after all."

THREE

THE temperature in the narrow corridor had risen to just over 47°C, but the line of sweat running down Torin's neck had more to do with exertion—inside her suit, it remained a chilly 13°. For the last half hour, her suit had been maintaining di'Taykan conditions and couldn't be reset.

At least the environmental controls worked.

Early on, an electromagnetic pulse had knocked out her mapping program. Fortunately, the homing beacon had been unaffected and she'd been moving steadily back toward the air lock through a maze of corridors. The builders had gone in big for dead ends, rooms with no recognizable purpose, and huge pieces of machinery that seemed as much historical as alien. Torin had looked down a ladder into the heart of a steam turbine and, shortly after, on a long straightway had raced against something that wouldn't have seemed out of place back on her family's farm—had any of the farm machinery ever tried to kill her.

The air lock was now only eight meters to her right.

Behind a wall.

She was standing at the bottom of an l-shaped area. Another dead end.

She had twenty-three minutes of air left.

There had to be a way.

Slowing her breathing, she mentally retraced her steps.

And smiled.

Three long strides toward the end wall and she released her boots. Momentum kept her moving forward. Feet up, she pushed off hard.

Negotiating the corner involved a bit of a ricochet, but she got twisted far enough around to hit nearly the right vector. "Nearly" equaling no more than a bruised shoulder. It wasn't pretty, but as long as it worked . . .

At the next T-junction, she flipped over, remagged her boots, and walked straight up the wall to a second-level gallery.

Visibility was bad. Particulates saturated what passed for atmosphere and had gummed up most of Torin's faceplate. It took her five long minutes to find the tube she'd remembered, seconds to confirm that it went in the right direction.

Air lock entry 22.86 meters away. One level down.

An earlier laser bounce had measured the tube at 16.3 meters. Which would put her on the other side of the wall she'd been staring at.

It was a tight fit.

Seven minutes of air left.

On the bright side, the tight fit allowed her to brace after impact, take up the shock with her knees, and keep from careening back the way she'd come.

Air lock entry 6.56 meters away. One level down.

Torin slapped down a shaped charge. It activated on impact.

With four minutes and twelve seconds of air, a thirty-second fuse delay took forever.

Stripping the suit of everything detachable, she jammed it in over the charge, and shuffled back.

Three minutes and forty-two seconds later, she shoved the rest of the debris through the hole, followed it, remagged her boots as she hit the deck, and jogged to the air lock.

As the door cycled closed behind her, she dug her gloves into the shoulder catches and dragged her helmet off the second the telltales turned green, sucking back great lungfuls of air less redolent of staff sergeant.

It took her a moment to identify the sudden sound through ringing ears.

Applause.

Torin turned, swept her gaze over the half circle of watching Marines and brought it to rest on Huilin and Jynett who were looking like anxious parents. "You two are a pair of sadistic sons of bitches," she said, unhooking her empty tanks, too tired to think of a Taykan equivalent.

Their eyes lightened.

Jynett pounded Huilin on the shoulder and ducked his return swing. "Thank you, Staff."

"You're welcome."

"You had seventeen seconds' worth of air left, Staff," Nivry observed, coming forward to catch Torin's tanks as they dropped. "Why the rush?"

"Well, Corporal, it's like this . . ." She paused long enough to remove her left glove. "I didn't want anyone to think I was hogging the simulation."

"Very considerate."

"Aren't I." A hoot of laughter spun her around. Her thrown glove slapped against Guimond's chest. "You're next, laughing boy."

"All right!" The perpetual smile broadened and he waved the glove like a trophy. "Thanks, Staff."

You couldn't not laugh with him, Torin thought, as she unsuited against one side of the fake air lock and Guimond suited up by the other. With only two hours of air, they weren't bothering to hook in the plumbing, so the whole procedure took half the time it might have—and twice the time it would have had there not been so many people helping out.

The Corps' hazardous environment suits were high-tech marvels that allowed a full range of movement and protected the wearer against almost anything an unfriendly universe could throw against it—up to and including most personal projectile weapons, although a hit anywhere but the head or torso left a nasty bruise. The helmet co-opted H'san technology and held two different shapes. Dropped off the back toggle, it collapsed down the back of the suit like an empty bag; snapped back up over the head, it became a rigid, impenetrable sphere capable of polarizing to maintain any programmed light level.

Helmet up, if the outside atmosphere held oxygen and nitrogen in any combination, the suit could filter in something essentially breathable to support the tanks. It recycled fluids, all fluids, almost indefinitely. Self-contained, they were comfortable for six hours, livable for eight, and, if breathing was still an option, got progressively nastier after that. They glowed under a number of different light conditions in order to make it easier for S&R crews to find the bodies. Marines loved them and hated them about equally.

August Guimond was the first Marine Torin had ever seen who looked happy putting one on.

"All right . . ." She let the suit drop, stepped out of the boots, and rolled the kinks out of her shoulders.

". . . let's say a two-and-a-half-hour turnaround, a little longer if the subject doesn't survive and we need to debrief. Even simulated deaths are meaningless if we don't learn from them."

Nivry's eyes lightened. "That's deep, Staff."

"It'll get deeper as the day goes on. Pack a shovel." Her suit in one hand and a cleaning kit in the other, Torin turned back to Huilin and Jynett. "Can that thing spit out another twelve programs?"

"No problem, Staff."

"Twelve *different* programs," she qualified.

"The Hazardous Environment Course 2 comes with an infinite number of nasties."

"How realistic. So," her voice reached out to include the entire team, "we'll spend today and tomorrow running through singles and then break into squads. Guimond, you won't need that much ammo for your KC. We're playing variations on 'find your way home,' not 'search and destroy.'"

The big Human looked down at the double handful of clips he was loading into bulging leg pouches and then up at Torin. "It's simulated ammo," he reminded her with a grin.

"True."

"And you had explosives."

"I fail to see the connection. Demolition packs are standard Recon equipment." She draped her suit over one shoulder and tossed a pack across to him. "Don't leave home without it."

"And the ammo?" he asked, snapping the demo pack to his belt.

Torin sighed. "Take what you think you'll need."

"Thanks, Staff."

"But . . ." Her attention expanded to once again include the entire team. ". . . if I get the impression any of you are becoming too dependent on the suits, we'll run a couple of minimals."

About to settle his helmet, Guimond paused. "So, Staff, you're saying you'd rather send me in naked with a knife in my teeth?"

Torin waited out a pause almost di'Taykan in its implications, then said, "Knife in your hand, Guimond. I'd hate to see you cut your head off. Now, check your system and get in there; we're all getting older even if the universe isn't."

"A five percent death rate, Staff Sergeant?" Captain Travik shook his head in dismay. "I think you're making the simulations too easy."

"These Marines were specifically chosen, sir. They're good."

"Still, five percent. I don't want General Morris to think I'm not taking your training seriously."

As the captain's only contact with the team so far had been in the briefing room, Torin figured General Morris would have grounds. On the bright side, if the captain wasn't involved, he wasn't screwing things up. "The programs were taken from the HE2, sir."

"Two?" His brow furrowed until it met his upper nose ridges. "Did I order you to run two?"

"You weren't specific about which simulations to run, sir. These were the best we had on hand."

The extra ridges smoothed. "The best; I see." He beamed in approval.

Torin suspected he'd just edited reality and made the HE2s his idea from the start—standard operating procedure for bad officers. As far as she was concerned, he could claim to be the guy who'd dreamed up close order drill just so long as he didn't put her people in unnecessary danger.

As for the HE2s: in the interest of getting a leg up on his next course, Huilin had picked up a bootleg copy of the advanced simulations and, together, using information they'd acquired on their last course, he and Jynett had managed to crack the instructor's code so it would run—nothing Captain Travik needed to know.

She glanced down at the report she'd just finished summarizing. "We'll be running individual simulations tomorrow as well, sir."

"Excellent."

"Will you be coming by?"

"I don't think so, Staff Sergeant." Shifting forward in the chair, his chin rose, his chest went out. "The troops'll stand a better chance if they're not worried about me watching them."

"I was thinking you might want to run the simulation yourself, Captain."

"Me?"

Is there another captain in the room? Calmly meeting his indignant gaze, she elaborated, "As your senior NCO, it's my responsibility to point out that it's been a while since you've suited up."

"Your responsibility?"

"Yes, sir."

"To point out that it's been a while since I've suited up?"

"Yes, sir." It was like talking to a primitive translation program that changed the pronouns and repeated everything said to it. Unfortunately, it was like talking to a primitive translation program wearing a captain's uniform.

"A while?"

"Yes, sir."

He stood, drawing himself up to his full height and

jerking his tunic down in the same practiced motion. His shoulders squared, his head angled slightly, his lips curled back off his teeth. Torin couldn't shake the impression he was staring into a vid cam only he could see. "Horohn 8 was a hazardous environment, Staff Sergeant, and I'm sure you've heard that I suited up there. In fact, I spent four hours in that *serley* suit; four hours fighting for my life while all around me, Marines were dropping like . . ." His nose ridges flushed lightly. "What is it that Humans have things dropping like?"

"Flies, sir."

"Yes, exactly. All around me, Marines were dropping like flies. When an officer comes out of that kind of a situation, Staff Sergeant, he doesn't need a hazardous environment course. He's survived the only course that means anything." The left half of his upper lip curled higher. "This mission is a mere moo two . . ."

"Sir?"

"A moo two." His ridges flushed darker. "Military operation other than war. MOOTW."

"Oh."

"Exactly. I won't be putting the mission in danger by not participating in your little drills, Staff Sergeant, and I resent the implication that you think I will. Continued insubordination will be reported to the general, don't think it won't."

"Yes, sir."

He stared at her for a moment, trying to work out just what she was agreeing with. Torin gave him no help. "Good," he said at last, hiding his uncertainty in movement. Dropping down into his chair, he propped one foot up on his desk and reached for his slate with the other. "Now, if you actually want those simulations to do some good, go have a word with your friend Mr. Ryder. He hasn't the benefit of your training or my experience. I'd just as soon not have to include the details of his death in my report, and I'm sure you won't want to be encumbered by his body while securing the alien vessel."

With the bleed off from the Susumi drive giving her power to burn, the *Berganitan* used an internal transit system indistinguishable in every way but size from the links on the stations. Unable to go directly from the Marine attachment to the shuttle bays, Torin found herself waiting at an isolated transfer point. As much as she hated to agree with Captain Travik about anything, his observation on the Navy's inability to draw a straight line had merit.

When the link finally arrived, a pair of emerging vacuum jockeys nearly ran her down.

One paused, turned, and smiled. "Staff Sergeant Kerr."

"Lieutenant Commander Sibley."

"You're not lost, are you?" The vacuum jockey glanced around the corridor as though trying to figure out exactly where they were. "You're a little off your usual beaten paths. And you know what they say, no one beats a path like a Marine."

"Do they, sir?"

"Oh, yeah. Beats it into submission and plants a flag on it."

"They don't say that around me," Torin told him after a moment's consideration.

He nodded. "I can understand that. *Are* you lost?"

"No, sir." When he indicated a need for more detail, she added, "I'm on my way to shuttle bay six to speak with Craig Ryder."

"You want some advice? Don't play poker with him."

"Hadn't intended to, sir."

"Hey, Sibley!"

Torin and the pilot both turned toward the voice. The di'Taykan who'd emerged from the link at the same time was waiting down the corridor by an open hatch, citron hair a corona around his head. "You coming?"

"Not yet, still not even breathing hard."

Too much information, Torin decided. "Excuse me, sir, but I'm holding up the whole system here." She stepped onto the link at the lieutenant commander's good-natured wave. He must have said something she didn't catch because as the door closed she heard the di'Taykan officer say, "No, we're going to my quarters because your quarters are such a disaster I can't find my *kayti*!"

Way too much information . . .

Craig Ryder's ship, the *Promise,* nearly filled shuttle bay four. Torin found it hard to believe he'd managed to dock it cleanly, but both the hull and the edges of the *Berganilan* that she could see appeared to be free of scrapes. Whatever else Ryder was, he was one hell of a pilot.

Without the cargo pods extended, the *Promise* looked like a Navy ship to ship shuttle crouched under a stack of cross-slatted panels. Considering the dimensions of the most basic Susumi drive, Torin understood why CSOs tended to work alone—two people would have to be very friendly to share the remaining space.

The hatch was open, and the ramp was down.

Curiosity may have made her approach quieter

than necessary, the only sound as she made her way up the ramp the soft and ever present hum of Susumi space stroking the *Berganitan*'s outer hull.

May have.

The interior of the salvage ship was smaller than she'd imagined. To her left were the flight controls and the pilot's seat. Directly across from the hatch, a half-circle table butted up to a wall bench. To her right, across the blunt end of the oval, a bunk and a narrow opening leading to—she leaned through the tiny air lock—the toilet facilities. It looked as though taking a shower involved closing the door and the toilet seat and standing in the middle of the tiny room.

Bits of paper and plastic had been stuck to the bulkhead over the bunk and a single white sock lay crumpled on the deck. A blue plastic plate, cup, and fork had been left on the table next to a small, inset screen. The pilot's chair looked as though it had been built up out of spare parts and duct tape—clearly tailored to fit only the dimensions of the builder.

Approximately five meters from the edge of the control panel to the bunk and three, maybe three and a half meters, from side to side, Craig Ryder's entire world was smaller than the smallest Marine Corps APC.

How could anyone live like that? She found her gaze drawn back to the sock. *Or more specifically, what kind of person would choose to?*

"I don't recall inviting you on board, Staff Sergeant Kerr."

Torin glanced down at her boots before turning. "I'm not on board, Mr. Ryder."

"You're on my ramp."

"Granted. I apologize for intruding." Half a dozen long strides brought her back to the shuttle bay's deck and almost nose to nose with Craig Ryder, close enough to smell sweat and machine oil about equally mixed. Bare arms folded, a wrench held loosely in one hand, he clearly wasn't moving, so she took a single step away. Common sense suggested keeping a careful distance—if it came to it, she needed enough room to swing. "The hatch was down, and the door was open."

"I wasn't expecting visitors." Unfolding one arm, he scratched in the beard under his chin with the wrench and smiled charmingly. Strangely, the two actions didn't cancel each other out. "You're a long way from the Marine attachment. Can I assume you're here for the pleasure of my company?"

"No."

"No?"

It was like looking at two different men—the one who'd been standing at the end of the ramp watching her descent under lowered brows and the one who'd just repeated her blunt response in tones of exaggerated disbelief. Given a choice, Torin would have preferred to deal with the former.

"I'm here," she explained, "because you're not hooked to the *Berganitan*."

"I hook to the ship, the ship hooks to me." Ryder shook his head. "A little too much give and take for my tastes. Since you couldn't call, what did you walk all the way down here for?"

"I'm here to assess your hazardous environment status."

"Excuse me?"

"I'm not being funny, Mr. Ryder." Although he clearly thought she was. The urge to wipe the smirk off his face was nearly overwhelming. She wouldn't have taken that kind of attitude from a Marine, enlisted or commissioned, but she had no idea of how to handle it coming from a civilian. "Look, we have no idea of what we'll face inside the alien vessel . . ."

He snorted. "We have no idea whether we can even get the locks open."

"Excuse me?"

"It's an *alien vessel*, Staff Sergeant Kerr. We might not be able to crack it."

Torin shrugged. "That's an engineering problem, Mr. Ryder, not mine. If I can't stop you from boarding with the Recon team, I need to know you won't be a danger to my people—no matter what we face."

"Staff Sergeant, do you know how I operate?"

She managed to keep her lip from curling. "No, Mr. Ryder, I do not."

"When we claim salvage, we deploy specifically sized cargo pods made up of those panels." His gesture took in the stack on the *Promise* and his voice picked up a strange, mocking tone, as though he objected to the necessary explanation. "The number of panels depends on the size of the salvage. Each panel adds a specific set of factors to the Susumi equation. Do you know what happens to a ship when the Susumi equation is off by the smallest integer?"

"Oh, yeah; specifically, it pops out next to unknown alien vessels and complicates my life." When he turned to face her, she met the indignation in his eyes with mild exasperation.

After a moment, he blinked and grinned. "Condescending question?"

"You think?" Torin stared up at the panels, noting the signs of hard use. "You're telling me that every time you deploy, you vacuum trot?"

He followed her gaze. "Every time there's a questionable reading, yes."

"And that happens?"

"Oh, pretty much every time I deploy."

She shook her head and transferred her gaze to his face. "You're insane."

"Me? *You* get paid to be shot at."

"That's not why they pay me, Mr. Ryder. They pay me to see that we achieve our mission objectives without losing personnel."

"Military speak," he snorted. "You get the job done without anyone getting killed."

Seventeen tiny metal cylinders, each holding a Marine she'd brought home. "I try, Mr. Ryder."

He sighed and tossed the wrench down into his tool kit. "Look, Staff Sergeant, I can guarantee I've spent more time suited than your entire team. I will not be a danger to your people. And . . ." A crooked finger rose to emphasize the point. ". . . should we run into someone who objects to our presence, I have every intention of hauling ass out of there and, if that's not possible, hiding behind the professionals. I'm there protecting my salvage—which will be no use to me if I'm dead."

He'd sounded sincere. But he'd previously sounded annoyed, charming, amused, mocking, and sarcastic—all within their short conversation. What made this last emotion any more realistic than the rest?

And what difference does it make? Torin demanded silently. *You don't have to figure him out, you merely have to endure him.* "Okay, you know how to work in a suit. I'd still like to see you come out for the team simulations, if only to get my people used to having you hide behind them."

"When?"

"Day after tomorrow. In the afternoon." That

would give them the morning to run the course without him, to shake down the squads, and make necessary changes to both personnel and equipment. She refocused to find him watching her from under the edge of thick lashes.

"So, what's happening tomorrow?"

"The remaining individual simulations—the ones you've convinced me you don't need."

"Maybe I'll come by anyway."

"You'd be a distraction."

"You find me a distraction, Staff Sergeant?" The question was almost coy.

"I find anything outside the mission parameters a distraction, Mr. Ryder." Weight back on her heels, Torin folded her arms and met his gaze. "You rank right up there with hangovers and hemorrhoids."

The skin around his eyes creased into laugh lines as his smile broadened. "You know, I was starting to think you didn't have a sense of humor."

"I don't. Day after tomorrow, afternoon; if you don't want to bring your own equipment, I'm sure we can find a suit to fit you."

Craig Ryder stood at the top of the ramp and took a couple of long steadying breaths before he stepped into the *Promise* and punched the inner hatch closed. That had been too close. Staff Sergeant Kerr had been one long stride away from being inside.

In his personal space.

His.

Bunk, bench, table, screen, dishes; he touched each in order, then spun the control chair once around and sat. The familiar sink and sway in reaction to his weight helped, but he still drifted a hand over each of the controls in turn before he leaned back and swung his feet up onto the precise place he'd rested them a thousand, a million times before—the place where his heels had worn the finish off the edge of the control panel.

His place.

After a long moment, he leaned back and closed his eyes. He hadn't quite made up his mind about attending the simulation although he suspected he'd go if only for the pleasure of continuing to annoy Staff Sergeant Kerr.

And to keep her from making a return visit.

"All right, then."

There didn't seem to be much else to say.

"Hey, Werst, Staff's sending me down to the armory to make sure the guys back at MidSector actually loaded what inventory says they loaded." Guimond grinned down at the top of the Krai's head. "She says I should take someone with me; you up?"

"No. I'm busy."

"Come on, you're sitting on your ass drinking *sah*, how busy is that?"

"I'm busy resting."

"Right, 'cause you'll be first through the sim in the morning which is at least ten hours away." He slid a long step to his right, just far enough to bend and peer into Werst's face. "Come on."

Werst's attention remained on the contents of his mug. "Fuk off."

"I'll go with you, Guimond." Orla stood and tossed her empty beer pouch into the recyler in one lithe move. She crossed to the big Human's side and rubbed her shoulder against his. "Maybe we can find something else to count while we're down there."

"I've still got the same one I had yesterday,"

Guimond grinned. "But we have to do the inventory check first. Staff says MidSector's not used to loading for Recon and she doesn't want us going in with our asses hanging out."

"Staff said that?"

"Those very words."

Johnston glanced up from the circuit board he'd pulled out of the food dispenser, magnification lenses silvering his eyes to a di'Taykan monochrome. "Who'd have thought Staff would be so articulate."

Golden brows drew in as Guimond turned to Orla, looking confused. "What's he talking about?"

She shrugged. "He's an engineer, who the fuk knows?"

"I, myself, am wondering," Dursinski put in from her place by the pool table, "if Staff's so worried about our asses, why's she not doing the inventory check?"

Nivry glanced up from her slate. "She got invited to dinner in the Chief's and PO's Mess."

"How do you know that?" Dursinski demanded.

"Harrop and I were going over squad assignments with her when the invite came in from some warrant officer. He's a friend from other trips on the *Berg*. Human, so, after dinner, they probably won't . . ." She dropped her attention back to her slate. ". . . have dessert."

"She doesn't really mean dessert, does she?" Guimond asked as he and Orla left the room. The hatch cut off the di'Taykan's laughter.

"What a fukking moron," Werst grunted.

Nivry caught Harrop's eye and shrugged. When making up the squads, the two corporals had decided to keep Werst and Guimond together—the Human's size and good nature making up for Werst's lack of either—and Nivry had drawn the short straw. "What do you have against him?" she demanded.

"You've got the double hooks," the Krai snorted, "you figure it out."

"Let's assume I got them for good looks—not brains—and you tell me."

"Whatever. Fine." Werst drained his mug, crushing it in one hand as he stood. "August Guimond's a big sweet guy, good-looking by Human standards, and everyone likes him—why don't we just paint a fukking target on him now and get it over with. You all know he's exactly the sort of guy who gets shot first when his squad hits combat." His voice rose an octave. "They shot Guimond! That lousy *serley chrika* shot Guimond!" And dropped back down to a growl. "Then we spend the rest of the mission winning one for poor August. No, thank you." He slammed the crushed mug into the recycler hard enough for its bounce to be clearly audible then, growling inarticulately, stomped out of the room.

"What was that all about?" Harrop wondered.

Nivry shook her head. "I have no idea."

Chief Warrant Officer Dave Graham waited for the heckling to stop before raising his stein. "Thank you. And here's to the riggers of Black Star Squadron, the best in the fleet!"

Torin raised her stein with the rest. As Dave sat down amidst renewed noise, she leaned toward him and said, "Should I be grateful a brand new, high and mighty chief warrant lowers himself to eat with a lowly staff sergeant?"

He grinned. "You should be grateful I lower myself to eat with a Marine."

"You know, I'd heard you were drinking accelerant again."

"How's the steak?"

"Great, thanks." She cut off another hunk of meat and chewed happily. The Navy ate well, that was for damned sure. "If I was your master chief, I'd be watching my back. You keep getting promoted at this rate and you'll have her job in five."

"I dunno, master chief's job gets pretty political. I think I'd rather keep my hands on the machinery. You can trust a thruster to be a thruster." He washed down a mouthful of braised *tabros* with a swallow of beer. "But people . . ."

"Speaking of, I think I met one of yours on the way in. I got a ride from MidSector with a Lieutenant Commander Sibley and I'm having a vague memory of black stars on his Jade."

"Yeah, Sibley's one of ours. Good pilot, but a little too fond of bad puns, if you ask me."

"I seem to have escaped unscathed."

"He must've been on his best behavior."

Torin remembered the multiple accelerations and angles as they left the station. "I wouldn't go that far."

"Well, he'll be out scouting for you when we reach the ship. Black Star and the Red Maces pulled flyby duty—orders came down this afternoon."

"Two squadrons?"

"It's a big ship. Brass wants to know as much as they can before they send you lot in."

"We lot appreciate that."

"Word is you're working with a patchwork team—no two Marines from the same unit."

"Word?"

Dave snorted and slathered butter over another thick slice of bread. "Fuk, Torin, gossip moves around a ship in Susumi faster than light. If you can't get the hockey scores, you've got to talk about something."

"Word's right, then. General Morris doesn't want the information that an alien ship's been discovered getting out to the media before we know what it is, so he decided moving individuals would be less noticeable. They're a good lot, though. With a whole sector to choose from, he could choose the best."

"Yeah, but you've only got four days, five tops, to build a team from scratch. Then you're heading in to gods know what."

"Marines are infinitely flexible."

"Makes it easier to duck."

"I'm personally in favor of ducking."

"I personally am impressed your General Morris got Captain Travik away from MidSector without him alerting the media." Dave grunted. "You planning on bringing him back in one piece?" Tone made *his* preference perfectly clear.

"That's my job." Her tone pretty much matched his.

"Word has it you were the general's special choice." When Torin rolled her eyes, he added. "So what did you do to piss off General Morris enough for him to stick you with the ego that walks like a Krai?"

Unable to separate certain Krai specialties from the more prosaic Human provided varieties, she waved off a tray of mixed cheeses. "Believe it or not, he gave me the job because he wants it done right."

"No, really." He grinned. "Did it involve unspeakable acts."

There were bodies everywhere, most stopped by fire, then shot. Against the south wall of the remaining building were places where the bodies were piled three deep. The smell of burning flesh could be ignored, but the smell of burning blood was very nearly overwhelming.

"You might say that."

Torin glanced down at her slate and shook her head. "Squad One, mission objective; find whatever it is that's sending out the BFFM signal and get back to the air lock with it, keeping Mr. Ryder alive while you do."

All heads turned toward the salvage operator.

"Mr. Ryder . . ."

"Staff Sergeant Kerr."

". . . your objective," she continued, ignoring the cheery interruption, "is to stay alive."

"I think I can do that." His smile had picked up that annoying intimate cast again.

"Corporal Harrop is squad leader. You will obey his orders. Corporal."

"Staff?"

"You will give those orders recognizing Mr. Ryder is a civilian."

"Civilian." Because of the helmet's faceplate, Harrop had to tilt his head to rake the other man head to toe with an unimpressed gaze. It took a while. "Right, Staff."

"Take them in, Corporal."

He'd come mostly out of boredom. And curiosity: And because he realized Staff Sergeant Kerr had been right. They had no idea what they were going to face inside that alien ship, and it was best to be prepared. But when she asked, he planned to make it clear that preparation was the least of his reasons.

She never asked.

She'd looked up, nodded, as though she'd never

doubted her logic would convince him to show, reminded the roomful of black uniforms who he was, and told him he was with Squad One. No surprise. No happy smile of recognition. He hadn't expected either, but he wouldn't have minded a little credit for voluntarily walking into a hazardous environment with a group of armed strangers.

Shuffling into the simulator's air lock beside Heer, the Krai engineer, Ryder leaned down and tapped him on the shoulder. "What's a BFFM, mate?" he asked when the Marine glanced up.

"A Better Fukking Find Me."

"We're looking for a Better Fukking Find Me?"

"You having receiver trouble? It's a Flishing 117, isn't it? I can take it apart without cracking a seal on your suit . . ."

"Thanks, my receiver's fine." He blocked the reaching hand with the back of his forearm. "You Marines are a literal lot, aren't you?"

Heer snickered. "You have no idea."

"Play poker?"

"Does a *gruinitan* go better with red sauce?"

"I'm guessing . . . yes?"

Torin had been surprised to see Ryder come through the hatch, HE suit draped over his arm. He'd brought the basics, borrowed tanks, and now, as she watched the air-lock door close behind him, she wondered why he'd come.

Probably bored.

She knew more than one Marine back on OutSector who ran the simulation chamber just for the hell of it. Given what Marines did for a living, she always thought the di'Taykan way of filling spare time made a lot more sense.

"Hey, Staff, will Ryder be going through again or does Squad Two get a different objective?"

Nivry's question snapped her back to the here and now. "Squad Two," she told them, "gets a wounded comrade to carry out."

"Who?"

"You'll know when they know."

Every eye in the squad turned toward August Guimond who was watching the action in the chamber like it was an adventure vid he'd heard good things about. None of the other Marines matched his size. Only Craig Ryder came close, and he wouldn't be there to carry the body.

After a moment, the pressure of half a dozen pairs of eyes drew his attention from the simulation. "What?"

"It won't necessarily be Private Guimond," Torin pointed out.

When those same eyes turned to her, she smiled.

Werst's upper lip came off his teeth. "Crap. Crap. *Serley* crap."

No one disagreed.

Four

STAFF Sergeant Kerr, report to my office immediately.

Torin tongued in an acknowledgment adding aloud for the pickup in her jaw, "We're in the midst of our last simulation, Captain, twenty minutes to endgame."

Captain Rose would have told her to take the twenty minutes. But then, in the same circumstances, Captain Rose would have been monitoring the simulation with her—after having run it once himself.

Immediately, Staff Sergeant Kerr.

"Yes, sir."

Squad Two had come up against enemy fire, and they were pinned down. Squad One was working their way through adjacent corridors trying to relieve them. Nothing in the briefing suggested the alien ship had to be empty. Granted, any aliens on board could be as cuddly as the H'san but a "hail fellow sentients, well met" kind of first contact didn't need to be practiced. Craig Ryder was currently flat on the deck—when the shooting started, Werst had dropped him down out of the target zone by simply kicking his feet out from under him and letting him fall. Torin made a mental note to commend Werst for his initiative.

Fuk; if they have to promote a Krai, why don't they promote Werst?

She punched in the simulation's override code, throwing open all channels as the lights in the training module came up. "Sorry, people, you were kicking simulated ass but the captain's called me away from the board. Get the gear stowed, then you can stand down. When I get back, we'll take a look at the vids; see if we can up our survival rate. Mr. Ryder, thank you for your participation; you're welcome to stay."

"Anything for the Marine Corps, Staff Sergeant."

Although she couldn't see his face through the reflections on the curve of the helmet, Torin could hear the charmingly supercilious smile in his voice as he pushed himself into a sitting position.

"But," he continued, "I'd better get back to my ship; I have a busy night planned."

"Fine." What made him think she cared what kind of a night he had planned? *Asshole.* "You're on your own, people."

"Good luck, Staff."

That had to be Guimond; from anyone else, it would have sounded like sucking up.

Wondering just what exactly Captain Travik had up his butt this time, she headed for the other end of the Marine attachment at a quick walk.

It hadn't sounded like an emergency.

The captain had sounded enthusiastic.

Experience had taught her that an enthusiastic officer was a bad thing; an enthusiastic idiot in a captain's uniform was a very bad thing.

"Staff Sergeant Kerr, what took you so long?" Captain Travik chewed, swallowed, and leaped up from behind his desk as she entered his office. "I've had a . . ." His lips curled back. "You're out of uniform."

Torin looked down at her combat fatigues and back up at the captain. "Simulations today, sir."

"I know that—but you were monitoring."

"Yes, sir."

"All right, then."

All right, then? Torin regarded him with some suspicion from behind a carefully neutral expression. The lights were at Krai levels, and the green filters made the mottling on his scalp look like lichen or moss—which she supposed was what it was meant to do from an evolutionary standpoint. It just looked damned weird in their present circumstances.

"What," he asked, nose ridges flushed with excitement, "do you think about a formal inspection?"

He really didn't want to know what she thought. Fortunately, he didn't want an answer to the question either.

"How often," he continued, "do combat Marines travel with a general? I want to give him the opportunity to see what we're made of."

"Due respect, sir, but combat Marines aren't usually made of anything that shows well in a formal inspection."

"Nonsense. A little applied spit and polish and they'll be fine."

Remembering the last time she'd heard that and what the ultimate result had been, Torin lost the next bit of the captain's announcement in the noise of battle, picking it up again at:

". . . dress uniforms, medals if they've got them."

He was salivating—which, given how fond Krai were of Human flesh, Torin found just a little disconcerting. Horohn 8 had netted him a Nova Cluster, and he clearly needed to show it off. She wanted to smack the condescending little bugger. "Sir, this mission was minimum kit; no one has their dress uniform with them."

"I do."

Of course he did.

"The rest of you can shine up your service uniforms. I'm sure the general will understand."

"You've already asked him, sir?"

"These are my Marines, Staff Sergeant, I don't have to ask the general's permission to hold an inspection and . . ." He stepped closer and poked a finger toward her chest. ". . . I certainly don't have to ask yours."

"Have you already asked the general to *attend,* sir?"

The finger withdrew. "Oh. I informed him of my intention. It's not like he has anything else to do on this tub. As I have no aide, myself, you can go over the details with his."

"Yes, sir."

Won't that be fun.

"Sir, it's irrelevant that the general is also traveling with a full dress uniform." And not really surprising. "The officers should be in service uniforms as well."

The ends of Lieutenant Stedrin's pale hair made short choppy motions in the still air. "But the general . . ."

Torin ignored the bristling. "The general doesn't need tassels and fringe, Lieutenant, he's a general—my people all know that. And the Marine Corps doesn't need to emphasize artificial divisions between the officers and the enlisted—not if we're going to function as a team when it counts." Maybe if this mission went in General Morris' favor, he'd be able to add a gunny to his staff. She shouldn't be the one explaining the facts of life to his aide. Closely following that thought, came the sudden and horrible realization that she, herself, was due for a promotion to gunnery sergeant.

"But, Captain Travik . . ."

"Excuse me, sir . . ." Rattled by promotion possibilities, the interruption emerged a little sharper than she'd intended. ". . . but the general is mission CO, not Captain Travik."

"I'm aware of that, Staff Sergeant."

"And you're the general's aide, sir, not Captain Travik's." Torin banished an unknown future and shrugged. "But it's not my place to tell you how to do your job."

Stedrin met her gaze. After a moment, his eyes lightened. "That's a load of crap."

He was learning. "Yes, sir."

The inspection was a stupid idea, but not necessarily a bad one. Traditionally, Marines spent the time before their carrier emerged from Susumi space wondering if maybe *this* was the time the engineers had forgotten to carry the one and popped them out directly in front of an object too large for the bow wave to clear. They'd remember the *Sar'Quitain* and the battalion of Marines who'd slammed into the gas giant with her. They'd speculate about the *Sargara-West*, and the Marines who'd disappeared into Susumi space with her never to emerge—although twelve years later unconfirmed sightings continued to make the news.

They were helpless during a situation that could be terminal, and they hated that helplessness.

Captain Travik had given them all something new to think about.

No harm, no foul. Torin watched from her place in the rear as the three officers moved slowly past the dozen Marines. *It's not as if they liked him to begin with.*

The "all clear" sounded as the *Berganitan* blew out of Susumi space right on schedule.

The alien ship remained exactly where Craig Ryder's equations had placed it.

"You know, I can't help thinking of the HE suits," Torin muttered a short time later as the first pictures came down to the Marine attachment.

Nivry's eyes darkened for a closer look. "Why?"

"The bright colors." Torin nodded toward the screen at the tiny image of the brilliantly yellow ship. "It makes them easy to find."

Forty-six hours of deceleration later, the *Berganitan* came to a full stop one hundred and eighteen kilometers away from the alien ship, maintaining the minimum distance required by both defensive and offensive systems.

The two squadrons got their orders to hit vacuum.

"All I'm asking is that you *try* to remember you've got a fukking big surveillance system bolted to the front of your bird."

Lieutenant Commander Sibley swallowed the last of his stim stick and shot Chief Warrant Graham an incredulous look. "Bolted?"

"Figure of speech; just remember it's there."

He grinned and shrugged the flight suit up over his shoulders. "Vacuum, Chief, no resistance. Aerodynamic doesn't count."

"Yeah, sir, I know that. But if you have to fire . . ."

"Can't fire you, Chief, you're in the Navy. And there's nothing to fire at, out there." An elbow waved more or less toward the air lock as he sealed his cuffs.

"Maybe some boffin'll want you to shoot off a sample, I don't know, but if you have to fire, that system's going to cut a chunk off your forward arc, port *and* starboard."

"You get that, Shylin?"

His di'Taykan gunner settled her helmet over cadmium hair. "I got it."

"She's got it," Sibley informed the chief. "Probably not catching. And since Lieutenant Shylin's going to be jigging your system—not to mention doing the shooting should it come to it—maybe you ought to tell her what you've done to my baby."

Graham folded his arms. "The lieutenant knows, sir. As does the rest of your wing. Now, I'm telling you."

"You still haven't forgiven me for what happened at Sai Genist, have you? I brought most of her back, and you've got to admit I did some pretty flying."

"Considering what you had left to fly, sir . . ." The chief showed teeth in a reluctant smile. ". . . yeah, you did."

One hand on the air-lock controls, Shylin twisted around to face her pilot. "You coming, Sib, or am I flying this thing from the back seat? Squadron's launching in five."

Dave Graham watched until the Jade dropped free of her bay and scratched at his cheek where the depilatory was beginning to wear off. No rigger, from the FNG to the master warrant liked to see the fighters go out—they all spent too long waiting for them, and their crews, to come back.

"Chief?"

He recognized the voice of his newest petty officer. "I'll be there in a minute, Tristir."

"Bay's empty, Chief. She's gone."

"I know."

The Krai rigger walked over to stand by his side. "At least this time, we'll get her back in one piece."

"Fuk, Tris, I wish you hadn't said that."

"One hundred and eighteen kilometers, Captain Carveg?" Arms folded, eyes locked on the vast expanse of yellow ship filling the screen, General Morris shook his head. "Couldn't you bring us any closer?"

The *Berganitan*'s captain shot him a look Torin recognized. "Considering the size of my ship and the size of that ship and the relative size of the galaxy, one hundred and eighteen kilometers is plenty close enough, General. And just so you know, we get one ping off it, any energy indication at all, and I'm backing up so fast you'll taste yesterday's lunch."

Torin had always liked Captain Carveg—unlike some, she understood the meaning of orbital support. And, it turned out, she had a way with words.

The general stared down at the much shorter officer for a long moment, then he nodded. "You are, of course, in command of the *Berganitan*, Captain."

"Yes, sir, I am."

Torin heard the silent, *this time,* on the end of that agreement even if no one else in the room did.

With the exception of the enlisted Marines, the same people were back in the same briefing room for the first data from the flyby.

"The general wants you there for the flyby, Staff Sergeant."

"Why?"

Lieutenant Stedrin stiffened but had clearly been instructed to answer if asked. "Captain Travik will be there, and General Morris wants you to have the same information the captain has. Did you have something better to do?"

"No, sir. Squad Two challenged One to a boom ball game. I was going to watch."

"Why?"

He'd mimicked her tone exactly. She didn't bother hiding the smile. "You can learn a lot about people watching them play games, sir. Organized sports is like stylized warfare—only no one gets killed."

The lieutenant snorted. "You've never played in my old neighborhood, Staff."

He was standing a careful distance from the general, not so close he was crowding, close enough if he was needed. At best, half his attention was on the alien ship, the rest was on the general. He was still remarkably tight-assed—which was something Torin had never thought could be said about a di'Taykan—but he took his job seriously and did it well. Both were qualities she appreciated.

"I've never understood the Human attraction to the di'Taykan." Torin began to stand, but Captain Carveg waved her back into her seat. "To the Krai, they're too tall, too colorful, that pheromone thing is too annoying . . ." She rubbed a hand over her muzzle. ". . . and they're far, far too skinny. We like a people with a little more meat on their bones. Just in case."

Definitely, a way with words. "I'll be starting my diet tomorrow, ma'am."

Her smile showed no teeth. "I was glad to see you back on board, Staff Sergeant. I feel like I owe you—and your people—an apology."

"You were following orders, ma'am. Fortunes of war."

"War is one thing," she growled, "political expediency is something else again. I never heard exactly how things ended—I don't suppose you can tell me—but I do know you were the general's ace in the hole then and I suspect you're here now because you're his best bet at keeping Travik alive. Bottom line, the general's only here—with all his hopes for promotion tied up once again in one mission—because he couldn't trust Travik as senior officer. Now me, I run my ship and I don't follow politics, but you wouldn't believe the garbage I got sent when Captain Travik came on board. The Krai need to stick together and that sort of *serley* shit. A number of my people still think joining the Confederation wasn't the best idea. Actually, a number of my people still think leaving the trees was a bad idea." They turned together to watch the captain making a nuisance of himself with one of the Krai scientists. "And the good news is," Captain Carveg observed dryly, "if those food wasters in Parliament insist on promoting the species, at least they won't be taking a decent officer off the line."

"I was thinking the same thing, ma'am."

Carveg didn't pretend to misunderstand. "Thank you, Staff Sergeant. Now, I'd better get back before the general convinces my XO to stuff my ship up that thing's bright yellow butt. I just wanted you to know that when you go in, I'm not going anywhere." She waved off Torin's thanks and headed back to the front of the room, pausing by Captain Travik to say a few words as she went. Torin would have loved to have known what those words were because they moved him back to Lieutenant Stedrin's side PDQ.

Lieutenant Stedrin didn't look very happy about it.

"G'day, Staff Sergeant. Is this seat taken?"

Torin glanced pointedly around at the empty seats between her and the clusters of people at the front of the room. Craig Ryder watched the motion, a smile creasing the corners of both eyes, and sat down anyway. She was pleased to see he had the brains to leave a seat between them.

"I wasn't lurking around behind you or anything," he said, leaning back and making himself comfortable. "I was just waiting until you finished your conversation with the captain."

Maybe if she ignored him, he'd stop talking.

No such luck.

"So, what are you doing way back here? No, wait, let me guess; General Morris told you to find yourself a seat where you could see everything and, for you, everything includes everyone. Am I right?"

"Does it matter?"

"Just wanted to prove I'm more than a pretty face, Staff Sergeant Kerr. Or can I call you Torin?"

She turned to face him. "You can call me Staff Sergeant Kerr. Or just Staff Sergeant if that's too much for you."

"The Marines call you Staff."

"They've earned the right."

"By doing a few simulations?" With exaggerated chagrin, he crossed both hands over his chest. "*I* did simulations."

"They earned it the moment they put on this uniform."

"Ouch." After a moment, he added, "Is this where you hand me the three white feathers?"

"The what?"

"You know, for cowardice because I'm not a Marine."

Torin sighed. "Mr. Ryder, you blind jump out of Susumi space in a vessel smaller than the average SRM. You secure potentially hazardous salvage in vacuum, with no backup, leaving you essentially screwed if something goes wrong. I do not think you're a coward."

He cocked his head and she could see a glint in the blue eyes. "You think I'm a scavenger who makes his living off the misfortune of people you call friends."

"It's like you were reading my mind, Mr. Ryder . . ."

"Call me Craig."

". . . but that doesn't make you a coward."

"Or a Marine."

"What makes you think we'd have you?"

"Ouch again."

"Lick your wounds a little quieter, please, they're starting."

"Are you smiling?"

She was. "No."

"Okay."

The two squadrons had set up in a grid pattern at one kilometer out. When the first flyby evoked no response from the ship, Captain Carveg had the flight commander bring Black Star Squadron in to five hundred meters while the Red Maces held their position.

"We might as well be circling a large yellow turd for all the notice it's taking," Sibley muttered, manually keeping his Jade an exact five hundred meters from every protrusion.

Shylin checked that the data stream was on its way back to the *Berganitan*. "Are we even sure this is a ship?"

"Scans say it's hollow inside."

"So's your head, but that only makes you a vacuum jockey with bad taste in men."

"Hey, did I know his family and yours have been feuding for generations? No."

"Coming up on alleged air lock coordinates."

"I've got it. Oy, mama." He flipped his ship so they could get a look at it from another angle. "That alleged air lock looks just like an air lock. You copy, Command? We've got a docking collar and, eyeballing it from here, it looks like it'll take a universal coupling."

"We copy, Black Star Seven. *Do you see anything that looks like external controls."*

"Negative. You think they left the key under the mat?"

"Could have. Find the mat."

They found the rest of the air locks—one larger, one smaller, three the exact same size, now marked in blue on the screen in the briefing room. Opposite the single aft air lock, portside, they found a ripple in the hull of the ship. The scientists receiving the data were momentarily excited until a continuing scan showed the ripple otherwise identical to the rest of the hull. They found no fighter bays, no shuttle bays, and nothing they could identify as an exterior sensor array. Close up, the ship did have a number of protrusions that looked more extruded than built, and these were now marked in red. Readings at the dimpled end confirmed it was indeed part of some kind of a propulsion system, but until those readings could be analyzed, not even the propulsion engineers could tell what kind.

* * *

"You know, I'm not one to cast disparaging remarks about the vast sums spent on military equipment and training, but you guys haven't found anything I didn't find with my two rubber bands and a gerbil."

That was just weird enough to merit a response. "What's a gerbil?"

"Small rodent."

"Okay. Two things: One . . ." Torin nodded toward the continuous stream of numbers rolling down one side the screen. ". . . they've barely started analyzing the incoming data. And two, those aren't my guys, they're Navy. You send in the Marines, you get an immediate response."

"Someone tries to kill you."

"It's not that easy."

"And good on that, since I'll be going in with you."

Torin twisted in her seat. "What if I promise not to touch anything—will you stay back with the science group then?"

"If you promise not to touch anything?"

"Yes."

Smiling broadly, Ryder tucked his chin in and looked up at her through thick lashes. "No."

"Very pretty. But it's not going to get you anywhere."

He blinked. Then laughed, loudly enough to turn a few heads. "Are you always this direct, Staff Sergeant?"

"No. Usually, I'm armed."

"Am I in . . ."

Torin cut him off with a raised hand, her attention drawn back to the front of the room by the sudden agitated clumping of the Naval officers. Captain Carveg held a hurried conference with her flight commander who snapped a series of orders into her headset, one hand raised to cover the line of sight to her mouth.

Whatever it was, she didn't want to panic any watching civilians—although as far as Torin could see, every scientist in the room but the Ciptran was involved in an argument of some kind. The big bug just sat holding his/her version of a slate in his/her hand, attention apparently divided between it and the screen—apparently because it was pretty much impossible for anyone to tell where any of his/her compound eyes were focused.

On the screen, six of the bright lights representing the fighters peeled away from the ship and disappeared in a double wing formation off the edges of the screen.

Torin could feel Ryder watching her. "What is it?" he asked quietly.

"The ship's sensors have picked something up. It's nothing big, the flight commander only sent two wings and didn't pull the others back in, but it hasn't identified itself as a friendly or she wouldn't have sent any at all."

"Do you think it's trouble?"

Captain Carveg was now speaking to General Morris.

"Always."

The general turned to Lieutenant Stedrin who unhooked his slate from his belt.

Staff Sergeant Kerr.

From his slate to her implant. Whatever was going on, they wanted it kept quiet. She tongued in an acknowledgment.

The general wants you to bring the Recon team up to combat readiness. You're to slip out quietly and join them.

So as not to panic the civilians.

She sent the affirmative, stood, and unhooked her own slate all in one smooth motion.

"What is it?" Ryder was standing as well, effectively blocking her way to the aisle. There'd be no trouble getting by him, but the result wouldn't be considered slipping out quietly.

About to input Corporal Nivry's code, Torin paused and adjusted her grip on the slate. "You'll know when they decide to tell you," she told him flatly. "I think you should get out of my way now."

He studied her expression for a moment longer, then, with a grin, spread his hands in surrender—a gesture he seemed fond of, Torin noted—and turned sideways, leaving room for her to get by but not without close contact.

One long stride put her very close to his left shoulder, where she said, so softly he had to cant his head to hear, "I could kill you and not make a sound doing it. They'd find your body sitting in this seat, looking surprised and beyond revivification. Get. Out. Of. My. Way."

For a big man, he could move quickly when he had to.

"Thank you."

The grin was gone. "Staff Sergeant, I'm sorry I . . ."

"Attention, **Berganitan,** *I are Presit a Tur durValintrisy of Sector Central News. I are needing immediate assistance!"*

Captain Carveg looked like she was about to take a bite out of something, preferably Presit a Tur durValintrisy. "Sector Central News, this is Captain Carveg of the *Berganitan,* narrow your bandwidth! You're jamming all ship's frequencies!"

"I are saying again. I are needing immediate assis-

tance. My ship are having difficulties upon exiting Susumi space!"

There was no mistaking Katrien syntax. The Katrien scientists seemed excited by the contact and more excited when the captain strode over to them. Actually, as far as Torin was concerned, the Katrien always seemed excited about something.

Staff Sergeant Kerr, General Morris says that's a negative on combat readiness. Stand down the team.

Torin sent the lieutenant an affirmative and an expression that clearly asked, *It's the media; are you sure?*

After a moment's exaggerated consideration, he nodded as a call code sounded from her slate.

Hitting audio only, she brought it up by her mouth.

"Staff Sergeant Kerr? What the hell was that?"

"That was exactly what it sounded like, Corporal Nivry. The media appears to have breached a class four security. When I know more, you'll know more."

"You think it was Captain Travik?"

The general certainly seemed to, although the captain appeared to be vehemently denying the possibility. Torin looked pointedly at Craig Ryder, standing barely an arm's length away. "I think we have to consider all possibilities, Corporal. Find the best hacker on the team and have them go over the attachment's security. I don't want a further breach."

"I'm on it, Staff."

"You think I had something to do with this?"

Torin replaced the slate on her belt and, turning only her head, looked over at the salvage operator. "No. The more people who know about the ship, the better the odds someone'll try to jump your claim—and you're way too paranoid to let it slip."

"But you said . . ."

"That we had to look into all possibilities." She refocused her attention on the officers at the front of the room. "You are not the *only* possibility, Mr. Ryder."

His sigh had force enough to move a strand of hair against her cheek. "And here I thought we were getting along."

There wasn't any point in responding to that.

He sighed again. "I shouldn't have blocked your way, should I?"

"No."

"I said I was sorry."

"I know."

"I meant it."

"Okay." Answering a gesture from the general, Torin left him standing there—hopefully reevaluating his place in the current scheme of things, but she doubted it. An ego like his had to be resilient.

"Staff Sergeant, I want you to accompany Commander Verite and the security detail she'll be taking down to meet our unexpected visitor. I want to know everything that's said."

"Yes, sir." She shot a glance at Captain Travik—who was looking petulant—and slid it over to Lieutenant Stedrin.

General Morris read her question from the motion. "I'm not sending the lieutenant, because I don't want to give this representative from Sector Central News too much credence."

"Yes, sir."

He didn't bother explaining why he wasn't sending Captain Travik. But then, he didn't need to.

"Hey, Sib, that ship's particle trail leads right back to the exact point the *Berg* exited Susumi space."

Sibley frowned over at the tiny ship surrounded on all planes by the six fighters, their extended energy fields all that was holding it together. It was smaller than an STS shuttle, smaller than the *Promise* would be without her cargo panels. "Is there even room in that thing for a Susumi engine?"

"Well, they sure as *sanLi* didn't take the long way out."

"Good point. And good piloting. Given the readings coming off it, I'm amazed they're not sucking vacuum."

The nine members of the security team were wearing side arms. Neither Torin nor the commander were carrying weapons.

"Sensors read three Katrien in there," Commander Verite said softly as they took up positions at the air lock's inner door. "No weapon signature, but if this is some kind of an elaborate trick, Staff Sergeant, I want you to get out of the way and let my people handle it."

"Yes, ma'am."

"Telltales are green, Commander." The crewman by the door had one hand on his weapon, the other about a millimeter above the release pad.

"All right." She checked her masker and nodded. "Open it."

Torin had been on Sai Genist when the media had landed—it was like being attacked with both hands tied, with the Marines helpless to do anything in their own defense. Fortunately, it hadn't lasted long. The vid crews seemed to believe that, while they were shooting, they were immune to what everyone else was shooting. They weren't. And the signal from their equipment made it easy for the enemy to lock in. Torin's platoon had been covered in debris, but the enemy's aim was so exact no Marine was actually injured.

Vid crews got smarter after that. At least the vid crews from that particular news company. She didn't think they belonged to Sector Central News although a number of the crew had been Katrien.

The moment they had room enough between the door and the bulkhead, the three Katrien pushed out into the corridor, all talking at once.

Torin recognized the one in front. Recognized the silver fur edging the dark mask and running in single lines down each side of the muzzle. Recognized the way the black vee ran up the collarbone and over both shoulders to spread into a dark cape that ended in a narrow triangle halfway down the spine. *And if that's not enough, they're the same fukking dark glasses.*

"Staff Sergeant Torin Kerr." The Katrien pushed right by the commander. "I are Presit a Tur durValintrisy, Sector Central News. I are thanking you for your help in leading us to this story."

The next Katrien out was definitely recording.

Torin could feel the eyes of the entire security team now locked on her rather than on their visitors.

"Staff Sergeant?" The commander's voice was a low growl. Things were about to get ugly.

"One minute, Commander."

There was a slow way to get to the truth, and a quick way. Torin chose the latter.

Katrien were small, barely a meter high. They were, like all of the Elder Races, noncombatants. They were also very fast, but they had to know they were supposed to start running.

Torin dropped to one knee and leaned forward until her nose was almost touching the damp black tip of Presit a Tur durValintrisy's muzzle. Reaching up, she pulled off the dark glasses and locked eyes with the Katrien. "Please, explain," she said softly in a tone that had once caused a new recruit to piss himself in fear.

A wave rippled down the soft gray fur of the reporter's throat as she swallowed. "We are interviewing Captain Travik, and he are saying he are leaving on a top secret mission with General Morris. We are knowing General Morris are using you, Staff Sergeant Kerr, on his previous secret mission, so we are watching all shuttles from OutSector for Marines of your rank. Once we are finding you, we follow and find out you are going to *Berganitan*, then we are following *Berganitan*. You are not giving away the secret mission. We are not intending to cause you trouble."

"Thank you."

Pupils constricted to pinpricks, she put her hand on Torin's wrist. "Glasses?"

"Of course." Torin returned them and straightened.

Presit a Tur durValintrisy shook herself and spun around to face the Katrien who was recording. "Are you getting that? I are threatened!"

Ears flipped up and then down, the Katrien equivalent of a shrug. "Staff Sergeant are saying 'please' and 'thank you.'"

Torin got the distinct impression that Presit a Tur durValintrisy was less than popular with her crew. Hardly surprising if the near fatal trip had been her idea.

"Right. Well. Looks like you're in the clear, Staff Sergeant." The commander signaled her security team to fall in around the news team. "If you'll all come this way, Captain Carveg and General Morris would like to speak with you."

Torin stepped back as Presit a Tur durValintrisy

swept forward and fell into step beside the commander, who was shortening her stride considerably. She found herself walking beside the third Katrien. Probably a male, but she didn't make assumptions. When she glanced down, it held up a hand.

"Durgin a Tar canSalvais. Call me Durgin."

She stroked her palm across his—a Tar, male. The skin was so soft it felt as though it had been dusted with powder.

"Nice you're not holding a grudge at least."

His ears flipped. "Hey, I are just her pilot. What are I caring if you are intimidating the *aururist*?"

The way the hair lifted off Presit a Tur durValintrisy's spine, Torin figured that had to be a very bad word. Now that she was getting a better look at it, that black triangle was too regular to be natural. It had to be dyed.

"Actually," Durgin continued, "I are thinking you are going to pick her up by the throat and shake her."

Torin's eyes narrowed as she watched the reporter mincing up the corridor. "Yeah. So was she."

FIVE

"GENERAL, General." The reporter raised a gently protesting hand, silvered claws glittering. "Protests are beside the point. Under laws of full disclosure if media are present, media must not be denied. If Marines are going into ship, we are going in with them."

"All three of you?"

"No. Durgin are pilot only. He are staying with my ship. I, Presit a Tur durValintrisy, and my crew, Cirvan a Tar palRentskik, are going in."

Her crew didn't look too happy about it.

"We don't know what's in there, Presit a Tur durValintrisy . . ."

She smiled winningly, showing many tiny points of teeth under the black line of her lip. "Call me Presit."

". . . but it will be dangerous. You'll be putting yourself and your crew in danger."

"I are not going in, in front, General Morris." The tiny points of teeth reappeared, and a purple tongue swept lightly over them. "But I are going in."

Teeth, tongue, body language; if the reporter had been Human, Torin would have said she was flirting with the general. She looked like she was about to rub against his leg.

By the time the security detail had escorted the

three Katrien back to the briefing room, the scientists had been cleared out. Only the three Marine officers, Captain Carveg and two of her officers, and Craig Ryder remained. As far as Torin was concerned, they should have tossed Ryder out with the other civilians—having reached the alien ship, there was no longer a need to suck up in order to get his Susumi equations. The general had probably gotten used to including him and hadn't even noticed he was there.

Hands behind his back, General Morris frowned down at his reflection in the reporter's dark glasses. "All right. You and your crew may accompany the science group into the ship. You will not go in with the Recon team because I will not have you exposed to unknown dangers."

"A compromise, General? According to law, I are not having to compromise." She lifted one hand and combed her claws through her whiskers. Alien body language or not, Torin recognized a smug gesture when she saw one. "But I will."

"Good. And now, the other matter—you said you followed Staff Sergeant Kerr to the *Berganitan* . . ."

"No, no, no," Presit interrupted. Leaning around the general, she showed teeth at Torin. This time, it didn't look anything like a smile. "I are only following Staff Sergeant Kerr until I know what ship she are taking. Then I are following that ship to *Berganitan*."

"Fine. You followed Lieutenant Commander Sibley's Jade to the *Berganitan*. How did you follow the *Berganitan* through Susumi space?"

Presit actually waved a tiny finger at the general. If Torin hadn't disliked the reporter so much, she'd have been enjoying this. "I are not having to tell you that, General Morris. Thanks to suspicious Parliament, full disclosure works only one way. You are having to disclose to me, but I are not having to disclose to you. But," she added as the general flushed puce, "it are no big thing. I are merely . . ."

Durgin trilled an interruption. Torin figured he objected to Presit's pronoun.

". . . locking on the tail end of the *Berganitan*'s Susumi signature," she continued, ignoring her pilot. "It are a tricky maneuver—we are having to be close enough to follow but not so close we are being swept up in the wake and destroyed—but are not a secret."

His broad cheeks lightening slightly to maroon, General Morris attempted to lock Durgin in a steely glare, but it kept sliding off the nearly black lenses of his glasses. "You're a pilot, you had to have known how insanely dangerous that was. You could have destroyed both ships. As it was, you nearly destroyed yourself and your passengers."

The pilot's ears flipped down and up. "Unfortunately," he began.

Presit cut him off, her glasses still pointed toward the general. "Durgin a Tar canSalvais are working for me. If he are intending to continue working for me, he are keeping certain things to himself."

Durgin's ears flipped again. "Yeah, what she are saying."

"Fine." Taking a deep breath, the general appeared to accept the situation the law had placed him in although his voice retained a snarl around the edges. "Owing to the unfortunate, near destruction of your vessel, Presit a Tur durValintrisy . . ."

"Please, Presit."

"Yes, Presit." He cleared his throat and continued through clenched teeth. "Captain Carveg has kindly offered all three of you quarters on the *Berganitan*."

"Where she are keeping an eye on us," Presit

murmured, summing up exactly what Torin had been thinking. "Still . . ." The fingers of her left hand made three quick passes through her whiskers. ". . . I are graciously accepting."

Captain Carveg stepped forward. When a Krai showed that much tooth, the more edible species usually found some distance to put between them. "If you'll just accompany Yeoman Sanderson," she said politely, her tone in complete opposition to her expression, "he'll show you to the guest quarters. This is a warship and space is at a premium, so I'm afraid your pilot and your crew will have to share."

"They are not caring." Leaning around the other side of the general, Presit waggled silver-tipped fingers toward Captain Travik. "We are talking later, you and I."

The captain nodded graciously, "I'd be honored."

"You'd be honored?" General Morris asked, turning slowly to face his subordinate.

"Yes, sir. The full disclosure law may require my compliance, but if Presit a Tur durValintrisy of Sector Central News wants to speak with me, I would be honored."

He sounded sincere.

Torin couldn't decide what she wanted to do more, puke or smack him, but it certainly explained why he was so popular with the press.

"And this one, General." Presit's attention switched to Torin, who met her gaze with bland indifference. "You are intending to deal with how she are behaving to me?"

"That are . . . is, between myself and the staff sergeant." He nodded at the yeoman, who stepped forward.

"Ma'am."

"So polite." She smiled up at the young Human. "You are leading us, so go. We are following."

Looking slightly confused by the syntax, Yeoman Sanderson led the way from the briefing room, the reporter and her crew close on his heels talking rapidly in their own language. Durgin fell in behind, occasionally interrupting. Cultural rules seemed to differ when communicating in Katrien as opposed to Federate.

General Morris rocked back on his heels as the door closed. "I don't suppose there's any way the locks on their quarters can malfunction until we're done here?" he snarled in Captain Carveg's direction.

Recognizing the snarl had nothing to do with her—which was lucky for the general—she shook her head. "Sorry, no."

"I can't believe they followed us through Susumi space."

"So it seems."

"That's insane."

"Yes."

"We have to get their equations. If they've actually found the sweet spot—and aren't merely the luckiest three S.O.B.s ever evolved—the information will have major military applications. Is there some way you can access their ship's logs?"

"Legally? No. Accidentally . . ." Captain Carveg smiled.

The smile suggested her people were already working on it.

"Good." Nodding, he repeated "good" to himself a couple more times, then turned toward Torin. "Now then, Staff Sergeant Kerr." His voice frosted over. "If I could have a moment of your time."

"Yes, sir."

They walked a short distance from the clump of officers.

"Is it true you threatened Presit a Tur durValintrisy?"

Torin met his gaze levelly. "No, sir. She made a statement, and I asked her politely for an explanation, saying both 'please' and 'thank you.' It's all on record."

"I'm not an idiot, Staff Sergeant." He clamped one hand down on a chair back. His knuckles whitened, his fingers sank into the upholstery. "I am well aware you're capable of saying *please* in such a way as to blister the finish off a tank."

"Yes, sir."

Sighing, he released the chair. "Don't do it again."

"No, sir."

"The scientists will want a day or so to interpret the data. See that our people are ready when they are."

"Yes, sir."

Recognizing a dismissal when she heard it, Torin waited until he'd rejoined the others, then she left the room. She was barely three meters down the corridor when she heard someone following, and a moment after that, Craig Ryder fell into step beside her.

"What?"

"Nothing. We're just going the same way. It's a free corridor. And," he spread his arms, "it's the only way . . . excuse me . . ." Spinning sideways, he allowed two of the *Berganitan*'s crew to go by. ". . . to the links."

"What are you so happy about?"

"Well, I'm just basking in the knowledge that there's now a life-form on this ship you dislike more than me." He hit the link call a second before she could, but when the car arrived, Torin slid past him to claim it.

"For what it's worth," she said, as the door closed, "if you were also a reporter, I'd dislike *you* more."

Staring at the closed door, Craig grinned and hit the link call again.

"She wants me," he said conversationally to the crewman who'd arrived in time to hear the parting remark.

The crewman stared at him for a moment and then burst out laughing.

The next afternoon, Captain Travik, having spent the morning stroking his own ego with Sector Central News, arrived at the enlisted quarters for a surprise inspection.

Torin managed to get him out before much damage had been done. "I want this place spotless by the time I get back," she snapped following the captain out the hatch. "And if it doesn't pass *my* inspection, you'll be doing it again."

"First, I'm reporting this incident to the general and then, I'm putting them all on report," Captain Travik snarled as she caught up. "Every last one of them. When I'm done, the corporals will all be privates and the privates will be . . . privates for longer!"

"It was an accident, sir."

"Which was an accident, Staff Sergeant?" he demanded cradling one hand against his chest. "The slammed locker or the spilled depilatory?"

Since Krai had minimal hair, the depilatory had been more of a waste of time in Torin's opinion. "Both, sir. You took them by surprise. You were the last person they expected to see."

"That was the point," he sneered. "It was a surprise inspection, and they attacked me."

"They *are* combat Marines, sir, and beyond that, they're Recon. First in, always facing the unknown, hair-trigger responses; if they'd actually attacked you, you'd be in Med-op right now. But you know about that, *you're* Recon." Amazed she'd managed to get that last bit out without gagging, she checked his expression.

The sulky look had vanished.

"Hair-trigger responses . . ."

"Yes, sir."

He tentatively flexed his fingers. "It was an accident?"

"Yes, sir."

"All right." They'd reached the door to his office. He turned and drew himself up to his full height—which would have been more effective had that not put the top of his head at Torin's collarbone. "For the sake of the team and because we're all Recon together, I will overlook their behavior."

"Thank you, sir."

"This time." His chin lifted, his nose ridges flushed. "But I'm still recording it, and if anything like it happens again, accident or no, I will not be so understanding."

"Sir, if anything like it happens again, I will personally hold the air lock open while you kick their collective asses into space."

Although she'd been gone only a short time, the enlisted quarters were gleaming when Torin returned. Standing just inside the hatch, fists on her hips, she swept her gaze up one side of the compartment and down the other, allowing it to freeze each member of the team indiscriminately. She didn't know exactly who'd done what, and she didn't care.

"Captain Travik has been convinced not to bring the whole lot of you up on charges." From the stiffening of certain shoulders, the fact that Captain Travik could bring charges hadn't occurred to everyone. "You lot are luckier than you deserve to be, and if you ever again put me in the position where I've got to kiss up to an officer—any officer—to save your sorry butts, I am going to make your lives so goddamned miserable you're going to beg to be dropped into the front lines stark naked and armed with a sponge just to get away from me. Do I make myself clear?"

"Yes, Staff Sergeant."

It wasn't exactly a unison response, but it was close enough.

"Something funny, Guimond?"

The big Human's smile disappeared. "No, Staff Sergeant."

"Good. The whole miserable lot of you are confined to the attachment tonight. No one goes into the *Berganitan*. Twenty minutes, simulation room, full HE gear." She stepped back through the hatch and slammed it closed.

"Problems, Staff?"

Only with lieutenants who lurk in corridors! Palm flat against the cool metal of the hatch, she counted to three before she turned. "No, sir."

"General Morris sent me to tell you that you're going in tomorrow morning."

"Thank God." It felt so good, she checked to see that Lieutenant Stedrin's masker was on.

He actually smiled, eyes light. "Natives getting restless, Staff?"

"That would be the polite way of putting it, sir."

"Well, they can keep busy tonight humping their gear to the shuttle. Navy's moving it to our lock right ASAP. We should have full hookup in thirty," he added glancing down at his slate.

"Do we have numbers on the scientists, sir?"

"We're still trying to get them to agree to six, but you can assume eight; plus Ryder and the two Katrien from the news vids. The general wants everyone on board and ready to go at 0830 tomorrow."

Nice to get the chance to sleep in. There were benefits to traveling with civilians. "Should I tell Captain Travik?"

"I've already done it." About to turn away, Lieutenant Stedrin paused, his eyes darkening. "You wouldn't happen to know why he tried to get the drop on me as I came into his office?"

Tried. Torin grinned. "He's Recon, sir. Hair-trigger responses."

"Weren't we supposed to be in the simulation room in twenty minutes anyhow?" Guimond wondered as the sound of the slammed hatch stopped ringing through the compartment.

"She's not as pissed about what happened as she's pretending," Nivry told him, yanking her locker open.

"Oh, yeah?" Heer pulled a sheaf of crumpled schematic diagrams out from under his mattress and began reattaching them to the bulkhead over his bunk. "Then why the CTA?"

"We're always confined to the attachment just before a mission," she reminded him. "And besides, she *is* pissed about the sucking up. Today's simulation is going to be fast and mean."

"And that's just the way Werst likes it." Frii tossed

his headphones onto his bunk and made exaggerated kissing noises at the Krai.

Who responded with a curt, "Fuk you."

"Fast and mean."

"You've still got seventeen minutes," Guimond said helpfully.

The di'Taykan looked intrigued, but when Werst shot him an unmistakable gesture, he turned to the big Human instead. "What *were* you smiling about, Guimond?"

He shrugged, smiling again. "I just thought that whole naked with a sponge thing was funny."

Werst snorted.

"You didn't think it was funny?"

"Moron."

"Corporal Nivry!"

Waving the others quiet, Nivry opened the channel on her slate. "Staff?"

"Simulation's been scrubbed. We're out of here tomorrow. I want the whole team in the armory in fifteen."

"We'll be there in ten, Staff."

"No need to suck up, Corporal, I'm as anxious to get out of this tin can as you are."

At 0820 Torin stared down at her slate, read the contents again, then looked up at the general. "Sir, I still think the civilians should be on a second shuttle. Our STS can back off, and they can attach the moment we've secured the immediate area."

General Morris shook his head. "They've studied the coupling, and they're afraid that once an STS has detached, it'll need a complete overhaul before we attach another."

"With all due respect, sir, what about being afraid of a defense system that suddenly activates while we're inside and blows them into overeducated sticky bits?"

"Several factors indicate the need for an overhaul, but there's been no data collected indicating a defense system. Their argument not mine," he added hurriedly. "Bottom line, Staff Sergeant, if they get themselves blown up, no one's going to blame you. And Captain Travik will be staying on the shuttle with them. For their protection."

And will thus have died valiantly should something happen.

It hung between them, unsaid but acknowledged.

"Too bad Sector Central News will have blown up with him," Torin muttered.

"I'm sure Lieutenant Stedrin will add a satisfactory obituary to his report."

The lieutenant's ears turned at the sound of his name. He crossed the compartment toward them, adding new information into his slate as he walked. "The pilot says they're clear to go, sir."

"Thank you, Lieutenant. Staff Sergeant . . ."

"Sir." Torin took a step back, snapped her slate into position on her HE suit, turned on one heel, and headed for the air lock. When she turned to cycle the inner door closed, Lieutenant Stedrin raised a hand in farewell. Although he remained the least di'Taykan-like di'Taykan she'd ever served with, she'd much rather have been commanded by him on this mission than Captain Travik.

Although, since I'd rather be commanded by a H'san's grandmother, that's not saying much . . .

The personnel compartments on ship-to-ship shuttles went straight back from the pilot's cabin. A double row of seats, back to back, ran down the center with a weapons station both port and starboard. Tsui and Jynett had proved to be the best shots during simulations, so Torin had assigned them the covering seats. With thirty seats to seat twenty-seven, they were almost at full configuration.

The scientists had filled the first ten. General Morris hadn't been able to hold them to eight—let alone the original six. In typical Confederation fairness-before-all-else, they consisted of two Katrien, two Niln, two Humans, two Krai, and two di'Taykan. The Ciptran had probably been left behind because there was only one of him/her. Because Presit and her crew had claimed seats side by side—although Cirvan was still standing and shooting vid—there were two empty places between the last starboard-side scientist and Torin's place in back of Captain Travik.

Military and civilians alike were wearing HE suits, helmets off, and the only one who seemed to be missing was Craig Ryder.

No loss. I've already got more deadwood than people I can use.

"G'day. Mind if I sit here?" He was suddenly at her left shoulder, nodding toward the empty seat next to hers.

Knew that *was coming.* "What if I said yes?"

"I'd sit here anyway."

"So why do you even ask?"

Ryder grinned up at her as he dropped into the seat and reached for his straps. "Just because you're a grumpy gus is no reason for me to be rude."

"I'm a what?"

Blue eyes gleamed. "But I'm sure you're very good at your job."

Torin opened her mouth and closed it again. There

just really wasn't any point. "Guimond, Orla; check to see that the civilians are belted in properly."

The two Marines stood and clumped forward, their heavy soles ringing against the deck plates. Torin stopped Orla as she passed.

"Special attention to the Niln," she murmured. "They're never entirely comfortable with their tails stuffed down a suit leg, so they never strap tightly enough."

"Got it, Staff." The di'Taykan glanced down at Ryder and her eyes lightened. "You want me to check him, too?"

"No need," Ryder answered before Torin could. "The staff sergeant'll do it."

"Go on," Torin told her.

Smirking, she clumped off.

Torin leaned down, one hand on each side of Ryder's shoulders, their noses no more than ten centimeters apart. "You want me to check your straps?" she purred. His eyes widened as her right hand dropped between them. "They seem a little . . . slack." A quick yank brought out a strangled yelp and a roar of laughter from the watching Marines. "That's much better." She straightened as he pawed for the release catch. "I wouldn't want anything floating loose."

"If it floats loose, it'll only be because you've broken it off," he muttered to more laughter as the straps released.

Torin figured his relieved sigh would be the last she'd hear from him for a while.

On the other side of the seats, Guimond had finished with his five scientists and was trying, unsuccessfully, to get Cirvan into his seat.

"I are just needing a few more things on record," Presit explained. "It are so important to properly set the scene. Don't worry, Private Guimond, I are sitting and strapped in before we are detached." The reporter craned her neck and pointed toward the back of the compartment. "You are telling me, what are that back there?"

"That?" Guimond peered toward the green leather bunk built into the rear bulkhead. "That's the Med-op, ma'am."

"The Med-op?"

"It's the medical station," Captain Travik rushed to explain.

Poor boy. Doesn't want his reporter's attention on someone else.

"Ah." Presit went to claw her whiskers and frowned down at the heavy glove. "It are for Marines or for Navy?"

"Both Marines and Navy personnel have been laid there."

"And some of them were even wounded," Guimond added, ingeniously.

As the scientists craned around in their seats to see what the Marines were finding so funny, Torin waved Guimond away and leaned over the seat backs, her mouth by Captain Travik's ear. "Sir, we need everyone in their seats. If you could convince your news people to stop recording for a moment . . ."

"Wait." Presit's raised hand held Cirvan where he was. "This are a ship-to-ship shuttle, Staff Sergeant; why are it carrying weapons?"

"All STS vessels carry weapons, ma'am." Torin turned her head just enough to see her reflection in Presit's glasses. "Because sometimes that second ess doesn't stand for ship."

The reporter's brow creased, her fur folding into dark and light bands. "Ship to shi . . . Oh. You are being funny, Staff Sergeant. Marines are all being funny." The black line of her upper lip curled up. "You are taking your act on the road?"

"We're *trying* to, ma'am. Sir?"

"I think you'd better sit your crew down, Presit." Captain Travik touched the reporter lightly on the shoulder of her suit, clearly enjoying the thought that they were his news people. "I'd hate for anything to happen to the recording."

"Ah, yes, the recording." Presit trilled something in her own language and Cirvan howled something back as he sat down. Which incited the Katrien scientists to add their two credits' worth in a register that made Torin's teeth vibrate.

She straightened and somehow resisted the urge to beat her head against the bulkhead.

"Captain Travik, this is Lieutenant Czerneda. We're green for detach. Waiting for your go."

"Staff Sergeant Kerr."

"Yes, sir." Torin dropped into her seat and slaved her slate to the shuttle with one hand as she tightened her straps with the other. "Johnston, your left foot's not secured."

"Fuk. Sorry, Staff."

The last telltale flashed as she slid the toes of her boots under the plastic loops. "All personnel are secured, sir, air lock is sealed."

"Lieutenant Czerneda, this is Captain Travik. We're green for go."

"Roger, Captain. Detach in three, two, one . . ."

A familiar shudder ran down the length of the shuttle closely followed by a series of loud cracks. Torin had long suspected the Navy pilots of feeding sound effects through the comm system. In a universe that included furniture in a tube and spreadable broccoli, there was no other reason for the clamps to sound as though they'd been broken off rather than released.

She swallowed as they dropped into zero gee and swallowed again before saying, "If you're feeling queasy, take the suppressant. No one wants to be chasing puke through the compartment."

Behind her, she could hear someone shifting in his or her seat. Could be the captain, could be either of the Katrien, they were about the same size.

"This shuttle are having no gravity generator?" Presit asked, her voice pitched a little higher than usual and almost loud enough to echo off the facing bulkhead.

"I *am* sorry." The captain sounded more smug than apologetic. Krai were virtually immune to all negative effects of zero gee; no nausea, no disorientation, no decrease in red blood cells, no bone loss should the lack of gravity be maintained over time. When the Confederation made first contact, they were planning a trip to a star almost three light-years away in zero gee the whole trip.

A repeated pressure on Torin's left shoulder turned out to be Ryder's shoulder nudging against hers. When she glanced over, he had the shuttle's schematics on his slate. "This thing's *got* a gravity generator," he murmured for her ears alone—although as the Katrien were talking again, it wasn't a particularly soft murmur.

"Uses a lot of energy," Torin told him. "Navy won't waste it if it isn't necessary. Might need it for something else."

He nodded appreciatively. "And there's a lot of something else in here, too. This shuttle's got more lethal bells and whistles than a H'san toilet."

"I wouldn't know. And you're in files you shouldn't be able to access."

"'Shouldn't' is such an interpretive word." Three fast screens went by; he lingered on performance variables. "Looks like the Navy bought next year's model. Do you Marines have this kind of fancy flight equipment?"

"Not likely. Marines just want the damned things to fly and drop explosives." She keyed her override code into her slate and his screen went blank. "If you survive this mission, I'm going to have to have you mind-wiped."

"You're joking."

She shrugged. "Okay."

"I mean about surviving the mission. What's to survive?"

"We won't know until we get there, will we?"

"Fair enough." He sighed, snapped his slate back on his suit, sagged within the confines of his straps, folded his arms, and stared at nothing in particular. After a moment, he focused his gaze on Torin's face. "Are we there yet?"

Torin ignored him.

"You're smiling, Staff Sergeant. I can see the corner of your mouth rise."

Oh, damn, she *was* smiling. There was nothing to do but continue ignoring him although she could feel his triumphant grin dancing between them. She pushed her chin against the collar of her suit, activating the HE's comm unit. Because the helmet detached, it carried almost no tactical equipment. "All right, Marines, suit check. Communications, first. Sound off by squad . . ."

They'd barely completed the checklist when Lieutenant Czerneda informed the compartment they'd be attempting first attach in ten minutes. Captain Travik unstrapped and stood, twisting in his foot loops to face the scientists.

"Doctor Hodges, *Harveer* Niirantapajee, I believe this is your area of expertise."

Torin figured he was being gracious for the news recording. Or sucking up for reasons of his own. He certainly seemed to manage better with civilians than with other Marines.

The two scientists, a Human and a Niln, unstrapped carefully. The Human, Dr. Hodges, pushed off the front bulkhead, flew the length of the compartment, turned just before Med-op, realigned himself, and snapped his boots down just before impact with the inside door of the air lock. A few Marines applauded, shouting out observations more or less complimentary, and Torin had to admit she couldn't have performed the maneuver much better herself.

Harveer Niirantapajee, her balance off with her tail down the leg of her suit, walked the entire distance hissing softly as she detached, swung, and reattached each booted foot.

Guimond dug his elbow into Werst's side as the Niln passed. "Looks like she tucks left." The snicker took him by surprise. "Hey, you're laughing."

"And you're pathetic."

"But funny."

Arms folded, slumped low in his straps, Werst growled something that could have been an agreement.

As the pair of scientists opened an instrument panel surface-mounted beside the air-lock's emergency manual controls, Torin stood and leaned over the seat back toward the captain. Under normal circumstances, she'd have subvocalized over the implants, but with the Katrien still talking, she didn't see much point. She'd have to shout to be overheard.

"Sir, do you think you should order helmets on, just in case?"

Travik looked confused. "In case of what?"

"Vacuum."

He glanced toward the air lock and reached for his helmet. "Good idea, Staff. Make it so."

"Sir?"

"Just give the order, Staff Sergeant."

"Yes, sir."

The civilians followed the Marines' example.

"Check each other's seals, people. You have no idea of the size of the report I'll have to write if one of you pops an eyeball." She slipped her feet out of the loops and flipped up and over to the captain's side. "Sir."

"I am capable of securing my helmet, Staff Sergeant," he sniffed indignantly.

"Yes, sir, but regulations are clear on this matter. I check you, you check me."

"Well, we wouldn't want you to have any trouble." His smile was a patronizing pat on the head. "Would we?"

"No, sir."

"You should tighten your right shoulder connection."

"Yes, sir." She resisted the urge to crack the seal on his tank. To give credit where credit was due, however reluctantly, he'd put himself together perfectly. *High marks for self-preservation.* Flipping back over the seats, she found Craig Ryder waiting for her.

"Odd man," he reminded her as she slid her feet back in the loops. "If you wouldn't mind."

The man got in and out of his helmet half a dozen

times a day when putting together a load of salvage. He no more needed his seals checked than she did. She checked them anyway. Hard vacuum was as unforgiving as it got.

Before she could move away, he checked hers.

"Just in case," he murmured, helmet to helmet. She nudged her comm system off group channel before he could continue. The pickup was sensitive enough to throw his opinion out to every Marine in the shuttle. "No offense, but I wouldn't trust that captain of yours to recognize a weak seal if it opened under his nose."

"Thank you." And back on again—no one had missed her. "Heer, that had better not be your emergency rations I hear you eating."

"Wouldn't think of it, Staff."

"I don't care what you're thinking about; stop it," Torin snapped, grabbing a di'Taykan scientist as he floated by, arms and legs flailing.

"It seemed significantly easier to navigate in zero gravity on the training vid," he complained, without even the expected double entendre about being grabbed. She sent him back toward his seat where two pairs of hands snagged him and dragged him back down to his straps.

Oh, this is *going to be fun.*

"Attempt first attach in three minutes."

"Weapons, people, we don't know what's coming through that door."

The Marines' weapon of choice was the KC-7, a fairly primitive, chemically-operated projectile weapon, impervious to electrical disruptions and solidly enough built that even nonfunctioning, it made a deadly club. Every Marine, no matter what their specialty or trade, qualified on the KC-7 during basic training or they didn't qualify to be Marines.

Unfortunately, projectile weapons were a bad idea in space, where shooting holes in the structure containing the life-support system was inevitably fatal.

On those rare occasions where the Marines were thrown into ship to ship fighting, they used a BN-4, a weapon which combined a cellular disrupter for antipersonnel use and a tight band laser operating off the same energy pack. The Marines called them bennys and those who preferred them to the KC never admitted it.

"Are weapons wise, Captain Travik?"

Torin's lip lifted. The full disclosure laws granted the reporter access to both the group and the command comm channels. The Others had forced Parliament to acknowledge the need for both Confederation-wide branches of the military but nothing could force them to like it.

"What," Presit continued, "if the aliens of the ship are coming in peace?"

"Then we won't shoot but we prefer to have the option."

Well, good for him.

"Did I ever tell you about the time I outshot half a dozen of the Others' top marksmen while I freed Horohn 8?"

"Yes, Captain. You are telling me three times already."

And good for her.

"Attempting first attach in three, two, one . . ."

If not for some creative cursing from *Harveer* Nirantapajee as she worked at the new control panel with a filament probe, contact would have been too smooth to notice.

The telltales flickered and turned green.

"We have a seal. Equalizing pressure."

Torin had put together a boarding plan that Captain Travik had approved and presented to the general as his own. She didn't give a damn who got the credit as long as she was able to implement it. "Squad Two, defensive positions."

"Opening inner door."

"Squad One; into the lock. Squad Two; maintain your positions, this side. If I can't talk you out of this, Mr. Ryder, stay with me."

"Oh, I'm right behind you, Staff Sergeant."

"And stay off the comm."

The air lock on a Navy shuttle held fifteen bodies—a few less if they were Dornagain, a few more if they were Katrien or Niln. Torin placed her people around the edges, and waited. After a short argument with his colleague, Dr. Hodges joined them.

The shuttle's inner door closed.

Torin hated how loud her breathing sounded within the confines of the helmet.

After the atmosphere had been pumped out—so many things reacted badly with oxygen—Dr. Hodges walked across the lock to the outer door where the telltales were already green. "I am now opening the outer door."

"Sounds like he's talking for fukking posterity."

"Tsui."

"Sorry, Staff."

The outer door opened.

The alien ship was even more yellow up close. Torin's helmet polarized slightly.

"I am now laying the sensor band against the ship." As he spoke, Dr. Hodges placed a strip of something about thirty centimeters long and no more than five wide along the center axis of the ship's outer door. Tiny red and green lights flashed up and down the length.

Never underestimate the power of a flashing light. Torin resisted the urge to snort.

After a moment, the lights changed their pattern, and the doctor removed it. "The door is now ready to be opened. Commence opening, *Harveer.*"

The Niln made no reply the comm could pick up.

The solid yellow acquired a thin black line.

"Come on, baby," Ryder breathed. "Papa needs a new O_2 scrubber."

There was vacuum on the other side.

Torin strained to see what they were facing.

The line grew thicker, and became an opening into what was unmistakably another air lock.

Once again, she noticed that this alien ship wasn't very alien. The first time she'd seen a H'san air lock, she'd thought it was a large bag of lime jelly. Which, in a way, it was, given that lime was also a color.

Oblivious to any potential danger, Dr. Hodges carried his sensor band to the inner door. "We're making history, *Harveer.*"

He was also making himself an obvious target, but that wasn't Torin's problem. She moved the squad forward as first the shuttle's and then the ship's outer door cycled closed. They were now inside the alien air lock. It was also yellow.

"Don't touch the walls, people. Defense systems could be on a contact trigger."

"Amazing," Dr. Hodges murmured, crouched over almost familiar controls set into the floor. "Equalizing pressure."

Torin thought she could feel the slight purr of working machinery through her soles.

The inner door of the alien ship opened as easily as the outer.

"They knew we were coming, so they baked a cake," Johnston muttered.

There was a general consensus in the following silence.

Frozen in place, they stared into a dull gray corridor approximately three meters wide. The light levels were low but bright enough, Torin decided, not to have them switch on lights. Frii was on point and di'-Taykans could adjust their vision to handle anything but total darkness.

Benny ready, Torin motioned for Corporal Nivry to grab the doctor—who'd made a try for the interior. She counted to ten, slowly, then checked the microfiber readout in her left sleeve. "Johnston, get your arm over here."

The engineer's readout was identical.

The atmosphere in the alien ship seemed to be exactly the same mix as the atmosphere in the shuttle had been. The temperature was off by point four of a degree, but that appeared to be correcting itself as they watched.

"What do you think, Staff?"

The corridor was empty.

"Scanners?"

"Readings show more empty corridors, Staff. No movement. No life signs."

"I think," Torin sighed, straightening, "that this is remarkably anticlimactic."

SIX

WHEN it became clear the shuttle was in no immediate danger, Torin sent a protesting Dr. Hodges back to his colleagues and brought the other squad into the ship; splitting the entire team into pairs. Even numbers stood with weapon ready. Odds dropped to one knee, giving the evens a clear shot as they followed the scans downloaded from Torin's slate to theirs.

"All right, people, we're going to set up perimeters here," Torin tapped her screen, "here, here, here, here, and here." The points indicated flared green. "And just because our scanners have picked up nothing but empty doesn't mean we . . . what the hell are you doing?"

Helmet hanging down his back, Ryder scratched at his beard with both hands. "Air's breathable, I didn't see any reason to stay sealed."

"The air may be breathable *here*, but we don't know what's around the next corner."

He shrugged. "I'm not going around the next corner, am I?" When she continued to scowl, he sighed. "Look, Staff Sergeant, someone had to be first. You do consider me expendable, don't you?"

"I don't consider anyone expendable," she snapped, "but you're as close as I've come in a while."

"Staff, should we . . . ?"

"No. We stay sealed until this area is secure."

"Is this great or what?" Guimond asked, staring down another hundred meters of gray and empty corridor identical to the hundred meters of gray and empty corridor just in from the air lock. "My whole battalion's been on station duty for two months now and I was so bored I almost requested a transfer to a sector where the Others were on the offensive." He glanced down at Werst who was deploying a perimeter guard. "Good thing I didn't, eh? I'd have hated to miss this."

"Oh, yeah," Werst grunted, securing the guard to the deck. "It's a thrill." He adjusted the sensors to take in the full width of the corridor, then activated them. If anything turned on, if anything changed, if anything moved—they'd know about it.

"What do you think? The crew's abandoned ship or they're hiding deep, waiting to see what we're going to do?"

"What crew?"

"Well, come on," Guimond swept the point of his benny from side to side, "you don't build these kind of halls in a drone, it'd be a waste of space." He switched back to group channel. "Staff, this is Guimond. Ready to test."

"Roger, Guimond. Test on my mark. Three, two, one, mark."

A small capsule tossed out in front of the guard hit the deck and shattered.

The area covered by the guard's sensors shimmered briefly blue and, had both Marines not been suited up, they'd have caught the faint smell of ozone.

"Guimond, this is Staff Sergeant Kerr. Perimeter test registered as capsule four; nitrogen and a nine-volt pulse."

"Roger, Staff. Perimeter point is secure."

"Head on back to the lock. Keep your eyes open."

"Roger, Staff. Guimond out. Not that there's anything much to see," he added, switching off as another pair began their test. "No doors. No panels. No light fixtures. Still, can't complain."

"You can't." Werst checked the settings one last time and straightened. "Come on."

"You're expecting trouble?" Guimond wondered, shortening his stride to match the Krai's. "No, wait, let me guess." His smile gleamed inside the curve of his helmet. "You always expect trouble."

"Only when things are too fukking good to be true."

"Like this ship."

Werst glanced up at the big Human. "Yeah. That, too."

"Can I ask you something?"

"Can I stop you?"

"Who's Roger?"

"What?"

"Why does the Corps use Roger to mean, 'I hear and understand'? Why not Angela? Or Fred? Or Werst even?"

"How the fuk should I know? It's a Human thing."

"It is?"

"It's not a Krai thing. Humans joined first; we got it from you."

"So maybe it's a di'Taykan thing."

"Only if it starts humping your leg."

As their footsteps faded in the distance, the floor on the other side of the guard quivered and the remains of the test capsule disappeared. Nothing registered on any of the sensors.

". . . because you haven't given me any reason to keep them here, Staff Sergeant. Empty corridors can hardly be considered a danger."

"Sir, scans show the walls are full of things our engineers can't identify. We can't even tell where the light is coming from."

"But it is light, and warm, and breathable over there?"

"Yes, sir. And that's what concerns me." Torin nodded as Nivry indicated the last pair had appeared around the corner. "Alien ships don't maintain life support identical to that in a Confederation Navy shuttle. It doesn't happen."

"Why not?"

"Sir, a Krai ship and a Human ship don't maintain identical life support." Years of practice kept the implied, "you idiot" out of her voice. "Something had to have created this for us."

"A friendly gesture."

"Or a trap."

"You've secured the area around the air lock?"

"Yes, sir. But . . ."

"No 'buts,' Staff Sergeant. I am the officer commanding. I believe there's no danger and I'm bringing them over."

"Yes, sir." Torin switched off the command channel. "He's bringing them over, people! Johnston, Heer; I want you free to hook up with the scientists. Tsui, Jynett; pair up."

"Should we desuit, Staff?"

Torin glanced over at Ryder who was leaning against the wall, arms folded, smiling broadly enough that fine lines bracketed both eyes. "No. And keep your helmets on. We've got two more species coming over. We'll see how the ship reacts to them."

"Ship's not reacting to anything, Staff Sergeant."

"Then what's that you're breathing, Mr. Ryder?"

He checked his sleeve. "Appears to be predominantly an oxygen, nitrogen mix—22.3 and 76.6 percent respectively. The remaining 1.1 percent is made up of . . ."

"No one likes a smart ass, Mr. Ryder."

"You'd be surprised, Staff Sergeant."

Fully aware that any possible response would only serve to further amuse their audience, Torin beckoned for Nivry. "Corporal, I want you to take three Marines out to the T-junction. I want one of you in sight of the air lock and the others wandering no more than two meters down either corridor. I want actual eyes and ears out there, just in case."

Nivry studied the hundred meters of featureless passage leading to the junction. "In case of what, Staff?"

"Of whatever, Corporal. Move."

"Moving. Guimond, Werst, Frii—you're with me."

"We just got back," Werst protested, as the other two fell into step with the corporal.

"Yeah? Well, nothing changed while you were gone. Come on."

As the four Marines started down the corridor, Torin moved the rest of the Recon team away from the air lock. If anything happened, she wanted them to have maneuvering room.

"And where would you like me, Staff Sergeant?"

The salvage operator's question had a distinctly mocking undertone. "In the *Berganitan*. Failing that, stay out of the . . ." She frowned. Was that music? "Frii, if you've brought your player with you and if you should have an earphone in, I'd like to remind you about the regulations concerning the wearing of players while deployed and I'd like to point out that the captain's already got me in a bad mood."

Silence. An absence of music.

"Uh, it's turned off, Staff."

"Good. Keep it that way."

And the lock still hadn't opened.

"What's taking them so long?" Dursinski muttered, shifting her weight from foot to foot.

Beside her, Tsui snorted hard enough to momentarily fog the inside of his helmet. "Reporter's probably trying to set up the best shot."

"That's enough, people. Telltales are green, they're . . ." Torin frowned. What were the odds of an alien ship using the same color codes as the Human-organized Confederation Marine Corps?

"Staff?"

"Private Huilin, what color do those telltales look to you?"

Out of the corner of one eye, she saw him turn his head to look at her, turquoise hair spread out so that each blunt end touched the inside curve of his helmet.

"They're green, Staff."

"And that doesn't strike you as strange?"

"Telltales are always green."

"Human; yes. And because the Confederation found us first, so's the Corps' and the Navy's. di'-Taykan telltales are orange . . ."

"Yuin."

"Orange to Human eyes." di'Taykans saw a much broader color spectrum although less fine detail.

"Staff, are you saying this is a Human ship?" Corporal Harrop asked as the inner doors began to open.

"I'm saying this ship is more than it seems. Odd

numbers turn around and face down corridor." Torin could tell by the way they moved, they thought she was being overly cautious. She didn't care what they thought, as long as they did what they were told. If nothing happened, it'd give them something to bitch about later in the barracks.

Ryder, who'd been standing about two meters down corridor, hurriedly shifted position. "You know," he murmured, having moved closer to Torin's external pickups, "you're giving paranoids a bad name."

Several snappy comebacks went to waste as Cirvan backed out of the air lock closely followed by Captain Travik looking heroic for the benefit of Sector Central News. Heroic quickly turned to surprise.

"Staff Sergeant Kerr, why are these Marines still in their suits? The HE does stand for Hazardous Environment, doesn't it?" He gave the camera a three-quarter shot, chin slightly lifted and continued before Torin could answer. "And I believe this is not a Hazardous Environment."

Neither the captain, nor the reporters, nor any of the scientists now spilling excitedly—and in the case of the Katrien noisily—into the corridor were still in their suits.

"Sir, I have reservations about this ship."

"Reservations?" Presit pushed her way past the two Niln and wrinkled her muzzle at Torin. "Then I are wanting a corner suite with an extra deep nest and full links." When Torin stared down at her blankly, she sighed. "It are a play on the word reservations, Staff Sergeant. Reservations as misgivings and as a promissory booking for a room. Human humor. It are important I are appealing to many species," she added, stroking her whiskers.

Torin stared at the reporter for a moment longer, then she switched her gaze back to the captain. "Sir, I can't help feeling that this isn't all there is."

"I understand your disappointment, Staff Sergeant."

"Sir?"

"You're a Marine, and we prefer action."

Which was when she understood he was still performing for the camera.

"Not only that, but it's your job to be cautious, Staff Sergeant. As an officer, it's my job to see the big picture. And the big picture says, you don't need those suits. Take them off."

"Sir . . ."

"That's an order."

"Yes, sir. Respectfully request permission to maintain suits until all gear has been removed from the shuttle." Given what the scientists had brought from the *Berganitan* and what they didn't seem to be carrying with them as they spread out from the air lock, that ought to take some time. By then, the other shoe might have dropped.

It hadn't.

Sealing up the front of her combats, Torin watched the two Niln scientists spraying what smelled like cheap Scotch on a section of wall delineated by what looked like a single fiber-optic strand. She shrugged into her vest, snapped her slate into place, reached for her helmet, and paused.

"I know what you're thinking."

Did the man not have anyone else to bother? And did he have to stand so damned close? Her brows drew in, and he took half a step back but maintained his smile as he continued.

"You're thinking that if they—whoever the 'they' on this ship are—can't show up with a welcoming committee they can at least take a shot at you, just so you know where you stand." Before she could respond, he held up a pouch. "Corporal Nivry's got the mess kit up and running; I brought you a coffee."

"A coffee?"

"Nothing like a little caffeine to put the day in perspective."

Maybe he wasn't so bad. "Thank you."

He fell into step beside her as she crossed the section of corridor the Marines had claimed as their own. "I notice you didn't disagree with me—about the shooting."

"You brought me a coffee. I'm not totally unreasonable."

"Good." Ryder dropped his voice to a low purr as they drew closer to other ears. "In case you're curious, the captain has made a preliminary report to the general saying that the Recon team has found this section of the ship deserted but that he'll be sending two patrols out beyond the established perimeter as soon as everyone's eaten."

"A civilian has no business listening to a military . . ." And then she realized and sighed. "He said it on vid, didn't he?"

"Yes, he did."

"And the general's reply?"

"Came through loud and clear. 'Good work, Captain. Carry on.' I expect Presit will do a couple of cutaways with the general later. She's really very good at her job. You should give her a break."

"Oh, I should break something," Torin muttered

under her breath. Fortunately a screaming match between the two Katrien scientists had drawn the news team away, leaving the captain standing by the mess kit, sucking down coffee and looking bereft.

"Everything all right, sir?"

"Why wouldn't it be?" he demanded, ridges flushing.

"No reason. You looked . . ."

"I looked like this is a colossal waste of my time, Staff Sergeant." He flapped his half-empty pouch toward half a dozen scientists sitting and staring at monitors. "That lot's accomplishing nothing much, and if the scans we took are right . . ."

"They are. " Although Torin had no idea where the "we" came from.

". . . then this place is going to be *serley* boring to explore." Finishing his coffee, he stuffed the pouch in the kit's recycler and pulled another. "I'm going to make major after this trip and, oh, aren't kilometers of gray corridor going to look exciting on the vids. It's not fair."

Okay, we've reached today's limit. "Don't whine, sir, it's unattractive in an officer."

Nose ridges moving through red to purple, Travik glared up at her, coffee pouch dangling from one corner of his mouth. "What?"

"Sets a bad example for the enlisted personnel. They're looking to you for leadership, sir." It took an effort but she managed close her teeth before adding, *not that I should have to tell you that.*

"General Morris will hear about that insubordinate comment, Staff Sergeant."

"Yes, sir."

Travik stomped away, jerked his slate up off his vest, and turned his back before he began talking.

From the angle of the bristles on the back of his head, he was seething. From inside the ship, contact with the *Berganitan* was patchy at best, so all communications were routed through the shuttle's system; Lieutenant Czerneda monitoring in case anything else attempted to make contact. Right about now, she was getting an earful.

"Was that wise?" Ryder asked. "I mean, it's none of my business, but he seems like he could be an officious little prick."

Torin shrugged. "You're right. It's none of your business."

"Looking on the bright side, you seem to have cured his boredom."

"All part of the job." Bending, she slid a tray out of the section marked with a big red H. Unlike field rations, designed to satisfy the nutritional requirements of all three military species, the mess kit's prepared meals were species specific. "I assume we're feeding you?"

"I tried to get my mom to pack me some sandwiches, but . . . thank you. " He took the tray out of her hands and peered through the clear cover. "Mystery meat and vegetables in a pita. Cup of soup—best not to look too closely at the puree. Pouch of juice and a pudding cup. All maintained at their intended temperature provided their intended temperature is lukewarm."

Torin snorted. "You sure you've never been a Marine?"

"I picked up a surplus mess kit a couple of years ago," he explained, dropping down to the floor beside her. "I can load it at any station and this stuff'll last indefinitely as long as it's sealed."

"Just one of the differences between us," Torin

noted, toasting him with her soup. "You pay to eat like this, I get paid to do it."

"Looks like Staff Sergeant Kerr and the civilian are getting along," Orla murmured speculatively, eyes darkening as she leaned past the Marine next to her in order to get an unimpeded look.

"Who else is she going to hang with?" Tsui asked. "If she hangs with us, we feel like we're being watched all the time, and I doubt she wants to hang with Captain Asshole. Besides, Ryder's okay; as long as you don't play cards with the son of a bitch." He poked a finger into his pudding, and the reaction by the di'Taykan took the conversation into a biologically unlikely direction.

STAFF SERGEANT KERR.

The bounce from the shuttle threatened to overwhelm her implant. Torin adjusted the volume then tongued in an acknowledgment.

You're pissing Travik off on purpose. Stop it. I don't want to hear any more complaints from him for the duration. Is that clear?

"Yes, sir." Not much point in subvocalizing since she didn't intend to say anything that couldn't be overheard. She glanced up at the captain. From his smug expression, he'd been expecting the general to contact her. "Sorry, sir."

Any problems?

"No, sir."

Good. Keep it that way and keep him alive. Morris out.

"Talking to yourself?" Ryder wondered, glancing from her to the captain and back again.

Corps business was none of his.

"Sometimes it's the only way to have an intelligent conversation," Torin told him.

"Corporal Harrop."

"Staff?"

"Take three Marines and relieve Nivry. I'll call you in as soon they finish eating. Captain wants to send out the entire team in two patrols."

"If we're coming back in so soon, why are we even going out?"

"You're going out because I told you to go out."

"But . . ."

"And in a minute you'll be cleaning out the recyler in the latrine because I told you to."

"Orla, Jynett, Dursinski, you're with me."

"This are Presit a Tur durValintrisy for Sector Central News reporting from a corridor inside a ship belonging to no Confederation species. With me are *Harveer* Niirantapajee, head of the Xeno-engineering department at Jinaffatinnic University on the Niln home world of Ciir. *Harveer* Niirantapajee, please tell our audience what you are discovered about this alien ship."

"Bugger all," the elderly engineer grunted, her nictitating membranes flicking across the golden orbs of her eyes.

Presit's smile tightened. "Could you elaborate?"

"We got in okay. Having established a door, there is, after all, a limited number of ways you can get a door to open. Once in, nothing. Scans show there's working parts in the walls but we can't get to them. We can't find panels, we can't make a hole. We can't even get a really good picture. The only thing we're fairly certain of, is that the ship is at least partially constructed of PHA—polyhydroxide alcoholydes."

"Which are?"

"Essentially organic plastic. Certain bacteria use PHA to store energy much the way mammals use fat."

"So, you are saying bacteria are building this ship?"

"No. I'm not."

Her tone moved the reporter on. "Are you being discouraged, *Harveer*?"

The membrane flicked across her eyes again. "As you said, the ship belongs to no Confederation species. It doesn't belong to the Alliance . . ."

"The Alliance; that are being our allies, the methane breathers."

"Right. Given that and given that we've only been working at it . . ." Her tongue touched a spot on the shoulder of her overalls. ". . . a little under two hours, don't you think it's early yet to be discouraged? Now, if you'll excuse me, I have to get back to beating my tail against this *scrisin* wall."

"Captain Travik, we're ready to send out the patrols."

"Well?"

"Well, what, sir?"

"Well, send out the patrols, Staff Sergeant. Do I have to do everything?"

"No, sir."

"Corporal Nivry, you'll take your patrol to perimeter point six. Harrop, to perimeter point five. You'll be running parallel to each other and pretty much parallel to the hull. Logically, there should be compartments of some kind between you, so both teams will run deep scans on the walls every three meters. Don't let your guard down."

"Uh, Staff, what are we guarding against?" Tsui asked, his smile a millimeter from mocking.

"Right now?" Her smile flattened his. "Me. Tomorrow, we'll see how much corridor we can map and still make it back before the shuttle leaves. Today, we'll concentrate on protecting our specialists while they pull data for the science team."

"Hey, Johnston." Tsui poked Squad One's other lance corporal in the thigh with the butt of his benny. "You wish you were still back with the eggheads instead of getting ready to hump that thing through never-never land?"

The engineer snorted and flexed the exoskeleton supporting most of the scanner's weight. "Oh, yeah, I'd much rather be listening to a pair of frustrated Katrien argue about solitons. Sounds like a fukking cat fight."

Arms folded—which had to be a human posture he'd adopted as Torin had never seen another Krai use it—Captain Travik exposed most of his teeth. "You don't make plans about future assignments without consulting your commanding officer."

"General Morris made it clear he wasn't to be bothered, sir."

"I was referring to *myself.*"

"Yes, sir. When I spoke of tomorrow's plans, I was referring to the boarding plan you downloaded and approved on the *Berganitan.*" Torin brought up the file and read from her slate. "Day one, secure the area and, should no hostiles be encountered, support the science team. Day two, should no hostiles be encountered, map as much of the ship's interior as possible. Day three . . ."

"I want you to consult with me before you implement!"

"Yes, sir." Hooking her slate back on her vest, Torin calmly met the captain's apoplectic gaze. "Tomorrow—before I implement tomorrow's plan—I will consult with you."

Travik stood there for a long moment, as the blood gradually drained from his facial ridges. "Good," he said at last. Then he spun on one heel and strode purposefully away.

"You're armed," noted a quiet voice at Torin's shoulder. "How do you keep from killing him?"

She watched the captain head straight for the news team. "Captain Travik is the officer commanding, Mr. Ryder. Marines are not in the habit of killing their officers."

"Okay."

"It's an acquired skill."

"Mind if I ask you a question?"

"I don't seem to be able to stop you."

"Why the helmet? We're not under fire."

"Among other things, my helmet contains a PCU—personal communications unit. I use it to maintain contact with the patrols."

"But doesn't the whole unit snap out so you can just shove it in one ear? I'm not saying the helmet doesn't look good on you." He met her frown with a grin. "I just wondered why. Does it give a feeling of security?"

Torin's tone would have told even a raw recruit that the conversation was over. "I don't like things shoved in my ears, Mr. Ryder."

"Okay."

Unfortunately, Craig Ryder was not a Marine. "Stop saying that."

"Why?"

Also unfortunately, *because I said so,* wasn't good enough for a civilian. *More's the pity.* Before Torin could come up with a suitable reply, a sudden shout from Dr. Hodges froze everyone in place and a second brought most of the other scientists running to his workstation just inside the air lock. *Harveer* Niirantapajee and both Katriens, who were working closest to the Marines, glanced up from their equipment but continued working.

"I'm too old to go scampering off every time his analyzer farts," she muttered in answer to Torin's silent question. "And these two won't leave me alone with their pretty new toy. But don't let us stop you from joining the fun."

"Fun," Ryder repeated, matching his stride to Torin's. "Fun would be blowing through the walls with explosives."

She considered discouraging him from dogging her footsteps, but since there wasn't anywhere else for him to go . . . "The di'Taykan are planning that for later."

"That's because the di'Taykan know how to have fun."

They reached the edge of the group a moment later to see Captain Travik installed at Dr. Hodges' elbow looking as though he were personally responsible for any successes. Cirvan had climbed up onto a crate trying to get more in his shot than the elbows of the taller species, and Presit was asking questions of the scientist—who ignored her as he dealt with the incoming data.

"What's he actually doing?" Ryder asked, sidestepping a stack of packing crates to get a better look.

"Don't know, don't care." Torin pulled her helmet forward and flipped the microphone down. "Nivry, Harrop; hold up. Something's happening here."

"You want us to head back?"

Torin glanced at the display on her slate. Both patrols were in the corridor designated NS2, separate but still in sight of each other. "No. Wait there until we know what's actually going on."

"Roger, Staff. We'll wait."

Straightening, Dr. Hodges thrust both hands over his head in triumph. "I have the numbers!"

"And that means?" Torin muttered.

"Seems to mean something to them." Ryder nodded toward the excited scientists. There was hurried movement away from the younger Niln's uplifted tail.

Waving off questions, Dr. Hodges aimed two beams of blue light at the wall, then caught up a strip similar to the one he'd used on the air lock door and rushed around his apparatus, accepting congratulatory pats from his colleagues as he ducked between the beams.

Ryder took a step closer and was pushed back as Dr. Hodges returned to his data, the spectators surging back and forth with his movements. "So what's his machinery do?"

Torin shrugged. "No idea. I do know it's damned heavy and, apparently, it shouldn't be dropped."

"Did you drop it?"

"Not personally." The light strip, now on the wall, lit up. For all Torin knew it might have been the same strip Dr. Hodges had used in the air lock. As far as she was concerned, one set of red-and-green flashing lights looked like another. She dropped her benny down off her shoulder and brought it around to the ready, just in case.

"Dr. Hodges. Dr. Hodges!" Whiskers quivering, Presit pushed herself between the scientist and Captain Travik. "Are you please telling our viewers just what it is you are doing?"

"I'm about to open an access panel. Now get out of my way."

As the reporter stepped indignantly back, Captain Travik stepped forward. "As the officer commanding this mission, I'd like to . . ."

"I said, move!"

Enjoying the captain's discomfort, Torin didn't see the actual moment the panel opened. When the cheering drew her gaze, a three-or-four-centimeter crack already ran halfway down the wall between the two beams of light. As it widened farther, all the hair rose off the back of her neck.

The deck shivered under the soles of her boots.

Grabbing a handful of Ryder's shirt, she threw him down behind the packing crates and followed him to the floor just as an explosion filled the corridor with flying debris and plumes of smoke. Ears ringing, she rolled up tight against the lowest crate, shoulder pressed hard against Ryder's back.

"Staff! What the hell was that?"

She snapped her mike down against her mouth. "Explosion by the lock! Report!"

"Area rippled. No damage. No casualties."

A second blast slammed up against the pile, sending the upper crates flying. A hunk of meat still wearing a bit of sleeve splashed against her boot. "We've got both!" Coughing, she checked her sleeve.

Combats had a lot of basic tech built in. "Pressure's holding; no hull . . . Craig!"

Twisting around, Ryder swept one arm up and slammed the debris off his forearm. It crashed and bounced, missing them both by centimeters.

"Staff? Staff Sergeant Kerr?"

"I'm here." Her eyes burned and her nose streamed. She wiped her face on the back of one hand while pulling a filter mask out of her vest with the other. "I say again, pressure's holding; no hull breach." A flick of the wrist unrolled the mask and she slapped it over her nose and mouth. The edges sealed.

"We're on our way!"

Metal screamed against metal.

"Be careful, there's a lot of smoke and the whole area's un . . . Fuk!" Her legs, Ryder's legs, the crate had all sunk into the floor.

And they were continuing to sink.

There was nothing she could grab. Nothing that wasn't sinking as fast as she was.

"Son of a fukking bitch!" Instinct brought his hands down to shove against the floor. They sank. And he couldn't pull them out again.

Something popped in his shoulder. He kept fighting.

Not like this. Not like this. Not like this.

"Mr. Ryder! CRAIG!"

Strong fingers turned his head.

"LOOK AT ME!"

The voice promised consequences worse than being swallowed by an alien ship if he disobeyed. Torin's face swam into focus.

"Stop it! It's not doing any good and it's pissing me off."

"Oh, that's comforting," he panted, panic shoved aside by irritation.

"Good."

Now he'd stopped thrashing, Torin grabbed for Ryder's right arm with both hands.

He jerked away.

"Staff Sergeant Kerr!"

"Nivry!"

"Staff! What's happening?"

"We're being sucked into the goddamned floor; that's what's happening!"

Still feeling a solid surface under her feet, she couldn't stand. She couldn't change her position. The pressure against her lower body was so slight, it couldn't possibly be holding her in place. But it was.

What had been the floor was now up around their waists.

The muzzle of her benny was under the surface. The trigger was up by her right breast. The angle was bad, but she forced her thumb through the trigger guard without touching her elbow to the floor.

"What are you doing?" Ryder coughed, eyes widening. He began to struggle again, leaning away from her.

"Fighting back!"

"You don't know what that'll do!"

"Well, I don't fukking like what's happening now!"

The weapon fired—she watched the charge drop—but it had no effect.

"Staff Sergeant Kerr!"

She stopped pulling the trigger. Took a deep breath. Coughed. Spat. Watched it sink.

"Listen up, Nivry: there were three scientists down by our gear. If anyone made it, they did." The floor was up by her shoulders. Torin could see a mark made by one of the pieces of heavy equipment, a black scuff against the gray. If she turned her head, she could see the piece of arm—di'Taykan or Human. It was too small a sample to tell for certain. Apparently, the ship didn't want it. "Deal with the civilian casualties, then get the team out." Her left arm was under, immobile. She held her right arm over her head.

"We're not leaving you behind, Staff."

"Glad to hear it, Corporal. Feel free to come back with the proper gear."

The floor touched her chin. It felt cool. She couldn't smell anything but the smoke she'd inhaled before she got the filter on. *What the hell does a floor smell like anyway?* Since she couldn't move her head, she stared into Ryder's eyes. They really were the most remarkable blue. Pity his nose had been running into all that facial hair.

"Take a deep breath," he advised.

"No shit."

She folded down all but one finger on her right hand.

The world went dark.

SEVEN

"STAFF Sergeant Kerr!"

No response.

Six running paces later, Nivry tried again. And six paces after that. Six paces after that brought them around the corner into NS1, the corridor leading to the air lock.

All twelve jostled for position.

"Fuk a duck," Guimond breathed.

It looked like the explosion had blown every piece of scientific equipment they'd humped off the shuttle into a barrier stretching wall to wall and very nearly ceiling high. Tendrils of gray-brown smoke pushed through the narrow opening and slowly dissipated. An HE suit had been fused across the front.

"Hey!" Orla took a step closer, her eyes darkening. "That's my suit!"

"We are so screwed," Dursinski murmured. "Those things aren't supposed to melt."

Johnston swung the scanner around. "It's not melted," he said after a moment. "Its molecules have been integrated into the molecules of the equipment behind it."

"And that's supposed to make me feel better how?"

The engineer shrugged. "It didn't melt."

"I don't care if it's stuck on with spit," Nivry snapped. "We're either going over or through. If there's anyone alive, they're on the other side of this thing."

"Not to mention," Werst grunted, "so is the air lock."

"Not to mention," the corporal agreed.

The darkness lasted thirty-one seconds—give or take the few seconds it took Torin to overcome panic and begin counting. The first twenty-eight seconds lasted forever; no sight, no sound, no smell, no touch, and only the bitter taste of burning chemicals in her mouth. At twenty-nine, she could move her legs. At thirty, her lower hand came free. At thirty-one, kicking and clawing for freedom, she dropped into dim gray light.

Her legs absorbed most of the impact. She rolled and would have come up on her feet had another body not slammed into the same space—knocking her flat and driving the breath out of her.

After a moment spent gasping, she slid her hand under a heavy, familiar shoulder and heaved.

Ryder flopped to one side, coughing out a curse as his head hit the floor, and Torin fought to catch her breath. *And wasn't that the perfect end to an unpleasant experience.* Still, it could have been worse. If the aliens did any probing during her trip through the flooring, they'd done it without her noticing and, as far as she was concerned, that was the preferable way to be probed—di'Taykan opinions on the matter aside. Hitting this new floor had left nothing more serious than bruises. Fortunately, Ryder's elbow had been moving fast enough that her vest had absorbed most of the impact.

The mask was gone. Wherever they were, the smoke hadn't come with them. The air was clear, odor free but for the stink of fear sweat that clung to her and Ryder. Torin could hear Ryder's breathing and her own blood pounding in her ears but nothing else. As near as she could tell—given the light levels—the ceiling above her head was as featureless as the floor that had swallowed them. Rolling her head to the right, she could see a wall—looking like every wall they'd seen on the ship and, for that matter, like the floors and the ceilings. To her left, Craig Ryder's profile filled most of her line of sight but a few meters beyond him, she could see another wall.

Wherever they were, the scenery hadn't changed.

And where the hell's the packing crate? It had been sinking as fast as they had, but it wasn't with them now.

Groping for the weapon that should have been lying along her right side, Torin realized that, although the strap remained over her shoulder, the benny was gone. *H'san on fukking crutches!* Drawing in her legs, she touched the knife in her boot—more for reassurance than because she planned on immediately using it—and sat up. Slowly. If anyone—or anything—was watching, she didn't want to startle them.

They were alone in what was essentially a cross section of one of the corridors—three meters by three meters by three meters of uninterrupted gray.

A moan drew her attention to her companion. "You all right?"

"I just got swallowed by a fukking floor!"

Apparently civilians, like officers, were inclined to state the obvious. "And you survived it." An obvious observation back at him. "Are you injured?"

"Physically? No."

"Then move on." Crossing her ankles, she stood.

Ryder propped himself up on his elbows and glared at her. "Mind if I take a moment to have a freaking reaction to the experience?"

Torin shrugged; it wasn't like she needed his assistance. "Take all the time you want."

The shuttle had to have been destroyed by the explosion or Captain Travik's implant would have been sending her his vital signs—or lack of vital signs. Considering how close he'd been to ground zero, he and his implant had likely been blown to pieces. Her orders from General Morris had been to keep the captain alive, but she had no intention of beating herself up over a death she couldn't have prevented nor mourning an officer the Corps was inarguably better off without. *And on the bright side, Sector Central News probably went with him, so there's nothing to stop the general from having him die a hero's death and everybody's happy.*

Her helmet mike, snapped down before the explosion, still nestled against the corner of her mouth.

"Corporal Nivry. Nivry, this is Kerr. Acknowledge."

No response. Not even static.

"Corporal Harrop. Harrop, this is Kerr. Acknowledge."

"What are you doing?" Ryder groaned as he got to his feet.

"Attempting to contact my Marines." Lips pressed into a thin line, Torin slid her helmet off and checked the display. The telltale was green; if that still meant anything, the unit was working. It was possible that the internal structure of the ship was blocking the signal. It was also possible they could hear her, but she couldn't hear them.

Nivry's code in the slate brought no results. Neither did any of the other eleven.

Hooked into the *Berganitan*'s system, she could have used the tracking program to find anything with a familiar energy signature—other slates, comm units, weapons, living bodies. Without the *Berganitan*, she'd need one of the big scanners.

Her slate's mapping function had been disabled. Her own position was as unknown as the teams'.

"What's wrong?"

"I'm not getting through."

"Why?"

"I don't know. You think it could have something to do with the alien technology we're surrounded by?"

"No need to be so sarcastic," he grumbled, staring up at the ceiling. "You sure they're alive?"

"Yes."

The inarguable response brought his attention back to her. "You don't know . . ."

"I know they were alive when we went out of contact, and that was less than five minutes ago."

"Look, I don't have to tell you that a lot can happen in five . . ."

"They're alive," Torin growled, daring him to argue.

Both hands lifted, he backed away.

She couldn't stop herself from taking another look around the cube.

No scanners. No weapons. No Marines. Just Craig Ryder, pacing from wall to wall, fists clenched as though he wanted to hit something. "We have to find a way out."

"No shit. What do you think I've been doing?"

"A pisspoor job. You're not even touching the walls."

"Well, excuse me for distrusting solid surfaces."

Torin rolled her eyes and crossed to his side. "All you have to do is . . ." Her hand stopped a centimeter from the surface. Muscles along her arm trembled; she couldn't bring herself to actually put flesh in contact with the wall. It felt as though she'd been stalled there for minutes although it couldn't have been more than five or six seconds at the most. Breathing slowly and deliberately, she continued the motion back to her vest and pulled off one of the recharge bars for her missing benny. ". . . tap on the walls with this."

The wall seemed to absorb the sound but was otherwise solid enough.

She could feel him watching her, so she turned, one eyebrow lifted. "Did you need to borrow a bar?"

He knew. She could see it in his eyes. He knew she'd stopped and he knew why.

But all he said was, "No, thanks." He pulled a screwdriver out of a pouch on his belt. "I'll use this."

"What a fukking mess." His upper body sandwiched between the top of the barrier and the ceiling, Werst waved a hand to clear the smoke from his face. "Primary damage is at the far end of the corridor but the entire area between the barrier and the air lock's filled with rubble. I see no survivors, but I can smell blood." His facial ridges spread slightly behind the translucent filter covering the lower part of his face. "Human, di'Taykan, Krai, Niln . . . everyone took damage. I'm going down."

Feet holding a convenient piece of pipe, he dropped over the inside edge. "This side's warmer, all right."

"Hot enough to block the scanners from picking up a thermal signature?"

"Probably. Air temp reads 33.4°C, and the barrier's warmer than that." He grabbed a protruding corner, tested the stability, swung around, found another hold, swung again, and dropped to the floor. Facial ridges clamped shut, he froze, counted to ten, and slowly straightened, glancing down at his sleeve. "Nothing's moving."

"Sensors show nothing's moving." Corporal Nivry's correction was a quiet buzz in his ear. *"Sensors gave no warning of the explosion or of what happened to Staff Sergeant Kerr. Be careful."*

"Always."

"And no snacking."

"Up yours."

Joining a multispecies military had forced the Krai to change their battlefield eating habits.

A soft thud and Orla crouched beside him. "I don't care what Johnston says, Guimond's never going to fit through there."

"Not my problem. Go left."

They found *Harveer* Niirantapajee and one of the Katrien scientists alive but unconscious in a sheltered triangle made by their half-slagged piece of equipment and the mess kit.

"Clear to casualties, Corporal."

Nivry nodded at Tsui and Dursinski who were carrying the patrol med kits. "Go."

As they reached the top, she sent the next two then waved ahead the four Marines needed to move the scanners.

"We should leave the scanners," Harrop murmured, watching Heer follow Jynett over the barrier at the wider of the two points. "We can come back and get them."

Nivry shook her head. "No. If that air lock's been blown, we'll need them to find our way out of here. I don't trust this place enough to leave gear where we can't see it."

"If that air lock's been blown, we're fukked."

Neither corporal mentioned that the shuttle pilot would have contacted them by now had she been able to.

Harrop nodded at the barrier. "Command should be on the other side. I'll watch the rear."

The situation's serious, he thought as Nivry slid through the narrower point, *when that gets no comment from a di'Taykan.*

Too bulky to be worn, the scanners were passed over the barrier from hand to hand, most of the weight on both sides held by the augmentation worn by Johnston and Heer. Once the scanners were safely on the deck, Guimond climbed to the same space, looked dubiously through it, then back at Harrop.

"Hey, Corporal, maybe we should widen this."

"There's a three-centimeter difference, between you and that space, Guimond. Now move."

Arms, head, shoulders . . .

Heer grabbed a double fistful of Guimond's combats while Johnston shoved from behind.

"Son of a . . ."

Chest.

Most of his descent was headfirst, then he swung in Heer's grip, and dropped.

Heads turned at the impact.

"Air lock's gone. Although Heer's still scanning it, looks like the shuttle went with it. There's a six-by-four-meter hole in the wall likely caused by the *something* Staff Sergeant Kerr mentioned. We've got two casualties—both unconscious—one dead Katrien and a whole lot of body parts that may or may not add up to the other civilians. What we don't have is either of our two missing personnel. Captain Travik wasn't in vest and helmet, but both the captain and Staff Sergeant Kerr were in combats and we've found no trace of uniforms. We all know this," Nivry's gesture took in the destruction, "was not enough to obliterate . . ."

"Big word."

"Shut up, Tsui. This . . ." She repeated the gesture. ". . . was not enough to obliterate two MCCUs. Have I missed anything?"

There was a negative response around the circle.

Nivry stared down at the one clear section of floor, her eyes so dark they'd lost almost all color. "So, considering one of Staff's last transmissions said, and I quote, *'We're being sucked into the goddamned floor!'* does anyone have any better ideas about where the staff and the captain are?"

No one did.

Nivry bounced a piece of wreckage off the area in question. Then stepped out onto it. And back. And took the time to breathe before saying, "Johnston, start scanning."

"If they're more than a meter and a half down, I'm not going to find them," the engineer warned, squatting and setting the scanner facedown on the cleared bit. "We haven't been able to go more than a meter and a half through any of these walls."

"Good thing this is a floor."

"But what happens if they're more than a meter and a half down?" Dursinski demanded.

"We start digging. Johnston?"

"Give it time. It can't interpret half the data coming back and that . . . Got it! Just over a meter of something solid—same organic metal combo that the walls are made of—then some open space, then two thermal sigs. Except they're both Human. Captain Travik should be showing three to four degrees higher."

"Maybe he's wounded and his body temp has dropped."

"No. These are Human—and look at that hot spot there, and there." He tapped the display. "That's a slate and that's a helmet PCU. I'd say we've found the staff sergeant and one of the civilians but not Captain Travik."

"No *serley* loss."

"Werst."

He snorted unapologetically.

"What now?" Johnston asked, straightening.

"We make contact." Nivry stepped out beside the scanner. "Staff Sergeant Kerr, this is Corporal Nivry. Acknowledge."

The only sound in the ruined corridor was the hum of the mess kit turning the remaining food into field rations and the hiss of *Harveer* Niirantapajee's labored breathing.

After a moment, she stepped back. "I can't get through to her slate either. Can we adapt the scanner to signal her?"

"Sure. I could hit her with a couple of different things, and if she's running a scan protect, she'll even know I'm doing it. Other than that . . ." Lifting his helmet, Johnston ran a hand back over his scalp. "We could probably burn through with the bennys."

"It'd drain the lot of them," Dursinski pointed out.

"We'd be disarming ourselves. I really don't think that's a good idea."

"Don't worry about it," Nivry told her dryly. "Given what happened the last time, we're not putting holes in these walls."

"How about a low-tech solution?"

Heads turned as Guimond slapped a metal bar into one palm.

"You're going to try and beat your way through?" Johnston asked, eyebrows nearly at his hairline. "Through a meter of a substance the entire science team couldn't get a scraping of?"

"No." Flipping the bar around, he tapped it against the floor. Three short. Three long. Three short.

Over the ambient noise came the sound of realization dawning.

Werst shook his head. "You're not as dumb as you look."

"Do you hear something?"

One ear cocked toward the ceiling, Torin frowned. "Tapping." They listened for a moment. Her frowned deepened. "It almost sounds like there's a rhythm to it." She snapped her slate off her vest.

Ryder snorted and began walking again, around and around the perimeter of their prison. "Vermin dancing in the pipes."

"Unlikely." Recording the ambient noise onto her slate, she boosted the gain and played it back.

"That was in the way of being a facetious observation."

"I know. Shut up."

Three short. Three short. Long short long.

"Son of a bitch . . ."

Her smile stopped Ryder in his tracks. "What?"

Smile broadening, Torin looked the civilian up and down. "You're what? A little taller than one point eight meters?"

"Why?"

"Because I'm a little shorter and I need to reach the ceiling."

"We already threw stuff at it," he protested. "It's solid."

"Yes, but we have a new situation." Slipping the strap of her benny off her shoulder, she uncoupled the ends. Holding the lighter piece, she whipped the heavier up against the ceiling. The thud sounded loud in the cube, but it wasn't enough to stop the pattern still tapping out of her slate. "Damn. They can't hear it."

Charging across to her, Ryder grabbed her shoulders and kept her from making a second attempt. "Who can't hear us?" he demanded. "Who?"

"The Recon team banging s s k, Staff Sergeant Kerr, into the floor up above."

"They're tapping out letters?"

She had to admire a man who didn't need a long explanation. "It's Morse code."

"They've found us?"

"Yes."

"They can get us out!"

No room for doubt; in spite of explosions and alien technology. Marines didn't leave their own behind. "Yes." He still had hold of her shoulders. She shrugged to remind him.

"Okay." Ryder took a deep breath, wiped his palms on his thighs, and started pacing again. "Okay," he said again, a little more calmly. Then he frowned. "What's Morse code?"

"A primitive communication system the anal

retentives in the Corps have dragged through the last four centuries."

"Why?"

Easy answer. "For situations like this. I need you to get down on your hands and knees."

Ryder looked startled, then he grinned, blue eyes gleaming even brighter amidst the unrelieved gray. "What?"

"They can see us; that message is aimed at me. They're probably scanning energy sigs with one of the engineering units. The PCU in my helmet has a noticeable signature." While Ryder connected the dots she'd given him, Torin flipped up the microphone and took off her helmet. "If I hold it under your body, they can't see it. When I bring it out again, they can."

"Visual tapping."

"If you like."

"These vibrations aren't doing the scanner any good," Johnston grumbled as a sweating Guimond stopped pounding and the gathered Marines waited for a reply. "And we don't know that she can hear us."

Nivry glanced up from the scanner's display and frowned at the engineer. "A few more minutes."

"There's a good meter between the top of the staff sergeant's head and the ceiling. What's she going to do to answer; stand on the civilian?"

The corporal ignored him. "Guimond try a . . . wait, something's happening."

Crouching, Johnston fiddled with the scan. "Looks like the thermal signals are joining."

"Now we know who the civilian is," someone snickered.

"Sig for the helmet PCU keeps disappearing and

reappearing. There." He pointed. "Now you see it, now you don't."

"She's answering."

"Well, if she isn't, I'd like a closer look at what they *are* doing."

The tapping changed.

"Sounds like they got your message." Craig shifted his weight from one knee to the other and back and tried not to think about how ridiculous this had to look. "What're they saying?"

"Give me a minute, Mr. Ryder, it comes through one letter at a time."

The situation had clearly stabilized if she was Mr. Ryder-ing him again. He had to hand it to the Marines, they had an interesting idea of a stable situation.

Air lock gob? No, gone . . . Torin reminded herself to send an apology to the gunny who'd taught communications back on Ventris. *Who knew I'd ever actually need to use this crap?*

When Ryder rose up onto his knees, she put a hand on his shoulder to stop him. He twisted out of her grip, the muscles across his back tight enough to march on.

"I need you for a few more minutes." She slid the words between the letters being pounded out above.

"No, I'm done . . ."

Torin understood his desire to do something, to not sit by and wait passively for rescue. Unfortunately, his options were limited, and if he started pacing again, she was going to have to break both his legs. "I can't do this without you," she reminded him.

"I don't . . ."

The tapping stopped.

Protest cut short, he looked up at the ceiling, then back at her, one corner of his mouth curling up. "Well?"

"Air lock's gone and the shuttle with it. And they've lost Captain Travik."

"Nice to get some good news with the bad." He stared down at his hands resting on his thighs and, exhaling with some violence, abruptly dropped forward. "What are you going to tell them?"

Torin forced herself to concentrate as he arched his back. "To look for another clean bit of floor."

"Found it."

Marines and the second scanner converged.

After a moment, Harrop straightened. "Nivry, ditch the small talk and tell the staff sergeant we've found Captain Travik and what could be another civilian."

"Could be?"

"Heer's reading five small separate sigs beside him."

"Four meters on the other side of that wall?"

Torin rocked back on her heels and stood. "That's what they tell me."

"Oh, that's just fukking great!" Ryder surged to his feet. "He might as well be four fukking kilometers away." He threw up his arms and spun around. "There's no way we can get to him. There's no way he can get to us. And even if your people up top had cutting tools, they couldn't get to us, so . . ." A thick finger jabbed toward Torin. ". . . don't bullshit me that they can because structural components around here don't seem to want . . ." He shouted a word at each wall. "To. Be. Fukked. With."

Settling her helmet back on her head, Torin walked forward. An arm's length from the wall, she paused and shouted.

By the time the noise faded, Ryder was at her side, arms folded. "What did you do that for?"

"No echo. When you were yelling, there was bounce off every wall but this one." Torin took a deep breath and stretched out her arm, holding her hand a steady centimeter from the wall's surface. Before she could think too hard about what she was going to do, she took a step forward. Her hand disappeared.

"Are you insane!"

"Could be." Given how much she wanted to scream, she wasn't going to rule it out.

Ryder grabbed her forearm and yanked. Nothing moved except a couple of small bones in her wrist.

She took another small step, and he snatched his hands away as her forearm disappeared.

"You're fukking kidding, right?"

Breathing heavily through her nose, she shrugged. "This seems to be an exit."

"It's a wall," he growled. "I'm staying right here."

They locked eyes for a long moment. Torin looked away first and shrugged again. "Suit yourself. If you change your mind, you know the way out."

"Take a deep breath."

Her heart was pounding so violently, she hardly heard him but she managed a smile. "No shit."

She'd intended to keep her eyes open, but at the last second, she closed them and threw herself forward.

It wasn't as bad as the first time but only because it was over a lot faster.

Momentum slammed her into another wall.

The bounce dropped her into a defensive position. A fast check confirmed everything working and no gear lost in transit.

Adrenaline buzzing, eyes flicking from point to point, she looked around. Another corridor; but no more than a meter and a half wide and the walls appeared to be made of welded steel. Stranger still, the welds were rusting. The same ridged black rubber used for traction in most station docks covered the deck. Strips in the ceiling emitted cold white light not quite strong enough to reach into the corners, throwing the first shadows Torin had seen on the ship. About a meter to her right, the corridor ended in a blank wall, but it continued another six, maybe seven, to her left before ending in what seemed to be an old manual hatch.

If she was under surveillance, it wasn't registering.

If she was in danger, it wasn't obvious.

The knife went back in her boot.

So where's a thousand Silsviss trying to kill you when you need them?

The great thing about an obvious danger was the option of fighting back.

The wall she'd come through was the same welded steel as the rest. Just as rusty. Just as solid.

Ryder came through a little faster than she had. Hit the steel a little harder. Took a swing at her on the way down.

Given the circumstances, Torin let it pass.

"What took you so long?" she asked, holding out a hand.

He hesitated a moment, breathing hard, then took it and let her help him to his feet. "Why so relieved? You think I wouldn't follow?"

She hadn't been sure. She'd seen the inside of his ship; he spent a lot of time alone in a small space, so it didn't take much to work out the reason for the pacing he had been doing in the cube. Two people in that small space and the ship runs out of resources a lot faster in an unforgiving environment. Having her in that cube with him had to have been working against years of survival conditioning. No wonder he'd been on the verge of panic. Given a choice between being alone in the cube and forcing himself through after her . . .

If he'd been one of her Marines, she'd have ordered him through and trusted training to overcome panic. As it was, she had to count on the fine Human tradition of not wanting to look like a coward in front of a crowd.

One shoulder lifted and fell. "You said you were staying."

"I changed my mind." He glanced down at their clasped hands, pulled free, stepped back, and swept the area with a disdainful gaze. "Oh, this is a big fukking improvement."

"There's a door."

Torin watched the tension go out of his shoulders as he turned. "Now, we're getting somewhere."

"It might be locked."

"I have a way with locked doors."

"No doubt."

"We seem to be heading in the general direction of your captain."

"Convenient." And it was. Torin began to have a distinct sense of déjà vu.

"Door looks low-tech. This looks like an older part of the ship."

"This looks like an entirely *different* ship. And if these walls are actually steel . . ."

"Corporal Nivry, this is Staff Sergeant Kerr. Acknowledge."

The silence was sudden and absolute as the staff sergeant's voice rang out over the group channel.

"This is Nivry." She could hardly hear herself over the shouting. "You disappeared off the scanner; first your signal, then Mr. Ryder's."

"We left the cube."

"How . . . ?"

"We went through the wall. We're now in what looks like a low-tech area and are advancing toward Captain Travik's position. Report."

"Harveer Niirantapajee has regained consciousness, but Gytha, the Katrien, is still out. We've patched up what damage we could see, but no one's really up on Katrien anatomy. The mess kit's still working; we're running everything edible through into field rations and we're bagging body parts. Most of the science team was at ground zero and there's not much of them."

"Careful with your labeling, then."

It got a bigger laugh than it would have under better circumstances.

"We've found four intact HE suits, and Heer and Johnston were checking to see that the air lock can attach another shuttle."

"Were?"

"We've got both scanners pointed at the floor."

"Point one back at the air lock, but keep the other on Captain Travik. We may need directions. See what can be done about boosting our comm signal—the sooner the Berganitan *knows we're alive, the better."*

Nivry stepped back as Johnston moved to reclaim his scanner. "We're on it, Staff."

"Good work. I'll check in when I've found the captain. Kerr out."

"She went through the wall," the engineer muttered as the exoskeleton took up the strain. Straightening his legs, he announced to no one in particular. "Sergeants and above; out of their fukking minds."

The hatch was locked. Ryder had it open before Torin snapped her mike up. She raised a hand to stop him from charging through and motioned for him to stand by the door, ready to slam it shut, while she checked the immediate area for unfriendlies.

He ignored her.

Which was when she remembered he wasn't a Marine.

It was a little too late to do it by the book, so she followed him through the hatch and stopped short.

If she hadn't known better, she'd have sworn she was standing in a dirtside warehouse. The kind that took advantage of the fact that the real estate came with an atmosphere and so there was never any need to clear the old crap out to make way for the new. Light levels were low, creating a shadow maze around the stacks of crates and pieces of equipment. The perfect location for an ambush.

She glanced at her sleeve. If her sensors were right, nothing was moving. They'd find out soon enough if her sensors were wrong.

"Holy fuk."

Ryder's voice held significantly more fear than that situation called for.

"What is it?"

"I've been here before." When Torin turned toward

him, his eyes had nearly disappeared under the depth of his scowl. "It's Customs Storage 23 at Port Julion."

Environmental controls weren't enough to stop a chill from sliding down Torin's spine. "Dirtside warehouse?"

"Yeah."

"You're sure?"

"Dimensions, lighting, even the fukking shipping crates are in the same place. Except that." Ryder pointed toward a familiar box of gray plastic. "That sank with us. Our backs were right up against it. So, why did it land way over here when we got dropped inside the magic cube?"

"Good question. Here's a better one. My guys said it was just over a meter between their floor and our ceilings—a straight line from where we sank up there to where we ended up down here. But we were in darkness for just over thirty-one seconds. What else happened while we were in transit?"

He stared at her for a long moment. "Thank you for sharing that. You think the ship pulled this place out of my head?"

Torin shrugged. "Got a better answer?"

"And the corridor outside?"

"That could have come from either of us—it's pretty much a generic piece of old station or ship, but . . ." Again, she reached for the benny that wasn't there. "We'd better hope they decided to stick with what's in your head."

"And why would that be, Staff Sergeant?"

He sounded insulted. Tough. "Ever been in combat, Mr. Ryder? Trust me, I've been in places I don't ever want to go to again. Captain Travik should be over that way. Come on." Moving carefully around blind corners, she'd covered about half the estimated distance when the shriek of protesting hinges spun her around. Holding the lid up with one hand, Ryder was about to reach into a red octagonal case with the other. "What are you doing?" she snarled.

"This case was never in CS23. If the ship put it here, I want to know what's in it."

Torin closed the distance between them with three quick strides, slamming the lid down with both hands. "Are you out of your fukking mind?"

Breathing heavily, staring at his hands as though surprised they were still attached, Ryder snarled, "My salvage, Staff Sergeant. Don't forget it."

"Alien technology, Mr. Ryder. Quite possibly the same technology that's blown up once already. Anything you find will mean squat if we've been blown into greasy smears on the deck. Touch as little as possible. Open nothing." Lips drawn back off her teeth, she leaned toward him. "Am I making myself clear?"

He leaned in as well. "At the risk of sounding childish," he growled, his breath warm against her face, "you're not the boss of me."

"True." She held her position, their eyes locked.

After a long moment, Ryder jerked away. "All right. You win. I open nothing."

"Thank you."

"Yeah, yeah, you're welcome."

He stayed close on her heels after that, which was, she supposed, an improvement.

They found Captain Travik in an open area, one arm bent at an impossible angle, a triangular flap of skin peeled back over one eye and still bleeding sluggishly.

The five thermal points beside him turned out to be the muzzle, hands and feet of Presit a Tur durValintrisy—her fur too thick for the scanner to read body heat.

"And the day just keeps getting better," Torin sighed.

"*Berganitan*, this is *B7*. We're at the air lock and it's a mess. Looks like there's pieces of the ship missing and pieces of the shuttle still attached. I can't tell if parts are melted or melded." Frowning at the wreckage, Commander Sibley brought his Jade in closer. "Sending visuals and data stream now. You want my opinion, we're not going to be using this entrance again, and if the internal damage is half as extensive, I doubt there's anyone left alive."

EIGHT

IT took seconds to seal Captain Travik's head wound. As she could do nothing about the triangular dent in the bone beneath the laceration, Torin ignored it. Familiarity with impact wounds suggested the explosion had flung a piece of debris at his head, and had he been anything but Krai, he'd have lost the top four inches of his skull. As it was, his med-alert had gone off, marking him for med-vac, so there was definite brain damage behind the dent.

Brand new damage, Torin snorted silently, turning her attention to the arm.

Grateful that the captain remained unconscious—for her sake as much as his—Torin took a deep breath, then gripped his arm above and below the joint, slowly straightening it.

"I heard Krai bones were too tough to break," Ryder said quietly, his hands working nearly wrist-deep in Presit's fur.

"The bone's not broken; the joint's been shattered." She frowned down at the information on her slate and shifted her thumb until she felt something move beneath it. "The pieces are in roughly the right position, but he's going to need internal fusing to hold things together."

"And until he gets it?"

"We do the same thing we usually do."

Ryder snorted. "Because this sort of thing happens all the time?"

"Injuries are a side effect of battle, Mr. Ryder." Releasing the captain's arm, Torin picked up her slate and added the new data to his medical file. A moment later, his sleeve tightened, then stiffened, holding his arm immobile at a ninety-degree angle. "The main function of MCCUs—combats," she added at Ryder's expression, "is to keep the wearer alive. The fabric's got a dozen or so functions built into it."

"Or so?" Her attention back on the captain's head wound, she could hear the grin in Ryder's voice. "I'd have thought a staff sergeant of your caliber would know for certain."

"I know. You don't need to." She checked the sealant before rocking back on her heels and standing. "How's the reporter?"

"No broken bones, no lacerations, no dark glasses, so it's a good thing it's a little dim in here, and she definitely uses a conditioner when she shampoos."

"Ryder . . ."

"Other than that . . ." He sat back, hands on his thighs, and looked up at Torin, "I haven't the faintest idea. You don't have her specs in your slate?"

"Why would I? No Katrien in the Corps. Her heart's beating, she's breathing." Torin shrugged. "Other than that . . . Nivry, this is Kerr. Is your Katrien awake yet?"

"Negative, Staff. We've stopped the bleeding and her vitals seem steady, but she's still out."

"Roger that. Let me know when she comes to. Any progress on reaching the *Berganitan*?"

"Negative. The air lock's fused—completely unusable—and we've determined we can no more get an unassisted

signal out through the hull than they can get one in. Heer thinks if we set a benny on narrow band and drain every charge we have, we might have juice enough to cut a pin-prick hole through the hull: big enough so the Berganitan *could pick up the energy signal, not so big we'd decompress, and easy enough to patch."*

"Considering what happened to Dr. Hodges, let's try to avoid poking holes in the ship if it's at all possible. There's no chance of cobbling something together out of all that scientific equipment?"

"Not unless you or Mr. Ryder can make a comm unit with a mess kit; everything else has been slagged."

"I can't even make a decent pouch of coffee with a mess kit. And since we're down here and the mess kit's with you . . ."

"Johnston may have something on that, Staff."

"Staff Sergeant Kerr, Johnston here. I was checking the site of the explosion—it left one fuk of a hole in the wall and at the back of it, we're scanning six centimeters of solid and then an area that reads like a vertical shaft. I suspect it's what Dr. Hodges was aiming for. It seems to go down to your level. Do you want us to start through?"

"What part of 'avoid poking holes in the ship' are you having trouble understanding, Johnston?"

"Yeah, but the material at the back of the hole is different. It's still a mix of metal and organic, but the explosion changed the organic part."

"How?"

"Layman's terms—it cooked it. I'm extrapolating a bit from available data, but if we smack this stuff hard enough, it's going to shatter."

Torin considered implications for a moment. As much as it would simplify things to have the team in one place, another explosion was on no one's wish list. "Let's make sure the shaft actually reaches this far before we risk it. I'll take a look and recontact. Kerr out."

"Take a look at what?" Ryder asked as she snapped her mike up. He was standing so close, he'd clearly been attempting to overhear the other end of the conversation.

"One of our engineers may have found a vertical."

"Down to this level?"

"That's what I'm going to find out."

"I'll go with you."

"You'll stay with . . ." Catching sight of his expression, Torin bit off the rest of the order. *Not a Marine,* she reminded herself. "Look, Ryder . . ."

"You know, you called me Craig while we were being sucked through the floor."

Had she? "Extenuating circumstances."

He grinned. "Look, I don't care what you call me, just remember I'm not one of your soldiers and I'm not going to ask how high on the way up. You want me to stay with these two." Still grinning, he folded his arms and nodded toward the floor. "Then ask me nicely."

Torin lifted her upper lip off her teeth. "Mr. Ryder, as an investigation of the location of a possible vertical is not going to require both of us, and because I have the PCU and can therefore stay in contact with the Marine engineer who needs the information, would you mind staying with Captain Travik and the reporter while I check things out?"

"You're being sarcastic again."

"Just get out of my way before I knock you on your ass."

"Now *that,*" Ryder stepped back as she approached, "sounded sincere."

The good news, Torin reflected as she made her way

around the crates toward the far wall, *is that our experiences thus far seemed to have caused no lasting trauma*—never a given with a civilian—*and he's regained his sense of humor. And the bad news is . . .* She froze as one of the lights flickered and then continued on more cautiously. . . . *he's regained his sense of humor.*

Directly below the point where the explosion had occurred there was an exact replica of the hatch they'd used to enter the room. More because it was procedure than because she thought it would do any good, Torin scanned for traps.

Nothing.

Yeah. Big surprise.

"Mr. Ryder, does CS23 have a hatch in this position?"

"Not that I remember. We've got one?"

"We do."

"Everything all right, Staff Sergeant?"

"Everything's fine, Mr. Ryder." She could hear him clearly although his voice had picked up a hollow, big-empty-room timbre. As the room was not empty, she assumed sound waves were being screwed with—certainly an effect well within the established tech level of the ship. Sound waves had shown them the way out of the cube. *We got to use them once; we don't get to use them again.* Which was either paranoia above and beyond the call or evidence of an emerging pattern. Since she could do nothing about either—yet—she wrapped her left hand around the bar latch and shoved it down. Metal hinges screamed.

"What the hell was that?"

"Bad maintenance. I've just opened the hatch."

"It wasn't locked?"

"No." No need. Her CSO had already shown

them, whoever *they* were, that he could get through the lock.

The hatch opened into a vertical shaft a meter square made of the same rusted steel plates. There were no lights, but the spill from the storeroom was enough for Torin to see two more hatches, once again identical to the first. *It's like the ship pulled out one hatch pattern and decided it didn't need any others.* One was in the bulkhead to her right, the other straight ahead. To her left, metal rungs had been welded to the steel and painted yellow, the paint dabbed sloppily over the welds. Definitely not military. The ship seemed to be sticking to what it had pulled from Ryder's head.

Torin looked up, way up, eventually losing the shaft in darkness.

"Johnston, this is Kerr. You reading my thermal sig in the shaft you're scanning?"

"Affirmative, Staff. Do I kick the wall down?"

"You sure you can get through it safely?"

"Not one hundred percent sure, no. But close enough for government work."

No point in bringing a specialist along and then not listening to him. Torin looked up again and then back throughr the hatch toward Captain Travik and the two civilians. "Do it. Safety level three. Once you're through, there's a whole lot of vertical above you, so keep an eye topside."

"This'll take time, Staff."

"Keep me informed. I'm exiting the debris field. Kerr out." Flipping her mike up, Torin hurried back to find the captain and the reporter lying alone where she'd left them. *Oh, fuk.* She reached for her absent benny, swore again, opened her mouth to yell, and spotted the missing Ryder bent half inside the packing crate that had accompanied them through the floor. *Kicking his ass is looking better and better.* Crossing silently to the crate, she leaned over and, close enough that her breath moved a strand of his hair, said, "What are you doing?"

He jerked back, his head missing the edge of the lid by centimeters. "You want another body to lug around, do you? Because if you do, keep that up!"

"You were to stay with the injured."

"I was looking for something we could carry them on."

She folded her arms. "Really?"

He mirrored the movement. "Yeah. Really."

Maybe he had been. It was a good idea and it wouldn't kill her to give him the benefit of the doubt. "Find anything useful?"

"No!" And then a little more calmly, "Nothing we could use as a stretcher, but remember when you said the di'Taykan were going to use explosives after lunch?" Holding out his left hand, Ryder slowly opened the fingers. Lying across his palm were a pair of demolition charges. "You weren't kidding, were you?"

"Actually, I was." When she went to take the charges, he closed his fingers around them.

"Not Corps equipment, Staff Sergeant. My salvage."

"And if we need them to get off this thing?" If they'd all still been in HE suits, she'd be tempted to blow a hole in the hull and start tossing both the living and the dead out for pickup by the *Berganitan.* Space represented a known danger. This ship . . .

"I expect to be compensated. At the going rate."

"Which is?"

"Depends on where we're going."

"Funny."

A half smile barely showed within the beard. "I'm not kidding."

"You know how to use them?"

"Try to remember what I do for a living. Most days, the bits you can salvage need to be separated from the bits you can't." He tossed the four-inch ceramic cylinders one at a time to his other hand and slipped them both into his belt pouch. "I'd bet I'm better at setting demo charges than you are at getting second lieutenants to run their platoons your way."

Torin snorted. "I doubt that." Still, he had a point. More relevantly, she knew where they were if she needed them and could retrieve them if the situation called for it. Craig Ryder was a large, well-muscled man but, her own abilities aside, she had twelve Marines working for her. "Given the unexpected way things have of blowing up on this ship, the Corps appreciates your willingness to take the risk of providing storage."

Ryder stared at her for a moment then shook his head ruefully when she smiled. "Nice."

There was nothing else in the crate but packing intended to protect delicate equipment in transit.

Explosives and bubble wrap.

"Mixed messages," Torin sighed, straightening. "That's what's wrong with the universe."

A noise from the captain drew her back to his side. "Sir?" She dropped to her knees. "Captain Travik?"

His eyes flickered open. *"Fleruke ahs sa?"*

Torin's implant, keyed to automatically translate both Krai and di'Taykan murmured an unnecessary, **Where am I?**

"We're a level below the air lock, sir. In . . ." An actual explanation was far too complicated. ". . . a storage facility."

"Explo . . . sion!"

"Yes, sir. There was an explosion. Then the floor opened up and we went through it."

"Telling . . . Gen . . . eral Morris."

Torin ignored the whiny tone. "I wish you would, sir. I'd be a lot happier if the *Bergani* . . . God damn it!" She sighed and looked up at Ryder. "He's gone again."

"You think there's brain damage under that dent?"

"Not for me to say."

"Brain damage *caused* by the dent."

She sat back on her heels. "I know what you meant."

"Okay. So, how can he contact the big *B* if you can't?"

"Officer's implants are a couple of grades higher than mine." Torin's left hand rose involuntarily to her jaw. "More memory and more power—maybe enough to get a signal through the hull."

Ryder squatted and studied the captain's face, pulling thoughtfully on the edge of his beard. "I've got an external mike in mine, tucked in under a molar . . . and what?"

"You have an implant."

"Yeah. Won the installation in a poker game."

Torin kept her voice quiet and nonthreatening. She had a feeling she should pace herself. "Have you tried to reach the *Promise*?"

"Nope. I figure this is your problem." His hands rose into a protective position at her expression. "Kidding. I've tried, no luck—not even static. It's only a seven-aught-four. So I was wondering," he continued when Torin didn't respond, "why can't you just reach in and activate the captain's implant and talk loud enough to be picked up?"

"Because Captain Travik is a Krai."

"So?"

Using only one finger, Torin pushed against the captain's chin just hard enough to open his mouth. Then she leaned back and picked up the broken arm of Presit's dark glasses.

"What are you doing?"

"Making sure you'll believe what I'm about to tell you. This is something we show the Human and di'Taykan recruits. Most of them have never worked with Krai."

The moment the end of the arm passed between the captain's teeth, his mouth snapped shut. As he chewed and swallowed the plastic, Torin held up what was left. "Never stick your finger in a Krai's mouth. You stand a slightly better chance of keeping the finger if they're conscious, but only slightly."

Ryder looked impressed. "How do they get the implant in there?"

"No idea; I'm not tech."

"He swallowed that plastic."

"And if there's anything organic about it, he'll digest that and pass the rest."

"So his implant's useless to us?"

"Unless he dies, then we have a three-minute window until it powers down."

"So, our best chance to contact the *Berganitan* involves holding a piece of bubble wrap over the captain's face?"

"Yes."

"Okay." Sighing, Ryder stood. "We're not going to do that, are we?"

"No."

The sound of debris hitting the floor of the shaft occurred simultaneously with Johnston's voice announcing he was through. After that, the debris came thick and fast, huge pieces falling and shattering. Then a moment of silence. Then Johnston again.

"We've got access, Staff. Waiting for orders."

"All right, everybody listen up. Given that the explosion destroyed the air lock and blew her shuttle to shit, Captain Carveg will assume that survivors will make their way to the next air lock and wait for pickup. My download of the *Berganitan*'s scan of the exterior put the next air lock down on the belly of the beast—maybe another seven levels and about four klicks aft and three and a half inboard. Since we're going down anyway, I want supplies and the injured brought to this position. Any questions?"

"Dursinski, Staff. Captain Carveg doesn't know we're alive, does she?"

"That's correct. Unless they've come up with something that can read through the hull since we left this morning, Captain Carveg has no way of knowing if anyone survived the explosion."

"Then how do we know she'll wait for us to get to the other air lock? We'll be moving injured personnel through unfamiliar territory inside an alien vessel—it's going to take time."

"You're Recon, Dursinski, moving through unfamiliar territory is what you do."

"But Captain Carveg . . ."

"Will have a shuttle waiting by that air lock until she knows we're dead."

"Speaking of the dead, Staff, what do we do with them?"

Body bags were standard equipment on combat vests. Every Marine carried one. Activated, the bag would use the single charge it carried to reduce its contents to fit inside a narrow cylinder less than two inches long. Marines didn't leave their own behind. Since she'd made sergeant, Torin had carried more cylinders than she wanted to remember—every one was one dead Marine too many.

Of the ten scientists, there were eight dead. Plus Cirvan a Tar palRentskik. Nine.

"You said you bagged them, Nivry; what in?"

"Depends on the size of the piece."

"Send someone down, I'm on my way up."

She'd taken only a single step toward the hatch when Ryder's hand on her arm pulled her up short.

"Are you going to tell them?"

"That they've designed this part of the ship around bits they pulled from your head? Yes," Torin added when he nodded. "I don't hold back information that might help keep my people alive."

"You don't think it'll distract them?"

"They're trained to stay focused while penetrating into enemy territory, Mr. Ryder. As long as it doesn't pin them down under a withering cross fire before calling in an air strike, I don't think your head will offer them much of a challenge."

"Bottom line, Staff Sergeant, if they get themselves blown up, no one's going to blame you."

Begging the general's pardon, Torin thought, staring at the dead, *but sure as shit someone's going to blame me if I just leave them here.*

"It's not like you were under fire, Staff Sergeant." She could hear the Board of Inquiry as clearly as if she was standing before them. *"You took the time to make field rations."*

Field rations. That would certainly solve the problem. And they probably wouldn't taste any worse.

"Staff?"

"What is it, Heer?"

"Werst and I would like to do ritual for the two Krai. They were spread around a bit, but if we run them through the mess kit, we can probably get four meals each out of them."

She frowned down at the engineer. "Did I say field rations out loud?"

Seven bags.

Torin ran her thumb along the edges the explosion had ripped in the wall. If more than five Marines died on the way to that other air lock . . .

"No one dies."

"Staff?"

"Bag them, Nivry. We'll carry them out."

"Harveer Niirantapajee." Torin looked down at the scientist sitting slumped against the wall, noting three field dressings and, through a singed hole in her lab coat, a glistening blister on one shoulder that had turned gray-green skin a muddy yellow. "I'm Staff Sergeant Kerr. Do you think you'll be able to climb down a vertical ladder or should we lower you?"

The elderly Niln got slowly to her feet and peered up along the line of her nose, nictitating membrane flicking across both eyes. "Not going to ask how I'm feeling, Staff Sergeant Kerr?"

All right. "Do you feel like you'll be able to climb down a vertical ladder, or should we lower you?"

They stared at each other for a moment, then the *harveer* snorted. "How far?"

"One level. About three meters."

"We're making our way to the next air lock?"

"Yes, ma'am."

"Where's your officer? Didn't you lot have an officer when we came in here?"

"Captain Travik is unconscious."

"And you're in charge." It wasn't a question, so Torin didn't bother answering it. "Just so we're clear, you're not in charge of me. It was agreed that the science team would operate independent of the military presence on this ship." Her tail, which had been moving slowly back and forth, began to speed up. "Our investigations were not to be interfered with. I did not agree with Dr. Hodges' procedure. Molecular unzipping . . ." Nostrils flared, her breathing had sped up to match the rhythm of her tail. "Dr. Hodges was a fine scientist. They were all fine scientists—although I believe the di'Taykan team's structural fluidity theory was way off the curve. Way off the curve!"

Anger in the face of death, Torin understood. She pulled one of the seven cylinders from her vest and held it down to the Niln. "If you'd prefer to carry this, *Harveer* . . ."

"What is it?"

"*Harveer* Ujinteripsani."

"*Harveer* Ujinteripsani?" Tail and breathing stopped together. An instant later, just as Torin was running through the little she knew of Niln physiology, breathing began again. Reaching out a trembling hand, *Harveer* Niirantapajee ran a vestigial claw down the length of the cylinder. "Returned to the egg. You did this?"

"Yes, ma'am."

"Thank you." Scooping it up, she slipped it into one of the many pockets in the overalls she wore under her coat, murmuring, "May the First Egg protect and enclose him." Then she sighed and looked around, as though she were actually seeing the extent of the disaster for the first time. "May the First Egg protect and enclose them all. Well, then, about that vertical descent." Leaning around Torin, she pointed an imperious finger toward Guimond. "You can put the big Human at the bottom to catch me, but I expect I'll manage."

They moved the gear down first, and then the injured. Torin would have moved *Harveer* Niirantapajee first, but the Niln had wanted to stay with Gytha a Tur calFinistraven, the Katrien scientist. Torin wanted Gytha moved last. The longer they waited, the greater the chance that she'd wake up and they'd have a better idea of what was wrong—not to mention the best way to drop her down nine meters and do the least additional damage.

Both med kits carried stretchers, a rectangle of smart fabric with a handle at each corner. In the end, they snapped it out rigid, using it as a backboard and immobilizing her for the descent in a webbing of rope.

Recon packs carried fifty feet of near weightless rope as part of standard gear. Spun by Mictock—Torin had no intention of asking how, only partly because it seemed obvious to anyone who'd met a Mictok—the rope didn't stretch, didn't bind, and damn near didn't tangle.

"How's it going, Werst?"

Hanging from his feet above the stretcher, one hand steadying the edge—the only way a Marine and the injured Katrien could descend the shaft at the same time—Werst carefully moved his right foot a rung down. "Keep her coming."

Braced on either side of the hole, Harrop and Jynett played out another bit of line.

A meter and a half from the bottom of the shaft, the stretcher came to rest across the inside of Guimond's forearms.

"You know, there's nothing to her under all that fur," he murmured as Werst reached down and unhooked the ropes. "She's so tiny and helpless."

"And quiet," Werst grunted. "I've never seen one quiet before."

"She's only quiet because she's unconscious."

"No shit."

They tipped stretcher and Katrien slightly to get them through the hatch, then Guimond reclaimed her.

"Remember, sentient species; no scratching her behind the ears."

"Shut up, Tsui."

He carried her through the maze of cases, emerging in the temporary infirmary to see Huilin kneeling beside Captain Travik with a pouch of water. The captain swallowed and grabbed the di'Taykan's arm. "It wasn't my fault," he said distinctly and slumped back down, head lolling to one side.

Huilin rocked back on his heels and caught sight of Guimond. "Just put her beside the other one," he sighed, shoving his helmet back far enough to allow a few strands of turquoise hair to escape.

"Where's *Harveer* Niira . . . Nyri . . . Where's the Niln?"

"Staff's got her and Ryder checking out packing crates on a 'look, don't touch' basis. She wants to know how good this reconstruction is and if there's stuff in here that couldn't have come from Ryder's memory, she wants to know if either of them recognize it. She says if we can get an idea of who else this barge has been in contact with, we can get an idea of where it's been and we'll have a better idea of whose side it's on."

"Okay, but what if they don't recognize anything?"

"Then the civilians are still out of the way while we make ready to move out. Win win situation." Tilting the helmet over one ear, Huilin granted momentary freedom to new bits of hair. "Fuk, I hate these things. She as light as she looks?" he added as Guimond squatted and set the scientist on the deck beside the reporter.

"Lighter."

"Good. 'Cause the captain's got that Krai bone density thing going, and he's gonna be no fun at all to hump around."

The rope holding the injured Katrien to the stretcher had been pulled tight enough that thick tufts of fur poked up through the spaces. It didn't look comfortable. Guimond freed one edge, then frowned over a second set of knots. Unable to tell which way they went, he moved the scientist's arm out from her body to allow him a better angle.

Her hand brushed Presit's shoulder.

Two sets of black eyes snapped open.

Guimond barely got out from between them in time.

"Staff? Guimond. The Katrien are awake."

"Good. Is that them I can hear?"

"Yeah, that's them."

"What the hell are they doing?"

"Uh, they were, I uh, guess . . . grooming?" He

winced at a particularly high-pitched burst. "Now, they're talk . . ."

A small black hand clutched suddenly at a handful of his uniform.

"Was that you, *Guimond?"*

"Yeah, Staff." Ears burning, he tried to ignore Huilin snickering.

A second hand joined the first although about ten centimeters to the left and in a significantly less sensitive region.

"Why is Gytha a Tur calFinistraven tied down?" Presit demanded imperiously.

"We're being tested." Torin made the statement in a tone so flatly inarguable, her entire audience blinked in near unison. "When Mr. Ryder and I sank through the floor, we spent more time in transit than the depth of the floor would allow for. During that time, the ship clearly lifted information from Mr. Ryder's mind." A truncated jerk of her head directed their attention to the surrounding storehouse. "We don't yet know if information was also taken from myself, Captain Travik, or Presit a Tur durValintrisy, but I expect we'll find out soon enough."

Perched near the top of the pile of gear, Orla shuddered dramatically, hair fanning out in a fuschia halo. "No offense, Staff, but given your simulations, I'd rather not end up somewhere out of your head."

"Better her head than the captain's," Tsui snorted.

Inclined to agree but not letting it show, Torin cut the general agreement off and continued. "Once we solved the communication problem, we got comm contact back. Mr. Ryder and I found our way through a seemingly solid wall . . ." She couldn't stop her gaze from drifting toward him. One corner of his mouth quirked up in appreciation of the understatement. "Since then, we've been given hatches. The first hatch was locked. Mr. Ryder dealt with it, and the rest have been merely latched. If holing the wall caused the explosion, Johnston found a place where the wall could be knocked down conveniently over a shaft enabling us to join up."

"That are all being coincidence," Presit scoffed from the edge of the group where she and Gytha were sitting so close their fur intermingled.

"No." Torin shook her head. "It doesn't feel like coincidence."

"And you are being who so that what you are feeling means so much?"

"What?"

"She wants to know why *your* feelings should define the situation," *Harveer* Niirantapajee sighed, shooting an exasperated look at the reporter.

"I are *speaking* Federate," Presit snapped, actually showing teeth.

Torin caught Werst's eye and he carefully covered his own.

The Niln slapped her tail against her leg. "You're speaking the Katrien idiosyncratic version of Federate. If you're going to learn a language, why don't you learn the syntax, that's what I've always wondered. Egocentric mammals."

"Enough!" The whip snap of Torin's voice sat both Katrien down again and cut off half a dozen other comments. "*Harveer*, thank you for the translation but there will be *no* interspecies conflict. And to answer the question, I'm defining the situation because I'm in charge."

"Who are saying . . ."

"They are." She jerked her head toward the twelve Marines.

Heads pulled almost reluctantly around, the two scientists and the reporter stared up at the mass of black uniforms.

Tsui waved.

"You want to wander around this vessel on your own," Torin told them, pretending she couldn't see Ryder grinning his stupid head off over on the other side of the team, "be our guest. You want a hope in hell of getting off this thing, you stay with us, you do as you're told, and I don't want to have to keep telling you that."

"We are not Marines," Presit muttered.

"That's for damn sure." Folding her arms, she swept her gaze over the remains of the boarding party, uniting them again. "Our mission objective is simple; we need to get to the next air lock as quickly as possible and pick up our ride back to the *Berganitan*."

"You're sure the *Berganitan* will still be there?"

"I am." Which she was, and her certainty was all they needed. "The closest air lock is seven levels down, a little over four klicks aft, and about three and a half klicks starboard. Hatch one opens into a passageway that goes forward a hundred meters, then drops into a descending vertical with no bounce and no disruption of airflow that'd indicate an egress—not to mention standard gravity and no visible rungs. Hatch two opens into an identical passageway heading starboard for seventy-five meters, then turns ninety degrees to head forward. This passageway, now paralleling the first, shows no bounce, no egress. Either *could*, eventually, lead us where we want to go, but I'd just as soon not wander randomly around—we need a map."

"Staff, what makes you think the ship'll give us what we need?" Nivry's hair was flicking back and forth. "I mean, maybe we'll solve the puzzle in this room and it'll give us . . . uh . . ."

"Piped-in music," Frii offered.

Nivry shot the other di'Taykan an irritated look but let the suggestion stand.

"It's given us what we've needed so far."

"Yeah, after it exploded and killed most of the science team."

"I don't think it meant to do that," Ryder said suddenly. "I think it saved your captain and the reporter because they were the only two not killed instantly. And I think it removed me and the staff sergeant because we were in danger. And now I think it's trying to figure out who and what we are."

Expressions changed as the assembled company considered new possibilities. Finally, brows knitted into a deep vee over the bridge of her nose, Dursinski shook her head. "It won't know we need to go out an air lock."

"It knows we came in an air lock," Torin said flatly.

"You're making this up as you go along, aren't you, Staff?"

"You got a better suggestion, Lance Corporal? Because if you do, I'll listen to it." Tsui ruefully shook his head and, arms folded, Torin watched the twelve Marines consider all that had been said. Heer and Johnston, the two engineers, looked intrigued. Nivry, Harrop, Frii, and Huilin looked reluctantly convinced. Dursinski looked worried and Werst pissed off, but both, Torin had come to realize, were pretty much a given regardless. Tsui, Orla, and Jynett seemed doubtful, but as long as they had no better ideas, they could do as much doubting as they liked. Guimond was smiling broadly. Torin decided she'd rather not speculate about the reason.

"Orla, you'll be staying with the captain. He regains consciousness, try and get him to contact the *Berganitan*."

"Why me?" the di'Taykan protested.

"Because if I remember correctly, which I do, you're pretty much the only one left who hasn't done something to piss him off. Heer, Johnston, you start scanning the cases. Mr. Ryder didn't know what was in them in the original storehouse so there could be anything in them now. Squad One, check the perimeter for anything resembling an access panel. Squad Two, sweep the room looking for anything that doesn't seem to fit. You find something, you check it against Mr. Ryder's memory." She stepped back and half turned, gesturing dramatically into the room. "Let's move, people; you really don't want to be around me when we run out of coffee."

She was surprised to find the three non-Human civilians beside her when the rush ended.

"We have very little equipment," *Harveer* Niirantapajee began without preamble, "but what we have we will use in an attempt to communicate directly with the ship." She held up a slate about half again as large as the military version. "I suspect that by your standards, I'm carrying nothing of practical value in here, but I do have a large memory and a great deal of processing ability as well as about half of the data I'd collected before the explosion."

"You said, we?"

Gytha leaned forward, muzzle wrinkled in what

Torin assumed was a smile. "I are carrying a second degree in fractal communications. Presit are being a professional communicator."

"And the three of you can work together?"

Presit looked dubious, but the Katrien scientist patted *Harveer* Niirantapajee on the shoulder. "I are working with her many times before. She are having—how are you Humans saying?—worse bark than her bite?"

"Close enough. Communicating with the ship would be very helpful, thank you." Torin watched them walk away, the Katrien keeping up a running commentary in their own language. As far as being stuck with civilians went, she supposed it could have been worse.

On cue, she turned to find Ryder standing behind her. "You walk too damn quietly."

"Sorry."

"Listen, I want to thank you for the support."

"Craig."

"What?"

"Thank you for the support, *Craig*."

"Don't push it." But she was smiling, and with the smile some of the muscles in her back relaxed.

"You know, I hate to put a damper on things, but we could be wrong. There could be no puzzle to solve in this room."

Torin took a deep breath and let it out slowly. At just past 1740 it had already been a very, very long day. "There has to be, because the alternative is trying to find a way to that air lock by wandering around inside an enormous ship that can change its configuration at will while carrying a wounded officer, escorting three civilians, with only three field rations and a little over a liter of water each."

"Four."

"What?"

"Four civilians." He smiled broadly and his eyes twinkled. "Although I'm flattered that you seem to be counting me among your people."

She had. And if he hadn't been so damned amused by it, she'd have let it go.

"I wouldn't be flattered," she told him, pulling her slate to check Captain Travik's vitals. "I'd forgotten to count you entirely."

"Ouch."

But a half glance toward him showed he was still smiling, and still twinkling. Annoying son of a bitch.

NINE

"WE plan to attach this comm unit directly to the side of the ship . . ." The science officer touched the screen and the image rotated one hundred and eighty degrees on the X-axis and ninety on the Y. ". . . with these pads here. Once attached, it will, in essence, act in the same manner as the shuttle's comm unit, boosting the signals of the Marines' PCUs and enabling us to communicate with your people."

"Seems simple enough," General Morris grunted, glaring at the three-dimensional rendering. "What's taking so long?"

Captain Carveg waved the science officer back and answered herself. "We don't just pick one of these off the shelf and slap it onto an RC drone, General. I've had engineers working since the explosion to adapt both the comm unit and the delivery system. We're talking about only a matter of hours here, so you've got little to complain about."

"I've got an officer in there who represents the entire Krai vote in Parliament, Captain. You'll excuse me if I'm impatient."

"You've got fourteen Marines in there, General. Not one."

He turned slowly, broad face flushed nearly maroon. "I don't much like your tone, Captain Carveg."

Her upper lip lifted. "I'm sorry to hear that, sir."

The tension in the room rose to near palpable levels. Four Naval officers and Lieutenant Stedrin froze in place—eyes locked on their respective leaders, Lieutenant Stedrin, at least, willing to shield his CO with his own body.

"Captain Carveg, we're picking up Susumi leakage at that portal we spotted earlier. Educated guess says it's about to reopen."

The voice of the watch officer over the ship's internal comm snapped the captain's attention off the general as though he no longer existed. "On screen in here, Commander Versahche."

The modified comm unit disappeared to be replaced by a familiar star field. The only thing missing was the alien ship usually hanging motionless in front of it.

"This is coming in from the buoy we set on the other side of the ship, Captain. When I emphasize the aurora . . ."

Soft green rays spread out against the stars. At their center was a shimmering green circle.

"I see it, Commander." Carveg stepped closer to the screen, facial ridges spread. "How far back behind the ship is that thing?"

"About one hundred and thirty-six thousand kilometers."

"Dangerously close."

"Yes, ma'am. Given the estimated size of the portal, there's no way the vessel coming through will be able to decelerate in time."

"Which means?" the general snapped.

"Which means," Captain Carveg repeated grimly, "that the vessel coming through is going to smack into the other side of the alien ship at a high speed, blowing themselves and very likely the alien ship, as well, into fragments. Commander Versahche, do we have any fighters out?"

"No, ma'am."

"Good. Get us to a safe distance and ready defense systems." With a last look at the screen, she pivoted on one heel and moved quickly toward the nearer of the room's two exits, bare feet slapping purposefully against the deck. "Yellow alert. I'm on my way to Combat Command Center."

After a stunned moment spent staring at the rapidly retreating back of the captain's head, General Morris charged after her, Lieutenant Stedrin at his heels. They caught up outside the conference room, the moving clump of three officers sending ship's personnel on their way to duty stations hard up against the bulkheads. "Captain! I will not allow you to abandon my Marines."

"General, one of two things is about to happen." Without breaking stride, or removing her gaze from the link station at the end of the passageway, Captain Carveg lifted her left hand into the air, first finger extended. "Either that ship is made of stronger stuff than anything in the Confederation and the incomer will bounce off its hide, in which case, we'll go back for your Marines because I assure you I am not abandoning anyone. Or . . ." A second finger joined the first, the three joints allowing it to snap erect with an emphasis a Human finger could never achieve. ". . . your Marines are about to become part of a large debris field traveling toward us at high velocity and as much as I have no intention of abandoning those Marines, neither do I have any intention of joining them in death." Reaching the link station, she slapped her hand over the call pad. "Captain's override, *car sanute di halertai.*" With her back against the access hatch, she looked up at the general, her expression carefully neutral. "You'll be able to watch the whole thing from the Marine attachment, which is where I respectfully suggest you go. Now."

"And do what?" General Morris snarled as the link arrived.

"Try prayer," she suggested, stepping back through the hatch. "Because that portal's going to open, and there's not a *serley* thing we can do about it."

Crimson hair keeping up a steady sweep from side to side, Commander Versahche fell into step beside the captain as she stepped off the link and onto C3. "We've got a problem, Captain."

"Does it have to do with the main engines being off-line?" she snarled.

"You noticed."

"Inertial dampers aren't that good, Commander. What's happening?"

"We don't know. For no apparent reason, we're as dead in space as our big yellow friend."

"We can't move?"

"Not a centimeter. Engineering's working on it, but there's nothing to actually work *on*. All available data indicates the engines should be working."

"But they aren't."

"No, ma'am."

"Wonderful." She took her place behind the captain's station, one hand resting over the communications touch pad. Each finger opened a channel to a specific area of the ship, pressure from her palm opened a channel shipwide. Her thumb dipped, then lifted. No need to urge engineering to work faster; if anyone knew the result of a vessel exiting Susumi space too close to another solid object, they did. The three screens in front of the commander showed five second sections of the surrounding star field, the alien ship, and the portal. Its aurora had brightened. "All right; any idea of what's coming through?"

"No ma'am. Only thing we can tell for certain, is that it's not one of ours."

"Not Navy."

"Not from the Confederation at all unless someone's put something new in vacuum and no one gave us the specs for it."

"Like that's never happened before," Carveg snorted. "You'd think we weren't involved in a shooting war out here. What about the Methane Alliance?"

"Again, if it is, it's something new. They use essentially the same Susumi drive we do, and this is subtly different."

The captain froze in place. "In what way?"

Before he could answer, another member of the C3 crew broke in.

"Captain Carveg, we just picked up a signal from the alien ship."

"From the ship or from the Marines, Ensign?"

"It was very brief, ma'am." Scalp darkly mottled, the young Krai had hands and feet both working his board. "I'm analyzing the little we got."

The aurora had grown so bright, the *Berganitan*'s screens dimmed automatically.

"Engineering?" Asking, not urging. Because she knew engineering was already busting their collective asses.

"Still nothing, Captain."

"Captain, we have a seventy percent probability that the signal came from Captain Travik's implant."

"And the message?"

"What little there was, was completely scrambled."

"Unscramble it."

The lieutenant monitoring the buoy cut off the ensign's reply. "Portal opening, Captain!"

"Engineering!"

"Engines are still off-line!"

"Vessel emerging from Susumi space! Speed registering as fifty-one thousand, four hundred and three point seven seven kilometers per second."

Screens flared, then went blank almost immediately.

"Buoy's fried. Vessel's bow wave has reached the alien ship."

Captain Carveg slapped her palm down on the touch pad. "All hands! Brace for impact!"

Except that at those speeds, impact should have happened before the words left her mouth. When it still hadn't happened a heartbeat later, she took a moment to breathe. "Anyone know why we're still alive?"

"Ma'am, last data from the buoy indicates that the alien vessel was absorbing the energy from the incomer."

All eyes turned to the lieutenant.

"You think the alien ship—what did you call it, Commander?—Big Yellow absorbed the incomer?"

"No, ma'am." Eyes on her screen, the lieutenant's voice held equal parts disbelief and awe. "I think it stopped it."

"Stopped it?"

"Yes, ma'am. Data fragments support the theory that the incomer's just sitting there, on the other side of the alien ship."

"All right." Palm back on the touch pad, a little more gently this time. "All hands, stand down from impact!" Palm up. "Lieutenant, let's get some unfragmented data; launch another buoy. Stealth mode."

"Aye, aye, ma'am, buoy away."

"Commander Versahche, have General Morris informed that his votes in Parliament are alive."

"Yes, ma'am."

"And until we know what's out there . . ." Palm down once again. "All hands, red alert!"

". . . heading for nearest air lock and . . . son of a bitch. He's gone again."

"You think they heard you, Staff?"

"No way to tell." Torin straightened and pushed Captain Travik's mouth carefully closed. "We don't know if his implant's strong enough to breach the hull. We don't know if he actually turned the damned thing on."

Orla's eyes lightened. "If you'd told me to activate *my* implant in that tone, I'd have come back from the dead to do it."

"Thank you. Should you get an implant, I'll keep that in mind." She rocked back on her heels and stood. "What made you put him in the HE suit?"

"It was his, and I thought it would be easier than carrying them separately. He's not hooked in, so I left him in his combats and got the arm of the suit to conform."

"Good thinking. Let me know if he comes to again."

The rest of the Recon team stood a cautious distance from the only sealed container in the room that hadn't scanned as a solid object, watching Werst direct the beam of his benny along the seam between box and lid. Without hinges, without a hasp, it was the only way in. As Torin returned from attempting to contact the *Berganitan,* he was just finishing the last side.

As she slid back into the position she'd vacated at Orla's summons, Guimond half turned and flashed her a welcoming smile. "Any luck, Staff?"

Other heads turned until there were as many eyes on her as on Werst.

"Well, I could offer you possibilities and speculation—but I won't. This much I know for certain; Captain Travik was conscious long enough to activate his implant. Unfortunately, he lost consciousness before he could tell me if the *Berganitan* replied."

Guimond's smile broadened. "That's great! They know we're alive."

"They know Captain Travik's alive," Tsui snorted. "But why would they wait around for *him?*"

Torin leaned far enough forward to spear the lance corporal with an icy glare. "Tsui, I don't really give a crap what your opinion of our OC is and that means, I don't want to hear it. Do you understand?"

"Yes, Staff Sergeant."

"Good."

"I'm through," Werst grunted in the sudden silence that had replaced the constant background noise of the benny. "Charge is down to twelve point four percent."

Standard operating procedure called for power packs to be replaced when the charge hit ten percent, not before. Packs carried in were to be carried out and inspected by the senior NCO who was responsible for ensuring both that all packs were accounted for and under the minimum charge. NCOs who consistently came up either under count or over charge were written up. Combat officers who recognized the reports were a load of crap tended to lose them, but they were exactly the sort of thing Captain Travik would enjoy passing on.

Captain Travik was unconscious.

Not that it would have made any difference.

"Open it," Torin told him. "Take cover, people. Huilin, Jynett, Dursinski . . ."

As Marines ducked behind other cases, the two di'-Taykan stepped forward wearing their HE suits, helmets up. Dursinski, also in her suit, held her benny pointed toward the crate. If anything unpleasant came out of it, the suits would keep them alive long enough to get it closed again.

Or at least they lengthened the odds.

"You're just not much of a risk taker, are you, Staff Sergeant?"

"It's my job to keep these people alive, Mr. Ryder."

"And, sometimes, doesn't that mean riding the whirlwind?"

Torin turned just far enough to meet his gaze. "I don't ride whirlwinds, Mr. Ryder. I beat them into submission."

One corner of his mouth lifted. "And just thinking of you doing that is turning me on."

"Turn yourself off again."

The lid slid clear.

Nothing emerged.

Inside, were thirty-six, medium gray, empty boxes. The interior of the case showed only smooth gray walls identical in color and texture to the walls in both the original corridor and the cube.

After removing the boxes, the entire company, with the exception of Orla and the captain, stared at the empty case.

Torin sighed. "Son of a fukking bitch."

"You're thinking that's the way out?" Ryder asked in much the same tone.

"Yes, I am."

Tossing one of the boxes from hand to hand, Guimond shook his head. "Uh, no disrespect, Staff, this thing's solid. See." He tossed the box back into the crate where it bounced noisily.

"Solid is a relative term around here," Torin reminded him wearily. Before she could tell him to remove the box, the lights dimmed and an earsplitting burst of static evoked some creative profanity in three languages as helmets were snatched off.

"What was *that?*" Nivry demanded, hair an emerald aurora around her head.

"Let's assume it was a suggestion from Big Yellow that we move on."

"Big Yellow?"

"There's a limit to how long I can refer to something as 'the alien ship' and that seemed the obvious name." Replacing her helmet over hair nearly as wild as the di'Taykan's, Torin nodded toward Guimond. "Take the box from the crate."

The big Marine shrugged good-naturedly, grabbed the edge with his left hand, leaned in, stretched, slipped a little, and froze. "Staff . . ."

It was the first time Torin had heard him sound anything but cheerful. From the sudden surge forward, it was the first time for all of them. By the time she reached the crate, she had to shove Marines out of her way in order to get a place by Guimond's side. The fingers of his right hand had sunk into the floor up to the first joint. When he turned to face her, his eyes were huge in a flushed face, pupils so dilated the irises had all but disappeared.

"I can' t . . . I can't get them out."

"Stop trying; you'll hurt yourself." She reached in and gripped his arm, stopping the constant jerk, jerk, jerk as he tried to pull free. The muscles under her fingers felt more like stone than flesh. "It's all right, Guimond, you've just found the way to the next level."

"I have?" He managed a wan smile. "Good for me. You want me to keep going?"

"I don't think you have a choice."

"We could cut his fingers off."

Giving Guimond's arm a last squeeze, Torin straightened. "Shut up, Tsui."

"No, really; six months or so with his arm in a regen sleeve and he'll grow a whole new se . . ." The last word got lost in a strangled squawk as Werst grabbed a fistful of combats at around Tsui's waist and lifted the larger Marine off his feet.

"What part of shut up," he growled, "do you not understand?"

"Werst, drop him."

"Unfortunate choice of words," Ryder murmured by Torin's ear as Tsui hit the deck, both hands yanking fabric away from his crotch.

"Deliberate choice of words," Torin told him, aiming her reply under the covering shouts of laughter and at least three voices telling Guimond what had happened. "All right, people," she cut the noise off as Tsui got to his feet, "listen up. This is our way out. Private Guimond is on point." A touch on his shoulder and she was pleased to hear a chuckle from within the crate. "But I want two Marines in there immediately, and I mean immediately after him. Tsui, Werst, you just volunteered. Huilin, Jynett, Dursinski, stay in your suits. Frii, you help Orla with the captain. Johnston, go find our civilians and get them over here. Someone bring me Guimond's pack, I'll take it through." A pause and she raised her voice just a little. "Let's *go*, Marines, we're moving out."

Clutching the edge of the crate so tightly that silver polish flaked off her claws, Presit stared down at the visible two thirds of Guimond's hand. "I are not going through there."

"Yes, you are," Torin told her absently, catching the end of the line connecting Tsui and Werst to Guimond and tossing it back into the group of Marines who secured it. "You ready?"

Tsui looked anything but ready. Werst grunted an affirmative.

"Heer, Johnston?"

"Scanners up and running, Staff."

Both scanners were reading a big fat nothing under the crate, as though reality ended halfway up Guimond's right hand. But that was about to change. Because it had to change. It had to become the way out. It had nothing to do with faith. It had everything to do with putting all the pieces together in the right order.

"Just relax, Guimond."

"Trying to, Staff."

There didn't seem to be any way around Guimond going through to the next level headfirst.

"You won't drop until your entire body is in the open so you'll actually fall no more than a meter." *Provided this works like it did the last time,* amended a snide voice in her head. Torin ignored it. "Tuck and roll and you'll be fine."

"Tuck and roll," Guimond repeated. "Right."

Under the circumstances, he sounded remarkably cheerful.

Stepping back, Torin nodded to Tsui and Werst. "Go."

Bending, they each lifted one of Guimond's legs. The moment they released the pressure against the crate, he began to sink.

He sank very fast.

Seconds later, Tsui and Werst hit the bottom together, and were almost instantly ankle-deep.

"Let the line play out," Torin snapped, as it began to tighten, "we've got plenty." Watching the line run into the crate, she began to count under her breath, ignoring the watch on her sleeve. It was more important that she *do* something than that the count be accurate to the nearest nanosecond. "One MidSector Station. Two MidSector Station." The top of Werst's helmet disappeared. "Three MidSector Station." The crate was empty again. "Four MidSector Station. Five MidSector Station. Six Mid . . ."

"Staff Sergeant Kerr, this is Private Guimond, do you read?"

The cheering was a little premature but she let it run anyway. "I hear you, Guimond."

"We came through fine and you were right."

"It's part of the job description." Never let the relief show. They had to believe she never worried. "But what—specifically—was I right about this time?"

"We're standing in what looks like a station corridor heading fore and aft and there's one of those three-dimensional signs on the bulkhead."

"One of *what* signs, Guimond?"

"The kind that tell you where you are. You know: you are here and this is how you get to docking bay seventeen."

Torin sighed. "Guimond, are you trying to tell me there's a map down there?"

"Uh, affirmative, Staff."

A map.

"Is the air lock marked on it?"

"Seems to be."

Things were looking up.

"Corporal Nivry." Torin motioned toward the crate. "They're your squad."

Nivry, Frii, Johnston . . .

"Staff, we have a problem."

"What is it, Corporal?"

"Johnston's scanner and the exoskelton didn't come through."

"Did he lose any body parts?"

"No, he's fine."

"Then it's a problem we can live with."

With Squad One on the lower level and their immediate area secured, Torin had the captain passed carefully down through the floor into Guimond's waiting arms. She'd half hoped, half feared that the trip would bring him back to consciousness but Nivry reported no change.

Both scientists attempted to take readings as they went through the floor. Although they were unsuccessful, at least *they* got to keep their equipment.

As Guimond announced he was back in position, Torin turned to the remaining Katrien. "Your turn."

"No." Presit stared into the crate, black eyes narrowed suspiciously. "I said, I are not going through there."

"You can't stay here all alone," Torin pointed out reasonably.

"I are not wanting to stay here all alone. You are getting me out a different way."

Waving away a cloud of shed fur, Torin stepped closer. "There is no other way."

"You are not knowing that!"

"I know it's frightening." She was using the voice she used on new recruits. The one that gave comfort and no options in equal measure. "But everyone else went through all right."

"I are not caring about everyone else. I are not going through that."

"Yes, you are." Abandoning reason, Torin grabbed the Katrien under the arms and swung her up over the edge of the crate. "Guimond, incoming at speed."

"Ready, Staff."

The reporter nearly folded in half, trying to get out of Torin's grip.

Torin let go.

"I are going to do you FOR THI . . ."

"Got her, Staff."

Squad Two stood grouped in an admiring half circle as she turned.

"If this situation comes up again," Orla murmured, her eyes so light they looked pale pink, "can I do that?"

"Sure." Torin held up a bleeding wrist. "She scratches. Mr. Ryder . . ."

He stared at her for a long moment, then nodded and jumped.

"Corporal Harrop . . ." The edge of the crate had been melted smooth by the benny. Torin ran her thumb up and down one of the curves. "Send your squad through on my word. Leave the line tied where it is; I'd rather lose it than risk . . ." She didn't want to think of what they might be risking; she certainly didn't want to say the words out loud. Not right before . . .

She tightened her grip. Adjusted the straps of Guimond's pack. Wondered why she hadn't just dropped it down.

And jumped.

Her gaze went straight to Craig Ryder when she landed, one hand against the new deck, her knees absorbing the shock. He looked like she felt. She very carefully arranged her features so that she looked like nothing at all.

A few seconds later, Heer came through stripped of scanner and exoskeleton. Torin's best guess was that the ship disliked being probed. No one else lost a benny; leaving her the only one without a weapon. At the moment, it was merely embarrassing. She could only hope it didn't become something more.

Corporal Harrop was the last through the crate. The rope dropped with him.

In a silence so complete even the Katrien had stopped talking, Torin lifted a loop off Harrop's shoulder and saluted the ceiling with it. "Thanks." Then she tossed it to the corporal. "Get this packed up again, we may need it later."

He glanced at the ceiling, shrugged, and began rolling the line as half a dozen conversations were resumed.

Torin hid a smile as she turned back toward the map; Recon didn't much worry about a line of retreat at the best of times. Which these weren't. *Although,* she admitted, tracing a mental line from "you are here" to "closest available air lock," *things* were *looking up.*

"Buoy in place, Captain Carveg."

"Thank you, Lieutenant." Returning to her position, she stared down at the screens. "Let's see what we've got."

The first screen showed a distant image of a ship similar to the *Berganitan* in that there was nothing streamlined about it. Built for the frictionless vacuum of deep space, it was never intended to go into atmosphere.

"Distance from the incomer to Big Yellow?"

"One hundred and eighteen kilometers, Captain."

"One hundred and eighteen?"

"Yes, ma'am. The incomer is not only exactly the same distance we are from the alien ship, it's in the same position relative to the ship."

The captain's lip curled. "Interesting."

"Yes, ma'am. Receiving second data stream."

The incomer now filled the next screen.

Commander Versahche's hair had flattened against his skull. *"Ablin gon savit."*

"Indeed. And how fortunate we're already at red alert." Visible armaments equaled the *Berganitan*'s. No way of knowing what they had hidden. "I think we must assume this is one of the Others' ships. Mister Potter, do the Others know we're here?"

"No, ma'am." The lieutenant answered without taking his eyes off his screen. "Big Yellow is directly between us and the enemy. They've launched no buoys and—should they have recently acquired tech capable of either penetrating or circumventing the alien ship—we haven't been scanned. Nor are they running any of the standard defense sweeps."

"Maybe their sudden deceleration has slapped the entire crew against the bulkheads hard enough to turn them to jelly." She took a deep breath and exhaled forcefully. "Lucky day for us. Not so lucky for them."

After a number of fatal attempts at diplomacy, the Rules of Engagement had been adjusted to allow for the destruction of any enemy vessel found in Confederation space—although enemy vessels weren't usually *found* so much as interrupted in the midst of destroying or co-opting Confederation property. Neither were they easy to destroy.

Her forefinger touched the pad. "Missile Control Room. I want four of the PGM-XLs, the ship smasher missiles, programmed to round Big Yellow every ninety degrees, targeted on the Others' ship."

Targeting data on enemy vessels went automatically to the MCR the moment one was sighted, although missiles were most often used to soften up a Marine landing site.

"Four PGM-XLs to round Big Yellow every ninety degrees. Aye, aye, Captain."

"Even if an ADS comes on," she noted to no one in particular, "it won't be able to stop four missiles impacting simultaneously."

"The battle'll be won before the Others know they're in a fight," Commander Versahche agreed.

"Best kind of battles to be in. When they send out a buoy, Mister Potter, I want to know about it before it clears the launch tube."

"Aye, aye, Captain."

"Without a buoy, would they be able to pick up the drone taking the modified comm unit to Big Yellow?"

"No, ma'am."

"All right." An open channel to communications led to the discovery that attaching the unit to the drone was not going well. "I don't care if you have to stick it on with spit. Get it done and get it moving!"

"Yes, ma'am."

She drummed the fingers of her right hand against the edge of the console and spent a moment wrapped in the reassuring hum of her ship. Propulsion remained off-line, but thousands of other pieces of machinery were working perfectly. Then, because she had the time, a luxury not often given in battle, she pressed her palm down on the touch pad and let the rest of the *Berganitan* know what was going on. Rumors traveled through the closed environment of a ship faster than a head cold and usually caused more damage.

"Captain Carveg, this is MCR. Four PGM-XLs programmed and ready to launch."

"Fast work, MCR."

"Not exactly complicated trajectories, Captain, but thank you."

"Weapons officer . . ."

The lieutenant commander at the station stiffened slightly.

". . . launch missiles."

"Aye, aye, Captain. Missiles away."

"Buh-bye." Lieutenant Commander Sibley waved glumly at the monitor mounted high on the wall of the "Dirty Shirt" as the ship plotted a graphic of the missile launch. "Now, doesn't that just take all the fun out of war."

A number of the other pilots in the flight officers' wardroom nodded glumly. On red alert, two squadrons of Jades were held launch ready, leaving two squadrons moaning about drawing the short straw. With the captain using missiles rather than fighters, they were even farther out of rotation.

The missiles rounded Big Yellow. The wardroom held a collective breath waiting for them to turn toward the target.

They didn't turn.

Instead, they continued on their original trajectory, bracketing the Others' ship at a distance before heading off into deep space.

"I bet that's made them a little curious about what's on this side of the fence," Sibley murmured, as the silence gave way to a cacophony of speculation and profanity about equally mixed.

"No bet." Shylin raised her mug in a mocking salute. "Looks like war is fun again."

"MCR, what the *chreen* happened?"

"As near as we can figure, Captain, Big Yellow wiped the program as the missiles passed."

"Captain Carveg, the Others have launched a buoy!"

"Well, so much for the decelerate into jelly theory. Stealth or open, Mister Potter."

"Open, ma'am."

"No real reason for stealth, I suppose." Her lip curled up off her teeth. "They know we're here."

In a nose-to-nose fight, the *Berganitan* could hold her own with anything but the largest of the Others' ships, those that Command had dubbed Dreadnoughts. They weren't facing a Dreadnought and with the alien vessel playing silly bugger between them, that was the first good news she'd had today.

Any battle would now depend mostly on small fighters. The question: would they be allowed to fight? With that question unanswered, she wasn't going to risk the lives of pilots and crews.

"Mister Potter, can we use our buoy to fry their buoy?"

"We *should* be able to, ma' am . . ."

"And from your choice of words, can I assume we *can't?*"

"Yes, ma'am."

Drumming her fingers again, she watched the Others' buoy arc up toward the top of the alien ship.

"I wonder what they're up to."

"The Others, Captain?"

"No, the Big Yellow aliens."

His hair beginning to move again, the commander turned far enough to see her face. "Do they have to be up to anything?"

"I doubt it's coincidence that they stopped that ship," she nodded toward the screen, "exactly one hundred and eighteen kilometers out. They redirected our missiles and now they're allowing the Others' to take a look at us. My people have a saying, Commander, if it looks like a vertrek, and it sings like a vertrek, roast it with a nice red sauce."

"Which means?"

"Which means, they're up to something."

"Captain Travik, sir, I need you to activate your implant. Now."

He blinked up at her, facial ridges spread wide as he struggled to breathe. "You don't tell me what to do . . . Staff Sergeant. I . . . am the Officer Commanding. Me. You aren't even . . ." His ridges fluttered and his eyes closed.

Torin glanced down at the medical data on her slate. It didn't look good.

"Staff, what do you think?"

Heer had attached the captain to the stretcher by tying his personal fifty feet of rope into a loose net. Rural Krai were still largely arboreal and Heer's family were farmers.

"Nice to know all that specialist training didn't wipe out your more useful skills."

He beamed. "The last year I was home, my net took first prize at the Vertintry Fair."

She managed an answering smile. He couldn't

know he'd evoked a cascade of memories, each more *country* than the last—pigs and poultry, plowing and preserves—thank God, the Corps had given her a way out.

It would take four Marines to carry the captain, one at each corner. The passageway they were currently in was just wide enough and, with any luck, would stay that way.

Crossing to the map, Torin turned to face the group, most of whom were finishing up the last dregs of their field rations. A quick glance at her sleeve told her it was now 20:14. It felt later. Barring any unforeseen circumstances, they'd be at the air lock in about three hours and back on the *Berganitan* an hour after that—an observation she had no intention of making aloud, nothing being more likely to bring on unforeseen circumstances.

"Listen up, people. I want Squad One on point." Glancing over, she met Nivry' s eyes. "Corporal, place your people as you see fit. As neither Mr. Ryder nor myself have a weapon, we'll be taking two of the places around the captain—if Mr. Ryder agrees."

He flashed her a disarming smile—less effective in Torin's opinion because he clearly knew it was a disarming smile. "Happy to help out the Corps."

"Corporal Harrop, in an attempt to keep the captain relatively level, I'll want Huilin and Orla on the other two spots. The rest of your squad will cover the rear. You've got ten minutes to finish eating and use the facilities."

"Facilities?" Presit scoffed, from directly across the passage. "There are being no facilities."

Torin held up an empty ration bag. "They reseal."

"I are not using a food container to . . . to . . ."

"You won't be eating out of it again, ma'am," Guimond told her helpfully.

"Go in pairs," Torin reminded them over the laughter, "and don't go far. Three meters forward of the map and that's it. And, ma'am . . ."

Even with her eyes squinted nearly shut, the reporter was unmistakably glaring.

"If you think you can hold it for another three hours, be my guest."

Back against the bulkhead, Guimond peered around a ninety-degree turn, then waved Werst forward. "So you still think there's no crew on this thing?"

"I never said there was no crew." Finger through the trigger guard, Werst went around the corner and up against the opposite bulkhead.

"Yeah, you di . . . Okay, maybe you didn't." They started moving up the new length of passageway, boots making almost no sound on the black rubber flooring. "So where do you think the crew is?"

"What crew?"

"So then you don't think there's a crew?"

"I don't *care*."

"I just think that if there's a crew, we should try communicating with them."

"We are. They set puzzles. We solve them. That's communicating."

"But it's not talking."

"Maybe we should all sit down and have a beer together."

"I think that's a perfectly valid way of solving problems."

"I think you're an idiot." He stopped and motioned Guimond forward.

The big Human nodded and slipped to the other side of what looked like a standard vertical opening. Then he leaned forward and looked.

"Oh, that's smart," Werst grunted. "Lead with your head."

Flipping down his mike, Guimond ignored him.

"Corporal, we've reached the first vertical."

"Roger that. Wait for backup before attempting a descent."

So far, the floor plan matched the map in her head.

"Cred for your thoughts?"

So she told him.

"You memorized the map? I thought you had . . . what? uh . . . *even* numbers scan it into their slates?"

"That's right." Even numbers only. Should something go wrong, it would leave half the team's slates unaffected. She hadn't told the rest of the Marines to memorize the map. They were Recon. She expected it as a matter of course. "The Corps issues slates that are pretty much indestructible, but they can't do anything to prevent, say, a strong electromagnetic pulse from wiping the memory. Fortunately, Mr. Ryder, Marines are trained to use technology, not to be dependent on it. The Corps has always believed that the most powerful weapon its people possesses is between their ears."

"So you're saying you could charge naked into battle and triumph?"

She could hear the grin in his voice and replied with flat sincerity. "That, Mr. Ryder, depends on what I'm fighting."

From not five feet behind her, the soft-voiced di'-Taykan conversation grew suddenly speculative. Torin ignored them with the ease of long practice.

"You really think we're going to make it out of here in three hours?"

"If that map's right, there's no reason why we shouldn't."

"How about them?" He nodded toward the three civilians walking ahead of them. "The *harveer*'s quite a few years out of the egg, and I doubt either of our furry friends have ever walked seven kilometers in their lives."

Even more than the Krai, the Katrien's feet were designed for climbing. Although Torin doubted either the scientist or the reporter had ever climbed the equivalent of seven kilometers either.

"They're not very big." The scratches on her wrist throbbed. "We can carry them if we have to."

"Still, maybe you should have the lads up front looking for a defensible place to catch some kip."

"If it comes to it, a passageway will do fine. There're only two approaches in a passage, making it easy enough to defend. I don't know about you, but I'm hesitant to lock myself into anything on this ship."

"Even after the map, you don't trust it?"

"I don't trust anything I don't understand."

"What am I looking at?" Captain Carveg leaned over the screens at one of the science stations.

"These are the last views Lieutenant Commander Sibley took of the air lock, Captain. And these are our most recent images."

"It looks like it's healing."

"The ship is partially organic, ma'am. The science team was able to determine that much before . . ."

"Before they blew that air lock and killed one of my shuttle pilots?" the captain snorted.

"Yes, ma'am."

"And what's so important about what I'm looking at?"

"This area here. Where the ship has, for lack of a better word, healed. Notice the beginnings of a ripple in the hull. A ripple like . . ." The screen split. "This. This is the ripple on the opposite side of the hull, pretty much exactly in the same relationship to the Others' ship as the destroyed air lock is to us."

"So it's possible that the Others were here previously—while making one of their smash and grab forays into Confederation space—landed a boarding party, left—because they didn't want to hang around in Confederation space where a stationary target is likely to get its ass blown off—and are now back to pick up their people who are stuck inside having also blown their air lock?"

"That's one theory, ma'am."

"I'm open to any others."

The silence stretched and lengthened.

"All right." She ran one hand back over her scalp. "Let me guess this next part. The closest air lock the Others can now use is the same air lock the Marines are heading for."

"Yes, ma'am."

By the time Staff Sergeant Kerr—and it would *be* Staff Sergeant Kerr because on a good day Captain Travik was a *serley chrika* with delusions of grandeur—got her people to the next available air lock, there had to be a shuttle waiting for them. Unfortunately, the next available air lock was dead center on the belly of the beast, visible to the Others. The *Berganitan*'s gunners could shoot an enemy shuttle off the spot without even trying. Captain Carveg had to believe the Others' could as well.

Unless Big Yellow made arrangements for a peaceful pickup.

Hopefully, there'd be someone left alive to pick up.

"So." Hands locked behind her, she rocked back on her heels. "There's an unknown number of the enemy inside Big Yellow with the Marines."

"There's an eighty-seven point two percent probability of it, ma'am."

"Then we need to tell them that. Where's that *serley* comm unit now?"

A graphic of the drone approaching the alien ship replaced rippled yellow hull. "Almost there, Captain. We should be able to open communications in seventeen minutes, twelve seconds."

"Good. Let's just hope we're the first to give them the news."

The next level down had red and green lights running randomly along the bulkheads.

"I wonder whose head these came out of."

"Who cares?"

The passage was about to end in a T-junction. According to the map, six meters starboard there was another vertical that would take them two levels down and into a passage that ran aft for a full kilometer.

"You know," Guimond murmured as they moved up on the junction, "they could have reconfigured this thing into one long corridor aft, and a single four level drop. I wonder why they didn't?"

Werst shot the big Human a look that suggested he'd like to see him on a serving platter with an apple in his mouth. "Maybe they wanted you to have something to chat about."

Guimond grinned. "Maybe."

A quick look showed the corridors empty both to port and starboard and a moment later they stood on either side of the vertical. About to lean into the shaft, Werst froze, and looked up at Guimond. Voice barely clearing his facial ridges, he muttered, "Did you hear something?"

Ten

"YOU'RE sure?"

"Werst recognized the language. The Others used bugs when they took Drenver Mining Station; Werst was there."

"Okay, have them hold just to this side of the vertical. Secure the entrance to the shaft and establish perimeters in the passageway; we'll regroup there."

"Roger, Staff."

Torin pulled her slate free and, one-handed, thumbed in the next level of the map. "And why am I not surprised," she muttered, switching to group channel. "Werst, take a quick look at the map from the bottom of the vertical."

"It's changed."

"Yes, it has." Instead of an essentially straight path, they now had options. Several corridors. Cross corridors. Chambers. Access . . . tunnels? Galleries? Shafts? Whatever the hell they were called, they were registering as about a meter square. "This isn't the interior of Drenver Mining Station, is it?"

"No."

"Good." Because they'd lost at Drenver. Not badly, 2nd Recar'ta, 1st Battalion, Delta Company had managed to rescue most of the station's workforce and not lose many Marines doing it, but the Others had taken the station. And still held it. Torin assumed it was on somone's list of things to get back. Trouble was, the bugs were good in enclosed spaces and—although they'd have to strip off most of their gear in order to fit—they could move like shit through a H'san in passages a meter square.

"Johnston, Heer, I want you to replace me and Frii on the captain's stretcher." The thought of the height difference brought a reluctant smile, but if there were bugs around they needed to free up as many weapons as possible and carrying the captain in comfort took a backseat to winning any potential firefights. Although the youngest on the team, the di'Taykan scored better than both the engineers in combat skills and she needed to be free to move around. The moment one of the engineers arrived, she'd make sure the civilians—a particularly shrill bit of Katrien conversation bounced off the walls and around the inside of her skull—didn't give their position away.

"Harrop, keep your Tailends sharp," she added, taking another look at the map. "The way this bastard layout's changing, the bugs could end up behind us."

"Roger, Staff. How the hell you figure they got in here in the first place? You think Big Yellow could be an enemy ship after all?"

"No. I don't." She could hear the entire team waiting for her response. "We all know their tells and we haven't seen any of them—outside or in. As to how the bugs got in here," nodding her thanks to Johnston, she handed over her arm of the stretcher, "that, people, is not our problem."

"All I can say is, it's about time!" General Morris stomped into the small ready room off the Combat Command Center and rocked to a stop, face flushed, in front of Captain Carveg's desk. "You have a situation here, Captain, and I very much resent being kept out of the loop."

"You're *in* the loop, General. All the main monitors are linked through to your office and you've been kept informed of any developments."

"I have been locked in!"

"Marines are always locked in their attachment during a red alert. If we have to drop you off, we like to know we're dropping all of you." It took an effort, but she managed to keep from sounding like she'd prefer to drop him out an air lock at the earliest opportunity. "As there's only the two of you, I'll lift the restrictions if you give me your word you'll stay out of the way."

"I do not get in the way," the general sputtered, cheeks darkening.

Captain Carveg lifted her upper lip, just a little. "Your word, General."

"Fine!" He spat it across the desk at her. "You have my word!"

"Thank you. Access extends to Lieutenant Stedrin as well, of course."

"And do you want his word, too, or will my assurances suffice?"

"Your word will be quite sufficient, General." As the di'Taykan lieutenant had been locked in with only the general for company, she very much doubted *getting in the way* would be on the top of his to do list. "I requested your presence just now because the modified comm unit has been attached to Big Yellow and we're about to contact your Marines."

"Finally!"

As lives were at risk, she decided to ignore the implication that members of her crew hadn't been working to the general's standards. "My people felt that, even amplified, implant to implant would be the most secure." She stood. "If you'll come with me, we've decided to bring the signal through to the communications station in C3."

Taking a deep breath, he fell into step beside her. "I apologize for my bad temper, Captain, but I'm sure you'll understand the stress I'm under here. Had I lost Captain Travik, the war effort would have lost the support of your people in Parliament."

"My people are on board this ship, General. I don't really care what a group of idiot politicians from my home world do."

"Those idiot politicians can see to it that the *Berganitan*'s docked indefinitely," he snorted, following her through the hatch into C3. "And that you spend the rest of your career watching the borders of the Confederation grow ever smaller."

Before she could answer—before she was even certain *what* she'd answer—the science officer in charge of the contact project crossed the room toward them, looked from her to the general, and finally decided where to deliver his news. "I'm sorry, General, but although Captain Travis is still alive and his implant is functioning, we can't raise him. You'll be speaking to Staff Sergeant Kerr."

"Thank God."

The general's response was quiet, almost prayerful, and Captain Carveg found herself smiling as she returned to her station. *Just when I'm convinced there's nothing to like about the man, he goes and says something like that.*

". . . and Presit a Tur durValintrisy."

The reporter is alive?

"Yes, sir."

Then, for God's sake, keep her happy, Staff Sergeant.

Torin glanced down the passage to where Presit sat sulking. She'd had to finally threaten to gag both Katrien before they'd shut up.

The last thing we need, the general continued, **is for this to look worse than it is in the media.**

"Yes, sir." Which could be, when necessary, a polite way of saying, "Fuk you." Torin couldn't remember it ever being quite so necessary before.

General Morris missed the subtext. **Remember, Staff Sergeant, it is vitally important to the war effort that Captain Travik come out of this mission looking good.**

"Sir, right at the moment, he'll be lucky if he gets out alive."

Alive's not good enough, Staff Sergeant.

"I'm sorry, sir, I didn't catch that. You're breaking up. The Others must be jamming the sig . . ." She tongued her implant off. "Asshole." After a moment, when it became clear he wasn't going to use the command codes to override, she moved silently up the passage to join the rest of the Marines. Gathering them close, she quietly filled them in on the situation. "They have the list of survivors, they know we're heading for the air lock, they know we have bugs. Conversely, we now know they're being held in place, there's an Others' ship being held on the opposite side of Big Yellow, and they aren't allowed to shoot at it. On the upside, they *will* pick us up at the air lock. On the downside, they tell me this is going to look really bad on the vids."

Tsui snickered first, then it swept the circle.

After a moment of low-voiced but inventive profanity—mostly having to do with where General Morris could stick his PR problem—Torin raised a hand for silence. "Listen up, people, this is what we're going to do. The perimeter pin's reading no movement in the shaft, so I'm taking Jynett and Werst down with me to see where the bugs actually are. Werst." She turned to the Krai. "I know you've been working point, but you're the only one with any actual bug experience."

He nodded, his expression so neutral it bordered on blank. "And the simulation?"

"Jynett and I are the only ones who've qualified."

"How do you know that?" Jynett whispered. "It never came up."

"I know everything, Jynett. Get used to it. The rest of you stay sharp. This area is secure now, but it may not stay that way. Maintain PCU silence and do your best to keep the civilians quiet. You might want to take a crack at that last bit, Guimond. They seem to like you."

He flashed her a dazzling smile. "Everyone likes me."

"Oh, puke," Werst grunted.

The vertical was no different than verticals on any station Torin had ever been on except that the low-gravity cylinder was only two levels long—far too small to be cost effective on a station. Holding a borrowed benny, she dropped in headfirst and caught herself on a loop just above the lower exit, her body swinging around until her boots touched the deck. Given the ship's on again off again solids, she maintained her grip on the loop.

Werst landed beside her. Jynett to the other side of the exit.

Over the years, the Corps' R&D had developed a number of small drones that could be sent in advance of personnel to search for the enemy. And over the years, the enemy had found every one of them. Once or twice, the drones had been the first the enemy had known there were Marines deployed in the area. Eventually, R&D had discovered what Marines in the field already knew—it was impossible to replace an informed set of eyes and ears.

On the other hand, there was no point in being stupid about it.

Torin flipped down her helmet scanner and unhooked the narrow cable that ran around the inside of the rim. Holding it about six inches back from the camera end, she crouched and poked it around the corner just off the deck.

No bugs. No movement.

Nothing but an empty corridor, a junction, and two closed hatches. Illumination seemed even spottier than it had up above, but at least this level had no red and green running lights.

Werst's facial ridges flared, Jynett's hair flattened, and even Torin could smell the lingering bug scent. Approximately a third of their language was scent based and to Human noses the dominant notes were cinnamon and formaldehyde—not exactly unpleasant but unmistakable in combination. The scent trail raised the odds the bugs weren't in suits, which meant they'd have to be just as careful about shooting holes in bulkheads or releasing toxins into the life-support system. Two definite pluses if it came to combat.

With any luck, it wouldn't.

Taking a perimeter pin from her vest, Torin set it so that it covered the approach from the bow and pointed the other two members of the team toward the first hatch.

No bugs.

The compartment looked like a repair shop as much as it looked like anything. Tools, accurate enough in their rough shapes but lacking details, hung from the walls, and disassembled equipment had been spread over the center bench. A fast glance showed nothing they could use. About to turn away, a familiar shape caught Torin's eye. It took her less than a minute to find all the pieces of her missing benny and less even than that to check it and reassemble it.

She checked it for traps, then she wrapped her hand around the grip. It responded instantly, showing a full charge—which was interesting because she distinctly remembered firing into the floor. At an interrogative lift of Jynett's hair, she shook her head and transferred the strap of the borrowed benny to the returned weapon, slinging it across her back. Until she knew for certain it had been returned unchanged, she was taking no chances.

"And put your damned helmet on," she growled at the di'Taykan as they left.

The second compartment was a mirror image of the first. The parts on the bench had all been shoved to one side, and the room reeked of an animated discussion.

Looked like the ship had borrowed a bug's weapon as well. And returned it.

So the ship knows what both sides are carrying. Would that be a problem? *And it allowed us to know that it knows.* Was that even relevant? *One thing's for sure,* Torin acknowledged as they covered the last few meters to the T-junction, *a good old-fashioned firefight is going to come as a relief after all this does it or doesn't it crap.*

Twelve meters up the starboard arm of the T-junction, they found a dead bug. Although it was always dangerous to extrapolate with an unfamiliar species, the sticky patch on one side of its abdomen looked remarkably like a field dressing. A bug's vital organs—heart, lungs, brain—were in its abdomen behind not only the thickest bits of exoskeleton but body armor as well. In order to gain access to the wound, two pieces of armor had been removed. From the position of the entry hole, it looked as if something had gotten in a lucky shot, angling up in through both armor and exoskeleton at the break where the first section of millipedelike legs appeared. The carapace had been cracked, fluids had been seeping out.

"She probably took the hit during the explosion that destroyed *their* air lock. They carried her this far, she died. When they moved on, they took her weapon but left her body armor because," Torin flipped a finger into the air "they want to travel quickly and because," a second finger, "they don't know we're in here."

"How do you figure that second one, Staff? We can't use this stuff."

"We can use this." Torin knelt and peered down at a section of the thorax cover. "In the simulation, this was a comm unit."

"No translation program," Werst reminded her. "Even if we can get it to work."

"And it doesn't look like it comes off."

"It won't have to." Ignoring Jynett's silent request for more information, she rocked back on her heels and stood. "I think we can safely say the bugs have left this area. Put a perimeter pin around that corner facing aft, another on this hatch here, and let's bring the rest down."

* * *

"You've got a little time if you'd like to examine the bug, *Harveer* . . ."

"Do I look like a biologist?" the elderly Niln snapped, cutting Torin off. Leaning heavily on Gytha's arm, her tail dragging, she shuffled past. "If there's time to *examine,* there's time to sit and contemplate the stupidity of leaving a comfortable lab in a highly regarded university in order to deny one's age by throwing one's self into an intriguing bit of fieldwork. I want that as my epitaph," she added as the younger scientist carefully lowered her to the deck.

"Yes, *Harveer.*"

"You're not going to argue with me? Tell me I don't need an epitaph."

"Everyone are needing an epitaph, *Harveer.*"

"And no one likes a fluffy smart-ass," she snorted, sagging back against the bulkhead.

"It are not unattractive," Presit declared thoughtfully. "At least it are having a shell and are not a species looking like it are skinned." A glance and a lifted lip made it quite clear what species she'd been referring to.

"Please keep your voice down, ma'am." Guimond told her earnestly. "There's more of them around, and we don't want you to get hurt."

She patted his arm, her hand looking even tinier than usual against his bulk. "I are thanking you for your concern, and I are remembering it for later."

"Are you blushing?" Nivry demanded as the reporter moved down the passage to join Gytha and the two Katrien began what was for them, a quiet conversation. di'Taykan didn't blush; their circulatory system wasn't set up for it, and they found it a fascinating Human response.

The pink in Guimond's cheeks deepened. "I can't help it, Corporal. They're just so damned cute."

"All right, Frii, hand it over."

"Staff . . ."

"Now."

Sighing deeply, he reached down in under the collar of his combats and pulled out his music card. After a last lingering look, he dropped it into Torin's outstretched hand. "It's the best on the market," he told her mournfully. "Best sound, most memory, great range. They could turn it on from the *Berganitan*. The Corps'll reimburse me, right? I mean, it's personal property destroyed during a military operation."

"Tell you what, Private, if this actually works . . ." Torin handed the card in turn to Johnston who began attaching it to the input end of the bug's exposed comm unit. ". . . I'll ignore all three regs you broke bringing it along and I'll personally file the reimbursement request with your company clerk."

Frii's eyes lightened. "And if it doesn't work?"

"We'll have bigger problems than you breaking regs."

Propped against a bulkhead, carefully situated to see both where they were going and where they'd been, Craig Ryder watched the Marines moving purposefully around the bug. Besides the staff sergeant, one of the engineers and a di'Taykan—*Who looks remarkably depressed for a species who invented flavored massage oil before the wheel,* he snorted silently—three others were peering through their helmet scanners and keying information into their slates. It seemed that time taken to turn the bug's comm unit into a weapon was also being used to gather information on the enemy. Now, had *he* been in charge, they'd be breaking speed records hauling ass to the air lock, but clearly the staff sergeant believed that whole gram of prevention thing. Not to mention, better safe than sorry.

Since sorry in this instance meant dead, he supposed he had to appreciate her thoroughness.

Not the only thing about her that he appreciated, either.

Although most of the rest of it was the standard stuff he appreciated on most women.

Actually, it had been a long while since he'd spent enough time with a woman to appreciate anything else. Sex and gambling both had a pretty narrow focus.

I've got to get out more.

Provided, of course, I get out of here.

Funny thing, though, he didn't feel trapped, hadn't felt the growing pressure of sharing limited resources in an unforgiving environment. Maybe it was the size of the ship. Maybe it was because they were actively moving toward a destination. Whatever the reason, he hadn't felt the familiar panic since Torin had led the way out of that cube.

His heart began to pound, and he hurriedly reburied the rising memory.

Maybe it was Torin.

She turned away from the bug and started toward him. As she passed, he fell into step beside her.

"Mind if I ask you something?"

He had a strange, speculative look in his eyes Torin wasn't sure she trusted.

"What's with all the sneaking around and whispering? You lot have state-of-the-art PCUs on your heads, why not use them instead?"

Not the question Torin had expected. *And I expected what?* "We in the Corps prefer to call it reconnaissance—not sneaking."

"No offense intended."

"None taken. To answer your question, we're not entirely certain the bugs can't pick up our PCU signals. We don't want them eavesdropping; even if they don't understand us—and we're not entirely certain about that either—they could use the signal to acquire our position."

The left corner of Ryder's mouth curled up, creasing laugh lines around his eyes. "And what *are* you entirely certain of?"

"That if they're close enough to hear a whisper, they're close enough to shoot," Torin snorted. *And what the hell am I doing looking at his laugh lines? Let's try to remember he's a civilian, shall we?* Emphatically not looking, she dropped to one knee beside Captain Travik. "Any change?"

Orla's gaze flicked between the staff sergeant and the salvage operator, then she glanced back down at the captain and shook her head. "Not really. He mumbled something about wasters of food out to ruin him—I think. My Krai doesn't go much beyond *gre ta ejough geyko.*"

"Sit on it and rotate?" Ryder translated, smiling broadly. "I wouldn't have thought you lot considered that an insult."

The di'Taykan grinned up at him. "We don't."

Torin attempted to ignore their continuing exchange but with little success. The years of practice she'd put in honing her skills at selective listening seemed suddenly insufficient. *I must be more tired than I thought.*

The captain's vitals were low but holding steady. There'd been only minor changes since the last time Torin checked his medical program, and his heart rate had even improved slightly. As she stood, she patted him on the leg almost fondly. Not the hero the general expected him to be, but he was doing a lot less damage unconscious than if he'd been up and giving orders.

Johnston had finished up at the bug.

The *harveer* seemed to have gotten her breath back.

The moment Harrop's squad returned . . .

As if summoned, Harrop, Dursinski, and Huilin rounded the corner.

"Everything still matches the map, Staff. Passage is heading aft, and we get a bounce at 570.3 meters. There's a vertical at 569, accessed through the starboard bulkhead, it goes down one level, ladder only."

Torin followed on her slate as Harrop made his report and tried to stop worrying about why the ship had changed the original configuration. Nothing she could do about it; not worth wasting wetware on.

"There's a cross corridor every 95.05 meters," the corporal continued. "Six in total. They bounce out at 80 meters ending in the passage, here . . ." He touched the map. ". . . that runs parallel to our main passage. No sign of bugs."

"Although that doesn't mean they're not down here," Dursinski muttered as he finished.

"We *know* they're down here," Torin sighed. A gesture brought the Recon team together, another sent them to their positions, ready to move out. She turned to the civilians, expecting to find them on their feet.

"Guimond?"

He shrugged. "I can't make them stand up, Staff."

"You're twice the size of all three of them put together, so, yeah, you can."

"We are still resting," Presit declared, folding her arms. "It are getting late, we are having a *very* full day." Her lip curled up off sharp points of teeth. "We are not moving until we are ready."

The two scientists looked more resigned than enthusiastic but had obviously been convinced to support the mutiny.

"And if we were alone on this ship, we could take our time. But we aren't. And if they," Torin jerked her head toward the body, "return, they will kill you."

"We are being killed, walked off our feet!"

"Ma'am, you need to understand that there is a difference between being killed and walking." Dropping her benny off her shoulder, Torin squeezed a burst off into the bug's head. It didn't make much noise as it blew, but rusty brown fluid covered both bulkheads and dripped from the ceiling. "That," she said, turning back to her astounded audience, "is being killed and I'm trying to prevent it from happening. We're leaving. Now!"

A few moments later, as the entire company began making its way to the next vertical, she felt Ryder's familiar presence at her side.

"Good shot."

"Not really."

"Well, I suppose the odds were in your favor that it wasn't going to duck," he allowed thoughtfully. "You learn about using visual aids in NCO school?"

"No, just something I picked up on my own."

"You knew it was going to do that?"

"Obviously." Then, because he was waiting, she added, "The helmet scans of Drenver Mining Station, the last place the Others brought in bugs, are part of the training simulation. After they've been dead for a while, the stuff in their heads becomes unstable. The scans are piss-yourself-laughing type funny . . . if you can disregard the fact that we're losing."

Harrop, back on point, had reached the first cross corridor. Raising his weapon to cover the new approach, he held his position and waved the march on.

The far end seemed darker than the distance would allow, Torin noted as she crossed. Not good. The light levels were already low. It wouldn't take much more dimming before only the nocturnal Katrien and the di'Taykans could see clearly. Torin had no idea how well the bugs could see in the dark, nor did she want to find out.

The second cross corridor was identical to the first.

No. Torin paused for a heartbeat. Not identical but she couldn't put her finger on the difference.

Her feeling of unease grew at the third corridor.

And the fourth.

As they approached the fifth, she moved up on point, waving Dursinski back.

Raising her benny to her shoulder, she peered through the targeting scope and sent a quick bounce.

Harrop had bounced all six cross corridors at eighty meters. Corridor five showed barely twenty. *Son of a fukking bitch!* The ship had changed the floor plan again.

Hand signals sent Nivry and Jynett on the run to the sixth and final corridor. As they raced off, she moved Werst and Tsui into position covering corridor five and got the rest of the march moving double time toward the vertical.

Then she turned back to the shadows.

The bugs racing out of them were almost expected.

The benny's cellular disrupter had to actually hit organic matter to work. Fortunately, it "splashed" on impact, widening the target area. Torin squeezed off two quick bursts, aiming for the shoulder joint in the lead bug's body armor, then as it jerked back, arm and weapon dangling, she dropped prone and began trying for their legs, forcing the bugs to either fold them in under their abdominal armor—becoming stationary targets—or to retreat. No fools, they chose the latter.

Tsui and Werst stood behind the slight cover offered by the corners, on opposite sides of the corridor, shooting diagonally. Under their covering fire, Torin scrambled back until she shared Werst's space.

The two engineers carrying the captain between them were past. Guimond pounded by carrying a Katrien under each arm, closely followed by Ryder holding *Harveer* Niirantapajee.

How nice he's making himself . . . She fired as a head and thorax suddenly appeared, driving the bug back. *. . . useful. And who the hell took him off stretcher duty?*

As the last Marine crossed, Torin tapped Werst on the shoulder. "Go!"

The moment he was clear, she followed.

It still seemed to be ninety-five point five meters to cross corridor number six.

Thirty paces along, Torin stopped and spun around, back against the wall, benny extended out from her right side. "Tsui! Break off!"

The lance corporal squeezed off another half dozen shots, then whirled and ran.

Torin held her position as Tsui raced past, waiting for the first bug.

"Staff! Break off!"

Thirty paces farther up the passage, Tsui held the wall.

They'd managed to leapfrog nearly all the way to the sixth corridor when the first bug appeared out of corridor five.

Torin dropped to her stomach and fired.

The bug threw itself back out of range.

A quick glance over her shoulder and Torin noted Captain Travik had nearly reached the vertical.

At corridor six, Nivry and Jynett had taken a bug out although from nine meters away, it was impossible to tell for certain if it was dead. Eventually, its head would explode and remove any doubt, but Torin had no intention of remaining around for the spectacle.

Jynett's right arm was smoking.

"Chemical weapon," she explained, firing at the sudden appearance of a bug in the shadows. "Tried to fukking eat through my suit. Couldn't quite. Suit's neutralized it now, I think."

"Make sure of it the moment you can." Over the years, Torin had taken a number of injuries and, in her experience, nothing delivered old-fashioned, scream-until-hoarse pain like a chemical burn. She jerked her head in the direction of the vertical. "Go. I'll hold here."

With two corridors to watch, the next set of leapfrogs became more complicated. Ten meters from the drop, the bugs swarmed out of corridor six.

Firing one-handed, Torin dropped her microphone. "Do it, Frii!"

His music card was everything he'd said it would be. Blasted through the dead bug's comm unit at full volume, the attack ran into a solid wall of sound.

The passage smelled suddenly of burned cork.

The final three Marines sprinted for the ladder.

Torin slid last, and as her head dropped below the level of the deck, the sound switched off. *Found another channel. Smart bugs.*

Almost before her boots hit the deck, she was moving out into the new passage.

Before she could speak, the hatch slammed, the two engineers were laser welding the seal, and Presit had a handful of Torin's combats.

"You are getting me out of here, now!"

"Guimond!"

"Sorry, Staff."

"Was anyone besides Jynett hit?" Torin snarled, glaring at the Katrien as Guimond led her away.

"Huilin and Dursinski. Aid kit stuff. Nothing to . . ." Something rattled in the vertical.

"Fire in the hole!"

Johnston and Heer dove out of the way as a muffled explosion buckled the hatch.

"Something to remember, people," Torin announced as she stood. "They've got ordnance with them. Did the welds hold?"

"Enough of them, Staff."

"And the hatch is jammed in its track now," Heer added. "They're not coming through here."

"Unless they've got a couple more of what they just dropped?"

"Well, yeah."

"Then let's not linger, people. We're on the right level, it's just a matter of getting to the air lock before the bugs." She checked the charge on her benny, noted that Guimond seemed to be keeping his bulk between her and the reporter, and finally took a moment to look around. "What's with all the fukking pipes?"

* * *

"Captain! The Others appear to be opening their launch bays!"

"Appear to be, Mister Potter, or are?"

"The Others *have* opened launch bays."

"Flight Commander."

"Launch bays open, Captain. Squadrons standing by."

"Captain!"

"I see it." Fighters, longer and narrower than the Jades, were dropping into space. *What would happen if we didn't respond?* the captain wondered as the enemy fighters began to gather into flights of three. *What would happen if we just sat here, and let them come at us? Would Big Yellow stop them?*

Maybe

Maybe not. It wasn't something she could risk.

"Flight Commander, launch squadrons."

"Aye, aye, Captain. Launching squadrons."

"Buh-bye scientific support," Lieutenant Commander Sibley chortled as he dropped his Jade with the rest. "Let's hear it for being back in the saddle."

"It," Shylin muttered. "You think we're going to be allowed to do any shooting, Sib?"

"Allowed?"

"Big Yellow stopped the missiles. Could as easily stop us."

"Could. Won't."

"You know something I don't?"

"Lieutenant, the amount I know that you don't could overload the *Berg*'s memory core."

"And you're modest, too."

"Aren't I?" Grinning, he turned to his wing frequency. "*Black Eight, Black Nine,* form up on me."

"Roger, B7. Eight *taking position to port."*

"Nine *to starboard. Ready to move in."*

"All fighters, enemy is advancing around the full 360 of Big Yellow." The flight commander's voice filled the double cockpit like the voice of God and Sibley hurriedly adjusted the volume. *"All fighters, advance pattern zeta."*

"Eight wings of them, eight wings of us, all evenly spaced out in two pretty, pretty circles. Oy, mama, I get the feeling someone's selling tickets to this." Sibley moved his wing into the forty-five-degree mark. "Step right up, ladies, gentlemen, and species undecided. Get a front row seat as we fill the skies with pyrotechnics."

"They're more ellipses than circles, Sib."

"I'm not going to argue with you, Shy."

"'Cause I'm right."

"Fighters are about to clear Big Yellow, Captain."

"Ours or theirs?"

"Both."

ELEVEN

"WHEN I find out whose head *this* came out of, I'm going to kick their ass."

When no one claimed responsibility, Torin snorted and ducked another pipe. The only passage leading away from the last vertical headed starboard in a series of fifty-six-meter diagonals no more than a meter wide, crossed and recrossed by pipes in a variety of diameters and colors. The lowest pipes were about shoulder height on Torin, the highest disappeared into darkness two or three levels up. Some of them were warm to the touch. Some of them made noise.

The lack of space had taken them down to two stretcher-bearers. At each corner, they had to lift Captain Travik's head until his body was nearly vertical in order to get him around the forty-five-degree angle. Various vital signs would fluctuate during the maneuver, but as they always returned to more or less the same position afterward, Torin figured they weren't doing much damage. Not that they had any choice.

On the upside, the civilians, now behind the stretcher party, got a series of short rests. *Harveer* Nirantapajee was visibly flagging and even the Katrien were saving most of their breath for walking. Sooner or later, they'd have to be carried, but Torin wanted to delay the inevitable as long as she could. Many

Marines had trouble taking the smaller species seriously, and she didn't want to reinforce bad attitudes. Nor, however, did she plan on allowing the march to be overrun by bugs because the civilians couldn't keep up.

"Why won't he just fukking die," Johnston muttered, inching backward, both hands at shoulder height gripping the forward stretcher handles. The captain sagged forward against the net. "Then we could bag him. Dust him and he'd be a lot easier to carry."

"A good officer would die," Heer grunted agreement at the other end of the body. "Fukking figures Travik would linger."

"You call that an *abquin*?"

Johnston jerked and narrowly missed hitting his head on a random "u" of yellow pipe. "Staff! Captain Travik's awake."

The captain's eyes rolled around in their sockets independent of each other while the two engineers lowered him carefully back to a horizontal position. "Sergeant, put that Marine on report."

"Captain?" Torin waved the stretcher carriers forward so the rest of the march could get around the corner then bent and wrapped one hand around the captain's chin. His skin felt cold and slightly clammy. "Sir? Can you hear me."

For an instant, his eyes focused on hers. "I won't," he snarled, upper lip curled. "And you can't make me." Then he blinked twice and his features sagged back into oblivion.

She sighed and straightened. "He's gone again, let's move on."

"They are wishing he is dead," Presit declared,

emerging into the new length of passage. "I are hearing them."

"Ma'am, fair warning." Torin waved the engineers and their burden forward. "No one likes a snitch." Rather than waiting for a response, she turned and shuffled sideways past the captain, shooting Johnston and Heer both a silent warning as she passed. Griping was a grunt's right, but they needed to keep their voices down unless they wanted every word repeated on Presit a Tur durValintrisy's "Voice from the Front." The torrent of chittering that followed her to her previous place in the march sounded less than complimentary even given the language barrier.

"Staff! Dursinski. We got bugs cutting us off!"

According to the map, the switchbacks opened up into a wide passage that would take them the remaining 1.79 kilometers aft. Which would do them no good at all if they couldn't get to it.

"Dursinski, which direction are they coming from?"

"Both directions. I think they know we're in h . . ." The sound of weapons fire sounded clearly over Dursinski's PCU. *"That's a big affirmative on them knowing we're here! We can't get out!"*

Fuk. Only one thing to do. "Fall back. We'll retreat to that last vertical and head back up a level." Provided Big Yellow hadn't changed the floor plan, they'd have room to maneuver up there.

"Roger, Staff. Falling . . . Goddamn it, Huilin! Cover your left side! . . . back."

"Staff."

"What is it, Johnston?"

"We sealed the hatch at the bottom of the vertical."

"I know. Now, you'll have to unseal it because they could hold us indefinitely at these goddamned angled corners. You heard what's happening, people. Nivry, you've just moved from tailend to point."

"Roger, Staff."

"So, now we are walking back," Presit sneered. She pointed an ebony finger up at Torin with such force the thick fur fringe folded back off her wrist. "You are having no idea what you are doing!"

"Shut up, you idiot. I'm so tired of hearing you complain." The scales on the Niln's throat began to flush a deep gold. "In fact, I'm just generally tired of hearing you."

Presit whirled on her, teeth bared. "You are not silencing the media!"

"No, I'm not. I'm silencing an annoyance with more hair than brains."

"We are needing to get along," Gytha began, but Torin cut her off with a touch on the shoulder and a quick shake of her head. When the Katrien stepped back, Torin stepped between the two combatants, her relative bulk impossible to ignore. "I've run out of dead targets to shoot in order to make a point," she said quietly.

"You are not meaning . . ." Presit's voice trailed off as she met Torin's eyes.

Torin raised a brow.

"Fine. We are walking back." She spun around and stomped off in a cloud of shed fur. "But I are registering a complaint with General Morris the instant we are rescued."

"You know," the *harveer* murmured to Gytha as they passed, the younger scientist having given an arm to the elder, "I'm thinking freshmen would be a lot easier to control if they let us carry weapons."

Ryder wanted to say something, she could feel it in

the air, but a pointed look got him moving after the others. Grinning, Guimond followed.

"And what are you two smiling at?"

Johnston and Heer exchanged essentially identical expressions as they carried the captain back to the corner.

"Nothing, Staff."

She stepped back as Harrop paused by her shoulder. "Go on, Corporal. I'm going to beat my head against a bulkhead for a moment."

"The general'll stand by you, Staff. No matter what the little hairball says."

"Thanks." Given their history, Torin figured the odds were about even that he wouldn't. "Now, get moving."

"Staff, Nivry. We got bugs at this end, too!"

As all eyes turned toward her, Torin allowed only mild annoyance to show.

They'd maneuvered their way back around three corners. If the map was right, and if the ship hadn't decided to rearrange the architecture, they were exactly halfway between in and out.

No way to avoid a firefight.

"How many bugs, Nivry?"

"Can't tell. Tsui took a hit trying to get around that last corner for a look."

"Is he bad?" Torin ducked around a pipe looping down from the tangle up above, paused, flipped down her helmet scanner, and tilted back her head.

"He's bleeding, but he'll live. We can hold them here indefinitely, Staff."

"Just like they can hold us." At maximum magnification, the light she'd spotted became a recognizable pattern. "Everyone fall back on my position."

"Roger, Staff."

"Dursinski, you copy that?"

"Roger, Staff. Falling back."

"Harrop. Take a look up there and tell me what you see?"

"Lotta pipes. No way out."

She reached over and thumbed an adjustment into his scanner. "Look again."

"It's a . . . well, it *could* be an access grille."

"Let's find out, shall we? Werst!"

He stepped back from the corner, benny remaining in firing position until Frii stepped into his place. By the time he reached Torin's side, he'd already slid his pack down off his shoulders. "Fukking obvious," he grunted at her raised brow. "We're trapped, and you're looking up. Where do I climb to?"

Torin pointed.

"Right." He wrapped a hand around the pipe Torin had ducked and swung himself up. Yellow, to blue, to red, to yellow to . . .

"Serley chrika!"

"Werst? You okay?"

"Yeah. Mostly. This pipe, it's fukking cold!"

"Which pipe?" Torin snapped. All she could see was the lower half of his right leg.

"Pinky-purple one." His tone suggested he was as much insulted by the color as hurt by the cold. "I'm moving on."

He disappeared and reappeared a moment later, a shadow against the light. "You were right, it's an access grille. Double toggles holding it in place. Should I go in?"

"Carefully."

Since she wasn't supposed to hear his grunted, "No shit," she didn't.

After a few moments, he returned and dropped as

much as climbed back to the passage. "You're not going to fukking believe it, Staff. Tube comes out in one of the Ventris Station wardrooms. Pool table, bar, big comfy chairs—and the door's been barred from the inside."

"And the bugs?"

"Not a whiff."

The door barred from the inside suggested a sanctuary—or would have were they not running around the changeable guts of a whacked alien ship. Still, it had to have taken the wardroom from Captain Travik's mind—there was nothing to say it hadn't taken the symbolism as well.

"Staff!" Dursinski threw herself into the passage after Huilin. "We got bugs one corner back." She wiped a dribble of sweat off her face and shook her head. "We're trapped. Trapped like rats."

"Cork it, Dursinski." Torin decided she didn't need to see the quick glances directed at the Katrien—who looked nothing at all like rats but were the only fur-bearing species present. "Nivry, where are you?"

"Two corners out. We'll be there in a . . . Tsui!"

"Got her!"

Up was their only option.

Although their hands and feet looked uselessly tiny poking out from the bulk of their fur, the Katrien, like the Krai were natural climbers. *Harveer* Niiranta-pajee was not.

"And I'm old. And I'm exhausted."

"We're not leaving you behind," Torin told her, indicating that Guimond should lift her to the first pipe.

"Who asked you to?" she snapped. "You there, Worst! Don't just hang there. Give me your hand."

"It's *Werst.*"

"Worst, best . . . what difference does it make? Just give me your hand!"

"You're going to be just like her when you're old." Ryder had moved back into place by Torin's shoulder.

Torin snorted. "Except I'll be taller. And tailless."

"And not half as smart."

"Ma'am, just climb."

Guimond was already halfway up, blocking the view but not the steady stream of sound.

"Is that the pipe you were burned on? It's considerably more pink than purple to my mind. How well does your species see that part of the spectrum? An educated guess says it's transporting some kind of liquid gas and . . . Young man, get your hands off my tail!"

The Katrien were strangely silent.

Maybe they just need someone *to be talking*, Torin reasoned as Werst took a rope attached to the captain's stretcher up over a pipe and dropped the free end back down into the passage. Heer took up a position only a Krai could hold, approximately halfway between the passage and the hatch.

Captain Travik remained unconscious while they hoisted him up into the access tunnel.

"Staff! He's jammed!"

"Unjam him!" Bruises would heal. Or he'd be dead before they had a chance to. Either way, no one else could make the climb while the captain remained stuck between two pipes.

"Staff!" Nivry's voice had picked up a shrill edge. "They just tossed a smoker! I think they're going to try to rush us this side."

"*Both* sides!" Dursinski yelled.

"Maintain a continuous fire along the floor! Frii, Huilin, steady bursts at a meter!"

"I can't see!"

"You don't need to *see*, the passage is only a meter wide!"

"What are they trying to prove?" Ryder demanded. With no room to pace, he stood shifting his weight from foot to foot. "They hold us here and they keep themselves from getting to the air lock. It makes no fukking sense!"

"Welcome to war. Start climbing."

"Tsui's hurt, he should . . ."

Torin grabbed his arm and shoved him toward the pipe. "Go!"

When the smoke cleared, Dursinski's passage held a small clump of still twitching legs.

"Nivry?"

"I don't know, Staff. They were making so much noise we must've hit something, but they've cleared any bodies." The corporal adjusted her grip on the vid cable and waved a hand under her nose. "Smells like roasted nuts."

"Do bugs *have* nuts?" Huilin wondered beside her.

"Maybe they roasted yours."

He laughed but made a fast, one-handed grab for his crotch. Just in case.

The packs went up quickly, Orla to Heer to Werst to Guimond. Once they were clear, Torin called the two Krai down and sent Tsui and Orla up.

"You're the fastest climbers. You'll be the last two on the corners. If I put Huilin by the liquid gas pipe, can you get by?"

Heer looked dubious. "It'll be tight."

"Just tell him not to grab anything," Werst grunted, "and we'll manage."

As Johnston, Harrop, and Jynett made the climb, the Krai replaced the two di'Taykan on the corners.

"Frii, up. Huilin, seal your helmet; you'll be covering our tracks."

"You want me to laser a hole in that pipe."

He was smarter than he looked, but then most di'Taykan were. "No, I want you to use your cutters on that pipe. We're not using lasers on an unknown gas."

"Okay, but why not just use a grenade? I mean, you made us carry them all this way."

"Because it'd be a waste of a smoker and we don't use the gas if we're not all in suits. We're in a closed environment, and I don't want us running into it later. Besides, it'd be rude not to use the free alternative kindly provided."

"Yeah, but, Staff, my cutters went up with my p . . ."

Torin held out the pair she'd pulled as the packs went by. "I'd do it myself, but you're in the suit. Nivry, Dursinski; now!"

Nivry squeezed off two more shots, but Dursinski whirled and ran for the pipes.

"What'll keep them from following us?" she demanded, as Torin boosted her to the first handhold.

"They don't climb for shit. They don't like the cold. And they've chased us up a level away from the air lock. Pick one."

She half twisted to stare down at Torin. "It's not cold."

"Yet. Climb!"

Nivry's foot had barely left the pipe when Torin grabbed it. "Huilin, right behind me. Heer, Werst, wait for my word and then haul ass." She squeezed her shoulders through between a red and blue pipe, wondered how Guimond and Ryder had fit, and pulled herself up to the pipe above the gas line. It was, indeed, a pinky-purple regardless of the *harveer*'s contrary opinion.

"In there, Huilin." Leg wrapped around a vertical, she bent and checked his seals as he wedged himself as far out of the way as possible. "If you're not through the pipe by the time Werst and Heer are at the access tunnel, leave it. This is just insurance; like I said, bugs don't climb for shit."

He grinned at her through his faceplate. *"What happened to the rule about not putting holes in the ship?"*

"It got beat by the desire to not have bugs put holes in us. Werst, Heer! Now."

She could feel them on the pipes as she dragged herself into the tunnel, two pairs of hands and feet slapping out a staccato rhythm. Benny across her back, she crawled forward on elbows and knees. It was a familiar means of locomotion—join the Marines, crawl around the universe. Uncountable sums budgeted for tech and somehow it always came down to that. Usually, it also came with mud.

"Blade's not making much of an impression."

"Then leave it."

"No, it's cutting. It's just slow."

"And on a flat surface the bugs aren't." She could hear Werst and Heer in the tunnel behind her. "I said leave it, before they start shooting at you."

"Almost got . . ."

It was a small explosion, strangely muffled. A ripple ran down the length of the tunnel.

"Huilin! Goddamn it, Huilin, answer me!"

"I'm okay. Mostly okay. I'm in the tunnel."

Torin's heart slowed closer to its normal rate as she crawled off the metal onto carpeting, rolled to one side, and stood.

Heer and Werst crawled past then, a long moment

later, the top of Huilin's helmet appeared. Torin helped him the last meter with a white-knuckled grip on his tank, hauling him up onto his feet and popping his seals before he was fully standing.

"First, what the fuk does mostly okay mean?"

His eyes were as pure a turquoise as his hair—every light receptor closed tight. "I got caught looking at the flash." His arm trembled under her hand.

"Well, it's a good thing you're di'Taykan then, it's a better ocular system for stupidity." She tightened her grip and shook him gently. "They'll open up again, just give them time. And until then, you've got an excuse to grope your way through the team." His hair started to lift but before he could reach for her, she snapped, "Second, what happened?"

"Gas started to pour out. It split the pipe and flooded down into the passage just when one of the bugs got off a shot." He shrugged. "Boom."

"Yeah. I got that part. And third . . ." This time when she shook him, it was a lot less gently. "What part of *leave it* did you not understand?"

"I wanted to get the job done."

"Admirable sentiment. Except when I'm telling you to do something else."

"Sorry, Staff."

"You're just lucky you didn't get yourself killed 'cause that would have really pissed me off." Still holding his arm, she turned the two of them toward the room. "Come one, let's . . . H'san on fukking crutches."

It really was one of the wardrooms on Ventris Station. It said so over the door. *Ventris Station. Wardroom Three.*

It held a bar big enough for captains to drink at without having to rub elbows with lieutenants—

although the bottles of booze behind it seemed to be part of the wall. There were a dozen big comfy chairs and four sofas. A pool table. Carpeting. Soft, indirect lighting. Deep burgundy curtains covered the wall opposite the bar.

"Don't tell me there's a window behind there," she sighed.

"Okay." Grinning broadly, Ryder opened the curtains instead.

They were looking out toward the *Berganitan*, impossibly tiny one hundred and eighteen kilometers away. *Could Human eyes even see one hundred and eighteen kilometers?* Torin wondered. *Even through empty space?* Space . . . She ran over the distance they'd traveled. "It can't be a window, we're nowhere near the hull."

"It doesn't seem to matter."

A Jade spun by, one of the Others' fighters in close pursuit.

Her eyes narrowed. "I've had just about enough of this crap. Has anyone taken a look at what's outside that door?"

"Corridor," Harrop told her. "Just like on the map."

Handing Huilin over to Frii, she checked her slate. According to the map, the corridor ran a quarter of a kilometer aft, then ended in a T-junction. The port arm ran a hundred meters then cornered and headed back forward. The starboard arm went two hundred meters then through a series of compartments. The next vertical appeared to be in the middle of the fourth compartment.

Aft. Starboard. Down. Just where they needed to go.

"I checked the door," Harrop continued. "It can't

be locked from the outside. I think the ship wants us to take a break, Staff."

"The *ship* wants us to take a break?"

He shrugged.

"And since when do we do what the *ship* wants?"

"Pretty much from the moment the air lock blew," Ryder snorted.

"No one asked you." Torin glanced down at her sleeve. 2343. Another two hours and seventeen minutes and it would be tomorrow. It *had* been a long day. Unfortunately . . . "If the bugs get to the air lock first, they'll use it and then destroy it so that we can't use it, trapping us on board."

Harveer Niirantapajee stared up at her from the corner of a couch. "Why would they do that?"

"Every enemy they take out of the fight is one less they'll have to face later."

"And you know this because?"

"Because it's what I'd do."

"If we are just talking to them . . ."

"You'd say what?" Torin asked the younger scientist. "Why can't we all just get along? Well, ignoring the immediate bug/Federate language barrier, if we could get an answer to that, we wouldn't be fighting this war. Or any other wars for that matter."

"Then why are we not using another air lock?" Presit demanded. "There are more than one. So this air lock are closer; let the bugs have it!"

In answer, Torin held up her slate. "The maps we were given—before we knew we were heading into bugs—have all gone aft of our original position. If we start for another air lock now, we'll be wandering blind. We have limited food and, more importantly, limited water." A sweep of her arm directed everyone's attention to the *window*. "Also, there's a whole different battle going on out there and we need to get off this thing while the *Berganitan* is still able to protect the shuttle." She swept an uncompromising gaze around the room. "Fifteen minutes, people, then we're moving out."

"Do you want someone on the door, Staff Sergeant?" Harrop asked before any of the civilians could make another protest.

He was so obvious, Torin grinned. "You lock it behind you when you came back in?"

"I did."

"Then I think we can ignore it for fifteen minutes." Crossing the room, she dropped to one knee by the end of the sofa where Tsui was sitting. "You okay?"

"I'm fine, Staff." He flexed the arm. "Bug just creased me; lots of blood but no real damage."

A gesture turned him in the seat so she could take a look at his field dressing. "Nice work. Who . . . What the hell is wrong with this thing?" Although the cushions looked soft, there was no give under her hand and the surface had the familiar slickness of the original walls.

"I think Big Yellow doesn't quite get it," Nivry offered, dropping onto the other end of the sofa and rapping it with her knuckles. "The stuff behind the bar is one big molded piece, too. It's like it took the visual part of the captain's memory but nothing else."

"Probably didn't want to go any deeper into the captain's head," Tsui snorted. "I mean, talk about a gross . . . invasion of an officer's privacy."

"Nice save," Torin told him, smacking his leg lightly as she straightened. The chemical burn *had* been neutralized before it breached the integrity of Jynett's suit—given the amount of damage it had done, without the suit it would have gone right through her arm. Huilin's light receptors were beginning to reopen. Dursinski was complaining of a charley horse. Captain Travik's condition seemed unchanged. All things considered, they were in pretty good shape.

A full circuit of the room brought her to the *window.* Coincidence only that Ryder was standing by it, arms folded, looking out.

"I don't see any more fighters," he said as she stopped beside him.

"There." Torin pointed at a distant moving point of light. "And there. At this distance and at their speeds, they're hard to spot unless you know what you're looking for."

One of the points flared suddenly.

"Saw that," Ryder said softly. "Any idea if it was us or them?"

"Them."

"How do you know?"

"I don't." She could feel his gaze on the side of her face but she kept her own eyes locked on the stars. "So as far as I'm concerned, it's always them."

"Shylin!"

The lieutenant kept her attention on her screen as the Jade flipped one eighty to come up behind an enemy fighter. "I see him."

"Then you think maybe you could do something about him?" Although there was no way to tell for certain, Lieutenant Commander Sibley thought there were bugs flying the fighters as well as bugs inside Big Yellow. They flew with a certain style that suggested non-binocular vision.

"Give me a minute, he's jamming the targeting computer."

"And isn't that the reason I bring you along on these little outings?"

"I thought it was for my witty repar . . . Got it ! PGM away and . . . Sib, he's shooting back!"

Sibley slipped the Jade sideways and down. "Looks like his bug buddy's taking out our ordnance."

"He's shooting at it; hasn't hit it yet."

"B7 *this is* B8, *I've got a double tail wagging; you think you could get one of them?"*

"On our way." Leaving their smart bomb to its own devices, Sibley pulsed full lower thrusters. "Ready, Shy . . ."

They popped straight up a fast hundred meters. Full upper thrusters to kill momenteum. Energy burst back along the X-axis meeting the enemy missile dead on.

The canopy polarized at the sudden flare, but by then the Jade had already moved forty-five degrees forward and down, away from the debris field.

"Thanks, B7, *we can handle the other one."*

"You sure, Boom Boom?"

"If you hadn't just saved my ass, I'd find that question highly insulting. Looks like your guy's getting away."

The Jade flipped in time to see their PGM taken out before reaching its targeted fighter. "Crap. Hey, bug buddy, those things are expensive! The Navy likes us to hit stuff with them!"

"He can't hear you."

"I think most bugs are roughly female."

"Whatever. Looks like she's trying to get in under the guns."

"B9! Herd dogs!"

"Roger, Seven."

The moment it had become apparent that Big Yellow wasn't going to prevent fighters from either side crossing its axes, the flight commander had divided the squadrons into offense and defense—half to try and take out the Others' ship, half to defend the *Berganitan* against enemy fighters.

Simultaneously—or so close to it there was little point in clocking the difference—the Others had done the exact same thing.

Black Star Squadron had drawn the defensive end of the stick.

As *Black Nine* moved to intercept the enemy fighter, Sibley tucked in behind, bobbing and weaving to avoid being target locked. Together, they herded it toward the *Berganitan*'s big guns. At the last possible instant, it sped up, slid in and down, flipped, and nearly skimmed the surface of the *Berganitan* as it raced away, firing at both fighters, secure in the knowledge they couldn't fire back without hitting their own ship.

"Fuk. That bug can fly."

"Good thing she was more interested in hitting us than the *Berg*." Sibley brought the Jade around. "At that range, even a bug couldn't have miss . . . Boom Boom! You're double tailed again!"

"Tell me something I don't know! A little help?"

"The second missile must've split." Shylin's fingers danced over the pad. "Get me closer."

"I'm trying. Boom Boom, level out so my gunner can lock!"

"I level and I'm toasted."

"No. We take one, your gunner takes the other."

"He won't have time to lock!"

"Tail's be right up your ass, he won't need to lock. He can reach out and smack it away."

The pause took them forty meters in three directions.

"B8 *leveling. Just don't fukking miss!"*

"Now, *I'm* insulted," Shylin muttered. "Got the lock!"

This time, they went right through the debris field. No way to tell for a long moment what or who the pieces had belonged to.

Then something big hit them all along the portside.

"B7! B7 *this is* B8, *respond!"*

"I'm a little busy right now, Boom Boom."

"Looks like that serley *piece of shit took out your port thrusters!"*

"You think?" As the galaxy spun wildly around him, Sibley locked his eyes on his instruments and fired the starboard thrusters, canceling their rotation and bringing the Jade more-or-less level—a position that lasted less than a heartbeat as Shylin fired one of the starboard guns and they were suddenly engulfed by another debris field. An unidentifiably soft object slapped into the canopy and stuck.

"Damn it, Shy!" There were days when he'd kill for a little air resistance. This was clearly going to be one of them.

"No choice; spin took us into the path of a bug. Us or them situation. I voted for us."

"That's because you're not flying this thing!" His fingers danced over the keyboards. "Give a two H'san burst on your PFU."

She squeezed the trigger. "One H'san, two H'san." And then she released it. "Better?"

"Much." This time when he got them straightened they were more or less facing the *Berganitan,* both wingmen hovering close.

"B7, *this is* Eight. *You need a hand."*

"No, thanks, Boom Boom." Sibley glanced up at the body part stuck to the canopy. "Got one."

"B7, this is B9. *Can you make it back to mother?"*

"It won't be pretty but I think so."

"Sib . . ."

"I see it. Boom Boom, we've got an enemy fighter moving in. Looks like they're going to try and finish us off."

"I'm on it. B9, *I'll chase off the bug, you get* Seven *back to the ship "*

"Roger, B8. *Will tuck* Seven *in safe and sound."*

"Unless you'd rather take out that second fighter."

"What sec . . . Fuk, Sibley, you've got eyes like a hurnatic."

"Yep, keep them in a jar on my desk. Don't worry about us, we'll get ourselves back. You go deal with the bad guys."

"Roger, B7. *Dealing."*

As both his wingmen peeled away, Sibley tried not to think of how vulnerable the loss of a quarter of his maneuvering thrusters made his Jade. They'd be sitting ducks if an enemy attacked while they were on their final approach to the launch bay.

Something flared in the distance, the pattern unmistakable against the stars.

Even without knowing, it hurt.

"One of theirs?"

Shylin checked her positioning data, her hair flattening. "No."

"What I don't understand," General Morris growled, glaring at the long view of Big Yellow on the center screen, "is why you don't launch another squadron, have them blow through the enemy fighters around the *Berganitan,* and then attack the Others' ship with superior numbers."

"General, the moment we set to launch, the Others

will know and they'll do the same, blowing through *our* fighters, and in the end we'll be in the same position only we'll both be short a squadron. As long as Big Yellow's holding us in place and keeping us from using our heavy ordnance, neither of us will commit all our fighters."

"The Others are an alien enemy, Captain. How can you possibly know what they're thinking."

Captain Carveg's teeth came together with an audible snap, but before she could answer, the flight commander turned from his station, eyes narrowed. "They're fliers, sir."

"Are you trying to tell me that cognitive patterns follow function?"

One shoulder rose and fell in a motion that might have been a shrug had it not been directed toward a full general. "How do you anticipate what the enemy will do on the ground, sir?"

"It looks bad, Chief. *Black Seven*'s coming in with no port thrusters and he's coming in fast. Seems like they're shooting at him out there and he can't fire back without losing his approach. Which you, of course, already knew," Tristir amended as the squadron's senior NCO turned a basilisk stare on her. She hurriedly added, "Emergency crews are ready—the fire team and two corpsmen are standing by."

"What's his ET . . ." A loud crunch and shudder that ran through the deck plate and up into his boots cut off the last letter. "Never mind."

It wasn't the worst landing Chief Graham had ever seen—worst was reserved for those landings when a crippled Jade smashed home so hard it took out some of the crew waiting there trying to help it. Worst was reserved for the Jade whose pilot found out when they reached the docking bay that the braking thrusters were slag and they hit so hard the fighter went right through into the ship and they had to seal off the section to prevent decompression—pilot, gunner, half a dozen of the emergency crew, and two poor bastards who'd just been passing by dead.

By those standards, this landing was merely messy.

Four canisters of foam sealed the bay along Black Seven's damaged side. Chief Graham popped the hatch the moment the compartment had been repressurized and entered in time to see Lieutenant Commander Sibley climbing out of his pod refusing the corpsman's offer of help.

"We sucked a little smoke, but we're fine. Aren't we fine, Lieutenant?"

"Oh, yeah." Shylin crawled from the rear section, eyes still watering, hair flat against her head. "We're fine."

The corpsman folded her arms. "You still have to go to medical, sirs."

"Not a problem, we know the . . . Chief!"

"Lieutenant Commander Sibley." Chief Graham crossed the bay and squatted by the Jade's damaged side.

"So, how fast do you think you can get it fixed?"

He straightened slowly and turned to glare at the pilot. "How fast can I get it fixed?"

"Well, yeah, there's . . ."

"How fast can I get it fixed? You didn't scratch the paint, sir; you had your port thrusters blown away and you're leaking enough radiation to scramble sperm you haven't thought of spilling yet. Get to decontamination, then get to medical, and stop being so goddamned anxious to get back out there and get yourself killed!"

Sibley opened his mouth, took a closer look at the chief's face and closed it again. Gathering up his gunner, he headed for the hatch. As it closed behind them, Chief Graham sighed.

"Would you fukking look at that; they *also* scratched the paint."

TWELVE

"C C HYDROPONICS Garden, Paradise Station. It was the first HpG I'd ever seen—blew me away that you could grow things without dirt." Torin leaned over the familiar/subtly wrong railing, and stared up at the central column with its rings of plants' roots hanging down in nutrient sprays, growing tips supported by fine filaments. Six levels high, it was an aesthetic not a practical design. The shallow ramp that circled the outside of the atrium was also edged with plants—the greens were too uniform to be real, but she had to give Big Yellow an "A" for effort.

"And you were worried about what would come out of your head," Ryder murmured by her left ear. "Me, I knew it couldn't all be death and destruction."

Torin looked just far enough over her shoulder to meet his gaze and asked flatly, "How?"

"Well, it's . . . uh . . ."

Behind them, a Marine snickered.

Pivoting on one heel, Torin swept her gaze over the gathered Recon team. "Listen up, people, we need to go down a level and this looks like the only chance we're going to get. Huilin, eyes?"

He squeezed them tightly shut and opened them again. The right looked darker than the left. "About seventy percent. Maybe seventy-five."

"Stay in the middle of the march. Harrop, your squad takes point. Keep alert; at the bottom of the ramp you'll be in a park of sorts and there's about two dozen places the bugs could be shooting from on that level alone. You hear or smell anything that could be bugs, you assume it is. Heer, don't eat that. It's not a real *gitern,* it's a part of the ship."

The engineer looked sheepishly down at the fruit in his hand. "Ship's partly organic, Staff."

"And it could be trying to get you to ingest it as a way to infiltrate the Confederation. You have no idea what you'd be shitting."

"You really think so?"

"No. Get rid of it."

Heer sighed and tossed it back into the tank with its parent plant.

A quick glance at Werst showed the other Krai staring challengingly back at her. His jaw might have been moving. Nothing she could do about it now if he'd eaten something and, besides, if it came down to a one on one, Big Yellow against a Krai digestive tract, smart money would be on the colon.

"At the bottom of the ramp, we head across the atrium on a diagonal. Keep moving until we're out of all this cover. Maintain PCU silence unless there's no other option, and keep the dialogue to a minimum. We clear?" Heads nodded. "Orla, get your goddamned helmet on." The patch of fuschia amidst the gray disappeared. "Go."

The back of Torin's neck crawled as they moved down the ramp. The public HpGs were *always* crowded. There should have been hundreds of people, dozens of races, every size and age, all milling about in a space that now held fourteen Marines, two scientists, a reporter, and a salvage operator. She should have been able to smell a dozen things but mostly the gardens. There should have been noise.

It was the lack of noise that bothered her the most. Unlike the Krai and to a lesser extent the di'Taykan, Humans relied a lot more on their sense of hearing than on their sense of smell, and silence was a warning more often than not.

It's too quiet.

And she was well aware that there was often truth in old clichés.

Exhaustion had momentarily shut up the Katrien although Presit seemed to be mumbling to herself as she followed Guimond down the ramp.

They were strung out across the park in a staggered diagonal when someone sneezed, someone else made a sound like wet fingers rubbing glass, the air filled with the smell of cinnamon and, an instant later, with weapons' fire. As Johnston and Heer raced for the dubious cover of a copse of tarrow—Captain Travik making them almost fatally slow—Torin dropped to one knee and began firing back along the incoming trajectory, hoping to buy them some time.

The moment the spiky, broad-leaved plants closed behind them, she dove and rolled, gouging through the pebble bed that provided the illusion of a traditional garden but still allowed the liquid nutrients to reach the roots. Under normal circumstances, leafy vegetation would not have been her first choice in a firefight, but these weren't normal circumstances and Big Yellow apparently had no more actual knowledge of plants than it did of sofa cushions—which made the tarrow difficult to get through but not totally useless as a protective barrier.

As she scrambled behind the triangular leaves, an energy bolt exploded in the pebbles by her right leg, throwing a hundred or so tiny missiles against her. Her combats absorbed most of the impact, but Torin could feel bruises rising along the length of her calf.

Heer bled sluggishly from a nick in the edge of his outer ridge and the back of Johnston's left hand had been scored in a cross-hatched pattern—probably by a leaf tip. The captain remained unconscious. Bright side to everything. Craig Ryder and *Harveer* Niirantapajee had actually dug down into the pebbles.

Smart. She wasted an instant wondering which of them had come up with the idea.

Torin could see Guimond, the Katrien, Orla, and Jynett in the next clump of garden—Jynett's HE suit a brilliant and unmistakable orange against the green—looking back, she could pick out Nivry, Huilin, and Werst. If Tsui had been walking as tailend, he should be . . . yes; the unmistakable spit of a benny came from up a branched palm.

Up was good. It gave him the best line of sight.

"Tsui, were they waiting for us?"

"Negative, Staff. I think they were just crossing the park at the same time."

Just? Torin doubted that very much. It wasn't coincidence that put both groups here—heading out of different passages, heading into different passages—at exactly the same time.

"Has anyone taken a look at the passage behind us?" Not the way they needed to go but preferable to a firefight.

"Way ahead of you, Staff. It's been sealed."

She'd be willing to bet that the passage behind the bugs had been sealed, too. The ship was dicking them around again. In the vids, this would be the moment both sides would realize it and decide to work together against a common enemy.

Torin jerked as a shot fried the edge of a leaf.

Unfortunately, they were in a war not a vid.

"I see you've got each other pinned down again."

"Ryder, get back in your goddamned hole!" Shoving him to one side, she stayed reclining half over his torso as she took a quick shot at the glint of bug armor across the park.

"You know, you're not light."

"Not now, Ryder." About to roll off, she froze, eyes locked on the center column.

Two Marines up the column could provide enough cover for the rest to get out of the park. If the bugs were smart, they wouldn't stick around to get shot at from the high ground, they'd make a run for the closest open passage. If the two Marines were in suits, they could drop smokers to keep the bugs in the passages and to cover their own fallback.

Two *bugs* up the column could do the same thing and the door was out in the open, exactly between the two lines. Inset into the column, it offered shelter once it was reached. Reaching it would be the problem.

And she had the shortest run on it.

"Dursinski, where are you?"

"Behind a bench about two and a half meters from the passage."

"I need you back here. I want two suits in the central column."

"Huilin and Jynett are closer."

"Huilin's half blind."

"It's not that bad, Staff."

"I'm not asking for your opinion, Private. Dursinski, move your ass. Drop back to Jynett's position and then move to the column on my signal."

"Why didn't the ship fry my *fukking suit . . ."* Dursin-

ski's complaint trailed off as the pattern of firing changed.

While the bugs were distracted by the movement, Torin pushed off Ryder's chest, ignoring his grunted protest. "Keep their heads down, people. I'm going over to open the door." Clearing the plants with only minor damage, she tucked her benny close and sprinted across the open area. No point in ducking; the bugs tended to fire low. The column would keep the bugs on the far end of their position from getting off shots but the rest . . .

An energy bolt nearly took her knee off.

"Sniper on the upper ramp!"

"I see him!"

"So stop looking and try fukking hitting him!"

Torin forced herself to dive and slide as her hind-brain kept insisting she wanted minimal contact with shiny, gray floors. She rammed shoulder first into the tower and flipped into the setback just ahead of a chemical impact. A single drop splashed up and hit under the edge of her right shoulder flash. Her combats had been woven from the same material the Confederation used to build ship parts and Torin had to believe they'd maintain their physical integrity long enough for her to get the job done.

Way back in the real HpG on Paradise Station, she'd tried the door and it had been locked, a sign announcing *Authorized Personnel Only* in the three local languages as well as Federate. Odds were good that the copy was also locked. Not a problem. Last time, she hadn't been armed.

Another shot splashed against the edge of the door as she switched her benny to laser and began cutting the lock.

"Keep their damned heads DOWN!"

"Bugs know where you are, Staff. And they know what we're trying to do. They're not bothering to aim."

Wonderful. If they got lucky . . .

Fortunately, the lock had only been designed to stand up to inquisitive teenagers.

After the next splash—evidence suggested they needed time to reload—Torin backed out a step and put her boot to the door. It slammed open just as an energy bolt went wild past her shoulder and up toward the atrium ceiling.

"Got her! Bug couldn't resist taking a shot at your ass."

"Must've been a di'Taykan bug."

"Shut up, Tsui!"

"Can the chatter," Torin snapped, tucked into the setback's one safe angle. "Dursinski, Jynett; you ready to run?"

"Ready, Staff!"

She spun out and aimed toward the bug position, squeezing the trigger as she yelled. "Go!"

No one moved at their top speed in an HE suit. Fully aware they were bright orange targets, both Marines gave it their best shot as the rest of the team hit the bugs with everything they had. Jynett's longer legs reached the setback two strides ahead of Dursinski, but they pounded up the interior stairs in unison.

"Fuk, there's a lot of them!"

"How many's a lot, Dursinski?"

"Uh, seventeen, twenty-three . . . thirty give or take. Some of them are so close together they're hard to count."

"So shoot them twice."

"Roger, Staff."

Sent in by General Morris to be pinned down by an enemy with a numerical advantage while attempting to keep a group of civilians alive.

Déjà vu all over again.

"We've got them pinned, Staff."

"You heard her, people. Move. Everyone into that passage before the bugs figure out a way around this." At least, this time, it wasn't turning into a bloodbath.

"I'm hit!"

If there was one thing in the universe Torin truly hated, it had to be irony.

"How bad?"

"Not good." Tsui's voice held as much anger as pain. *"And I'm hung up on this fukking tree!"*

"Going back for him, Staff."

"Roger, Nivry." Torin could hear the corporal moving behind her. Somehow the gravel ground out a different sound than it did for those moving out of the battle.

"Staff. Dursinski. Bugs are on the ru . . . fuk!"

A flurry of shots rang both up and down the column.

"Bug on the way to your position, Staff! She's inside our range!"

"I'm on it."

Actually, it was anyone's guess as to who was on whom.

Trying for the legs under the armor, Torin threw herself out of the setback and slid round the curve of the column on her belly. The bug was up on her side sliding toward her, legs safely pointed away, torso folded back nearly flat against the abdomen. Torin's first shot ran harmlessly above the floor. The bug's hit high on the column—right about where Torin's head would have been had she been standing.

Torin flipped onto her side and kicked out hard as she passed.

The bug started to spin but managed to get the

curved claws on her lower arm around Torin's ankle as the upper arms swung her weapon around.

The helmet scans from the Marines on the Drenver Mining Station had shown that in hand-to-hand with a bug, the bug always won. But this was a new position for them, and as the claws closed, Torin realized that in bending so far back, she'd opened the waist joint in her armor. A thumb switched the benny to laser.

A moment later, torso and head fell free of the abdomen.

Torin kicked again with her free leg and took out the braincase on the next spin.

Eyes watering from the overpowering stink of cinnamon, she cut the claw off her boot.

"Staff! I can't get to Tsui. That ablin gon savit *of a sniper's got us both pinned down."*

"Dursinski?"

"Yeah, I can see her. She's moved to a one-eighty from the door, Staff, second level. But the angle's fukked for us. We can't hit her."

"I've got her."

"How?"

Another time, she'd have a chat with Dursinski about that tone. "I'm going to give her a target she'll have to break cover for. Nivry, get ready." Flipping her helmet scanner around to the side, Torin rose from behind the dead bug, studying the fake plants on the second level from the corner of one eye. The bugs on the mining station had been derisive of binocular vision. As far as the sniper was concerned, the stupid mammal was looking the wrong way.

There. A glitter in the green as she rose to aim.

Nivry's first shot appeared to catch her under the upper armpit. The second spun her head around.

Torin didn't wait to see if there was a third; she was already sprinting for Tsui's position.

He was missing his left foot, sheared off clean just above the boot. Fortunately, the wound had cauterized—so it hadn't been the bugs emitting the smell of burned pork. When he'd fallen, the strap of his benny had got hung up, twisting him around so that his good leg had been jammed in the deep vee of a lower branch. The only way he could free himself would have involved pushing off from the trunk with the bloody remains of his other leg.

He was about to do just that as Torin reached him. She grabbed his calf as gently as possible and swung his leg out from the tree while freeing the spray tube of emergency sealant from her vest with her other hand. Nivry arrived an instant later, benny still covering the sniper's position.

"I hit her high, Staff, both times. I can't be sure she'll stay down."

"We'll have to risk it." The tube empty, Torin tossed it aside, snapped off Nivry's tube, and kept spraying. The two together wouldn't seal things as tightly as she'd like, but they'd have to do.

"I can't feel my foot." Tsui sounded mildly put out by the realization.

"Because it's not there." The second tube hit the gravel, and Torin motioned Nivry around the other side of the tree. At 1.87 meters, the di'Taykan corporal had height enough to free the trapped leg.

"Oh. So I guess you're telling me I'm a foot shorter."

"Shut up, Tsui."

He snickered, then moaned as the shock suddenly wore off.

"Now, Nivry." Digging her boots into the gravel,

Torin braced herself, not so much catching the injured Marine as directing his fall onto her left shoulder, minimizing the chance of his injured leg hitting her body. Two careful strides took her back out onto solid deck.

Panting and swearing softly in three languages, Tsui struggled to get down.

Left arm between his legs, Torin tossed her benny to Nivry and smacked him on the ass with her right. "Stop it! Or you can walk to the painkillers."

"Fukking hurts . . ."

"I know." Shifting his weight across her back, she started for the passage. Three steps to get her balance and then she was running. As she passed the column, she snapped, "Dursinski, Jynett; give me a ten count and then smoke them."

"Roger, Staff."

Torin counted strides. One, two . . . Nivry fired at something behind them. *Goddamned bugs just don't give up.* Under normal circumstances, she appreciated tenacity but this was becoming too fukking much. Five, six . . . Tsui'd stopped swearing, but he was holding fistfuls of her combats tighter than he needed to keep from falling. Seven, eight . . . *Where the hell is that passage?* Nine, ten. . . .

The smoke canisters hit and blew.

Firing ahead of her now and behind, the sound of HE boots slapping deck.

She almost stumbled on the lip of the hatch but caught herself and Tsui at the last moment, then straightened and rolled the injured Marine into waiting arms. Breathing heavily, she slumped back against the wall, one hand held out to Nivry for her benny.

"We have a way out of here?" she demanded of no one in particular.

"Passage conforms to the map, Staff."

"Perimeter pins set?"

"At the first corner."

Nice thing about working with Recon, they had the right answers to those kind of questions.

Dursinski and Jynett pounded by a moment later, then Werst and Guimond backed into the passage in a swirl of smoke.

"Close it."

Facial ridges shut tight, Werst shoved Guimond behind him and slapped the hatch controls.

Torin half expected the doors not to work, but with a familiar purr they slid into place. Big, open spaces in stations made people nervous, so builders always set decompression doors into the exits. Big Yellow had reproduced them here and, dogged down from inside, they provided a barrier the bugs didn't have the ordnance to get through.

Probably didn't . . .

She drew in a deep breath and let it out slowly as the adrenaline buzz of combat began to die. Her gaze slid over the captain—any relevant change meant he was either conscious or dead. The former would be obvious, the latter . . . He was a Marine and she'd fight to get him out alive because of that, but only because of that, and General Morris could just deal. She continued scanning down the passage. Kneeling on the deck beside the med kit, Frii had Tsui's stump up over his thigh and was applying painkillers directly to the raw tissue. The rest of the team were checking their weapons, changing charges if necessary—still edgy, still psyched. Huilin had his benny a little close to his eyes, but his hands snapped the old charge out and the new one in with confidence. The Katrien had rushed for Guimond as soon as he came in and were both pressed up against his side grooming with short swipes of curved fingers and chattering almost quietly to each other. *God help me, it's becoming a comforting sound. Harveer* Niirantapajee appeared to be asleep. "Anyone else hurt?"

Harrop shook his head. "The plant life did more damage than the bugs."

"I'm sweating like a pig in this thing, Staff." Dursinski pulled at a fold in her HE suit. "Can I take it off?"

"No. If Jynett hadn't been in hers, that chemical burn would have taken off her arm. Be thankful for the extra protection."

"I'd be more thankful if I wasn't sitting in a puddle," she muttered as Torin dropped down by Tsui's side.

Ryder watched Torin murmur words of encouragement to the wounded Marine and shook his head. Back against the wall, he slid down until his ass touched the deck, then he stretched out his legs. "Okay," he muttered, just loud enough for the Marines on either side of him to hear, "first she ran across open deck to the column. Then, having set up cover for our retreat, she took out a bug in hand to whatever the hell those things the bugs have are. *Then* she set herself up as a sniper target, ran toward the sniper, and carried that man pretty much the length of the park, saving his life. And yet, no one seems too impressed."

"She'd say she's just doing her job," Harrop grunted, draining the charge from a nearly empty power pack into another.

"That's what she says. But what do you guys say?"

"About her doing her job?"

"Yeah, about that."

Orla exchanged a glance with the corporal and shrugged. "She's pretty good at it." Her eyes suddenly lightened as a thought occurred. "You like her, don't you?" The accompanying gesture made the di'-Taykan's definition of "like" obvious and mildly obscene.

"Staff?" Tsui wet his lips, and Torin braced herself for one of the "what's it all mean" questions that always seemed to follow a major injury. "How come whenever we meet up with the bugs we're in a configuration out of one of our heads?"

It took her a moment to regroup. "Configuration?" She smiled down at him. "Big word."

"I'm serious."

"You're stoned on painkillers."

"Well, yeah, but it's still a good question. How come?"

"I don't know. Those switchbacks may have been made by the bugs or, since they've got the advantage of numbers, maybe Big Yellow's giving us the terrain."

He sighed. "I don't think I want to play this game anymore." Dark brows suddenly snapped in, and he clutched at her arm. "Staff, where's my foot?"

She closed her fingers over his. "Totally disintegrated. Not even a toenail left."

"Good." Muscles visibly relaxed. "It's just, I don't want this ship to have it. You know?"

"I know." And with any luck it was a lie that wouldn't come back to haunt her. Torin had no idea where Tsui's foot was. Finding it hadn't been high on her to-do list at the time, and she sure as hell wasn't going back out to look for it. *Let's just hope it's not waiting for us at the air lock.*

As his eyes began to unfocus, she lifted his hand off her arm and laid it on his chest. His fingers were warm, his injury not as bad as it looked. He'd spend a few weeks with a regen tube around his leg and then, brand new foot. Thing was, she had to get him to a regen tube. *And to do that, I have to get him to the air lock and off this fukking ship.* Fourteen Marines. Two of them on stretchers. Four stretcher carriers. Thank God, Tsui was Human and not another Krai. Eight Marines. Against thirty bugs, give or take.

Coming to a decision, Torin picked Tsui's weapon off the deck where Nivry had left it and stood. With the amount of painkillers careening around his system, he wouldn't be using it any time soon.

Ryder was sitting between Harrop and Orla about twelve meters from the closed hatch. There were deep circles under his eyes and a few lines she hadn't noticed earlier. *So. We're all tired.* Stepping over Orla's outstretched legs, she held the benny out toward the CSO. "I want you to learn to use this."

He looked startled. "The gun?"

"Yes, the gun."

Orla snickered—no surprise, di'Taykans could turn a court-martial inquiry into innuendo—but even Harrop looked amused. Torin decided she didn't want to know.

"Isn't it against the law for a civilian to carry a Marine Corps weapon?" Ryder asked scrambling to his feet.

Torin stepped back to give him room. "Yes."

"Okay." He seemed a little taken aback by the blunt response. "I figured I'd be carrying a stretcher."

"You will be, but if we're in another firefight, I want the weapons with the people who can use them. Tsui's out, and even if the other three were bigger, I couldn't ask them." Her lip curled slightly as she glanced over at the pair of Katrien and the Niln. Funny how easily those species who'd evolved past violence had been convinced to allow the less evolved to commit violence for them the moment diplomacy had failed with the Others. "Which leaves you."

"Me?"

"Unless I'm talking to myself and Orla . . ." Her gaze slapped down on the di'Taykan. "What's so damned funny?"

"Nothing, Staff."

"Harrop?"

"It's him." The corporal jerked his head toward Ryder's back, implication clear: *It's him, it's not you.*

"I see. Well, as much as I hate to remove Private Orla's source of amusement . . ."

Orla suddenly became very interested in her boots.

". . . I think maybe we should talk over here." Grabbing Ryder's arm, she pulled him diagonally across the passage to the other wall, which didn't put enough distance between him and the di'Taykan but did, at least, mean she could ignore whatever it was they had going on. "Have you ever fired one of these?"

"No. Not going to ask me if I'm willing to?"

"No. I think you're smart enough to realize that reaching and holding the air lock is going to take every weapon we've got, and if it came to it, you'd rather be unevolved and alive."

An eyebrow rose at *unevolved,* but all he said was, "That's the nicest thing you've ever said to me."

"Don't let it give you a swelled head." She shoved the benny into his hands and twisted the barrel. "This is the laser, it functions pretty much like every cutting tool you've ever used." Reaching out, she tapped a small screen. "This is your remaining charge. The MDC is point and shoot." She twisted the barrel again. "This is your charge for that."

"MDC?"

"Molecular Disruption Charge."

"I can see why you use the short form. What's it do?"

"Simple explanation?"

"Yeah, please."

"It causes organics to explode at a cellular level. We use them in situations like this, so we don't inadvertently hole a bulkhead and die sucking vacuum."

Ryder frowned down at the benny then up at Torin. "Isn't Big Yellow partly organic."

So it was. And it had definitely been hit on a number of occasions. She had a sudden flash of her benny spread out over the "workbench." "The ship found out what we were shooting—us and the bugs—and did something to protect itself."

"What?"

"How the hell should I know? Can we continue?" When he nodded, she lifted her weapon and thrust a finger through the trigger guard. "Same trigger works for both. If it's locked, and that one is, press on the pad just ahead of the trigger guard; it's species-keyed to Human, di'Taykan, and Krai. Don't forget to check the lock, don't forget to check the charge; empty, these things make crappy clubs. This is how you change the power pack."

Ryder snapped his pack in and out, gave the barrel a couple of experimental turns, and stared at the data stream. "That's it?"

"Essentially."

When he looked up, his eyes had crinkled at the

corners. "How come they spend so much training you lot if that's it?

"How to shoot's the easy part," Torin snorted. "They train us to know when."

"Okay. When?"

"When I tell you to." Body still squared off against Ryder, she turned her head. "Frii?"

"We can move him now, Staff."

"Then let's go, Marines. Air lock's not getting any . . ."

She was looking at Heer, saw his facial ridges clamp shut an instant before she smelled the cinnamon. When the panel popped out above her head, she'd already pivoted more than halfway around. The grenade came as a bit of a surprise—it didn't look like a smoker.

She caught it one-handed, swore at the heat, saw Ryder go to one knee, stepped up on his raised leg, and threw it back down the vent. It hit the retreating bug in the face and rolled under her thorax.

Good guess that *Oh, fuk* in bug smelled like lemon furniture polish.

Torin dropped, grabbing Ryder's shoulder, taking him to the ground with her.

"FIRE IN THE HO . . ."

The deck lifted, slamming them together. Then it lifted again, throwing them against the bulkhead. Teeth clenched to keep from biting her tongue, Torin felt the bulkhead buckle under her shoulder. Then she was falling. They were falling.

A bounce. A hand grabbed at her arm. A blow against her helmet canted it forward over her eyes.

She landed without ever being totally out of contact with the ship—or engulfed by the ship. Both were an improvement on the last time.

A feather touch against her cheek made her think of antennae, but grabbing for it she stubbed her fingers through Ryder's beard. Which explained the yielding surface she'd impacted against.

Her helmet was jammed tight. Torin jerked her head back out of it and shifted around, ignoring the grunts from beneath her until she was sitting half astride Craig Ryder's hips. She could just barely make out his face in the spill of light from above. He seemed to be grimacing. "YOU OKAY?"

The ringing in her ears drowned out all but the question. When he nodded, she stood. The wall or possibly the deck had fallen in after them, leaving a jagged hole half the diameter of her head about four meters up. An easy climb but nowhere to go.

Harrop's face appeared, plunging the area into total darkness. Before Torin could use several choice words she'd been saving, his helmet light came on. His eyes were wide, and his lips were moving.

"I CAN'T HEAR YOU!" Touching both ears, Torin shook her head. "WAIT!" Bending around Ryder, who chose that moment to stand, she braced one boot on a twisted support beam and yanked her helmet free. Most of the photoelectric coating would have to be replaced, but the PCU seemed to be working fine. She cranked the receiver's volume and tried not to shout.

"What's the situation, Harrop?"

"Orla's nose is bleeding and Tsui slammed his stump into the deck—no other casualties."

"And the civilians?"

"Gytha's having hysterics, but Presit's calming her down."

That didn't change Torin's opinion of the reporter, but it was a nice surprise. The universe had been short of those lately. "No sign of the bugs?"

"None."

She heard him that time around the PCU, so she took off her helmet and blew out her ears.

"You guys are never going to make it out this hole, Staff. Hang on; Johnston wants to scope it out."

The engineer's opinion matched Harrop's. "Unless there's another way up, we'll have to cut—if the ship'll allow it."

Torin took a good look around. They appeared to be in a one-by-three-meter hole in the wreckage. "Cut," she growled. "And if the ship's got a complaint, it can take it up with me."

"So, what did the general say?"

Torin tongued off her implant and sagged back against a bent piece of bulkhead. "He said we should get to the air lock as fast as possible. Man's a military genius."

"Could be worse; he's not using the override codes and insisting on a play-by-play."

"He's probably forgotten he has the override codes. I doubt he's used his implant much, if at all, in the last few years—that's what aides are for."

"He tell you what's been happening out there."

"Oh, yeah, generals always take the time to keep staff sergeants fully informed. I got the impression the fighters from both ships are still going at it, though. If they weren't playing with live ammo, the vacuum jockeys would probably be pissing themselves with joy. The whole breed's insane." Reaching out, she grabbed the hand tapping against his thigh. "Stop it."

"I don't do well sharing a small space."

"I know. Stop it anyway."

He jerked his hand away. "And you're doing so well yourself."

Biting back a profane suggestion, Torin spread her hands. "Sorry." Not a gracious apology, but he was right. *And if I'm not out of this hole soon, I'm going to start fukking shooting my way out.*

"I have the feeling you don't do well with being helpless."

Letting her hands drop, she closed her eyes. "And I have the feeling you wouldn't do well with a boot to the head."

"So what about Marine Corps vacuum jockeys?" Ryder asked after a moment's silence.

Torin opened her eyes. She couldn't see his expression. *Okay. If he wants to make polite conversation . . .* "What about them?"

"They insane, too?"

"Oh, yeah. It's a whole vj thi . . . Son of a fukking bitch!" Jerking away from the bulkhead and up onto her knees, she ripped open the seal on her vest, scrambling beneath it for the tab that would open her combats. Given the myriad bruises she'd been collecting, it had been easy to ignore the itching on her upper arm; not until the itch suddenly, painfully became a burn did she remember the chemical spill. "God fukking damn it!"

The tab finally lifted. She yanked it down to her waist and dragged her right arm clear. "JOHNSTON!"

The engineer's laser shut off.

"AID KIT! NOW!"

It had taken over an hour for the chemical to work through her sleeve. It was moving a lot faster through flesh.

"Torin, what's wrong."

Right hand clutching a fistful of fabric, teeth clenched, forcing herself to breathe—in and out, in and out, filling her lungs each time—she turned just enough for him to see. A chemical burn was worth a thousand words.

"Son of a fukking bitch!"

"Yeah." In and out. In and out. "Said that."

Boots pounded against deck plates.

"Staff! Kit's too big for the hole."

"Chem kit!" They could drop it into her left hand or . . . "Ryder."

He surged up onto his feet. "I've got it." She heard it hit his hands. He dropped to his knees beside her and shoved the kit into her line of sight. "What do I do?"

"Rip the film off. Slap the unit, sticky side down over the burn."

"It may not fit."

"Then fukking hurry!" Contact was a minor pain lost in nearly overwhelming sensation. Analysis and treatment were supposed to be instantaneous. Instantaneous turned out to be a relative term, depending on which side of the treatment defined it.

When the neutralizing agent finally hit, the sudden absence of pain was so intense Torin swayed into a warm, solid barrier, realized what it was as an arm rose to steady her, and swayed out again.

"It would kill you to collapse for a minute?"

Beginning to breathe more normally, she swung her head around and up to meet his gaze. "I get to collapse when the job's done. Not before." A few drops of neutralizer ran out from under the unit and down her bare arm, pulling her attention with it. She noticed that the handful of fabric her right hand clutched wasn't covering her leg. She had no idea when she'd shifted her grip. Opening her fingers, Torin patted the crumpled handful smooth and looked up to find Ryder staring at her. "When the job's done," she repeated.

"What if we die in here?"

"Not going to happen."

"Because you say so?"

Torin snorted. If he'd been a Marine, he wouldn't have had to ask. "Yeah. Because I say so."

"Staff! You okay?"

"We're fine. Keep cutting."

THIRTEEN

TORIN scrubbed both hands over her face and looked back down at the map. "You're sure?"

"Positive." Nivry tapped the screen. "We follow this passage to here, then there's some kind of weird engine room shit to cross and the air lock's right here."

"No bugs?"

"None."

"How are you sure?"

Nivry glanced down at the small hand clutching her sleeve. "It's what we in Recon do, ma'am. We go out and we find the enemy."

"How?"

"How do we find them?" When Presit nodded, she grinned. "Well, usually, we know we're close when they start shooting at us."

The reporter snatched her hand away and stared up at Nivry with accusing eyes, her ears flat to her skull. "That are not being funny!" she snapped, and flounced off, the silver tips of her fur trembling indignantly.

"Shouldn't have asked the question if she didn't want to hear the answer." Torin watched her go with as close to a neutral expression as she could manage, then looked back up at Nivry. "ETA on the air lock?"

Emerald hair flicked back and forth, then . . . "Even with the stretchers and the civilians, we're no more than an hour away."

"I'll let the *Berganitan* know."

". . . and Captain Travik?"

He's alive, sir.

"Good. Arrange it so that he's first onto the sh . . . Staff Sergeant Kerr? Staff Sergeant Kerr! Damn it." General Morris rubbed his left hand over his forehead and glared at the science officer. "You've lost the signal again, find it."

"Sir, it's gone out at the other end."

"And isn't that signal booster of yours supposed to stop that?"

"Yes, sir, but . . ."

"I don't want excuses, Lieutenant. I want to talk to my Marines."

Who don't want to talk to you. Taking pity on her officer—who faced a choice between telling the general that Staff Sergeant Kerr had cut the signal or outright lying to a direct question from a superior—Captain Carveg stepped down from her station and said, "We'll launch the shuttle now, General."

She thought he might push the matter, but after a long moment, he turned to face her.

"I want your best STS pilot flying it," he growled.

"Sorry. You'll have to settle for second best. Lieutenant Czerneda was my best STS pilot, but she's dead—along with three fighter crews."

"Four, Captain," a voice announced grimly from one of the stations monitoring the battle.

"Thank you, Ensign." She took a step closer and stared up at his face. "Four."

His face began to darken. "And your point, Captain?"

"My point, General," her toes worked to find purchase on the deck and she forced them to relax before she said, "is that my people have been doing their best, and we don't need you to ask for it. Flight Commander, launch squadron."

"Aye, aye, Captain. Squadron away."

"Any response from the bugs?"

"No, ma'am."

"Launch shuttle."

Fingers drumming against the table, Sibley locked his eyes on the monitor currently showing the signal coming in from the buoy.

"Sib, stop it."

"Stop what."

Shylin put her hand over his and flattened it. "Stop that."

"They're going to respond." He jerked his chin toward the image of the Others' ship. "There's no way they'd fight so hard and then just let us pick up our grunts and go home."

"They're still fighting. The Marauders and the *Katray Sants* are still out there."

"Not what I meant. They're going to attack the shuttle."

"It's got a full squadron riding shotgun."

"I know."

"You don't think they'd have launched by now if they were going to try something?"

"Yeah, I do. And that's what bugs me." Sibley pulled his hand out from under his gunner's and, without taking his gaze from the monitor, pulled a stim stick from the breast pocket of his flight suit.

"Don't you think you've had enough of those?"

"No."

"Your fingers are turning orange, and you're never going to get to sleep."

He looked down at that. "Sleep?"

"Yeah, you remember, it's what you do when you're in bed and not fukking. You know, the stuff you do between crash landings and going out again."

One eyebrow rose. "Not a lot of sleeping going on right now, Shy."

She looked around. With the exception of the three squadrons currently deployed, most of the *Berganitan*'s vacuum jockeys were in the "Dirty Shirt." The flight officer's wardroom wasn't exactly crowded, but it bordered on full. Crews from the two squadrons that had already been out were mostly staring into coffee or talking quietly about the empty places at their tables. Some, like Boom Boom, sitting beside her with a mug of *sah* held loosely in one foot, had their slates out and were writing home. Just in case. The virgin crews were watching the monitors. Waiting for their turn.

"Forget I said anything," she sighed.

"Captain! The Others have opened missile tubes one through six! Firing missiles!"

"Unless the rules have changed, missiles aren't a problem." She glared down at the relevant screen and muttered, "Anyone know if the rules have changed?"

"Yes, ma'am."

C3 went completely silent and, if only for an instant, all eyes flicked away from monitors and data streams.

"That was a rhetorical question, Ensign."

His ears flushed crimson. "Yes, ma'am, but I'm

reading life signs in the missiles. I think they're actually specialized fighters."

"And Big Yellow allows fighters."

"Yes, ma'am."

"Good work, Ensign. Flight Commander, alert your squadrons!"

All eyes were on the monitors now, coffee and letters home forgotten.

"These are new," someone muttered. "Fuk, they're fast."

"And it ain't like the fighters were slow," someone else added.

The Marauders and the *Katray Sants* had been pulled away by the Others' fighters, leaving the shuttle and her escorts alone in space.

"Maces are moving to intercept."

Fifteen to six, Sibley thought, stim stick forgotten in the side of his mouth. *Oy, mama, why don't I like those odds?*

The missile/fighters closed the gap rapidly and made no attempt to avoid the Jades swooping in at them. They roared on by, maintaining the same close diamond formation.

"A hit!"

One of the diamond's outer points spun away from the rest, leaving a trail of debris. Three Jades raced in for the kill. Another point was hit with the same result. Another wing peeled off after it to cheers in the "Dirty Shirt," but somehow Sibley didn't feel like cheering, although other times, other missions, he'd have been yelling advice and bad puns at the screens with the rest of them.

Nine Jades; one wing holding position around the

shuttle, the other two racing after the four missile/fighters.

"They're going to take out the shuttle." He almost didn't recognize his own voice.

"Well, they're going to try," Shylin snorted, her hair flicking back and forth. "But if they want to survive the attempt . . ."

"They don't."

One of the pilots seemed to realize the same thing; a Jade moved directly into the path of the enemy. Both ships were destroyed, but the three remaining enemy fighters were through the debris field so fast it did no damage.

The shuttle was taking evasive action but, given the comparative speeds between hunter and hunted, it needn't have bothered.

All three enemy fighters detonated on impact.

The explosion stopped all conversation, all speculation. The brilliant white light blanked out all but two of the monitors and the entire wardroom held its collective breath until they came back on-line. The shuttle and the two closest Jades were gone without even debris enough to mark their passing.

"Stupid fukking bugs," Boom Boom said at last.

Shylin leaned in closer to her pilot's shoulder and muttered, "You know, I really hate it when you're right."

"Yeah." Sibley fished out another stim stick and bit down without tasting it. "Me, too."

"Captain Carveg! The Others launched an STS shuttle of their own just before their missile/fighters impacted."

Her fingers clutched the edge of her panel, grip

tightening with every flash that told her two more of her people weren't coming home. "No fighter escort?"

"No, ma'am. The shuttle has been covered in a stealth material; it's almost impossible to see unless you know what you're looking for."

Her lip curled. "They thought we wouldn't see it until too late."

"Yes, ma'am."

"They think they can get it to the air lock while we're preoccupied with our losses. Flight Commander, move the remainder of the Red Maces to the attack. If you can't blow the damned thing up, cripple it. Keep it from getting to Big Yellow. And keep a better watch on the Others. Even if we couldn't see the shuttle, those things aren't small and there should be an energy spike when they open the shuttle bay doors. It happens again, and I want to know about it." She glanced around C3, but General Morris wasn't in the room. He had a definite knack for being around when he wasn't wanted and vanishing when he was. "Yeoman White, find the general and tell him he should contact his people and let them know the bugs are probably close on their collective ass. Only say it politely."

"Aye, aye, Captain."

"Communications, punch through to the staff sergeant's implant, but don't let the general know you did it. Or that you can do it."

"Aye, aye, Captain."

Due respect, General . . . The sound of weapons' fire nearly drowned out her next words. *. . . but we already knew that.*

* * *

"Listen up, people; the good news is, we won that round. The bad news is, we're running low on ammo."

"Staff? I volunteer to go to the *Berganitan* and get more."

Torin moved a little ahead so she could see Tsui's face as she walked. "And you'd just be completely screwed if I had a way to send you, wouldn't you?"

He let his head fall back down onto the stretcher. "Wouldn't have volunteered if you had a way to send me," he pointed out faintly. "But I could use a beer."

"Couldn't we all."

They'd run into the bugs again on their way to Nivry's "weird engine room shit." The lights were low enough that the Marines had helmet scanners in place, the passage had begun to look like a mechanical access route, and the front of the march was halfway across a T-junction when the sudden smell of furniture polish had let them know they weren't alone.

The bugs had been the more startled. Torin suspected it was because Big Yellow was also screwing around with their maps, moving corridors, shortening passageways, joining two sections that hadn't been joined before. They'd probably thought they were on a direct route to the air lock with no chance of running into the enemy.

There'd been a fast flurry of shots exchanged, and the bugs had retreated.

No casualties.

As fights went, it was one of the better ones.

"How's your arm?"

In moving up beside Tsui, Torin'd also moved up by Ryder who carried the foot of his stretcher. She slowed until he caught up, then matched his stride. "It's all right."

"Really? It didn't look *all right.*"

The gleam of the field sealant showed through the hole in her sleeve—the burn had been deep enough that had it been on either the front or the back of her arm instead of the side, it would have taken out a muscle group. "It aches, but I can use it."

"You were very brave."

Eyebrow raised, Torin turned to face him. It could have been a condescending remark, but after spending the last few hours in his company, she didn't think it was. "You're not used to seeing people get shot, are you?" she asked dryly.

"No, I'm not." One corner of his mouth lifted into a wry smile. "You know, most people aren't."

She considered that for a moment, then nodded. "Good."

A decompression hatch at the end of the passage opened into the upper wall of a well-lit, two-level chamber. Six-by-six grates covered the ceiling, allowing glimpses of a maze of pipes and wires through their mesh. Metal stairs led down to a textured deck. Four large tanks sat along one fifteen-meter wall in black cradles, digital readouts of pressure, temperature, and volume flashing on each. Large pieces of gray machinery that no one could actually identify squatted in rows down the center of the deck.

"Area's clear," Werst announced from an identical platform on the other side of the room.

"You heard him, Marines. Let's move. Air lock's twenty meters on the other side of Private Werst."

The deck vibrated as they crossed it, as though they were near the combustion chamber. A faint smell of ozone hung over the whole space.

Torin kept her people moving as quickly as possible; the last thing she wanted was prolonged exposure to what appeared to be four hydrogen tanks. She had no doubt this was just another scenario created for them—the system appeared far too primitive to be an actual working part of the ship—but, because of its availability, hydrogen *was* the default fuel and should anything happen, should the bugs reappear, the last thing she wanted was a stray shot damaging one of those tanks. Big Yellow had proved willing to blow part of itself up before.

They were three quarters of the way across when Werst yelled, "Enemy above!"

Above? *It's a fukking drop ceiling. Those things aren't weight bearing!*

Sliding along on a piece armor, only arms and head visible around its edges, the bug was a moving shadow behind the grates.

"Take cover!"

Marines and civilians dove under and behind the big gray machines. They didn't look likely to explode, but then, neither had that original section of wall.

The MDCs were defused by the grate. Anything that got through hit the armor.

"Stop firing! You're just wasting your fukking ammo!" Who was tallest and closest to the stairs? "Huilin, Frii; get to Werst and boost him high enough to get through the grate!" She could hear the two di'-Taykan moving.

The bugs had fired energy bursts in the hydroponics. *They can't be stupid enough to fire that weapon in here.*

A short burst dropped everyone to the deck.

Okay. They can.

When Torin looked up again, a metallic blue cylinder, small and familiar, was falling through a smoking hole in the grate.

The grenade hit one of the gray machines and bounced.

Torin spun around in time to see it roll past Guimond and the three civilians and disappear under a tank.

Time slowed to a crawl as Dursinski dropped to her stomach and batted it out with the muzzle of her benny. She grabbed for it with her free hand but it skittered away, taking an odd bounce on the textured deck, spinning around and almost disappearing again into the thick fur of the reporter flank's. Presit reluctantly shuffled her leg aside and picked up the grenade, holding it in both hands, her eyes squinted nearly shut as she tried to see what she had.

Guimond had his pack off and combat vest undone.

Standard operating procedure for a grenade in a sensitive area. *If you can't throw it back at the bastards, wrap it in your vest then get some distance. The vest will contain most of the explosion.*

Cinnamon.

Presit sneezed.

Guimond grabbed the grenade from her hands and threw himself down to the deck on top of it.

The explosion lifted his body, shaking it like a small animal in a predator's jaws.

On Torin's slate, his med-alert went off, then settled down to the steady beep of the locator. She keyed in the code that would turn it off. She knew where the body was.

Time sped up again.

"NO!"

Somebody had to yell it; the only question had ever been who.

The rage in Werst's voice spun all heads around.

From the handrail around the platform, he leaped out onto the grate. Gripping with fingers and toes, he raced toward the bug.

Torin didn't waste breath calling him back. He wouldn't have listened. *Rage, but no denial,* she thought as he crawled across the ceiling. *He expected this, or something like it.*

Werst reached the hole the bug had blown through the grate and shoved his benny into it, pulling the trigger again and again.

Another energy burst went off.

"If that bug's got more than one grenade . . . !" Dursinski yelled.

"She'd have dropped it already." Torin's voice filled all the spaces in the room, leaving no place for panic. If the bug had more than one grenade, she'd have tossed them down in a pattern, one right after the other, and they'd *all* be dead.

The grate Werst clung to peeled away from the ceiling, screaming a protest. Hanging upside down, he reached around the jagged edge and fired one more time. The bug made much the same sound as the grate and pitched forward through the hole, all four arms flailing wildly.

One caught Werst across the small of the back.

She missed the machines and hit the deck with a wet crunch.

Hanging from his feet, Werst swung, once, twice, his helmet flying off his head to clatter against a tank. The grip of his toes alone wasn't enough to support his weight. He twisted in the air, hit the top of a machine on all fours, and slid off to the deck.

"Harrop, the bug! Nivry, Guimond!"

Torin was at Werst's side a heartbeat later but, even so, he was already on his hands and knees crawling toward the remains of the bug, pushing his weapon ahead of him, his finger still hooked around the trigger. "She's dead, Werst. You got her. Let it go."

He snarled a Krai profanity and kept crawling.

"Werst!" When he jerked to a stop, she wrapped her hand around his right wrist, pinning his weapon to the floor. When he tried to roll out of her grip, when his left fist jabbed out toward her face, she was ready for him. "That's. Enough."

And it was because she said it was. She used the words to fill him as she used them to fill a room, leaving no space for questions or doubt.

His facial ridges flared once and with a sound halfway between a growl and a whimper, he collapsed into the circle of her arms.

A heartbeat later, when Torin felt muscles begin to tense, she let him push away. He had his own places to store grief, just as she did. Just as they all did.

"Wasn't enough he had the *nice guy* fukking target painted on him," Werst growled, glaring at nothing over Torin's shoulder, "he had to go like a fukking hero."

"Guimond saved a lot of lives."

"And that makes it better?"

Torin snorted. "Only time makes it better and there never seems to be enough of it."

She wasn't telling him anything he didn't know, but the snort drew his focus to her face. He stared into her eyes for a moment, then he nodded and looked away. "You're a big *serley* comfort, you know that, Staff Sergeant Kerr?"

"Just doing my job." His meaning had been clear on his face, the words used were irrelevant. "When you're ready to talk about it . . ."

He nodded.

"And otherwise; are you all right?"

"Yeah, I'm . . ." As he moved a leg, his ridges clamped shut and the mottling on his skull suddenly stood out in bold relief. "I broke a *serley* toe!"

"You're lucky you only broke one," Torin told him, standing. Huilin had been carrying one of the med kits, but he was still on the far platform. He—or he and Frii—had cut a section free near the hatch and, standing on the handrail, he was tall enough to make sure any other bugs trying that route would find an unpleasant welcome. The other kit . . . "Dursinski!"

"Right here, Staff."

"Werst's broken a toe."

"That's what he gets for not landing on his head." But she was on her knees with the med kit out before she'd finished talking.

"If there's one broken . . ."

"Yeah, yeah, I'll check the others."

The bug was next. Harrop poked it with a boot as she approached. "Not that I'm an expert on these things, Staff, but I'm pretty sure it . . ."

"She."

"What?"

When you forget the enemy is a person, you react to their weapons not them. That's dangerous. The little we know suggests the bugs are female. Not the time for a lecture, so Torin merely repeated, "She."

"Okay. I'm pretty sure *she* was dead before *she* hit the deck. Werst did a lot of MDC damage on the lower thorax. That windmilling as she fell was a last hurrah. She could have finished us if she'd dropped three or four grenades." He pushed back his helmet and glanced toward Guimond's body. "Why do you figure she only dropped one?"

"Maybe they thought the ship would endure one

grenade but not two. Maybe, it's a bug honor thing, strip off your armor . . ."

"She was on a piece of armor."

"Yeah, but she wasn't in it. Maybe you win points by stripping down and dropping a grenade on the enemy—this *is* the second time they've tried it."

"Seems to be a bit of a suicide mission."

"That might be the point." Torin shrugged, suddenly not so much tired as weary. "Maybe they've had budget cuts back home and they can only afford one grenade each."

"Fukking budget cuts," Harrop grunted. "So what do we do with her?"

"Leave her. If her people want the body, they know where it is. Take her weapon, though. R&D'll want it."

"Give me a break, Staff, it's covered in bug guts!"

"Welcome to another glorious day in the Corps, Corporal Harrop."

And, finally, Guimond.

Welcome to another glorious day in the Corps.

She pushed past the wailing Katrien and dropped to one knee through the cloud of shed fur. Fortunately for them, they expressed their grief at a lower decibel level than regular conversation. Nivry had turned Guimond over, still had one hand on his shoulder. His combats had contained the explosion although the force of it had collapsed his chest and forced blood from every visible pore. The blue of his eyes was strangely untouched amidst all the red. *And isn't that a fukking cliché.*

"If he'd had his vest done up . . ." Nivry murmured.

Torin shook her head. "It wouldn't have mattered."

Small fingers dug into her shoulders. "You are not going to him immediately! You are letting him die!"

"He was dead the moment he grabbed the grenade from your hands," Torin told the reporter bluntly as someone, she neither knew nor cared who, pulled her away.

The ring of Marines split to let Werst limp in to Guimond's side.

"The *serley* bastard's still smiling," he grunted.

Which seemed like as good an epitaph as any. Torin brushed Guimond's eyes closed, rocked back, and slid her hand into an inner pocket in his vest. The body bags were a smarter fabric than the stretchers and, unfolded, held what amounted to one massive MDC. Even given Guimond's weight, it took only moments to get the body into the bag. Torin wiped the blood off her thumb and ran it down the seal. *We're just too fukking good at this.*

She sighed deeply and stood.

"We will not forget. We will not fail you."

"Fraishin sha aren. Valynk sha haren."

Although Heer was the ranking Krai, no one was surprised when Werst spoke. *"Kal danic dir kadir."* Leaning on Heer's shoulder, he bit a small piece from the back of his forearm. *"Kri ta chrikdan."*

The bag stiffened, then flattened.

Torin bent, picked up the tiny canister of ash, closed her fingers around it, and looked down at her sleeve. From the moment the grenade had fallen until the moment she could hold Private First Class August Guimond in the palm of her hand—seventeen minutes, twenty-three seconds. Bracing herself against the weight, she slipped the canister into her vest, then bent and picked up Guimond's pack. "All right, people, let's haul ass to that air lock."

"This are it? So efficient you are dealing with death! You are not care . . ."

Torin had a fair indication of what her expression must have been when Ryder stepped between her and the Katrien.

"Let it go, Torin. Presit doesn't mean what she's saying. She's grieving."

She could feel the Marines behind her. "And we're not?"

"I didn't say that."

They locked eyes. Torin looked away first, making it quite clear she conceded *his* point, not the Katrien's.

A short choppy wave got the march moving, Nivry, Werst, Johnston, and Heer carrying the captain, Presit and Gytha, clinging so closely to each other fur merged between them, *Harveer* Niirantapajee, whose visible scales had turned a yellow-gray, Orla and Ryder carrying Tsui, Jynett, Dursinski, and Harrop bringing up the rear. Torin moved along the line between the two corporals, her gaze never resting for more than a moment in one place. The bugs had proved they were resourceful, the ship had proved it was not to be trusted; she had a lot to watch for.

She reached the metal stairs just after Werst, let the two Katrien pass, caught the *harveer* as she stumbled stepping onto the lowest tread.

"Can you make it?"

"Do I have a choice?"

"I can have someone carry you."

"No," she snapped, fingers hooked around the handrail, both feet placed carefully on one step before she tried the next. "Your lot are carrying enough."

It might have been sympathy, but it might as easily have been criticism—neither tone nor facial features gave Torin any indication of which. Empty air where Guimond should have been passed next, then Orla and Tsui's stretcher. She beckoned Jynett forward to take one of Orla's handles and moved into place beside Ryder herself. Until she noticed the di'Taykans' smirks, it didn't even occur to her it would have made more sense to do it the other way.

On the other hand, di'Taykans were known to smirk at weather reports, so fuk it.

Ryder looked from one Marine to the other. All four were wearing similar blank expressions. He'd seen men die before but he'd never seen a return to business-as-usual quite so quickly. Made sense, he supposed. *Can't have a war stop to acknowledge every new dead guy; damn thing'd never end.*

And he supposed the four Marines around him, Torin particularly, had had a lot of practice carrying on with big empty holes where people used to be.

He hadn't.

"Did he have any family?"

At that moment, *he* could only mean one person.

"His parents run an import/export business off New Horizon." Torin would be writing them a letter when she got the rest of the team safely back to the *Berganitan*. Another one of Captain Travik's jobs she'd be doing.

"He has a younger brother who's studying to be a teacher," Orla offered in the pause.

"People said his mother must've spent her whole pregnancy in the centrifuge," Jynett said, grinning. "No one could believe he was station born."

"Big boy."

"Mmmm."

This time the smirks were closer to satisfied smiles.

"He had this joke," Tsui snickered, hanging white-knuckled onto the sides of the stretcher as it rose up another step. "How many dirtballs does it take to screw in a lightbulb? Dirtballs don't screw in lightbulbs, they screw in gravity wells."

"What's a lightbulb?" Orla wondered.

"Hey, I never said it was a good joke. It was just his."

"He was going to re-sign at the end of his three years. He said he was happy in the Corps."

"He was happy cleaning the crappers."

"He was always happy."

Struggling to keep the stretcher level as they reached the top platform, Ryder shook his head. "You guys only knew him for a week."

"No." Torin waited until Ryder had hold of both handles, then she stepped away. "We knew him his whole life."

"Captain Carveg!" Face flushed, General Morris pounded into C3 and up to the captain's station, gripping the edge of the console with beefy fingers. "What's taking so damned long to launch that next shuttle? I ask your people a simple question and they shoot me a line of crap about constructing new defense systems. If I had a couple of Marine pilots here . . ."

"You'd be welcome to risk their lives in whatever way you pleased. But you don't. You have Navy pilots, my pilots, and before I tell them to launch, I'm going to see to it they have a fighting chance." She frowned down at the left screen. "Lieutenant, rotate B section of the grid twenty percent and run the simulation again."

"Aye, aye, Captain."

A satisfied nod and then she glanced up at the general. "Besides, General, this is the last STS shuttle we have and we thought you might like it to actually arrive at the air lock."

"What do you mean, it's the last shuttle you have?"

"Under normal circumstances, we carry four, but Mr. Ryder's *Promise* is using one of the bays. We've lost two, one at the first air lock, one on the way to the second. We have one shuttle remaining. It's not that difficult, General." A flick of her wrist turned a screen toward him. "Now that we know what we're up against, we can protect ourselves. We've deployed two dozen linked drones to fly in a defensive pattern round the shuttle, half a kilometer out. All six of those missile/fighters could impact simultaneously with minimal effect and they could keep doing it at thirteen-minute intervals all the way to Big Yellow and back."

"Why thirteen minutes?"

"That's the maximum time the drones need to reboot. It takes the missiles twelve minutes to cover the distance between their own launch tubes and Big Yellow, so unless they're going to throw a steady line of those things, we've got it covered."

"And at the air lock? Which seems to be inside your thirteen-minute maximum?"

"They won't blow the air lock, they need it to get their own people off. And before you ask, they need to get their own people off because they've got the only information about Big Yellow. I'm betting the Others can no more scan it than we can."

The general's eyes narrowed. "Based on what?"

"Based on them being as dead in the water as we are."

"Then what about their regular fighters? Couldn't they shoot out the drones?"

She wouldn't have minded so much if she'd

thought he was asking for information, but his whole bearing insisted he was asking to find fault. It had been years since she'd wanted to bite someone this badly. "They could, General, but we'll have Jades out there stopping them."

"All right. Fine. Good work." He rearranged his features into an expression resembling composure, clasped his hands behind him, and rocked back on his heels. "But when do you launch, Captain; that's the question."

"Flight Commander?"

"Ready to launch now, Captain."

Her lips curled off her teeth in a Human approximation of a smile. General Morris should know what it really meant. "We're ready to launch now, General. Flight Commander, launch fighters, launch shuttle, deploy defensive drones."

"Aye, aye, Captain. Fighters away. Shuttle . . ." The pause went on just a little too long.

"Flight Commander?"

He raised his hand, listened intently for another long moment, then slid one side of the headphones back. "The shuttle controls are unresponsive, Captain."

"Unresponsive?"

"Yes, ma'am. Crews are running diagnostics now, but . . ."

"But you expect they have the same problem the engines have?"

"Yes, ma'am."

"What?" General Morris glared from one to the other, his face beginning to flush again. "What's wrong?"

"Big Yellow is fukking us around again. The shuttle will no more launch than the main thrusters will fire."

Arms folded, the general put himself squarely in

Captain Carveg's line of sight. "You're taking this very calmly."

Captain Carveg glared up at him, lips curled. "Trust me, General, if screaming and biting would do any good, I'd be screaming and biting. Engineering's been working all hands since the beginning, but nothing's changed. If that *serley* ship's frozen the launch controls, that shuttle's not going anywhere."

"These things don't have a manual override?"

"What?" she snorted. "A big crank to open the launch door and some greased logs to help roll the shuttle out into space? No, the only manual override these things have involves pushing an actual sequence start switch instead of sitting back and letting the computer do it." She ran one hand back over her scalp. "Not that a big crank and greased logs aren't looking good right now."

"Captain! Buoy picking up an energy spike. The Others are opening . . ." His voice trailed off as he peered down at his screens.

"Opening, Lieutenant?"

"Nothing, ma'am. But there was a spike."

"The Others attempted to launch another shuttle, and Big Yellow shut them down, too."

"There's, uh, no way to know that, ma'am."

"We'll know if they never launch another shuttle. General Morris, you're going to want to talk to your Marines in private. Do you need someone to take you to Communications?"

"No. I can find my way."

"I'll have the comm officer begin trying to get through now. He should have contact by the time you arrive." The edge of the forward screen creaked, and she reluctantly loosened her grip. "Tell them this is a temporary setback. I'm not giving up."

"You'll go get them yourself?"

"If I have to."

"Captain! The Others are launching more fighters."

"Match them ship for ship, Flight Commander."

"Aye, aye, Captain."

She glared down at the screens, at the image fed from the buoy. Knowing it was foolish to put motivations on the movements of fighters two hundred and thirty-six kilometers away, something in how they were being spit out of the launch bays gave the impression that someone inside was intensely pissed off. "And I know exactly how you feel," she growled.

"What do you mean, she's not ready?"

Chief Graham tossed a tester down to the Krai working inside the Jade and turned, one hand gripping the edge of the open panel. "What I mean, Lieutenant Commander Sibley, is that we're replacing all your port thrusters, plus all the couplings, rebooting your whole goddamned propulsion system, and hopefully convincing your new thrusters to fire when you want them to and turn off when you don't."

"Chief, the squadron's going back out."

"And until your ride's fixed, you're not."

Hands deep in the pockets of his flight suit, Sibley stared at the parts of his Jade spread out on the mech deck. "How long?"

"That depends, sir." Dark brows drew in. "How long do you plan on standing here taking up my time?"

"Well?" Shylin fell into step beside him as Sibley came out into the passage. "How long?"

"Would you believe eight inches?"

"No."

"As big as a baby's arm?"

"Sib."

"Chief says it'll be done when it's done."

"Did you tell him the rest of the squadron's going out?"

"He knows."

"Did you pull rank?"

"On a chief warrant officer?" They'd reached the link, and he slapped the call button. "Do I look suicidal?"

FOURTEEN

"THIS makes no spatial sense."

"This whole day's made no sense," Torin reminded the engineer. "Not spatially, not any other 'ly' you care to suggest. What's the specific nonsense this time?"

"The air lock opens out into space. This," Johnston rapped his knuckles against the pale gray bulkhead, "is the hull. Except that the air lock is on the belly of the beast, so this," he stomped on the deck, "should be the hull. Except that the room where Guimond bought it is a level below. We came up a flight of stairs to get here."

"Yeah, I remember. What's your point, Johnston?"

"My point, Staff, is that this isn't right."

"Neither was the window in the wardroom. Hell, neither was the wardroom. Is this a working air lock?"

"As far as we can tell."

"Then don't sweat the weirdness, Lance Corporal Johnston. Can you get it open?"

"Me? No. But the *harveer* seems pretty confident. She worked with Dr. Hodges on the program that opened the first air lock, and she says the minimal readings she can take here are exactly—to the decimal point—the same. All she has to do is reproduce the codes on her slate and then use her filament probe to interface with the lock."

"*All* she has to do?" Torin glanced down at the elderly Niln, oblivious to the discussion going on above her head as she worked. "She has to get a Confederation slate to interface with an unknown alien technology. I can't even get this year's slate to interface with last year's desk." She clapped him lightly on the shoulder as she left. Tsui was resting comfortably, but Captain Travik's life signs were slipping. He hadn't regained consciousness since the switchbacks, and Torin had a strong feeling he never would.

Keep the captain alive. Make him look like a hero. She'd pretty much screwed the pooch on both mission objectives. General Morris wasn't going to be too happy with her.

General Morris can kiss my noncommissioned ass.

August Guimond was worth a dozen Captain Traviks.

The two Katrien were slumped against the wall in an exhausted heap. At first Torin thought they had their eyes closed against the light, then she realized they were sleeping, the edges of their blended ruffs rising and falling. As she watched, Presit whimpered. Without waking, Gytha combed at her fur until she settled. No surprise they were tired, they'd now been up and at a high stress level for about twenty-three straight hours.

Poor little thi . . . Torin cut the thought off short. They were not poor little things, they were adult members of a sentient species both of whom had considerably more formal education than she did. *And if even* I'm *falling into the cute furry darlings trap, it's no wonder they get away with being so obnoxious.*

Although in all honesty, Gytha was a sweetheart

and Presit wasn't any more obnoxious than any other reporter Torin'd had the misfortune to meet.

You're doing it again.

If the shuttle wasn't there in half an hour, she was taking one of the three sums provided to sergeants and above. She'd need a clear head if the bugs attacked and fuzzy thoughts about the Katrien indicated anything but.

Leaving the civilians, Torin moved out to check the perimeter. Emptying out the remaining food and water, the ropes and the med kits, they'd snapped all the packs together into two barricades three packs wide and two high coming out from both bulkheads twenty meters down the passage from the air lock. Made of the same fabric as the combats, they were of small but psychologically necessary protection. Harrop and Dursinski had pulled the watch. The hatch leading back to the tank room had been welded shut.

Laser charges were holding; MDCs were nearly spent.

Ryder sat, back to a bulkhead, talking quietly with Orla and Huilin. Given they were di'Taykan who'd been forced to go twenty-three whole hours without sex, Torin could guess the content of their conversation.

Directly across from the air lock, Heer was patting the wall with one hand, and holding his slate up to his face with the other. "There's something here," he said when Torin asked. "The *Harveer* copied one of her programs to my slate and had me running auxiliary scans around the lock. When I turned with the scan still running, I got one strange reading off this wall."

"A *strange* reading? What would you consider a normal reading on this ship?"

"Not strange in that way, Staff. Strange in that it resembled a piece of the code defining the air lock."

The section of wall looked as gray and blank as any on the ship. "It can't be a second air lock." She pointed across the passage. "Not if that's the hull."

"I don't think it's a second lock, I think it's a . . ."

A two-meter-by-a-meter-and-a-half piece of the bulkhead slid sideways. Behind it was a small access tunnel and a ladder leading down.

Heer looked up at Torin and grinned. "I think it's an access tunnel."

"And one without a bug in it. Nice change." She dropped a perimeter pin. It stuck to the deck as it landed and registered no movement on the lower level. "Spatially, this ought to make Johnston happy."

"Staff?"

"Never mind." A half-turn checked out the available Marines. "Orla, Huilin, got a job for you."

Ryder shot her an indecipherable glance which she ignored. Not everything was about him. In fact, not much of anything was about him.

"Staff, Orla. You've got to see this."

"On my way."

The lower level had four hatches and four control panels built into the bulkhead defined as the hull by the air lock up above. "Escape pods?"

"Well, they're not like any we've ever seen, but it's our best guess. Look." Orla pressed her hand against one of the hatches and a section twelve centimeters by eight cleared.

Torin leaned forward, staring through the window into a gray padded interior. It looked like no escape pod she'd ever seen either, but—in a weird way—it looked like all of them. They could probably fit both

Katrien in it with no difficulty, but of the larger species there'd be room only for two di'Taykan and their total lack of issues concerning personal space. To get two Humans or two Krai into them, they'd have to be under heavy fire with no other chance of survival. In Torin's experience, no other chance of survival settled *issues* pretty damned quick.

Given the way the last twenty-plus hours had gone, too few escape pods to save all her people were high on the list of things she didn't want to see. The one thing she knew for certain was that Big Yellow had an agenda, and this didn't look good.

"Should we get the *Harveer* and see if she can open them, Staff? Just in case?"

"No, not right now. She's still working on the lock and after that, I'd like her to have her rest a bit before she has to face a vertical ladder. She's old, and it's been a long day. And, Huilin, put your goddamned helmet on."

He sighed deeply but obeyed. "It doesn't fit under the HE's helmet, Staff."

"When you've got the HE's helmet on, you can take your combat gear off, but not before."

"We going to guard these things, so the bugs don't get them?"

"No, the air lock's more important. They try to rush us and we'll need all weapons. We'll set 2Ps at twenty meters both directions keyed to my pin at the foot of the shaft. The bugs show up, we'll know it."

"I'm out of pins, Staff."

"And this is my last."

"All right, hang on." She flipped her mike. "Heer, drop a perimeter pin down the shaft."

"You not sure you're moving, Staff?"

"Just do it."

Nearly out of 2Ps, nearly out of MDCs. If the shuttle didn't get there soon they'd be out everything but smart-ass remarks.

"The new thrusters are DK-7s, your old ones are sixes. The new ones are a fraction of a second more responsive, try to remember that."

Sibley sealed his flight suit and grinned up at Chief Graham. "It's on my list and I'm checking it twice."

"A fraction of a second means something at the speeds you're traveling."

"I know that, Chief."

"I should be replacing *all* the sixes with sevens, but for some reason the FC wants to give you another chance to get your ass shot off."

"Well, you know what they say, ass not what you can do for the Confederation."

The chief sighed and folded his arms over a barrel chest. "No one says that, sir."

"I just did." Sibley slapped the hatch release and motioned Shylin ahead of him into the docking bay, continuing the gesture and turning it into a jaunty wave back at the chief.

"Try to bring your ride back in one piece this time," Graham growled as the hatch closed.

Because if the Jades came back in one piece, so did the crews flying them.

"Think we can catch the squadron, Sib?"

His fingers danced over the thruster pad. "As easy as catching crabs on shore leave."

"And thank you for that image."

The rest of Black Star Squadron were nearly under the belly of the alien ship, having been sent to guard the air lock.

"Why would the Others destroy the air lock?" Shylin muttered, eyes locked on her tracking screens. "They want to use it, too."

"Why did the Others invade in the first place? Why do the H'san and the Mictok keep getting themselves blown to ratshit attempting a diplomatic end to the war? Why did I get that tattoo on my ass? Answer these and other skill testing questions, and you've solved the secrets of the universe."

"Just how many of those stim sticks did you have?"

"Not enough. Looks like the rest of the team's seeing some action up close and personal."

An enemy squadron had joined the Black Stars outside the air lock. Maneuvering under the four-kilometer breadth of the ship, both sides tried for a clean target lock that would keep them from blowing up their own fighters.

"Sib! Unfriendly, starboard, four o'clock!"

"Got her. Moving to engage. She's not reading us yet."

"Target locked and . . . she's firing!"

A pair of missiles streaked out from the enemy fighter.

"Taking evasive action!"

"She's not firing at us."

Both missiles raced toward the fight under Big Yellow.

And then she fired again and there were four.

"Fuk! She's got as much chance of hitting her guys as ours! Can you get them?"

Each missile split into three smaller warheads.

"What, all *twelve*?"

"Black Group, this is *Black Seven*! Disengage! Incoming ordnance! Repeat, incoming ordnance! Bugs are firing into melee."

"Black Seven, *this is* Black Leader. *Bugs can't be firing into melee; they'll hit their own people."*

"They don't care, Skipper! You've got a dozen little bangers moving in fast. Get out of there, now!"

"Black Group, this is Black Leader. *You heard the man! Move."*

"Must've looked out his fukking window," Sibley muttered.

"Evasive action, Sib. This time she's aiming at *us*!"

By the time they straightened out, most of the squadron had cleared out of the blast zone.

"Boom Boom! Disengage!"

"Don't tell me, tell the bu . . ."

Something slammed into the hull and bounced. The double impact filled the passage with sound. The Katrien woke shrieking. Fingers slid under trigger guards as bennys rose looking for an enemy.

"What the fuk was that?" Werst demanded when the sound faded.

All eyes turned to Torin. "That was opportunity knocking." She shoved the last empty coffee pouch into her pack. "You didn't answer, so it's buggered off to find someone who appreciates it."

"Oh, I'll fukkin' appreciate it," Werst growled.

"And would the universe end if you just told them you didn't know?" Ryder asked under cover of the snickering.

Torin stared at him for a long moment. "Theirs would," she said at last.

* * *

"We only lost one of the Jades, Captain. *Black Star Eight*."

Captain Carveg sighed deeply and drummed her fingers against the edge of the screen. "Good thing Lieutenant Commander Sibley was where he was when he was."

"Yes, ma'am."

"And the enemy fighters?"

"One of the enemy fighters was destroyed with *Black Eight*. Another took damage but got clear."

"So they can also thank Lieutenant Commander Sibley." She looked down at her fingers as though she didn't recognize them and forced them to still. "What did they think they were doing?"

Those of the C3 crew who could look up from their screens, exchanged uncertain glances.

"Risking collateral damage to win," a lieutenant commander offered when the continuing silence seemed to indicate it hadn't been a rhetorical question.

"Win what?" the captain demanded. "They destroy some magic number of our fighters and get their engines back? Have they got information about Big Yellow that we don't? This makes no *serley* sense!"

"This whole war makes no more sense than a H'san opera."

Captain Carveg spun around in her chair and glared at the general. He was smiling, and she had to work very hard at not taking it personally. "Have you spoken to your people, sir?"

"No. I had an idea." When he paused, the room paused with him. "The *Promise*. The CSO's ship." When no one seemed enthused, he continued more forcefully. "It's using up one of your shuttle bays, I say we use it to get my Marines. Hell, we'll use it to get Ryder, so he'll certainly have no grounds for complaint." Brows drawing in, his smile faded as he took a closer look at her face. "What? You've got to have pilots left; how hard can it be to fly?"

"Flying it isn't the problem, General." *And thank you for that sensitive assessment of my flight crew.* "Craig Ryder's got his ship locked down so tight we might not even be able to break the cipher to get the air lock open. And, if we'could get in, preliminary investigation suggests we'll blow the engines if we try to start them without his code."

"You've had your people working on it."

It wasn't exactly a question, but since he seemed to resent the preempting of his idea, and the last thing she needed on top of everything else was a sulky general, she said only, "Yes."

"So have your ship override his system! Goddamn it, Captain, you're sitting on a Confederation destroyer—use it!"

"Ignoring for the moment, General, that you do not give orders concerning my ship while on *my* ship, the *Promise* is not hooked up to the *Berganitan*."

"Why the hell not?"

She spun her chair around to face him full on and got to her feet, the dais giving her enough height to look him in the eye. "Why the hell should it be? I certainly didn't anticipate having to use it and, frankly, sir, if *you* did, I wish you'd told me back when it would have done some *serley* good!"

"Standard Operating Procedures . . ."

"Do not cover civilian ships in military shuttle bays because civilian ships aren't permitted to use military shuttle bays." She drew in a deep breath and slowly released it. "If there's any way we can use the *Promise*—and my people are continuing to work on it—we will. I no more want to leave those Marines there than you do. And believe me, sir, it's not because I give a fuk about what the Krai in Parliament will say about the loss of Captain Travik."

"I believe you, Captain Carveg."

Something had occurred to him. He couldn't possible be looking so *serley* happy because she'd thrown in a *sir.*

"And now, if your communications officer will see about raising Staff Sergeant Kerr, I'll see what I can do about having her get those codes from Mr. Ryder.

"Well?"

Ryder shook his head. "The air lock and the control panel both need a retina scan as well as the codes."

"Yours?"

"No, my mother's. I keep her left eye in a jar under my bunk. You know, you ought to bottle that look, you could sell it to weapons manufacturers."

"Ryder."

"Yeah, mine." He rubbed a hand over his face. "I'm sorry. I'm tired."

"Your mother's eye would be more useful," Torin muttered, and passed the bad news on to General Morris.

We'll keep working on it, Staff Sergeant. There has to be someone on this ship who can bypass a civilian security system.

Ressk's voice rose out of memory. *"You know there isn't a sys-op I can't get into. I could be useful on this kind of a mission."*

Except he'd be trapped on Big Yellow with the rest of the team.

Staff Sergeant Kerr?

"Sorry, sir. I was trying to think of a way to get Ryder's eye to you."

Yes. Well. How's Captain Travik?

The urge to ask "Who the fuk cares?" was intense. "He's alive, sir."

Good. We'll let you know if anything changes at this end. Don't worry, Staff Sergeant, I have complete faith in your ability to maintain discipline under these trying circumstances.

"Yes, sir." Torin tongued off her implant and lifted an eyebrow in Ryder's direction. "And they say I'm paranoid." No point in mentioning that his paranoia had just got them killed; he knew it. She could see the realization on his face. "It's not your fault; you couldn't have anticipated this when you locked up."

He shrugged and a corner of his mouth curled up in a self-mocking smile. "I just don't like people touching my stuff."

"Who does."

"Staff, we got bugs!"

"On my way." She hurried down the passage to the rhythm of weapons' fire, wondering why the perimeter pins they'd left at the corner hadn't given them more warning. "Frii."

He glanced up as she passed.

"What the hell are you singing?"

"It's di'Taykan electro pop, Staff."

"Well, pop it back where you found it."

He grinned. "It sounds better with the music."

"Let's hope." She dropped behind the left barricade with Harrop. "Hold your fire until you're sure you can hit them," she ordered, loud enough to be heard by Dursinski as well. "We're going to need more than bad language to stop them when they make their try for the air lock."

"So far they're just keeping our heads down," Harrop told her, checking the charge on his benny. "Letting us know they're there."

"How many?"

"Hard to say but two definitely; one shooting high, one low."

"They took out the perimeter pin," Dursinski added. "We had no warning."

"They did or the ship did. It doesn't much matter." A sudden vision of a perimeter pin sinking into a previously solid deck flashed through Torin's head. Lifting her hand, she rocked forward onto the balls of her feet, wishing she could lift those as well.

"How long are we going to have to hold them, Staff?"

"Good question." Harrop shot her a questioning look and Torin switched to the group channel. "Listen up, people; Big Yellow has decided to prevent the *Berganitan* from launching her last shuttle. Which means they're going to have to come up with another way to get us off this thing. Which means, we'll be here a while yet."

"Goddamned Navy."

"I doubt they're happy about it either, Dursinski. Huilin, Orla; you two get up here and double our strength on the barricades. The rest of you, stay sharp."

"Staff, we got something going on back here, too."

"What is it, Nivry?" The other corporal was standing by the sealed hatch to the tank room. "We got bugs cutting through?"

"I can't tell."

Neither could Torin when she laid her hand against the hatch and felt the faint vibration. "Could be some kind of sonic cutter, I suppose. All we can do right now is keep an eye on it."

"Staff . . ."

"Captain Carveg told me she wasn't leaving without us," Torin said, answering the question Nivry didn't ask. "She'll find a way."

"Why do you think Big Yellow let one evac shuttle launch but not the other?"

"Probably took it that long to figure out how to jam the controls."

Or both ships only got one chance and they blew it. But although that felt more likely, she wasn't planning to say it out loud.

And who said they only got one chance?

"Mr. Ryder, leave the benny and come with me."

She walked past, assuming that he'd follow, and the strength of that assumption pulled him to his feet.

"They're escape pods," Ryder said, studying the interior.

"Yes, they are. And you're going to get in one, get to the *Berganitan,* get into your ship, then come back and get us."

He straightened so quickly, he had to reach out and steady himself against the hatch. "You're insane."

Torin folded her arms. "What makes you think so?"

"What makes me think so?" When she made it clear she was waiting for an answer, he sighed. "Okay, to begin, there's two stretchers, eleven standing Marines and three civilians—I have a one-man operation. You've seen the inside of my ship." One hand slapped his chest. "*I* barely fit inside."

"You're right, I saw inside your ship and there's plenty of room for the stretchers and the three civilians."

Which wasn't the problem and they both knew it, but they had a way to go before they needed to pick at psychological scabs.

"And the eleven standing Marines?"

"Grab enough HE suits from the *Berg* and we'll ride in the salvage pens."

Ryder stared at her for a moment. Then he spun on one heel, walked six paces out, spun again, walked six back. "Okay, I was just talking before, but you really are insane."

"It's one hundred and eighteen kilometers; a little under half an hour's travel time in an STS. From what I saw of the *Promise*, you should be able to do it in an hour. We'll be fine."

"No inertial dampers."

Torin shrugged. The space between Big Yellow and the *Berganitan* buzzed with enemy fighters; inertia would be the least of their problems. "You've got straps, don't you? To keep the salvage from crashing around? We'll strap in."

Six out, six back. He wiped his hands on his thighs. "All right, given that we've established your lack of sanity, what makes you think Big Yellow will allow me to launch? I could easily be locked down, just like the shuttle."

"Won't happen."

"What makes you so fukking sure? And, God help me, Torin, if you say it's your job to be sure, I won't be responsible for my actions."

"You won't be locked down because Big Yellow was in your head." She kept talking as he walked away, and back, and away. "Based on that visit, the intelligence behind this ship wouldn't assume for an instant that you'd do something like this. Even after you launch, it would never believe that you'd willingly share your cabin with five people. You could hook up to the air lock and open the doors and it would know that at the last minute, as the first tiny Katrien foot stepped into your space, you'd freak and run away."

And back. "How the hell do you know that?"

"That you'd freak and run away?"

He opened his mouth. Closed it. Finally said, "No. How do you know what Big Yellow believes?"

A partial smile. "Because that's what I'd believe if I'd gone into your head."

"But you don't believe it, or you wouldn't be suggesting I ride to the rescue." Six paces away, seven back. A step into her personal space. Not threatening, although Torin suspected that was how he'd intended it. "So what makes you think that I wouldn't have done it then but I'll do it now? I'm a civilian, remember. You can't order me into that padded coffin. You think I'll do it for you? Just because you're asking me to?"

"No." She locked her gaze on his and held it. He was standing so close she could feel his breath on her face. "Because I expect you to."

One corner of his mouth curved up in a mocking smile. "And you find people live up to your expectations?"

"Yes."

She meant it. It wasn't bullshit, it wasn't bravado. Ryder found himself searching her face for any doubt; for the tiniest indication that she didn't think he could pull this off.

All he saw was a frightening certainty. A complete faith. In him.

And he saw that she believed that would be enough.

"You know, you really have a fukking huge ego." Seven paces away, six back. "I mean, you expect me to change a basic, intrinsic part of who I am . . ." Six away, six back. ". . . of who I've been for years—based on the strength of your personality alone and the vague possibility that when all this is over . . ."

Protests trailed off as one of Torin's eyebrows slowly rose.

"Fine." He threw up his hands in surrender and turned to the nearest escape pod, ignoring the voice of reason that kept asking what the hell he thought he was doing. "Do you know how to operate these things?"

"Actually," she admitted, and he found himself wishing she'd smile like that more often, "I haven't the faintest goddamned idea."

Opening the pods turned out to be relatively simple.

"Fortunately," Heer muttered, peering at the pressure pad running across the bottom of the control panel, "it defeats the purpose of escape pods if they're too complicated to get into."

"And to operate?" Ryder demanded

"Usually you don't operate them. You just pop out and drift until someone rescues you, or you lock onto the nearest planet you can exist on."

"You mean live on."

"Nope." Heer punched a sequence into the pod's control panel and didn't elaborate.

Torin figured it was time she stepped in. "You'll be

picked up by one of the Jades and taken to the *Berganitan;* no drifting, no rescues, no planets."

He shook his head although what precisely he was denying remained unclear. "We don't even know if I can breathe in there."

"We'll know that as soon as Heer gets the hatch open. If you can't, you'll wear Huilin's HE suit."

"It'd never fit."

"Or you can hold your breath until they pick you up. Your choice." There'd be further argument; Torin could see it in Ryder's eyes, but Heer postponed it.

"Got it." Stepping aside, Heer pushed his thumb against the same place on the contact pad three times. With a wet, sucking noise, the walls around the hatch folded in. "Okay. Maybe not."

"Maybe not," Ryder repeated to Torin. "You hear that?"

"He'll figure it out. Won't you, Heer?"

"It's *chrick.*" He flashed Ryder a broad smile. "Trust me."

"Nice try, but I know what it means when you guys show teeth."

The wall had closed entirely over the hatch. A faint shudder vibrated through boot soles, and Torin thought she heard a distant pop.

"Command, this is *Black Seven;* there's something being extruded from Big Yellow not far from the air lock."

"Extruded, Black Seven?"

"Roger, Command. Extruded. Popped out like a big yellow zit." Sibley corkscrewed the Jade to avoid an enemy fighter and swung around for a closer look. "There's a section of hull suddenly rising up in a half circle a little less than two meters across at the point where it joins the . . . Shit! Shylin!"

"I see it." She counterfired to take out a PGM almost locked on their tail.

"B7, *does this half circle of hull appear to be a weapon?"*

He rolled his eyes. "It appears to be a half circle. That's it. Nothi . . . Hang on, it's still coming "

"B7, *we repeat, does it appear to be a weapon?"*

"Not unless they're setting up for a game of zero gee dodgeball."

"Say again, B7."

When the round section of hull remained attached to the ship with only a thin umbilical cord, the yellow coating suddenly slid off a gray sphere and remerged with the ship. Floating freely, the sphere moved slowly out into space.

"It could be a mine," Shylin said thoughtfully. "I'm reading energy but no life signs."

"I need better than a 'could be,' Shy."

"Then get me closer."

They were moving in when an enemy fighter swooped in off their Y-axis and hit the sphere with two energy bolts at close range, destroying it.

There wasn't so much an explosion as a sudden brilliant absence of sphere.

"B7, *are you hit?"*

"That's a negative, Command." Blinking rapidly to clear his vision, tears running from eyes still seeing a full spectrum of spots, Sibley managed to match course with the enemy fighter although he had no idea how.

"Target locked."

"Let's blow up a bug for Boom Boom."

This time, the force of the explosion threw the debris field into the belly of the alien ship.

* * *

The impact was gentler than the last one had been, but there were more of them. The constant patter, patter of heavy items hitting the ship's hull almost sounded like rain.

Working on the second pod, Heer ignored it, but Ryder grabbed Torin's uninjured arm. "They blew it up."

"Sounds like."

"This may come as a surprise to you, but I don't want to die."

"No one does." She dropped her voice to match his. "But we all will unless we get off this ship. The bugs'll kill us quickly, or thirst will do it slowly, but we *will* die. You're our only chance."

"But no pressure, right? Torin, we don't even know who blew up the pod. It could have been the vacuum jockeys from the *Berganitan*."

"Yeah, it could have been, but that means they saw it and know it came from near our position. General Morris will contact me to find out what I know about it, and I'll make sure that our side, at least, doesn't blow you up."

"That's not very comforting."

Torin shrugged.

"This is where you tell me I don't *have* to go."

"Waste of breath; you had to go from the moment I made it clear you were our only hope. You have to go because you couldn't live with yourself if you didn't."

He stared at her for a long moment. "You actually believe that, don't you?"

Smiling, Torin shrugged.

One corner of his mouth twitched. Then the other. "You know," he said conversationally, "you're very good at your job."

"And which part of that job would you be referring to?"

"Inspiring the troops to get their collective asses blown off."

He was still holding her left arm just above the elbow and a deep breath would be enough to bring their bodies together.

Staff Sergeant Kerr?

Torin jerked back, pulling her arm from Ryder's grip, trying unsuccessfully not to feel like her father had just caught her making out on the couch. "Sir?" She mouthed, *General Morris,* at Ryder who seemed to be trying not to laugh. The bastard.

One of Captain Carveg's pilots has reported a sphere extruded from the ship near your position.

Extruded? "Yes; sir. It's an . . . General? General Morris? Sir?" The implant remained unresponsive.

"So the booster unit is gone?"

"Yes, Captain. Engulfed by the alien ship."

"Engulfed?" When the communications officer nodded, the captain sighed and rubbed a hand across the back of her neck. That wasn't good. "And we still don't know what that sphere was or if we can expect more of them."

"No, ma'am. We lost contact before the staff sergeant could pass on that information."

"But it could have been a mine?"

"Yes, ma'am."

She stared down at the screen where Big Yellow blotted out twenty kilometers of stars and tiny red and white lights zipping back and forth represented the fighters from both sides. "Mines are definitely just what we need floating around out there. Flight Commander?"

He shrugged, the movement worn down to almost nothing by the last few hours. "It might be smarter to blow them while they're still attached to the ship."

The captain sighed again. "It very well might."

"But you don't know *why* General Morris stopped transmitting."

"No, I don't." Her arms folded, Torin watched Ryder pace. "Maybe the *Berganitan* blew up. Maybe the galaxy got sucked into the ass end of a black hole, and we're all that's left. I do know that if we sit here with our thumbs in our mouths we *will* die, and I will *not* allow that. You give me a retina on a stick, and I'll get in the escape pod myself but otherwise . . ."

He stopped pacing in what had become a familiar position; face-to-face and too close for comfort. "I never said I wasn't going."

"Good."

"I wouldn't trust one of those ham-handed Navy pilots to fly the *Promise* anyway."

"Okay, this time, I've got it."

Torin turned gratefully toward her engineer. In another moment they were going to start smiling at each other again, and she honestly didn't think she was up to it. The subtext was rapidly becoming a distraction. "Show me."

Heer pushed his thumb against the contact pad three times.

"And how was that different from the last time?" she asked, one eyebrow rising as the pod's hatch sighed open.

"This time, I pressurized it." Arm stuck into the pod, he checked the readout on the sleeve. "Pod has the same atmosphere as the ship which had the same atmosphere as the shuttle—a compromise mix for all species present. Which means," he continued, removing his arm and turning to the CSO, "you won't freeze or asphyxiate before they blow you up."

"That's a big help," Ryder muttered.

"Hey, look at the bright side. If you'd been stuffed into a di'Taykan's HE suit you'd be humping the first sailor you saw at the end of the trip. Not necessarily a bad thing but . . ."

"Heer."

"Right." The Krai engineer twisted around until his feet were on the deck, both hands holding the upper lip of the opening, and his body arced back, allowing him to examine the pod without putting any weight inside. "There appears to be a self-contained air supply and a scrubber, but other than that, there're only two controls. Logically, the big button launches the pod, and the T-bar unlocks the hatch when you get where you're going."

"You're assuming one fuk of a lot."

"Not much choice." Heer straightened. "He can go any time, Staff."

Ryder looked from the pod to Torin. "You know, if you'd say, 'Don't go,' then I could say something like, 'A man has to do what a man has to do,' and leave a hero."

"Or there's always that retina on a stick option."

"I might have known she'd get all mushy on me," he muttered to Heer as he folded himself through the hatch. "It's not exactly roomy in here."

"You won't be in there long."

When he reached for the hatch, Torin was already there. She wanted to say something as she closed it but couldn't think of anything that wouldn't sound trite—he knew he was their only chance to live, he knew he might die—but she watched him through the window as the walls around the hatch folded in. And stood there until she heard the distant popping sound of the pod being extruded from the ship.

"Staff, we're getting a little more action from the bugs."

"On my way." Spinning around, she glared down at Heer. "What are you grinning about?"

"Not a thing, Staff Sergeant."

All the way up the ladder, Torin listened for pieces of an escape pod impacting against the hull.

FIFTEEN

BOUNCING against the padded interior of the pod, Ryder looked for straps, and couldn't find any. He didn't mind the bouncing, he worked in zero gee most of the time and, to save money, ran the artificial gravity generator in the *Promise* only enough to maintain muscle tone and bone mass. Considering he was floating out to an uncertain fate, as likely to be blown up by a vacuum jockey supposedly protecting his way of life as he was to reach the *Berganitan* and save the day, he had to admit he felt remarkably relaxed.

Probably because he was on his own.

Granted, Big Yellow was the size of most stations but deep down, he'd always known it was still a ship. He turned a slow somersault. He did better on his own. No big deal.

But the trip back . . .

". . . as the first tiny Katrien foot stepped into your space, you'd freak and run away."

The muscles across his shoulders knotted as tension returned.

Being blown up on the way to the *Berganitan* would almost be preferable.

Almost.

His fingers sank deep into the padding, and he felt something give.

"I think this definitely proves it," he muttered, pulling his hand away from the five impressions he'd gouged into the wall. "Some guys'll do anything to impress a girl."

And some girls were pretty damned hard to impress.

Torin threw herself up the last few rungs of the ladder and out onto the upper deck. "Talk to me, Harrop!"

"The good news is, they haven't thrown any ordnance. Either they're afraid they'll damage the lock, or they're out. Bad news, they're doing a lot more firing. I think they're getting ready for a charge."

"I agree. Heads up, people. Bugs incoming. The packs aren't much of a barrier, but we can't let them get by. Jynett, Frii, join the others at the barrier. Johnston, Werst, get the captain off his stretcher and add it to the barrier. Heer, help me with Tsui."

The injured Marine was up on his elbows fumbling for his returned benny.

Torin took a quick look into his eyes. His irises were so dark a brown it was difficult to tell, but his pupils appeared to be at a normal dilation. "Neural blockers working?"

"I hope so; I can't feel my whole fukkin' leg."

"Good." She grabbed one end of the stretcher and motioned Heer to the other. "Let's get him down by the tank room. He can guard the hatch."

"It's sealed!" Heer protested as they ran crouched over, trying to stay under stray energy bursts coming from the bugs.

"Now," Torin amended. They slid to a stop by Nivry and set the stretcher down. "Sitting or lying, Tsui?"

"Sitting."

She slipped her hands into his armpits. "Heer, get his legs. Mind the stump. Nivry, the stretcher. On three."

A quick glanced showed Johnston and Werst were being a lot less careful with Captain Travik. Johnston hoisted the top end, Werst the bottom, and they both kicked the stretcher clear. The captain didn't quite bounce as he hit the deck.

Torin sent Nivry forward with Tsui's stretcher.

"You hear anything coming through, you let me know!" she told him as Heer propped his stump up and he checked the charge on his benny. "You see anything, you shoot it *and* you let me know!"

His teeth were a brilliant white arc, slightly chipped on the right side. "You worry too much, Staff."

"Yeah, it's what I do. Heer . . ." She grabbed the engineer by the arm and dragged him to the edge of the open hatch leading to the lower level. "You and Johnston are in charge of the civilians." Three quick strides took her across the corridor, half a dozen shorter ones brought her back with the Katrien who clung silently to each other. As much as she'd come to hate the sound of their voices, the silence was disconcerting. Johnston crossed behind her, one arm half guiding, half carrying *Harveer* Niirantapajee.

"The bugs break through, you get them down below and into an escape pod."

"What if they come up from below?"

"If they could, they'd be there now, flanking us. No one charges a fixed position, even a piss poor one if they have an option. Once the pods are launched . . ."

"We're back up here to help kick bug butts."

Torin looked from the Human to the Krai and saw identical expressions. "Your choice," she told them.

"But don't spend your lives stupidly or you'll answer to me—if not in this life then the next."

"Staff Sergeant Kerr, I are not . . . are not . . ." Presit stared down toward the barricade, now stronger by the stretchers but still a fragile bulwark.

"It'll be okay." Torin pulled the reporter's attention back to her. "We do this for a living."

"I are not wanting to die."

"Well, I are not intending to."

Presit bristled at Torin's mocking tone and looked better than she had in hours.

Some people just prefer being annoyed. And annoying civilians seemed to be a big part of her job. "Stay low," Torin reminded the two Marines, as she turned. "The bugs seem fixated on this whole brain in the head thing and keep shooting high."

As she reached the barricade, a flurry of shots slapped into the packs and sizzled overhead.

"Here they come!"

"Command, this is *B7*. We have another extrusion out of Big Yellow."

"Roger, B7. *Is this second extrusion identical to the first?"*

"Shy?"

"Not exactly." The lieutenant bent over her screens, cadmium hair flicking back and forth. "But until you stop flinging us around, I won't be able to identify the difference."

He dropped the Jade fifteen meters, forty-five degrees to the Y-axis. "When I stop flinging us around, we go boom."

The yellow coating slid off the sphere and back into the ship.

"B7, we repeat, is the second extrusion identical to the first?"

"That's a good question, Command." Straight up. Full port thrusters for six seconds. "And as soon as we know, we'll let you know. Shy!"

"I've got her."

The bug fighter went spinning out of control and as the other fighters concentrated on getting out of her way, Sibley brought his Jade in for a tight swoop around the sphere.

"I'm reading life signs inside!"

"You catch that, Command?"

"Roger, B7. *What species?"*

"Insufficient data."

"Get the data!"

"Oh, yeah, easy for you to say," Sibley muttered, slipping his Jade under the arc of two incoming bugs. "It's getting a little crowded out here."

His maneuver threw one bug off enough that her shot merely skimmed the sphere.

"Oh, crap!" Ryder spit the words out through clenched teeth. His inner ear told him he was spinning and damned fast, too, given the pressure pushing him into the walls.

Sibley locked onto the tail of the second bug swinging into the attack and she broke it off before they could get a lock.

"Command, this is *B7*. I don't know who's inside, but the bugs don't seem to like them much."

"The bugs are shooting at the sphere?"

"Well, duh."

"B7, we didn't copy that last transmission."

Grinning, Sibley spun his Jade one-eighty to give

Shylin a clear shot at an enemy fighter. "I said, that's an affirmative. The bugs are shooting at the sphere."

"Lieutenant Commander Sibley, this is Captain Carveg."

"Now you're in for it," Shylin muttered.

"If the bugs want that sphere destroyed, I want it picked up and brought in."

"Aye, aye, Captain." He burned upper thrusters for three seconds, dropping straight down out of a missile lock. "Uh, got any ideas how we can do that without getting our asses burned?"

"B7, *this is* Red Mace One. *We're moving in to cover you."*

"Does that answer your question, Mr. Sibley?"

"Yes, ma'am."

Maneuvering over the sphere wasn't the problem. Canceling its spin, however, was a little trickier.

"Equal and opposite force?"

Shylin shook her head. "Given the way the first one went up, I wouldn't want to risk a shot."

"Okay, we extend an energy field, let it transfer momentum, and I correct our spin."

"We'll be sitting *rinchas* while we're spinning," Shylin reminded him. "I won't be able to get a shot off, and the Maces'll have our lives in their hands."

Sibley barely touched the starboard thrusters, then goosed portside to bring them into position. "What's the point of having friends if you can't take advantage of them? Right, *Red One*?"

"Don't worry about it, Shy. We'll keep you in one piece; your bastard pilot owes me money."

"Extending field . . ."

Double impact against opposite sides of the pod.

Ryder rubbed at a dribble of sweat running into his beard. All of a sudden, he desperately had to piss.

"Round and round and round she goes." Stars, bug fighters, Jades, and Big Yellow circled by; once, twice, three times. Sibley's fingers danced over the controls canceling the spin without sending them around the other way. "Where she stops nobody knows—but me."

"*Ablin gon savit,*" Shylin muttered as they slowed. "You actually figured out how to fly this thing."

They hung motionless in space for a moment, then he locked onto the *Berganitan*'s coordinates and hit the thrusters.

"*Red One*, this is *B7*. I'm taking my ball, and I'm going home."

"*Roger,* B7. *We have you covered.*"

MDCs gone, Torin switched to laser and dove out from behind the barricade under the reaching arms of the incoming bug. Slicing through the joint in the armor where the thorax joined the abdomen, she hit the deck, rolled, slid, and kicked out hard. To her surprise, the top half of the bug separated from the bottom half. As she rose to her knees, dripping with bug blood and stinking of cinnamon, Dursinski and Huilin took out the pieces.

The sudden silence made her ears ring.

The bugs had made it almost all the way to the Marine position. They'd been advancing behind their own dead.

"Good thing they're so explosive," Torin muttered, crawling back behind the barricade. "And I gotta say *that's* an observation I never thought I'd make."

When she went to stand, an energy bolt sizzled

past her right ear, close enough so her PCU reacted with a painful burst of static.

"They've retreated, but they're not giving up."

Torin dropped to a crouch. "I noticed. Anyone have numbers on remaining unfriendlies?"

Dursinski scratched at the chemical neutralizer dribbling down her cheek. "I saw six go back."

"Yeah, six." Werst grunted, ridges flared. "And there's nine maybe ten bodies."

Fifteen, maybe sixteen. Half of the thirty they'd faced in the garden. And if the bugs were willing to keep spending lives, they weren't going to last through many more charges. And there would be more charges, she was certain of that. Once the bugs regrouped, they'd try again.

"Stay sharp, people."

No need to tell them to consolidate the dregs of their ammo into a single power unit. No need to tell them to stay sharp either, but they needed her to say something.

Huilin had Frii tucked into the crease between bulkhead and deck. Blood stained the chest of the younger di'Taykan's combats almost black.

"How is he?"

Huilin shrugged. "I've got a tube in and he's breathing okay, but this is way beyond first aid. When we get back to the *Berganitan* they're going to have to rebuild the whole front of his throat."

He looked up at her as he said it and Torin read the challenge in his eyes.

"We'll get back to the *Berganitan*," she told him, her fingers wrapping around Frii's for a moment. "You have my word on it."

"All of us?"

She let Frii's limp hand slide from hers and fought

the urge to touch Guimond's cylinder. "All of us," she answered grimly.

The captain's vitals were unchanged.

The Katrien were talking again, a series of high-pitched, overlapping short shrieks and howls. It could have been Katrien hysterics. It sounded like Katrien conversation. The *harveer* appeared to be in shock, her leg joints drawn up against her stomach, motionless but for the trembling in the tip of her tail. There wasn't any comfort Torin could offer, so she moved on.

Tsui licked his lips as she crouched beside him. "I'm having an intense craving for a cinnamon donut."

"Yeah?" Torin scraped a congealed bit of bug off her thigh with her thumbnail. "I, personally, may never eat French toast again. You said the vibration's getting stronger?"

"That was a while ago, Staff."

"I was busy." Palm pressed against the hatch, she frowned. "There's a throbbing under the vibration."

"Yes, there is." Tsui frowned. "It seems familiar. It's like a sound I've heard a thousand times, but I can't put my finger on what it is."

"It *is* a sound you've heard a thousand times."

And it was the reason the bugs were so riled up and ready to die.

Big Yellow had started up its engines.

"B7, this is Command. Cut fields and release the sphere into shuttle bay one."

"Roger, Command. Shuttle bay one, it is. If we get there in one piece," he added under his breath. "What the hell's bugging the bugs?"

The one hundred and eighteen kilometers back from Big Yellow had nearly doubled. In spite of his escort, Sibley had needed to use every flying trick he had to keep from being destroyed. Normally, the bugs would have pulled back when they came within range of the *Berganitan*'s guns, but the mass of Jades and fighters were so intermixed, the big guns were useless.

"Now would be the time for a few Jades to peel off and take out the Others' ship," Shylin noted grimly.

"And which of our escort would you like to lose?" Sibley asked her. "I, myself, would just as soon not get my ass blown off."

Up ahead, the shuttle bay doors were opening.

"I guess as long as they're not launching a rescue mission, Big Yellow's willing to release control. *Red Leader,* this is *B7*; am flipping ninety degrees to release."

As the sphere seemed to have no propulsion system, the only way to get it into the *Berganitan* was to line it up on the doors, and give it a push—hard enough to get inside before one of the bugs got in a lucky shot, not so hard it was moving too fast for the emergency docking equipment.

As he began the flip, he caught sight of something out of the corner of one eye and trying for another look, cranked his head around so hard, he nearly self-inflicted more damage than the bugs had managed.

"Uh, Command, is that a big net?"

"Affirmative, B7.*"*

"You want me to toss this thing into a big net?"

"The item is too smooth for the docking clamps. Is it a problem?"

"Uh, negative, but I'm outside the foul line, so it's a three-point shot." He juiced the top thrusters, released the grapples and vectored away. The sphere continued along its original course. "And an object in motion will remain in motion unless acted upon by an equal or opposite force."

"Sib, are you all right?"

"Me?" A quick slip sideways took them out between *Red Three* and *Four.* "I'm having a ball."

"Captain, we have the sphere in the shuttle bay. Pressurizing now."

She surged up out of her chair. "Tell them I'm on my way."

"Aye, aye, Captain."

"Captain!" Lieutenant Potter's voice stopped her at the hatch. "Security reports General Morris and Lieutenant Stedrin on their way to the shuttle bay."

A little tired of having the general show up in C3 without warning, she'd had security tracking him. "Delay him," she snapped. "I don't want him there first."

Totally featureless and smoothly gray, the sphere hung in the net about a meter off the deck. Half a dozen technicians crowded around it with handheld scanners and portable science stations, and behind them an equal number of security personnel stood with weapons drawn.

"Can I assume proper quarantine procedures were followed?" Captain Carveg snorted, glancing around.

The senior science officer jumped at the sound of her voice and hurried over. "It's absolutely clean, Captain," he assured her. "Not so much as a micro on it. And, if we compare it to the preliminary reports of the science team on Big Yellow, it's the same combination of metals and polyhydroxide alcoholydes as the original corridor just inside the air lock."

"Then I suggest we don't use cutting tools on it."

"We weren't planning to, ma'am."

"Good." She walked forward until she stood a body-length away, security and science alike moving aside for her. "What's in it?"

"An excellent question."

The science officer jumped again as General Morris' comment boomed out and echoed around the shuttle bay.

"You might think about switching to decaf, Commander," the captain muttered as she turned.

If General Morris was annoyed she'd arrived first, he wasn't allowing it to show. He crossed quickly to her side, Lieutenant Stedrin behind his left shoulder, and stood rubbing his hands together expectantly. "Well, is it Captain Travik?"

The commander glanced from his captain to the general to his slate. "It's, uh, Human, ma'am. Sir."

The general smiled broadly. "No Human scientists survived, so it's got to be one of my Marines. Now, we'll find out what's happening. Might even be Staff Sergeant Kerr."

"The staff sergeant would never leave the Recon team, sir," Lieutenant Stedrin murmured, leaning toward the general's ear.

Captain Carveg's estimate of the lieutenant rose.

"Well, whoever it is, it's a Marine. Get it open, Commander."

"I'd be happy to, sir, but I don't know how."

With the return of gravity came the unwelcome realization that the hatch was now on the bottom of the pod. Straddling it, Ryder stared down at the T-bar. He had no way of knowing which ship he was on. If he'd been taken prisoner by the Others, being upside down was the least of his problems.

Unfortunately, there was only one sure way to find out.

He bent, took hold of the bar, and twisted it counterclockwise a hundred and eighty degrees. It snapped into place. Releasing it, he straightened.

A tech kneeling under the sphere threw herself backward. "Commander!"

"I see it." A dark crack now outlined an area about a meter square. "Filters, everyone. Captain."

"Thank you." As she slapped the disposable filter over her mouth and ridges, she turned to check the watching Marines. The lower half of both faces bore an unmistakable sheen. General Morris might have a knack for showing up and being a pain in the ass, but at least he came prepared. Although the odds were better Lieutenant Stedrin had come prepared.

The hatch sighed open.

Ryder stared down at a familiar square meter of deck. It looked exactly like the deck he'd parked the *Promise* on. *So I'm either on the* Berganitan, *or the North Fleetrin Shipyards really do have the lowest prices in the universe.*

He was probably no more than a meter and a half up. Less than his own height. So he jumped.

"You!"

Ryder moved out from under the sphere and straightened. "And g'day to you, too, General," he replied, adding, as the other man pushed past him to look up into the sphere, "You're shit out of luck if you think I brought friends."

"Nothing!"

"Told him," Ryder remarked conversationally to the area at large.

General Morris slapped the side of the sphere with enough force to start it swinging. "Why you?" he demanded.

Before Ryder could answer, Captain Carveg stepped forward, her expression suggesting she'd had about as much of General Morris as she could handle and was about ready to chew a piece out of him. "You're going back for them in the *Promise*, aren't you?"

He was safe and he was going back. He was out of his mind. "Yes, Captain, I am."

The first energy bolt in some minutes hit the packs, was partially absorbed by the fabric, arced over an area that had been previously fried, and fizzled out to nothing.

"When we get out of this, remind me to send a nice thank you note to the company that makes these packs," Harrop muttered, picking himself up off the deck.

"I hate to discourage good manners," Torin told him, "but I suspect the bugs are nearly out of juice. That shot had nothing behind it."

Dursinski sat slumped on the deck, head between her knees. "So, when they run out, do they give up or what?"

"What," Torin answered calmly. "A final flurry of shots to keep our heads down, then it's hand-to-hand."

"Hand-to-claw." Dursinski's lower lip went out. "That is so unfair."

"Claw-to-laser," Werst snarled.

She glanced down at her charge. "Yeah, and in thirty seconds when that runs dry?"

Werst snapped his teeth together with enough force so the sound jerked Huilin up out of sleep.

"Oh, sure. Easy for you. And then what? What if Ryder doesn't get back before Big Yellow finishes warming up? What if the ship takes off with us still in it? What then?"

Torin reached over and took the younger woman's chin between the thumb and forefinger of her left hand, lifting her head until they were eye to eye. "Then, we find the control room and learn to fly this thing. We turn it around. We bring it home."

"We can do that?"

"We're Marines. We can do whatever the fuk we put our minds to."

The packs jerked three times in quick succession and one of them started to smoke.

"It's your flurry of shots, Staff!"

"Marines! Incoming!"

"You want to put my Marines in your salvage . . ." Flushing, General Morris searched for the word, finally spitting out, "Enclosure?"

"Yeah, my enclosure; and we haven't got time to discuss it." It had been a long day, and he was pretty much running on pure adrenaline. In another minute he was going to shove the general out of his way. "Unless you can think of a better way to bring them home, I need eight HE suits and I need them twenty minutes ago."

"That's insane!"

"Look, I don't need your blessing, I just need the damned suits! Or a better idea." He paused pointedly, leaning in closer. "No? Fine." A half pivot, another officer. "Captain Carveg?"

"The Navy will supply you with as many suits as you need, Mr. Ryder."

"The Corps can look after its own, Captain. Lieutenant!"

"Sir." Lieutenant Stedrin pushed through the crowd of Naval researchers.

"Get Mr. Ryder those suits."

Power struggle. Use it wisely, Ryder thought. "Three di'Taykan, three Human, two Krai. Bring them to the *Promise.*"

Stedrin glanced at the general who, lips pressed into a thin line, nodded. He watched Stedrin's retreating back for a moment, then stepped back deliberately out of Ryder's way. Body language clearly saying, *You leave because I allow it.*

And he can just keep thinking that.

He was almost to the hatch when the general stopped him.

"Mr. Ryder, Captain Travik . . . ?"

"Is still unconscious," he said, turning and walking backward. "Which puts a limit on how much your pet gnome can fuk this up." Which was when he realized that referring to the captain by the derogatory description might not have been a good idea. He flashed Captain Carveg his most charming smile. "No offense."

She shrugged and the Krai around her relaxed. "None taken. I met him, remember? As it stands right now, we can still open the launch doors to let you out, but I'd hurry before Big Yellow figures out what you're up to."

"Yes, ma'am." One hand on the hatch.

"Mr. Ryder . . ."

This time, he didn't bother turning. "General, write me a fukking note."

"You can't talk to me like that!"

"Yeah, I can." Through the hatch. His hands braced on either side, he leaned back into the shuttle bay and locked eyes with the general. "I don't work for you. I'm not doing this for you. I'm doing this because . . ." Which was when he realized that he didn't owe General Morris an explanation and he grinned. ". . . Staff Sergeant Kerr told me to."

The *Promise* wasn't exactly as he'd left her, but then, he hadn't expected her to be.

"You weren't exactly subtle about trying to get in, were you, mate?"

The sailor shrugged. "Yeah, well, sorry about the scorch marks. After the last shuttle got locked down, we got a little desperate."

"And before?"

"Security doesn't like question marks."

Ryder ran his fingers down five parallel scratches. "You lot ever hear of privacy or personal rights?"

"Not on a warship, buddy. You want privacy you've got to get it cleared by three levels of noncoms and signed off by an officer." As she turned to go, she raised her wrench in a sloppy salute. "Fukkin' impressive security system."

"Yeah, well, I don't like people messing with my stuff," he muttered, punching in his personal code. At first he was afraid they'd damaged the lens on the retinal scanner, but after a moment, the hatch swung open.

The tiny air lock's inside door was also closed and locked, but it, at least, had only the dents he'd put in it himself.

The doors stayed open behind him to save time

when the HE suits arrived. And because he was afraid if he closed them, he'd never open them again.

As he stepped into the cabin, the lights came up, air circulation increased and his implant announced it was 0312. He'd been up for just over twenty hours. No wonder he felt like he'd been pureed. Three long strides took him across to the small galley. He reached for the coffee and pulled out a pack of caffeine lozenges instead. Same boost, fewer pit stops.

Which reminded him.

When he stepped out of the head, there was a Katrien standing in his air lock, peering curiously around the cabin.

". . . first tiny Katrien foot stepped inside and you'd freak."

Fuk off, Torin.

"You want something, mate?"

The pointed face swiveled around, close enough that Ryder could see his reflection in the dark glasses.

"You Craig Ryder?"

"That's right." He crossed to his chair and gripped the back, stopping himself from advancing and forcing the much smaller male out of the air lock, down the ramp, and off his ship. If he couldn't handle one of them . . . His fingers sank through worn vinyl and deep into old foam.

"Durgin a Tar canSalvais. Call me Durgin." He started to step forward, his nose wrinkled, and his foot went back down where it had been. "I are Presit's pilot. They are telling me Cirvan was killed?"

"Sorry."

Durgin's ears drooped. "He are putting up with a lot from that . . . how are you Humans calling it?"

"Prima donna?"

"Bitch." A flash of teeth. "You are bringing her back?"

" 'Fraid so."

He grinned—showing a lot more teeth—and reached into his belt pouch. "I are bringing this for her. It are her small recorder. You are giving her this when she comes on board and she are in a corner talking and not chewing on you."

"Good." If she was outside in a corner of the cargo corral, even better.

Holding out the recorder, Durgin slowly stepped into the cabin.

A trickle of sweat rolled down Ryder's back. He had a Katrien foot . . . two feet . . . an entire Katrien in his ship and although he could feel the familiar panic rising, he hadn't *freaked.*

And a very military word, by the way, Torin.

His heart began to pound and he tightened his grip. The back of the control chair creaked. *Air lock's open. Either one of us can leave any time.*

That helped. It'd mean piss all later on, but right now, it helped.

Setting the recorder down by the coffeepot, Durgin glanced over at the control panel. "You are having a panel of H'san controls?"

"Yeah, well, I got them cheap. It's not that much of a size difference."

The Katrien snorted and held up a hand. "Not for you." Back in the air lock . . .

Almost off my ship.

Durgin paused. "You fly alone?"

Ryder managed a tight grin. "Usually."

Durgin's ears rose and fell, but all he said was, "Good luck."

* * *

Lieutenant Stedrin paused at the door to the general's office. From the condition of the room, he'd taken out his anger on a few inanimate objects. "General Morris, sir?"

The general slowly turned his chair to face the door. He looked more weary than angry. The second stim must have been wearing off. *Once Mr. Ryder's left, I'll see if I can get him to sleep.*

"Sir, the HE suits are on their way over to Mr. Ryder's ship. I need your permission to give him the codes for the PCUs."

General Morris frowned. "For the PCUs?"

"Yes, sir. When he's close enough, he'll need to contact Staff Sergeant Kerr."

"Captain Travik is still in command."

"Due respect, sir, Captain Travik is unconscious. He won't be much help when it comes to docking or loading."

"He hasn't been much help just generally, has he?" Leaning back in his chair, the general dragged both hands over his face, pulling the skin down into temporary jowls. "He's been unconscious through the whole damned mission and in front of a reporter, too. Oh, she'll have a great story, won't she?" Eyes narrowed, he glared up at the lieutenant. "Do you have any idea how much political trouble this thing's going to cause?"

"A lot, sir?"

"A lot, Lieutenant. What do you figure the odds are that Travik'll regain consciousness and do something heroic before he's dragged back here in disgrace by a goddamned civilian salvage operator? A civilian."

"It's no disgrace to be wounded, sir."

"Well, it's not a great honor either." Both hands slapped down on his desk. "If he was dead, at least it would be a tragedy instead of a farce. You have my permission to give Mr. Ryder the PCU codes. In fact," his lip curled, "give him the codes for Staff Sergeant Kerr's implant as well. Who knows what else she'll tell him to do if given the opportunity."

"What's taking so long?" Dursinski demanded scratching at the sealant over the chemical burn on her cheek. "We're going to be taken halfway across the fukking galaxy any minute!"

"First, stop scratching. Your fingers are covered in bug guts and you're going to get that thing infected." Torin glared at the shorter woman until her hand dropped back to her side. "Good. And second, odds are the *Berganitan* doesn't know the engines have started up. Right from the beginning their scans have been worthless, and I doubt they're suddenly working now."

Dursinski snorted. "Goddamned Navy."

"Stedrin's probably got Ryder filling out forms in triplicate before he'll issue the suits," Huilin snickered. "Fuk, there's probably a 'civilian request to rescue Marines' form."

"Yeah, I'd laugh," Nivry sighed, sliding down the bulkhead and landing awkwardly on the deck, "but there probably is.

Graceless di'Taykan were exhausted di'Taykan. The Humans were in much the same shape. Only Werst and Heer showed any kind of energy. Torin suspected they'd been snacking on bugs, but she didn't want to know for sure.

"Bugs have withdrawn," Nivry continued. "I don't think there's more than seven or eight left."

"I can't believe we're kicking bug ass."

Tsui, Frii, and Harrop had all taken major wounds.

Torin had stopped counting the minor ones. And Guimond was dead. "I think we took out their command structure early on. There's been no direction to their attacks."

"You mean besides straight at us," Nivry snorted.

"Yeah, besides that. Still, nice to know we've got something under control."

The vibrations could be felt through the decks, through the bulkheads—probably through the ceiling although Torin had no intention of checking. A small puddle of blood from where a bug's claw had cut through an artery along with half of Harrop's thigh, trembled constantly.

"Ryder'll tell them about the engines," Orla murmured, her eyes dark. "Ryder'll hurry back."

Which would have been comforting except that Ryder didn't know.

SIXTEEN

THE suits were on board. The *Promise* was sealed. He could leave any time.

He was sweating so heavily, the controls felt greasy under his hands.

". . . the intelligence behind this ship wouldn't assume for an instant that you'd do something like this."

"Yeah, and it might be right."

"What was that, Promise?*"*

"Nothing." He took a deep breath. Dried his palms on his thighs. Told himself he was their only chance. Torin's only chance. Torin, who expected him to get the job done. *So let's not think about the trip back until we fukking get there.*

"Berganitan, this is Craig Ryder on the *Promise;* open the launch doors."

"Promise, this is *Black Star Seven.* I'll be your point man for the trip back to Big Yellow. Follow me and ignore the rest of the squadron; they'll be out there trying to keep you alive."

"I'm on you. And thanks for the pep talk, BS7.*"*

"He's got your number, Sib," Shylin snickered.

"B7's fine, *Promise.* No BS out here."

"My mistake, mate."

Sibley flicked the comm channel closed and snorted. "I wonder what he's up to."

"What do you mean?"

"He has to know he'll get sweet fuk all for doing this."

"If it works, they'll give him a medal."

"Yeah. That and a thumbprint'll get you a cup of coffee." Sibley shook his head. "He's got something in the bag."

"Cynic."

"Not even; I've played poker with him."

The trip back to Big Yellow turned out to be as uneventful as the trip in to the *Berganitan* with the sphere had been busy. The bugs still had three full squadrons of fighters out, but they had no real interest in the salvage vessel. Even their one-on-one encounters were more for appearances.

"Our lot's no better," Sibley noted when Shylin pointed it out. "There's a limit to how long you can keep it up when nothing changes. Both ships are locked down and we're too evenly matched for anyone to get the upper hand. No one, not even a bug, wants to risk being killed for no reason."

"That's more philosophical than usual, Sib."

"Yeah, well, I'm tired. I'm out of stim sticks." He shifted inside his webbing. "And my damned flight suit is crotching me."

"Lucky flight suit."

"That's the best you can do? And you call yourself a di'Taykan."

"Hey, I'm tired, too." Hair barely moving, she checked her screens. "You'd think the bugs'd find the energy to go after the *Promise*."

"I doubt they see the point. With that Susumi engine taking up all the room, the cabin's not much more than two meters square, so it can't be going in on a rescue. Fuel and ammo are finite. At this point the bugs'll wait to see what he does when he gets where he's going before they commit."

"What *is* he going to do when he gets where he's going?"

"Damned if I know."

Torin snatched her slate off her vest as the low, pulsing tone began.

"The captain," she answered when she looked up and saw Nivry's unspoken question. "I'm heading back to check on him, keep an eye on things up here."

Nivry turned and stared toward the corner with the one emerald eye that hadn't swollen shut. The bugs were still there—they could both hear and smell them talking—but no one had fired so much as a warning shot in almost half an hour. "You think they're going to try something the moment your back is turned?"

"Always," Torin snorted.

In spite of the blood loss, Frii's and Harrop's vital signs were holding steady. Tsui's blockers wouldn't last much longer, but he was fine except for the missing foot.

When Torin sank carefully down beside Captain Travik, favoring the knee a bug had clipped, he looked no different, but all of his numbers had redlined.

"And?"

She glanced up to see Werst crouched across the captain's body. No. Not body. Not yet. "He's dying."

Werst nodded. "Smells like he's dying. Mind you, he's smelled like he was dying from the beginning."

"Thanks for telling me."

He snorted. "You knew."

She supposed she had. Any blow hard enough to damage a Krai skull had to have pulped the brain behind it. Immediate med-evac might have saved him.

The vibrations had very likely finished off the jellied parts of his brain.

"If you wanted to make him a hero for General Morris, you should've thrown his body on the grenade."

"Believe me," Torin sighed, "if I'd had time, I'd have done it. He'd be a lot more useful as a dead hero than just dead."

"Marines, this is the Pomise. *Come back."*

Ryder's voice blaring out of every PCU snapped people out of sleep up and down the passage. A sudden burst of formaldehyde and cinnamon seemed to indicate that even the bugs had heard.

"Ryder, this Kerr. What the hell took you so long?"

"What?" She could hear the smile in his voice. *"You started starving in an hour and a half?"*

Was that all it had been?

"It's a little more serious than that." The bugs were all in a day's work, but the engines . . .

"You sure they're engines?" he demanded after she filled him in.

"Ryder, I've got two engineers in here and a Niln with a fukking armload of degrees. They're engines. Get us off this thing."

"That's what I'm here for. But I'm going to need some help hooking up."

The *Promise* came with what the manufacturers advertised as a universal lock—a flexible, ribbed tube guaranteed to seal to any solid surface on contact. Unfortunately, the four small thrusters on the end of the tube came with a safety feature that kept them from firing within three meters of organics—which was how their software recognized Big Yellow.

"You're going to have to throw something out, hook onto

the tube, and drag it in. Once there's contact, it should seal."

"Should?" Dursinski protested loudly.

"And what are we supposed to throw?" Nivry demanded from the barricade. "Bug parts?"

"Too organic."

"Good. 'Cause that's called indignity to a body and they charge you for stuff like that."

"So you're allowed to shoot them, but you can't toss them around?"

"Everyone shut up."

"Torin, we don't . . ."

"You, too, Ryder." She tapped her fingers against the edge of her slate and worked through the variables again. It might work. It should work. "All right." A deep breath and she straightened, shaking off the last couple of hours. *"Harveer,* can Johnston use your slate to open the lock?"

The elderly scientist peered from Torin to the engineer and back. "He's a bright boy. Probably."

"Good. Jynett, Orla; take the civilians down to the escape pods. If worse comes to worst; launch all three of them."

"No." Her fur dull, Presit pulled away from Gytha's grip, showing a hint of her old animation for the first time since Guimond died. "I are not moving away from a story. I are not even hearing the other half of . . ." When words failed her, she waved a tiny hand toward Torin's helmet. ". . . that."

"Ma'am, if it's a choice between having you carried away from your *story* or watching your eyeballs explode as you spontaneously decompress, I know what I'd choose." The pause lasted just long enough for Presit to begin to bristle. "If you'll go to the pods, you can take Private Frii's helmet with you and listen to everything on group channel."

"Uh, Staff . . ."

"She deserves to get the end of the story." Torin scooped up the helmet and offered it to the reporter. "Well?"

"I don't think eyeballs explode during spontaneous decompression," Johnston muttered away from his microphone when the civilians were safely out of sight.

Torin flicked her mike up. "Who cares. Get the lock pressurized and the door open."

Her slate began a steady hum.

"The rest of you stay where you are. Werst, you're with me."

The hum stopped.

They stared at each other over the captain's body.

"You refuse," Torin told him, her voice so low he leaned forward to hear, "and we use the suit without the captain. You agree, and we may be able to make him the kind of hero General Morris needs."

"We'd be doing this for the general?"

"Fuk him. We'd be doing this to keep Parliament from tying the Corps' hands. Be nice to achieve something worthwhile today," she added when he frowned. *Be nice if we could salvage something from Guimond's death.* But she didn't have to say that out loud.

Werst's ridges clamped shut. "If it goes wrong?"

"I'll take the heat."

"Fuk that, too. And the rest of the team?"

"They just have to play dumb."

He snorted. "Shouldn't be too hard for most of them." All at once, he grinned, showing an ivory slash of teeth. "Hope I can get the *serley* accent right."

Her own teeth clenched together, Torin pushed down on the captain's jaw and reached into his mouth. It was beginning to cool. She found the ridge that ran under his left molars and activated the implant.

Microphone down, Werst bent over the captain's mouth, their lips almost touching in a parody of tenderness.

No! I will not allow one of my Marines to take that kind of risk. I will . . .

". . . be the one to get that tube."

"But, sir, you' ve been unconscious . . ."

"Krai are tougher than you think, Staff Sergeant."

"Yes, sir, but . . ."

"Don't argue with me, Staff Sergeant Kerr. I'm the one giving the orders. I'm in command here, not you."

"Yes, sir."

They flipped up their mikes at the same time and sat back.

"Nailed the accent," Torin told him, pushing the captain's jaw shut. "We lost the implant after the *I will* but that was plenty. It's only important that Presit hear the whole speech, we just need the general to believe he's alive. Get him sealed up and ready to go." She rocked back on her heels, stood, turned, and found, as she knew she would, every pair of eyes in the passage locked on her.

Moving deliberately, so they all could see her do it, she flipped her mike back down. Long silences would not help the story. "Huilin, get out of your HE suit. There's nothing to tie off to in the air lock, and Captain Travik wants me to anchor him."

Huilin's eyes were dark and under the edge of his

helmet his hair was in constant motion. "The captain's regained consciousness?"

Torin slowly raked her gaze over the Marines, her expression silencing any other questions. "You heard him. He seems to feel it's his duty to get the tube. He also seems to think if he's going to risk his ass, so should I. Get out of the suit. Now."

Her voice moved his hands to the seals . "Why . . ."

"Because it's the only one I have a hope in hell of fitting in. Dursinski's too short and Jynett's integrity has been compromised. Move it, Marine. Time's wasting."

The suit puddled around his legs. Huilin glanced toward the vertical that led to the escape pods and back to Torin.

He knew.

They all knew. Although Torin suspected the whispering she'd heard had been Nivry filling Dursinski in.

They'd known her for eight days in Susumi space and for thirty hours on Big Yellow. They trusted her to get them through battles alive, but trusting her in this was a whole different ball game.

"It's my suit, Staff," Huilin said, at last. "I should go."

"Did I ask for volunteers? Just give me the damned suit."

I won't involve you lot any more than I have to.

They heard the subtext. It echoed around the suddenly quiet passageway so loudly, Torin was afraid Presit would hear it one level down.

After a long moment, Johnston made the decision for all of them. "I'll have the lock open by the time the captain's ready, Staff Sergeant Kerr."

"Good. And I'll need someone's rope." She stripped

off her combats and held out her hand for Huilin's suit.

Torin, what the fuk is going on in there?

The sudden blaring of her implant made her drop the captain's body. It was a damned good thing he only had to sound alive. Hauling him back up again, she half turned and nodded to Werst.

"Close the inner door, Lance Corporal Johnston."

Johnston scowled in Werst's direction, but all he said was, "Closing the inner door, Captain."

Torin? Answer me, damn it. Captain Travik is not seriously heading out to save the day? He was a fukking vegetable when I left.

She tongued her implant on and subvocalized so the suit mike wouldn't pick it up. **Trust me.**

Trust you? The heavy sigh came through loud and clear. **Do I have a fukking choice?**

No. Stay on group channel. And then aloud, "Ryder, Captain Travik and I will be working on command channel for clarity. Were you given the codes?"

"I have the codes. What I don't have is all day; move your collective ass."

"Keep your goddamned pants on," she muttered, watching the panel of lights as the air lock depressurized. Which was not an image she needed. Stuffed into an HE suit a di'Taykan had been wearing for hours had her so horny that Ryder's voice alone was nearly enough to overload the circuitry. The series of lights Johnston had told her to watch for flashed green, and she laid her glove against the pressure pad.

The door slid open the way a thousand air lock doors had slid open all her life.

Moving carefully, she centered herself and Captain

Travik in the opening and set her boot magnets at full power.

"I see you." A short pause, and he added, *"Both of you."*

Torin smiled and adjusted her grip on the captain. *And thank you for playing.*

It was good to see the stars.

"Torin, Sibley says you might want to think of hurrying. Bugs are moving in."

"Roger that." She resisted the urge to look for the bugs. It wouldn't make a damned bit of difference if she knew where they were.

With the bulk of Big Yellow behind her, the *Promise* looked absurdly small. The floating end of the universal lock was smaller still.

With one end of the rope tied around the captain's waist and the other around hers, Torin flipped him over so his boots were pointing toward the universe and threw the already stiffening body toward the tube. Her aim didn't need to be exact. When he was closer to the tube than Big Yellow, she punched his boot codes into her slate. Part of her job was ensuring that the captain's equipment functioned properly.

Magnetic soles worked fine.

"What the *sanLi* are they doing?"

Sibley took a look straight up through the canopy. "Putting their best foot forward? Booting up the air lock? Proving they've got sole?"

"You done?" Shylin sighed.

"For now."

"Well, I don't know about soul, but the little guy's got balls the size of . . . Bugs!"

The Jade slid to the left, dropped six meters, and fired as a shot streaked by their portside. A touch on the upper right thruster flipped them around. Another touch on the lower left stopped the spin.

"Target's taking evasive action."

"Let it. We've got two more closing on the *Promise.*" He goosed the Jade up and in. "Ryder, you want to remind your Marines they're not alone in the universe?"

"No shit. You think that's why people keep shooting at us?"

All Ryder could see was the middle bulge of the tube, but the instruments showed the end had nearly reached Big Yellow. "Could be your sparkling personality."

"Mine?" Torin wondered. *"Or the Corps'?"*

"Is there a difference?" A bug fighter streaked past almost too quickly to identify. It was amazing how the old panic, the panic he could feel bubbling and roiling beneath the forced, teeth clenched, surface calm, kept new panic at bay. At least if he got blown to component atoms by something that looked like a cross between an ant and a cockroach, he'd die alone in his ship.

His one-man ship.

Alone.

The way it was supposed to be.

"Securing first point of UAL and manually activating the seal. You sure this thing'll stretch to fit?"

Torin's voice helped.

"The brochure said 'one size fits all.' "

"Yeah, well let's hope it wasn't written by the same moron who sizes lingerie."

A sudden vision of what Staff Sergeant Torin Kerr wore under her combats caused an involuntary smirk. "You never struck me as the lingerie type."

"I have hidden depths."

"That, I never doubted." The UAL controls green-lined. "We've got a seal." He stared down at his hand on the panel. An inch to the right were the main thruster controls. He wouldn't even have to move his arm.

"Craig?"

And it came as no surprise she could read his thoughts in the silence.

"Tell your people to pressurize." He watched his fingers curl into a fist. "I'll deploy the salvage pen."

"Roger. I'm switching back to group channel. Any time you think you can't do this, contact me."

"I can do this."

"Glad to hear it. Kerr out." Torin propped the captain up against the inside of the lock and stepped in front of him to keep him from falling. "Marines, we are leaving. Johnston, get this thing pressurized. I want wounded and civilians moving, and moving fast, the instant the door opens."

"I'm sorry, General, we still can't raise Captain Travik."

"Why not?"

"He's not answering, sir."

General Morris placed both hands on the edge of the console and leaned into the comm officer's space. "I heard him not ten minutes ago!"

"Yes, sir. But he's not answering now."

"If you're still being blocked, why don't you blast the signal through that salvage ship the way you did with the first shuttle? It's practically sitting right there on the hull."

"We can't, sir. It's a civilian vessel and its comm unit isn't set up to handle that kind of amplification."

"Why the hell not? Why wasn't it set up before it launched?"

"We didn't have time, sir."

"So you're telling me I still can't speak to the officer commanding?"

"Yes, sir."

"Goddamned Navy." General Morris rocked back on his heels and fixed the comm officer with a basilisk glare. "Fine. If you can't raise the captain's implant, I suppose it's too much to hope you can raise the staff sergeant's—so get me Ryder," he continued without waiting for an answer. "Unless your tin can and piece of string don't reach that far!"

"I'm a little busy, General." Ryder swiveled his chair around so that he was staring at the air lock. "What do you want?"

"What do I want? I want a full report on the situation!"

Both inner and outer doors were still closed. The lock itself was unpressurized. He was alone in the cabin. A full report to General Morris would keep things that way for a good long time.

"Ryder! Goddamn it, answer me!"

One hand reached back for the comm controls.

"I think you're forgetting that I don't work for you, mate."

"Remember, the ship's AG field stops at the outer hull. I want one Marine to a civilian, one helping Tsui, two carrying each of the stretchers. You drop your baggage, you grab an armload of suits, you haul ass back to Big Yellow." A shadow flickered over the thin membrane of the tube. No way to tell if it was a bug fighter or a Jade. "I want a minimum of time spent in this worm casing." And what was taking the goddamned pressurizing so long?

"Staff Sergeant Kerr, we are not being carried . . ."

"Yes, you are. We don't have time for sloppy maneuvering in zero gee."

"Captain Travik! I are asking you . . ."

"The captain can't answer you, ma'am." Torin glanced back at the corpse. "Saving all our lives took everything he had. He's drifting in and out of consciousness again."

"Black Seven, *this is* Red Three. *We've got bugs heading toward your position."*

"So stop them," Shylin muttered, her fingers dancing across her targeting data.

"They appear curious rather than hostile. We see no attack patterns."

"Yet."

"Roger, *Red Three. B7* out." Sibley took the Jade down over the tube, around and under the deploying salvage pen. "You know, Shy. You're starting to be a real downer."

Clutching her helmet in both hands, Presit surged forward as the air lock door opened, took one look at eighteen meters of ribbed tube stretching out to the *Promise*'s lock, and her toes clamped down on the edge of the deck.

"I are not . . ."

Before Torin could speak, Nivry grabbed the reporter from behind. "Yeah, you are."

Three long strides took her to the edge of the hull, and a graceful dive—made less graceful than di'-Taykan norm by an armload of squirming Katrien—took them both out of the AG field and to the *Promise* just as the outer lock opened. She caught herself on the edge of the lock and practically threw a vehemently protesting Presit into Ryder's arms.

Torin grinned at his expression and began to strip out of Huilin's suit.

Nivry back. Huilin and Gytha.

Huilin back. Orla and the *harveer.*

Two shadows passed over the tube almost too fast to register.

"Keep it moving, people."

Orla back.

Heer and Werst with Tsui on the first stretcher, Tsui protesting all the way that he could manage without a foot in zero gee.

"Tsui."

He tilted his head enough to see her around Heer.

"Make sure nobody touches Mr. Ryder's stuff and," she raised her voice loud enough to be heard inside the *Promise,* "gag that reporter if she doesn't shut the fuk up!"

The torrent of Katrien protests shut off.

Tsui grinned into the sudden silence. "You got it, Staff."

Still standing at the outer edge of his air lock, Ryder tossed a smile in Torin's direction. Torin, in turn, tossed Huilin his suit. And blamed any visceral reactions on residual pheromones.

Frii.

Of the serious casualties, only Harrop remained on Big Yellow.

"They're going for the tube, Sib!"

"I'm on them!"

A hard burst with both left and right upper thrusters, intended to drop the Jade down behind the bug, put them into a spin. Sibley swore, corrected, and raced to intercept.

"What happened?"

"Forgot about the new lefties. I hit them too hard."

Fingers gripping the edge of the panel, right thumb a whisper above the fire control, Shylin shook her head. "We may not get a lock."

"We have to."

Her hair flipped forward. "You got anything encouraging to say that's not a cliché?"

"At this hour? I doubt it." He fought to get everything he could out of the Jade. "Goddamned bug is not getting away."

"Target has flipped one-eighty. She's coming back at us, Sib."

"Good." Teeth clenched, he headed the Jade right down the bug's throat. "We'll use less fuel catching her."

One piece of the debris hit the *Promise*. The others passed to the left of the tube.

"Son of a . . . ! Torin!"

Nivry, Orla, and the stretcher holding Harrop were between them, but there was no mistaking the terror now in Ryder's voice.

"This thing won't take a direct hit from a thrown turd. If it punctures . . ."

If it punctured with both air locks open, it would at the very least decompress the smaller ship, killing everyone on it and probably sucking two or three Marines into space before the emergency protocols closed the inner doors.

She kept her own voice vaguely disinterested. "What do you suggest we do about it, Mr. Ryder?"

Nivry and Orla had Harrop inside. She could see

him now. More importantly, he could see her. When she locked her gaze to his and lifted a deliberate brow, he grinned and shook his head. "I suggest we don't throw any turds."

Torin nodded. "I can support that idea."

"So." He leaned against the ship and folded his arms. "The Marines teach you to be calm in the face of disaster, or are you naturally like this?"

"The Corps believes in making use of natural ability."

He flinched as another shadow passed the tube, but it was a minor movement. Had she not been watching him so closely, she'd have missed it.

"And what do you believe in?" he wondered.

Then the two di'Taykan were pushing past him and launching themselves down the tube. Nivry landed, took three running steps to kill momentum and was safely inside Big Yellow.

Another shadow, closely followed.

Orla hit the AG field with her feet still in the tube, turned the landing into a shoulder roll, and bounced upright. "I meant to do that," she muttered as she went inside.

"Captain Travik, you are coming inside now!"

About to tell Ryder to get his door closed and the tube cast off, Torin tried to remember why it had seemed like a good idea to give Presit that helmet. A quick glance at the body reminded her. The Corps had also taught her to make use of available resources. She flipped down her mike. "Presit's right, sir. You can't ride in the cargo pen, you're injured. There's room inside."

"I ride with my Marines." The voice was barely audible; the upper class Krai accent unmistakable. If this

backfired, Werst could always join her in a fulfilling career in musical theater.

"But, sir . . ."

"I'm the officer, Staff Sergeant. I give the orders."

"Yes, sir."

The mike went back up. She looked down the tube toward Ryder, ignoring the Katrien who continued to babble about or to Captain Travik. "Thanks for coming back." She couldn't see past him, but she knew how crowded the small cabin had to be. Even if she hadn't known how he felt about sharing the space, she'd have seen it in the way he rocked back and forth, muscles rigid. A muscle had to be damned rigid to see it from eighteen meters away. "And as much as I'd enjoy standing here talking to you all day, get your ass inside." She reached out and tapped the tube. "Dump this. Get the salvage pen below the lock and as close to the hull as you can. Once we're in, just concentrate on getting us back to the *Berganitan* in one piece."

"Just?" He looked like he was about to launch himself toward her.

"Just keep doing what I tell you, and everything'll be fine."

Half a smile showed in the shadow of his beard. "Words to live by, then?"

"People do. I've been thinking . . ."

"When did you have time?"

"Shut up. Did you give your implant codes to anyone on the *Berg*? Then run mine into the program the *Promise* uses to contact you," she continued quickly when he shook his head. "You can talk to me any time you need to with no one else being the wiser."

"How did you know I . . . ?" He shook his head

again, more in wonder this time. "Never mind. Stupid question. It's your job to know."

"You're not part of my job—but I think I'll keep you alive anyway." Stepping back, she reached for the lock controls. "Inside. Now." The tone that had terrified a thousand recruits pushed him into the ship as effectively as if she'd reached out a hand and shoved. "Close up and go." Hand raised, she didn't touch her controls until she saw his door close.

And that was all she could do for him right now. He had to get through the next bit without her.

She had problems of her own.

"Uh, Staff. You better come see this."

Already suited, Dursinski had remained on guard at the barricade.

Sealing the front of a mercifully pheromone-free suit, Torin ran to join her.

The bug was standing in the center of the passage. She wore no armor. She carried no weapons. All four arms were spread. The air smelled of cinnamon and melted butter.

"What the fuk's she doing?" Dursinski's benny took a bead on the bug's head.

Torin pushed it down. "She's surrendering."

Werst limped up beside them and snorted derisively. "The Others don't let their soldiers surrender."

"Granted, but this lot has lost contact with their ship. They have no leaders left alive. They recognize the sound of an engine and they know what it means as well as we do. They're desperate. They don't want to die."

"Who does?" Dursinski sighed.

Two more bugs came out into the passage, armorless, weaponless, carrying vaguely familiar gear across their arms. Behind them, two more.

"And," Torin continued, "they've got their own suits."

"You can't trust them, Staff." Nivry's voice came from behind her left shoulder.

"They're the enemy," Werst agreed.

"I don't trust them." She handed her benny to the corporal and stepped beyond the barricade. "But I'm not leaving them here."

"This is fukkin' weird," Johnston muttered, shrugging his suit up over his shoulders.

Settling his tank, Heer glanced over at the five surviving bugs getting into their own suits under the supervision of Dursinski's and Jynett's weapons. "This is fukkin' history," he amended, ridges flared.

"I flunked history."

"And now you're part of it. Weird or what?" He tucked his head into the collar ring and came up with his emergency rations tube in his mouth. "Soup's on and life is good."

Johnston grimaced as the other engineer swallowed with every indication of enjoyment. "You want to talk about weird . . ."

"Salvage pen's in place. Any time, Torin."

"First group's on their way."

The first group consisted of four Marines and two bugs. Torin, the captain's body still propped behind her, opened the outer doors and motioned them forward. The bugs' reaction transcended both the lack of a common language and the bulk of their suits. They took one look and backed up, pushing Marines and weapons both out of their way.

"We don't have time for this. Nivry."

Torin grabbed the back of the corporal's suit as she

stepped out into space. A push and release sent her angling down into the pen.

"Johnston."

"But . . ."

"Now."

Two Marines safely loaded reassured the bugs.

When we get a minute, I'll have to find out what "you guys are fukking idiots" smells like, Torin mused, pitching the last of the first group. "Half done, Ryder. We're . . ."

As she closed the outer doors, the background vibrations moved suddenly to the foreground. "Fuk!"

"Torin?"

"Not now!"

Inner doors open.

"Get in here! Move!"

Everyone remaining in Big Yellow surged forward.

Inner doors closed.

"Here!" Torin tossed the loop of rope still connecting her and Captain Travik. "Grab hold!"

The three bugs imitated the Marines.

Torin slapped the outer control panel.

"Staff! The pressure hasn't . . ."

"Just hang on!"

The outer doors opened. Five Marines, three bugs, and the rope sucked past her into space. Torin's boots held but only just. "Another chance for you to be a hero," she muttered, grabbing Captain Travik's body with both hands, aiming him toward the clump of Marines now tethered in the pen and throwing him as hard as she was able.

The outer door began to close.

Torin released her boots as the rope around her waist jerked her out through the rapidly disappearing opening. She swore as the door slammed her injured arm and spun her around, Marines, bugs, pen, *Promise,* all spinning against a background of stars.

"Get your thumbs out of your butts and pull us in!" she snapped. "Ryder! Get moving!"

"But you're . . ."

"Six meters from a ship that's about to fire main engines!"

The first two bodies on the rope were in the pen.

"My engines . . ."

"Are one thousandth the fukking size!"

Three. Four.

She'd stopped spinning and was now moving steadily toward the pen.

Two bugs holding as much to each other as the rope slipped inside.

They were probably thinking they should have stayed with Big Yellow. Not that she blamed them.

Below her, below the salvage pen, the *Promise* began to move.

Too goddamned slow! Her breath sounded unusually loud in her ears.

The rope jerked violently.

Someone screamed.

Torin threw out her arms and instinctively grabbed the body that slammed into her.

"I thought I told you to hold on!" she gasped, hoping the rib had cracked and not actually broken.

"Sorry . . . Staff . . ." Orla's voice sounded wet and bubbling.

"You hurt?"

Her boots touched the outside of the pen.

"I . . . don't . . . I don't . . . I . . . I . . ."

There was no mistaking the sound of someone puking into a comm unit.

As the rope dragged them down into the pen, Torin

reached around and hit the external controls for Orla's cleanup suction, passing her off to reaching hands in almost the same move.

"We lose anyone?" she asked as Nivry pulled her to a strap beside the captain's body. The bugs were strapped along the back wall, the Marines to the sides just above the angled sections that kept the pen from being rectangular.

"Acceleration drove the edge of the pen into Huilin's thigh. Bone snapped, but it didn't break the skin and his suit's fine. He'll . . ."

The universe became brilliant yellow-white light.

Torin's helmet polarized instantly, going completely opaque. Still, she could see nothing but glowing blotches burned into her eyes. The temperature inside her suit began to rise. "Marines! Sound off by number!"

Only eight of the original twelve, but she heard from all eight. Huilin and Orla both sounded like shit, but they were alive.

She had no way of checking on the bugs.

She was sweating now. Squinting, she could just make out the readout on the left curve of her collar. Environmental controls placed the highest temperatures where her suit was touching the pen. "Marines, loosen your straps. Move out from the sides but do not, I repeat, do *not* unstrap completely."

One of the great things about vacuum, it didn't hold heat.

"Torin!"

Her helmet beginning to clear, still tied to the captain, and unable to tell the bugs to move away from the pen, she headed back to physically shift them. "We're still here." One bug was totally unresponsive; alive or dead, Torin couldn't know. One clutched at her in terror. Pain shooting along her left side, she barely managed to break free.

"What the hell happened out there?" she demanded, dragging herself back one-handed along the rope to her place between Nivry and the captain.

"Big Yellow's gone."

And that meant, the rules had changed.

Seventeen

"CAPTAIN Carveg! Our engines are back on-line!"

"Captain Carveg! The Others' ship has simultaneously sent a message to every fighter!"

"Captain Carveg! Mr. Ryder reports he has surviving Marines, scientists, and bugs on board."

The last report shut off the noise in C3—from chaos to quiet in an instant. All eyes lifted from monitors and data streams and turned to the captain.

She alone was looking at the lieutenant charged with monitoring the *Promise.* "Mr. Ryder has bugs on board?"

"Yes, ma'am. He says the last five bugs surrendered and are in suits in the salvage pen with the Marines."

"Prisoners of war."

Not entirely certain it was a question, the lieutenant answered anyway. "Yes, ma'am."

"Right." Captain Carveg straightened in her command chair, adrenaline banishing exhaustion. Those species who fought for the Others—or *were* the Others, no one knew for certain—never surrendered. And now Staff Sergeant Kerr was returning to the *Berganitan* with five. Things were about to get interesting. "Engineering, I want full maneuverability five minutes ago!"

"Aye, aye, Captain."

"Flight Control, let our pilots know the bugs are likely to attempt some kind of unified attack."

"Aye, aye, Captain."

"Lieutenant Demoln, see that Mr. Ryder is kept informed." She reached out and slapped her palm down on the touch pad. "All hands, battle stations!"

Torin was really beginning to miss the quiet inside Big Yellow. "Sir, Captain Travik saved the life of Presit a Tur durValintrisy, Sector Central News' star reporter. She'll make sure everyone knows it. Even without Big Yellow, you've got what you needed. Captain Travik is a hero."

"And he commanded the mission that captured five of the enemy," the general added thoughtfully.

"They weren't exactly captured, sir. They surrendered."

"Perhaps."

Perhaps? Torin sagged back against the side of the pen, the material no longer hot enough to damage her suit. The stim she'd taken had cleared her head and washed the fatigue from her body but it hadn't changed the fact that it had been a very long day.

"As far as the public needs to know, they were captured. We don't need to tell all we know, Staff Sergeant."

She glanced over at the captain's body, her tone carefully neutral. "Yes, sir."

"We can count on the captain to say anything he feels is in his best interest."

She could see the general, sitting at his desk, fat fingers spread on either side of the raised comm unit.

"Pity that reporter's crew person got killed."

"As well as nine scientists, Navy Lieutenant

Czerneda, and Private First Class August Guimond. Sir."

"All deaths are . . ."

"Strap in tight, mates!" Ryder's shout over the group channel cut the general off in mid-platitude. *"We're about to be swarmed."*

"Never a bug zapper around when you need one," Sibley muttered, slamming on his thrusters and moving away from the salvage pen to give himself more room to maneuver. "Looks like every bug out here's heading this way."

"B1 *to squadron. Heads up, team, we're about to be visited by every goddamned bug with wings."*

"Didn't I just say that?" He switched to the squadron's frequency. "You got a number on every goddamned bug, *B1*?"

"Five squadrons minus the ones we've taken out. A whole fukking lot of bugs."

"Roger that. Tell me, how did we get so popular?"

"Maybe they're attracted to your sparkling personality, Sib. Defensive pattern 12-4-2, people. We let the bugs come to us and hope the rest of the group knocks a few out before they get here."

"They're not having much luck," Shylin observed dryly.

Although the Jades were significantly more maneuverable, the bug fighters flew a lot faster in a straight line and they were heading right for the *Promise.*

Black Star Squadron had lost three Jades—Boom Boom's *B8* had been destroyed, *B2* and *B11* had been grounded; *B2* with no loss of life, but *B11*'s gunner had taken a jagged edge of the control panel in the throat. The twelve Jades remaining in the squadron moved into a two-on defensive pattern, four pairs defending the *Promise*'s four main axis points, two pairs free to go where they were most needed.

Sibley found himself beside *B6*, matching the *Promise*'s speed a half a kilometer out from the stern of the cargo pod.

"I've got fifty-two bugs on my screen, Sib. There's no way twelve of us will be able to stop them."

"Well, not with that attitude."

Light flared in the distance.

"Now there's fifty-one," Sibley grinned. "Piece of cake."

"They're moving too fast to be locked."

"Then they're moving too fast to lock—they'll have to slow down to get a shot off." Lifting his hand, he ran though a quick series of finger exercises, then laid them over the complex keypads that controlled the Jade's thrusters. "I'm ready. Bring 'em on."

"Maybe not," she declared with more energy than he'd heard in hours. "Sib, I need Flight Command."

"Group, this is Flight Command! Gunners who have a shot, lock missiles on the bug fighters' trajectories. Repeat, lock missiles on the trajectories, not the fighters."

"We know where they're going, and we know they're taking the shortest way there, so we let missiles and bugs run into each other—very smart, Shy. There's gonna be pats on the head for you."

"How nice for me," Shylin replied absently, feeding the last of the data into her targeting computer. "Permission to fire two remaining PGMs."

Sibley grinned. For a regulation question it had sounded a lot like a statement. "Permission granted. Fire away."

Forty-eight. Forty-two.

The flares of light made a pattern of destruction against the stars.

"You'd think seeing other fighters blow would bug them just a little. Enough to try something else."

"They know there's more of them than there are PGMs remaining."

"Would they be . . ."

"*Ablin gon savit!*"

"What?" He jerked against the restriction of his webbing.

"We lost a Jade in a debris field." A moment later on the small side monitors that showed Jades in the field, a call sign began flashing. "*Red Nine.* Jan Elson and Dierik."

The webbing felt like it was getting tighter with every second that passed. "I fukking hate waiting. You know, I once saw Dierik eat half a dozen pouches of that crap the grunts call field rations."

"Probably enjoyed them, too."

"Said it reminded him of his *jernil's* funeral."

More flares. Closer now.

Thirty-seven.

"And why the hell can't I take evasive action?" Ryder demanded, his screens showing three dozen bug fighters plus one still heading right for him.

"You're easier for the Jades to protect if they know where you are. You start changing your trajectory, and half their attention switches to you. Just let our people deal with this, Mr. Ryder. It's what they do."

Yeah, well, under normal circumstances, he'd be heading for Susumi space and the hell with sucking small fighters in with him. Unfortunately, he had live cargo in salvage pens and although the field would extend to cover them, they wouldn't survive even a short jump.

Not that the odds of them surviving thirty-seven enemy fighters were a lot better.

We are all going to die.

Too late to stop himself from thinking about exactly how many "we all" were.

Crap.

Denial was a wonderful thing—while it worked.

His muscles had knotted so tightly it felt as though daggers had been driven into the back of his neck, and every time he had to move his arms, pain shot from his spine to his shoulders. He *knew* he had six people in the cabin with him, but as long as they were quiet, he'd been able to ignore them. The Katrien had helped by locking themselves in the head with Presit's small recorder when he'd told them they were going out the air lock if they didn't shut the fuk up about the light levels.

Two of the Marines were unconscious. The Niln was sleeping; snoring anyway. He could feel Ken Tsui's gaze on the back of his head.

Carbon dioxide levels were rising.

He couldn't breathe.

He had to turn around. Had to. Not a good idea.

The only thing he could hear was his own heartbeat.

His fingers were trembling as he had the *Promise* contact Torin's implant. Never very good at subvocalizing, he had no idea what was about to come out of his mouth and no desire to have either the general or the *Berganitan*'s comm station listening in. The eavesdroppers behind him were plenty.

"Torin."

I'm here.

All at once, the situation didn't seem so dire. Her voice gave him a new focus. He wished he knew how she did it but, for now, it was enough to be able to draw a full breath. "Jades took out nearly a third of the bugs. Still three dozen coming in, though."

We can see them.

She sounded bored. As if being strapped into a salvage pen while three dozen enemy fighters blasted through a mere dozen defenders was something she did every day. Ryder grinned. Maybe it was.

"Navy says we should trust them to do their jobs."

As Dursinski would say, Goddamned Navy.

Dursinski. He had a sudden vision of her, blonde brows drawn tight into a worried frown. Since she seemed happiest with something to worry about, she was probably ecstatic right about now.

"Is everyone okay?"

Yeah, most of them are sleeping.

"Sleeping?"

Why not? You get those bugs to climb in here with us and we'll kick ass; until then, it's been a long . . .

The *Promise*'s small port polarized too slowly to prevent purple-white dots from dancing across his vision. "Torin!"

"We're fine," she snorted, switching back to group channel for her answer, her tone making it quite clear she had no intention of allowing her people to be anything but fine. "You might not be aware of this, but it takes more than bright lights to damage a Marine. We've been highly trained to deal with loud noises, too."

Someone snickered. It sounded like a di'Taykan. Nivry probably. The Corps had to have put her through at least one leadership course and this situation was tailor-made for that last lesson in Combat Morale, *"If you're going to die anyway, see to it that your people die with dry underwear and a smile."*

"We don't usually get to watch the vacuum jockeys work from such good seats," Torin continued before Ryder could respond. "Maybe we'll finally find out why they get the big . . ."

Not so bright this time, although the salvage pen rocked.

". . . bucks."

"So if there's three bugs for each of us, why the fuk are there five bugs on me!" Unable to take either hand from the thruster controls, Sibley jerked his head toward the stars.

"At least they haven't got a clear shot off." Shylin's hair stood out from her head in a cadmium nimbus. "And . . . I've . . . got . . . Damn it, Sib." The salvage pen was now straight up. "How am I suppose to take them out when you keep . . ."

The Jade slid down forty-five degrees to port and flipped ninety degrees.

"Saving our collective ass?"

"Yeah. That. I need a clear target; we've only got small stuff left."

"The AR-67s?"

"One."

"We had four!"

"Now we have one. And after that it's PFUs only."

"And after that we throw cocktail weenies—get ready."

A one-eighty flip and a short burst on the rear thrusters.

Shylin's shot hit the bug fighter a glancing blow,

spun it into another fighter's path, and sent the two of them careening out of control.

"You know for a cadmium-haired sex maniac, you're a decent shot."

"Thanks. For a . . ."

"Superior officer."

". . . Human, you're a decent pilot."

"Was that an insult?"

"Up to you."

Starboard thrusters. Full topside. The bottom of the Jade skimmed the side of the pen.

"Fuk!" Dursinski twisted around in her strapping. "I could read 'made by the H'san coalition' on the bottom of that thing!"

"You can read?" Werst snorted.

"Up yours."

Morale seemed fine, Torin noted.

"Squadron's down to ten. *B5* lost starboard thrusters, *B3* lost power. She's drifting, but the bugs are ignoring her."

"Great time to be an odd number." Sibley slid them between two fighters, throwing one off course. The other got by. "Ryder! Heads up!"

"Heads up? Oh, that's helpful, mate. Just bloody helpful." An early shot had fried a rack of the *Promise*'s processors. Fire control was now manual. So was the coffeemaker, but with green smoke gathering under the ceiling, that didn't seem as crucial somehow. *Not that I'd turn down an offered double double . . .*

One of the port thrusters had taken a direct hit from debris, and although it continued to fire, its angle had to continually be adjusted.

If he'd been an inch shorter, he wouldn't be able to handle the board.

"Can I help?"

Goddamn it! He didn't have enough going on—what with being the fukking center of attention and all? He had to have someone breathing down the back of his neck? Breathing his oxygen. Limited oxygen.

"Ryder!"

He jerked, realized two new trouble lights were flashing red, that the two systems he'd been monitoring were fluctuating wildly, that he was sitting frozen in place by a panic attack.

And he realized that he didn't want to die, that the odds of being killed by the *Promise* blowing apart around him were significantly better than by half a dozen unwelcome passengers sucking up his oxygen, that he needed help.

Turning, he found Tsui gripping the back of the control chair, balanced on his one remaining foot.

Fuk! The Marine really had been breathing down the back of his neck.

And so what. Ryder surged up out of the seat and practically threw the smaller man down into it, grabbing his wrist and slapping his hand down by the thruster control. "Keep that between seventy-five and seventy-nine degrees! Use your other hand to code in seven-slash-slash-three every time that bar lights up red."

"What am I doing?" Tsui demanded as Ryder moved to the other side of the board.

"Does it matter?" He glanced down at the stump of the Marine's left leg. "Doesn't that hurt?"

"Neural blockers," Tsui explained. "I'm good for another twenty minutes. After that . . ."

". . . we'll be in the clear or we'll be in pieces."

* * *

"A great big hunk of the *Promise* just blew by."

"Important hunk?" Shylin asked without looking up.

"Apparently not."

Ninety-degree flip, two seconds of forward thrusters; a last instant deflection of one of the enemy's small missiles from the salvage pen.

"I'm guessing they don't care there's also bugs in that pen."

"I think that's the point, Sib."

"Take out the prisoners before they talk?"

"Or whatever it is that bugs do."

He brought them around for another run. "You ever get the feeling we're playing by different rules?"

"You and me?"

"Us and . . ."

The bug fighter didn't bother slowing down to take a shot. It hit the side of the salvage pen farthest from the *Promise,* cutting through the metal latticework, shearing off the last third of the pen.

Torin had been the last one into the pen, the closest—but for Captain Travik—to the end and the bugs. She didn't see the fighter approach, but the impact jerked the strap up against her cracked ribs and turned her bones to jelly. The universe slowed. The pen begin to tear. The fighter slammed past. She saw stars through the deck plates. Realized her boots were attached to the piece breaking away.

The universe sped up again.

Boot release.

Boot release.

Boot release!

Pain.

Fingers of her right hand locked around a broken strap, Torin dangled into space, the rope around her waist only a meter long and ending in a charred fray.

The bugs were gone. The end of the pen was gone. Captain Travik's body was gone. The piece of deck that had been under her boots was also gone and had nearly taken her with it. Fortunately the straps had held until she got the magnetic field off. On the down side, the ribs that had been cracked were now definitely broken and every breath was agony.

She brought her head around so she could stare into the ruin of the pen.

Only the captain and the bugs seemed to be missing.

"You lot must fukking live right. Well, don't just stand there staring," she added through clenched teeth. "Pull me in." The only response was a continuing stunned silence as every eye stared out at the stars wheeling by as the *Promise* continued the spin begun by the impact. "NOW!"

Shock fled, chased off by a more immediate danger.

Her boots firmly locked, Nivry leaned out to the extent of her straps, grabbed Torin's lifeline and yanked.

The pain Torin'd been feeling in her upper arm exploded.

"Staff?"

She didn't remember making a noise, but it seemed she had. "The chemical burn. Should've grabbed on with my other hand."

"Your other hand?" Nivry set her into the pen. "You should be *dead*."

"Well, thank you, Corporal."

"No. I mean . . . Look!" A gloved hand gestured past Torin's shoulder.

"I don't think so." She couldn't open the fingers of

her right hand. Her brain knew that she was safe, that her boots were remagged and firmly connected to the deck, that Nivry had pulled out new straps and she'd been resecured, but her body wasn't taking any chances. *Fine. Good. Smart body.*

A quick glance at the readouts running along her collar showed Huilin was unconscious—"Johnston, you're showing a small leak. Find it and patch it! Heer, give him a hand." Everyone's respiration and heartbeat was up, and most of the suits were dealing with extra liquids.

No surprise.

"Staff Sergeant Kerr! What's going on out there! I want a full repor . . ."

"With all due respect, sir . . ." Standing stiffly at attention, Lieutenant Stedrin lifted his hand from the general's desk. ". . . this is not the time."

General Morris stared from his inoperative comm unit to his aide. "What the hell do you think you're doing, Lieutenant?"

"Preventing Staff Sergeant Kerr from telling you to get . . . stuffed. Sir."

Torin!

Torin didn't know what miracle had cut off the general, but this was a voice she wanted to hear.

Torin, are you all right?

"More or less. We lost the bugs, and the captain. Everyone else is still here. You?"

AG field's out. We got knocked around, but no one's badly hurt. I don't have the kind of external visuals you lot do, but it looks like the bugs are trying something new!

The skin between her shoulder blades tightened.

"Oh, that's just fukking great."

* * *

"Now that's more like it! Think you can outfly me? Dream on, bug breath!"

"Sib! All the fighters are moving away from the *Promise*. The squadron's following!"

"And we're driving them right into the rest of the group!"

"That doesn't make sense!"

"They took out the bug POWs! You saw the bits go spinning into space."

"They can't know they've got all of them."

"Then . . . Oy, mama." The Jade flipped one-eighty. They came around just as a large hunk of debris hit its thrusters and turned into a fighter.

It began to accelerate straight toward the broken end of the pen.

"I'm not reading any weapons."

Sibley raced disaster back toward the salvage ship. "It doesn't need a weapon. Remember how they took out the shuttle."

"They're going to ram . . ."

"Rams eat oats and does eat oats and little lambs eat ivy."

"What?"

"Human thing."

"Uh, Staff. I think you'd better turn around."

Something in Nivry's voice overcame the fear paralysis—part of it anyway. Fingers still clutching the broken strap, Torin turned.

The bug fighter was some distance away but closing fast.

"Ryder, now would be a good time for evasive action."

Love to, but I've lost most of my power relays.

"So use the rest."

Hey, if you don't like the way I'm driving, you can get out and walk.

"It might be safer," Torin acknowledged as the fighter grew rapidly larger. And just because she couldn't stand and do nothing, she swung her benny around onto her hip.

"Sib, we don't have anything big enough to stop it! And we're low on fuel. If we've got to do much maneuvering . . ."

"Won't be a problem," he interrupted, "'cause I've got a plan."

"Which is?"

He dropped the Jade into the bug's trajectory and hit all thrusters.

"Oh. Good plan. And we're ejecting at the last minute?"

"You are. I'm staying in case she blinks."

"Compound eyes don't blink, Sib."

"I know." Amazed by how calm he sounded, he reached out and hit the release for Shylin's half of the pod. As it blew clear, sealing him into his own small space, he forced his hands away from the thruster controls as the bug fighter filled his forward port. "Buh-bye . . ."

"Vacuum jockeys; goddamned show-offs," Dursinski muttered, her voice cracking with emotion.

"Convinced me they're worth what they're paid," Werst grunted.

Torin nodded and opened her eyes. She'd see that final explosion every time she closed them for months. But that was how it should be—sacrifice should be remembered. Honored.

Torin! All fighters have flipped one-eighty and are heading back!

She sighed. She could feel the Marines around her thinking, *"A single ship attempting to ram failed. They'll ram with everything they've got now."*

And the Others' ship is . . . Fuk!

Which, in Torin's professional opinion, was a fairly accurate assessment of the situation.

The Others' ship loomed suddenly to the rear of the pen, blocking out an impossibly huge section of the stars.

"This is it. We're going to die."

Eyes narrowed, Torin glared out at the ship. "Not until I say so, we aren't."

"Get real, Staff, you can't stop . . ."

The *Berganitan* swooped in over the *Promise,* angling her bulk between the surviving Marines and the enemy. While she might have been small next to Big Yellow, she was immense at this range and kept coming for what seemed like hours although it couldn't have been more than minutes.

"Saw 'made by the H'san coalition' on the bottom of that, too," Dursinski muttered.

Torin's temperature and radiation gauges shot into the black, and her suit began to overheat.

Then the destroyer was past and the Others were on the run.

"Staff Sergeant Kerr, this is Captain Carveg. Sorry we had to come in so close, but we wanted to hit the Others where they wouldn't expect it. You lot all right?"

The temperature gauge began to drop as empty space wrapped around them again.

"We got a little cooked, but we're okay."

"They're running for Susumi, so we'll be back in a few minutes to pick you up."

"We'll be here, ma'am." And so much for the one loose end. There was nothing like the backwash from a destroyer to wipe the memory off a slate. And off the suits . . . "Marines, check your environmental controls."

"Staff, my clock's out."

"You got an appointment somewhere, Jynett?"

"I'd like to have a chat with my recruiting sergeant," the di'Taykan sighed, her hair fanning out to connect with the reflected stars on her helmet. "But I guess it can wait."

"Glad to hear it."

By the time Torin stood on the *Berganitan*'s shuttle deck and pushed her helmet back, she could hardly stand the smell of herself. The panting she'd had to do in order to breathe around her broken ribs was probably the only thing keeping the stink bearable.

Stripping carefully out of the suit, she was pleased to note Captain Carveg had made sure that the closest Navy personnel when the di'Taykan Marines broke seal were other di'Taykans. The release of trapped pheromones was so strong it roused Huilin out of his stupor as they laid him on a stretcher, and he grabbed the nearest corpsman's ass.

Fortunately, the *Berganitan*'s scrubbers cleared the air before much of it reached the Humans and the Krai.

Tsui, Harrop, and Frii were already in Med-op, the *Promise* having been a lot easier to unload than a salvage pen with no air lock.

"Staff!"

She turned, took too deep a breath, realized the problem the instant the fog cleared from her vision. "Go with the corpsman, Werst."

"I'm fine!"

"You broke your toe. Go."

"You're next, Staff Sergeant."

Another turn. A more careful breath. And the sudden realization that long lines of red ran out from the cracks in the seal over the chemical burn, down her arm, and dripped off her fingers. She could see that the pair of corpsmen, an AG stretcher between them, were waiting for an argument. It didn't seem worth it to give them one.

Torin?

It seemed the backwash hadn't wiped her codes from the *Promise*. Activating her implant, she subvocalized, *Fine. You?*

The medical officer working on her arm, glanced up, assumed Torin was talking with one of her own officers, and continued repairing the damage done by the chemical burn.

They won't let me see you. Some crap about both of us needing to be debriefed.

No crap. Policy.

More crap. I'm a civilian.

Later.

"Can I take it from your smile that your general is pleased with you?" the doctor asked as she tongued off her implant.

Was she smiling? She was.

"Too bad he's not pleased enough to give you more time in here," he continued, stepping back. "I've bonded the ribs, but they'll be tender for a while, so no rough stuff. And lots of fluids—you may be a litltle light-headed from the loss of blood."

Light-headed. Good. There was a medical explanation.

* * *

Ken Tsui was being fitted for a regeneration tank that would extend down from his left knee; Torin couldn't get in to see him. Frii and Harrop had been fully tanked the moment they'd arrived in Medical. The doctors were cautiously optimistic they'd both make it. Huilin's leg had been bonded, and he'd been given a sedative that should keep him under until the *Berganitan* reached Susumi space. The rest were being checked over, cuts and bruises and minor injuries attended to.

Torin motioned the corpsman out of Werst's cubicle and stepped in.

"They hosed us down first," he grunted, bare feet swinging half a meter above the deck. "You'd think they'd build these fukkers Krai size."

"That is Krai size," Torin snorted. "On a Human table, I can't touch the deck."

"You're here to tell me I can change my mind, aren't you?"

She opened her mouth and closed it again as he kept talking without pausing for a reply.

"I can read it on your face, Staff." He scratched up under his robe and shook his head, facial ridges clamped shut as he locked his eyes on hers. "You do what you have to to get the job done—you don't like that you had to involve me. Don't worry about it. The captain's a hero, the mission was a success, we weren't where Guimond could throw himself on a grenade to save eighteen people for no good reason." His facial ridges began to slowly open as the words spilled out, more words than Torin had heard him speak the whole time she'd known him. "I had a buddy once. Knew him most of my life. We joined up together, went through Ventris together. He was Krai, not

Human, but big and friendly and didn't have a bad thing to say about shit. He died our first time out. Antipersonnel missile took his big, fukking, friendly head right off.

"Why is it the big, fukkin', friendly ones who die, Staff?"

"They're not the only ones who die, Werst, it's just we miss them more than the short, fukkin', cranky ones."

He grinned reluctantly. "So you're not going to miss me when I get it?"

Torin tightened her fingers around the cylinder in her hand. "No more than everyone else I lose."

Lieutenant Stedrin glanced up as Torin entered the outer office. "General Morris will be with you in a minute, Staff Sergeant. The reporter is still with him."

"Thank you, sir." She walked over to the edge of the desk. "I'd like to also thank you for taking General Morris off the comm unit."

He jerked and his pale eyes darkened. "How did you know . . . ?"

She hadn't. Not until this instant. Which she was not going to mention. "It's my job to know these things."

"What things?"

"What officers can be depended on, sir. I hope you didn't get in too much trouble on my behalf."

"He was annoyed," the lieutenant admitted reluctantly, pale blue hair flipping back and forth over the points of his ears.

Torin raised a single brow.

"Okay, he was furious." Stedrin shrugged, the graceful motion pure di'Tayakan. His small rebellion seemed to have loosened his body language. "But there's just him and me out here and he needs me, so, hopefully, he'll get over it before . . ." He surged up to his feet as the door opened.

"I are happy I are having had this talk with you, General." Presit—her fur brushed, her nails repainted, her dark glasses back in place—minced out of the inner office. "I are looking forward to integrating earlier vids of the brave Captain Travik into our full story."

Face wreathed in smiles, the general followed close behind. "The resources of the Corps are at your disposal, ma'am."

"I are thanking you, so much." Her head turned and Torin found herself staring at her reflection in the reporter's glasses. "And the Staff Sergeant?" she asked, her tone as pointed as her teeth.

"Will be dealt with."

"Good."

"Lieutenant Stedrin, if you could escort our guest out of the Marine attachment."

"Yes, sir!"

Torin had never heard a response snapped off with such perfect military delivery. Lieutenant Stedrin was reinforcing his chances of forgiveness with a little spit and polish.

When the outer door closed, General Morris stepped back, clearing access to his office. "Staff Sergeant Kerr . . ."

Torin took up the usual position in front of his desk, staring at the usual spot on the wall.

"At ease, Staff Sergeant. I hate it when you do that."

"Yes, sir." She dropped into a perfect parade rest—the lieutenant wasn't the only one who knew when to smooth off any rough edges. "Do what?"

"Stare at the damned wall. Makes me feel like I'm not in the room." He sighed deeply, dropped into his chair, and laid both hands flat on his desk. "Why did I bring you on this mission, Staff Sergeant?"

Hers was not to question why. *Because you're my own, personal, two star pain in the ass.* "To keep Captain Travik alive, sir."

"Yes, to keep Captain Travik alive. Which he isn't. Still, his final acts of heroism were enough to generate an amazing amount of good PR—essentially keeping him alive."

The general seemed pleased and he'd damn well better be—it wasn't every day Torin *essentially* raised the dead.

"Presit is more than willing to put the captain back onto his media pedestal and then crank it up a few levels. I suspect she's motivated as much by his actions as by her dislike of you and her belief that elevating the captain is the best way to get under your skin."

Interesting. Although the statement could certainly be taken at face value, it was possible the reporter knew more of what was really going on than Torin had thought. *You are thinking you are so smart, Staff Sergeant. I are making sure you are getting none of the credit.*

Not that it much mattered what her motivations were as long as the result was the same.

Leaning forward, General Morris' voice dropped into a low growl. "Did you actually threaten to blow her head off, Staff Sergeant Kerr?"

"No, sir."

"Not in so many words, sir," he mocked. "Fortunately for you, she seems content to have me deal with you." The fingers of his right hand drummed out a slow beat. "Don't do it again. The Corps is not in the habit of making idle threats."

Idle threats. No doubt the general's word choice came out of a few hours spent in the Katrien's voluble company.

"As welcome as the media coverage is," the general continued, "it won't bring Captain Travik back to life and that means he can't be promoted to command rank."

"Yes, sir. The way I see it, we all win."

"Explain yourself, Staff Sergeant."

"I have every confidence that the general can use the amazing amount of good PR to placate the Krai in Parliament to the extent that the captain's intended promotion will be forgotten."

"Yes." The single syllable dripped suspicion. Torin was willing to grant he had precedent for the emotion. "But how do *you* win?"

"Captain Travik would have been promoted for political reasons." She dipped her head just enough to meet his gaze. "Political officers in command positions aren't good for the Corps. Sir."

He stared at her for a long moment. His eyes narrowed. "Are you *sure* your parents were married, Staff Sergeant?" he asked at last.

Torin kept her face expressionless. "Yes, sir."

"When we get back, I suggest you check the paperwork. For now, tell me why—Captain Travik's heroism aside—this whole mission wasn't a total waste of time."

"Two reasons, sir. First—as regards the enemy. We kicked ass."

"And that would be your professional, combat NCO's opinion?" the general snorted.

"Yes, sir." Answer the question not the tone. "We

learned more about how the bugs fight and how they think. How they react when they've lost their leadership. Intelligence can use the data to extrapolate cultural practices. We brought back one of their weapons. Next time we meet them, we'll be better prepared and they'll have nothing but the knowledge of getting their ass kicked. Second—as regards Big Yellow; granted, we learned very little about the ship or the species who built it. We don't know why it was here, where it came from, or where it was going. But . . ." She drew in a deep breath and let it out slowly. "But I think it was on a fact-finding mission and I think it learned the best about us."

"The best?"

"Yes, sir." She held out her arm, opened her fingers over his desk, and let Guimond's cylinder fall from her hand. "One life, freely given, so that eighteen could live. I can't think of anything I'd rather have an alien intelligence learn."

The general picked up the cylinder and turned it over and over between his fingers. Maybe he was remembering the thirteen she'd handed him at the end of the last "special" mission he'd sent her on. Maybe he was just staring at his reflection. Torin couldn't know.

"All right, Staff Sergeant." He closed his fingers, enclosing the cylinder in his hand much as she had. "Let's go over the whole thing from the moment the shuttle blew."

"Yes, sir."

"Dave."

Chief Warrant Officer Graham looked up from his phase welder, waved, and powered down. "Torin."

He pulled off his safety glasses as he walked over to the hatch. "What brings you into the depths?"

She nodded past him at the empty docking bay. "That. Well, not that specifically, but I wanted to thank the pilots who saw to it we got home. But Marine Corps staff sergeants don't just walk in on Navy pilots, so I hoped you would pass it on for me."

"*That* specifically, then. This was Lieutenant Commander Sibley's bay. He's the one who slammed his Jade down the bug's throat."

The explosion played out again on the back of Torin's eyes. It was never a stranger. "We saw a half pod eject."

"His gunner. We picked her up just before we got you. She's still tanked—di'Taykan." He shifted his glasses from one hand to another. "They feel these things more, you know."

The two noncoms locked eyes for a long moment—grieving, anger, understanding, shared.

The *Promise* no longer quite filled shuttle bay four. The damaged salvage pen was one bay over—without the stacked panels the ship had a little more headroom. Considering the damage she'd taken, she didn't look bad. Or good, for that matter.

The hatch was open and the ramp was down.

The only sound as Torin made her way up the ramp was the soft and ever present hum of Susumi space stroking the *Berganitan*'s outer hull. Which was drowned out as she reached the top of the ramp by a stream of inventive profanity.

She stopped, her boots carefully on the ramp side of the tiny lock and leaned inside. "You need some help?"

Ryder was lying on his back, half under the control

panel, both muscular arms raised and buried elbow deep. She almost expected him to jerk up and crack his head, but he just lifted it enough to be able to see her and grinned. "Why aren't I surprised that you can fix one of these things?"

"Sorry, I can't. But I have friends on the *Bergani-tan.*" Friends who right now were mourning the losses of their Jades and the crews who flew them. "If you want me to put a word in . . ."

"Thanks, but Captain Carveg has already offered to send over any help I need."

"Captain Carveg's a good captain, but I doubt she knows who the best mechanics are."

" 'Cause she's not a staff sergeant?"

"Sad but true. I'd have been by sooner, but this is the first downtime I've had."

"Me, too."

"I know, the *Promise* told me. You've haven't taken my codes out of her system."

"Son of a bitch, I knew I was forgetting to do some-thing." He slid out into the limited floor space, stood, and held out his hand. "Come in."

In his place, she'd have thought it insulting to be asked if he was sure, so she didn't ask. The cabin was small enough to put them very close. Small enough to force the issue. She could smell the mix of sweat and grease coming off him and it seemed to be having the same effect as di'Taykan pheromones.

"So." Blue eyes gleaming, he scratched his beard with the charred edge of the processor rack. "What would you have done with the captain's body if the bugs hadn't conveniently removed him for you?"

Torin shrugged. "Brought him back to a hero's wel-come."

"A dead hero's welcome."

"You can't tell the exact time of death without a molecular autopsy and they don't put heroes under the knife. That implies something might be wrong, that he might not be the hero a two star general desperately needs him to be." She spread her hands. "He died to save us all."

"Your slate had his medical information in it." His teeth were brilliantly white in the shadow of his beard.

"True." Shifting her weight to one hip, she folded her arms. "You know, it's not that easy doing a vacuum trot from a damaged salvage pen into an unpressurized shuttle bay.

"A terrible accident?"

Another shrug. "Who can say what would have happened?"

"I'm betting you could."

The beginning of a smile to answer his. "I was just doing my job."

To her surprise, he stepped back and glanced around the cabin, his expression suddenly serious. "You think I'm a coward? Because of . . . you know?"

"No. You overcame your fear. Isn't that the definition of bravery?"

"You're the Marine," Ryder snorted. "You tell me."

"I *am* telling you."

"And what are you afraid of?" he asked after a long moment.

All things considered, he deserved an honest answer. "Failure."

"Not being able to do your job?"

"I get it wrong and people die."

"You said, back in that hole on Big Yellow, that when the job's done . . ." His smile returned as suddenly as it left. "It *is* done, isn't it? I mean, I wouldn't want to start anything that'll get me whacked. You probably know twenty-five ways to kill a man with your bare hands."

"Twenty-six," Torin told him as he closed the distance between them. "But you'll like the last one."

Bitching amongst themselves, a maintenance crew worked to clear the huge net out of the shuttle bay. No one seemed to know why it had been put there or on whose order although a couple of the di'Taykans had a few athletic suggestions for its use.

No one noticed the twelve large gray canisters stacked along one bulkhead.

AUTHOR'S NOTE

In September, 1944, the 1st Marine Division attacked the small "wretched" Pacific island of Peleliu. The westernmost of the Carolines, Peleliu had an oven-hot climate, a convoluted terrain, an *"ungodly scramble of coral cliffs,"* mangrove swamps, and 10,000 dug in and well-armed Japanese soldiers.

Lack of both time and ammunition made the Navy's preliminary bombardment short and essentially ineffective. As the amphibious landing craft approached the beach, the enemy opened fire with antiboat guns and heavy machine guns.

It was said to be as deadly a landing as the Marines would ever face.

After the slaughter on the beach, Colonel Lewis "Chesty" Puller, led his men in a *"gallant but fruitless series of frontal assaults"* on the cliffs and sharply angled hills the Marines called Bloody Nose Ridge.

At one point during the six-day battle for the ridge, an excited subordinate reported to Colonel Puller, "We've had such heavy losses we have nothing better than sergeants to lead our platoons!"

"Let me tell you something, son," Puller replied calmly, "in the Marines, there *is* nothing better than a sergeant."

—from A FELLOWSHIP OF VALOR, THE BATTLE HISTORY OF THE UNITED STATES MARINES by Col. Joseph H. Alexander, USMC (Ret.), published by Lou Reda Productions for The History Channel and A&E Television Networks, 1997

Tanya Huff

The Confederation Novels

"As a heroine, Kerr shines. She is cut from the same mold as Ellen Ripley of the *Aliens* films. Like her heroine, Huff delivers the goods." --*SF Weekly*

VALOR'S CHOICE

0-88677-896-4

When a diplomatic mission becomes a battle for survival, the price of failure will be far worse than death...

THE BETTER PART OF VALOR

0-7564-0062-7

Could Torin Kerr keep disaster from striking while escorting a scientific expedition to an enormous spacecraft of unknown origin?

To Order Call: 1-800-788-6262

DAW 19